Irresistible

Greeks

Secrets & Seduction

Irresistible *Greeks*
COLLECTION

May 2016

June 2016

July 2016

August 2016

September 2016

October 2016

Irresistible Greeks
Secrets & Seduction

LYNNE   JULIA   ANNE
GRAHAM JAMES McALLISTER

First Published in Great Britain 2016
By Mills & Boon, an imprint of HarperCollins*Publishers*
1 London Bridge Street, London, SE1 9GF

Irresistible Greeks: Secrets & Seduction © 2016 Harlequin Books S.A.

The Secrets She Carried © 2012 Lynne Graham
Painted the Other Woman © 2012 Julia James
Breaking the Greek's Rules © 2012 Anne McAllister

ISBN: 978-0-263-92236-3

24-0516

Harlequin (UK) Limited's policy is to use papers that are natural, renewable and recyclable products and made from wood grown in sustainable forests. The logging and manufacturing processes conform to the legal environmental regulations of the country of origin.

Printed and bound in Spain
by CPI, Barcelona

THE SECRETS SHE CARRIED

LYNNE GRAHAM

Lynne Graham was born in Northern Ireland and has been a keen romance reader since her teens. She is very happily married to an understanding husband who has learned to cook since she started to write! Her five children keep her on her toes. She has a very large dog who knocks everything over, a very small terrier who barks a lot and two cats. When time allows, Lynne is a keen gardener.

CHAPTER ONE

CRISTOPHE DONAKIS opened the file on the Stanwick Hall Hotel group, which he expected to become the latest addition to his luxury hotel empire, and suffered an unanticipated shock.

Ironically, it took a great deal to shock Cristophe. At thirty years of age, the Greek entrepreneur and billionaire had seen a lot of bad behaviour and when it came to women in particular he was a complete cynic with low expectations. Orphaned at the age of five, he had survived several major setbacks in life, not the least of which had included foster parents whom he loved but with whom he had not a single thought in common, and a divorce, which still rankled for he had entered his marriage with the best of good intentions. No, what caused Cristophe to vault upright behind his desk and carry the file over to the window to avail of the best possible light was a glimpse of a startlingly familiar face in a photograph of the Stanwick executive staff… a face from his past.

Erin Turner…a pocket Venus with pale hair that glittered like polished silver gilt and eyes the colour of amethysts. Straight off, his lean, darkly handsome features clenched into forbidding angles. Erin occupied a category all of her own in his memories, for she had been the only woman ever to betray him and, even though almost three years had to have passed since their last meeting, the recollection could still sting. His keenly intelligent gaze devoured the photograph of his former mistress standing smiling at the elbow of Sam Morton, the elderly owner of Stanwick Hall. Clad in a dark business suit with her eye-catching hair restrained by a clip, she looked very different from the carefree, casually clad young woman he remembered.

His tall, powerful body in the grip of sudden tension, Cristo's dark-as-night eyes took on a fiery glow. That fast he was remembering Erin's lithe form clad in silk and satin. Even better did he recall the wonderfully slippery *feel* of her glorious curves beneath his appreciative hands. Perspiration dampened his strong upper lip and he breathed in deep and slow, determined to master the near instantaneous response at his groin. Regrettably, he had never met another Erin, BUT then he had married soon afterwards and only in recent months had he again enjoyed the freedom of being single. He knew that a woman capable of matching his hunger and even of occasionally exhausting his high-voltage libido was a very rare find indeed. He reminded himself that it was very probably that same hunger that had led her to betray his trust and take another man into her bed. An unapologetic workaholic, he had left her alone for weeks while he was abroad on business and it was possible that he had invited the sordid conclusion that had ultimately finished their affair, he conceded grudgingly. Of course, had she agreed to travel with him it would never have happened but regrettably it had not occurred to him at the time that she might have excellent, if nefarious, reasons for preferring to stay in London.

He studied Sam Morton, whose body language and expression were uniquely revealing to any acute observer. The older man, who had to be comfortably into his sixties, could not hide his proprietorial protective attitude towards the svelte little manager of his health spas. His feelings shone out of his proud smile and the supportive arm he had welded to her spine in a declaration of possession. Cristo swore vehemently in Greek and examined the photo from all angles, but could see no room for any more innocent interpretation: she was at it again…bedding the boss! While it might have done him good to recognise Erin's continuing cunning at making the most of her feminine assets, it gave him no satisfaction at all to acknowledge that she was still happily playing the same tricks and profiting from them. He wondered if she was stealing from Morton as well.

Cristo had dumped Erin from a height when she let him down but the punishment had failed to soothe an incredulous bitterness that only increased when he had afterwards discovered that she had been ripping him off. He had had faith in Erin, he had trusted her, had even at one point begun to toy with the idea that she might make a reasonable wife. Walking into that bedroom and finding another man in the bed he had planned to share with her, along with the debris of discarded wine glasses and the trail of clothes that told its own sleazy story, had knocked him sideways. And what had he done next?

Lean, strong face rigid, Cristo grudgingly acknowledged his own biggest mistake. In the aftermath of his discovery that Erin had cheated on him, he had reached a decision that he was still paying for in spades. He had made a wrong move with long-term repercussions and for a male who almost never made mistakes that remained a very humbling truth. With hindsight he knew exactly why he had done, what he had done but he had yet to forgive himself for that fatal misstep and the fallout those closest to him had suffered. Handsome mouth compressed into a tough line at that reflection, he studied Erin closely. She was still gorgeous and doubtless still happily engaged in confidently plotting and planning how best to feather her own nest while that poor sap at her elbow gave her his trust and worshipped the ground her dainty feet trod on.

But Cristo knew that he had the power to shift the very ground in an earthquake beneath those same feet because he very much doubted that the reputedly conservative and morally upright Sam Morton had any awareness of the freewheeling months that Erin had enjoyed in her guise as Cristo's mistress, or of the salient fact that at heart she was just a common little thief.

That bombshell had burst on Cristo only weeks after the end of their affair. An audit had found serious discrepancies in the books of the health spa Erin had been managing for him. Products worth a considerable amount of money had gone missing. Invoices had been falsified, freelance employees invented to receive pay cheques for non-existent work. Only Erin had had full access to that paperwork and a reliable long-term employee had admitted seeing her removing boxes of products from the store. Clearly on the take from the day that Cristo hired her, Erin had ripped off the spa to the tune of thousands of pounds. Why had he not prosecuted her for her thieving? He had been too proud to

parade the reality that he had taken a thief to his bed
and put a thief in a position of trust within his business.

Erin was a box of crafty tricks and no mistake, he
acknowledged bitterly. No doubt Morton was equally
unaware that his butter-wouldn't-melt-in-my-mouth employee played a very creditable game of strip poker. That
she had once met Cristo at the airport on his birthday
wearing nothing but her skin beneath her coat? And
that even the coat had gone within seconds of entering
his limousine? Did she cry out Morton's name and sob
in his arms when she reached a climax? Seduce him as
only a very sensual woman could while he tried to give
the business news his attention instead? Most probably
she did, for she had learned from Cristo exactly what
a man liked.

Disturbed that he still cherished such strong memories of that period of his life, Cristo poured himself a
whisky and regrouped, his shrewd brain swiftly cooling
the tenor of his angry reflections. The phrase, 'Don't get
mad, get even' might well adorn Cristo's gravestone, for
he refused to waste time on anything that didn't enrich
his life. So, Erin was still out there using her wits and
her body to climb the career and fortune ladder. How
was that news to him? And why was he assuming that
Sam Morton was too naïve to know that he had caught
a tiger by the tail? For many men the trade-off of as
much sex as a man could handle would be acceptable.

And Cristo registered in some surprise at his predict-
ability that he was no different from that self-serving
libidinous majority. I could go there again, he thought
fiercely, his adrenalin pumping at the prospect of that
sexual challenge. I could really *enjoy* going there again.
She's wasted on an old man and far too devious to be

contained by a male with a conventional outlook. He began to read the file, discovering that Erin's wealthy employer was a widower. He could only assume that she had her ambition squarely centred on becoming the second Mrs Morton. Why else would a scheming gold-digger be working to ingratiate herself and earn a fairly humble crust? He was convinced that she would not have been able to resist the temptation of helping herself to funds from Sam Morton's spas as well.

Her healthy survival instincts and enduring cunning offended Cristo's sense of justice. Had he really believed that such a cool little schemer might turn over a new leaf in the aftermath of their affair? Had he ever been that naïve? Certainly, he had compared every woman he had ever had in his bed to Erin and found them all wanting in one way or another. That was a most disconcerting truth to accept. Clearly, he had never got her out of his system, he reflected grimly. Like a piece of baggage he couldn't shed, she had travelled on with him even when he believed that he was free of her malign influence. It was time that he finally stowed that excess baggage and moved on and how better to do that than by exorcising her from his psyche with one last sexual escapade?

He knew what Erin Turner was and he also knew that memory always lied. Memory would have embellished her image and polished her up to a degree that would not withstand the harsh light of reality. He needed to puncture the myth, explode the persistent fantasy and seeing her again in the flesh would accomplish that desirable conclusion most effectively. A hard smile slashed Cristo's handsome mouth as he imagined her dismay at his untimely reappearance in her life.

'Look before you leap,' his risk-adverse foster mother

had earnestly told him when he was a child, fearing his adventurous, rebellious nature and unable to comprehend the unimaginably entertaining attraction of taking a leap into the unknown. In spite of all his foster parents' efforts to tame his passionate temperament, however, Cristo's notoriously hot-blooded Donakis genes still ran true to form in his veins. His birth parents might not have survived to raise their son but he had inherited their volatile spirits in the cradle.

Without a second thought about the likelihood of consequences, indeed merely reacting to the insidious arousal and sense of challenge tugging at his every physical sense, Cristo lifted the phone. He informed the executive head of his acquisitions team that he would be taking over the next phase of the negotiations with the owner of the Stanwick Hall Hotel group.

'Well, what do you think?' Sam prompted, taken aback by Erin's unusual silence by his side. 'You needed a new car and here it is!'

Erin was still staring with a dropped jaw at the top-of-the-range silver BMW parked outside the garages for her examination. 'It's beautiful but—'

'But *nothing*!' Sam interrupted impatiently as if he had been awaiting an adverse comment and was keen to stifle it. Only marginally taller than Erin's five feet two inches, he was a trim man with a shock of white hair and bright blue eyes that burned with restive energy in his suntanned face. 'You do a big important job here at Stanwick and you need a car that suits the part—'

'Only not such an exclusive luxury model,' she protested awkwardly, wondering what on earth her colleagues would think if they saw her pulling up in a vehicle that undoubtedly cost more than she could earn in several years of employment. 'That's too much—'

'Only the best for my star employee,' Sam countered with cheerful unconcern. 'You're the one who taught me the importance of image in business and an economical runabout certainly doesn't cut the mustard.'

'I just can't accept it, Sam,' Erin told him uncomfortably.

'You don't have a choice,' her boss responded with immoveable good humour as he pressed a set of car keys into her reluctant hand. 'Your old Fiesta is gone. Thanks, Sam, is all you need to say.'

Erin grimaced down at the keys. 'Thanks, Sam, but it's too much—'

'Nothing's too good for you. Take a look at the balance sheets for the spas since you took over,' Sam advised her drily. 'Even according to that misery of an accountant I employ I'm coining it hand over fist. You're worth ten times what that car cost me, so let's hear no more about it.'

'Sam…' Erin sighed heavily and he filched the keys back from her to stride over to the BMW and unlock it with a flourish.

'Come on,' he urged. 'Take me for a test drive. I've got some time to kill before my big appointment this afternoon.'

'What big appointment?' she queried, shooting the sleek car into reverse and filtering it out through the arched entrance to the courtyard and down the drive past the immaculate gardens.

'I'm having another bash at the retirement thing,' her boss confided ruefully.

Erin suppressed a weary sigh. Sam Morton was al-

ways talking about selling his three country-house hotels, but she believed that it was more an idea that he
toyed with from time to time than an actual plan likely
to reach fruition. At sixty-two years of age, Sam still
put in very long hours of work. He was widowed more
than twenty years earlier and childless; his thriving hotel
group had become his life, consuming all his energy
and time.

Thirty minutes later, having dropped Sam off at his
golf club for lunch and gently refused his offer to join
him in favour of getting back to work, Erin walked back
into Stanwick Hall and entered the office of Sam's secretary, Janice, a dark-haired fashionably clad woman
in her forties.

'Have you seen the car?' she asked Janice with a self-
conscious wince.

'I went with him to the showroom to choose it—
didn't I do you proud?' the brunette teased.

'Didn't you try to dissuade him from buying such an
expensive model?' Erin asked in surprise.

'Right now, Sam's flush with the last quarter's profits
and keen to splurge. Buying you a new car was a good
excuse. I didn't waste my breath trying to argue with
him. When Sam makes up his mind about something
it's set in stone. Look at it as a bonus for all the new clients you've brought in since you reorganised the spas,'
Janice advised her. 'Anyway you must've noticed that
Sam is all over the place at the moment.'

Erin fell still by the other woman's desk with a frown.
'What do you mean?'

'His moods are unpredictable and he's very restless.
I honestly think that he's really intending to go for re-

tirement this time around and sell but it's a challenge for him to face up to it.'

Erin was stunned by that opinion for she had learned not to take Sam's talk of selling up seriously. Several potential buyers had come and gone unmourned during the two years she had worked at Stanwick Hall. Sam was always willing to discuss the possibility but had yet to go beyond that. 'You really think that? My word, are half of us likely to be standing in the dole queue this time next month?'

'Now that's a worry I *can* settle for you. The law safeguards employment for the staff in any change of ownership. I know that thanks to Sam checking it out,' Janice told her. 'As far as I know this is the first time he's gone that far through the process before.'

A slight figure in a dark brown trouser suit, silvery blonde hair gleaming at her nape in the sunlight, Erin sank heavily down into the chair by the window, equal amounts of relief and disbelief warring inside her, for experience had taught her never to take anything for granted. 'I honestly had no idea he was seriously considering selling this time.'

'Sam's sixtieth birthday hit him hard. He says he's at a turning point in his life. He's got his health and his wealth and now he wants the leisure to enjoy them,' Janice told her evenly. 'I can see where he's coming from. His whole life has revolved round this place for as long as I can remember.'

'Apart from the occasional game of golf, he has nothing else to occupy him,' Erin conceded ruefully.

'Watch your step, Erin. He's very fond of you,' Janice murmured, watching the younger woman very closely for her reaction. 'I always assumed that Sam looked on you as the daughter he never had but recently I've begun to wonder if his interest in you is quite so squeaky clean.'

Erin was discomfited by that frankly offered opinion from a woman whom she respected. She gazed steadily back at her and then suddenly helpless laughter was bubbling up in her throat. 'Janice...I just can't even begin to imagine Sam making a pass at me!'

'Listen to me,' the brunette urged impatiently. 'You're a beautiful woman and beautiful women rarely inspire purely platonic feelings in men. Sam's a lonely man and you're a good listener and a hard worker. He likes you and admires the way you've contrived to rebuild your life. Who's to say that that hasn't developed into a more personal interest?'

'Where on earth did you get the idea that Sam was interested in me in that way?' Erin demanded baldly.

'It's the way he looks at you sometimes, the way he takes advantage of any excuse to go and speak to you. The last time you were on leave he didn't know what to do with himself.'

Erin usually respected the worldly-wise Janice's opinions but on this particular issue she was convinced that the older woman had got it badly wrong. Erin was confident that she knew her boss inside out and would have noticed anything amiss. She was also mortified on Sam's behalf, for he was a very proper man with old-fashioned values, who would loathe the existence of such rumours on the staff grapevine. He had never flirted with Erin. Indeed he had never betrayed the smallest sign that he looked on Erin as anything other than a trusted and valued employee.

'I think you're wrong but I do hope that nobody else has the same suspicions about us.'

'That car will cause talk,' Janice warned her wryly. 'There's plenty people around here who will be happy to say that there's no fool like an old fool!'

Erin's face flamed. She was suddenly eager to bring the excruciating discussion to an end. She had grown extremely fond of Sam Morton and respected him as a self-made man with principles. Even talking about Sam as a man with the usual male appetites embarrassed her. Not only had the older man given her a chance to work for him when most people wouldn't have bothered, but he had also promoted and encouraged her ever since then. It was purely thanks to Sam that she had a decent career, a salary she could live on and good prospects. Only how good would those prospects be if Sam sold up and she got a new employer? A new owner would likely want to bring in his own staff and, even if he had to wait for the opportunity, she would not have the freedom to operate as she currently did. It was a sobering thought. Erin had heavy responsibilities on the home front and the mere thought of unemployment made her skin turn clammy and her tummy turn over sickeningly with dread.

'I'd better get on. Owen's interviewing therapists this afternoon,' Erin said ruefully. 'I don't want to keep him waiting.'

As Erin drove the sleek BMW several miles to reach the Black's Inn, the smallest property in Sam's portfolio—an elegant Georgian hotel, which incorporated a brand-new custom-built spa—she was thinking anxiously about how much money she had contrived to put by in savings in recent months. Not as much as she had hoped, certainly not nearly enough to cover her expenses in the event of job loss, she reflected worriedly. Unfortunately she could never forget the huge struggle she had had trying to get by on welfare benefits when her twins, Lorcan and Nuala, were newly born. Back then her mother, once so proud of her daughter's achievements, had been aghast at the mess Erin had made of her seemingly promising future. Erin had felt like a total failure and had worked out the exact moment that it had all gone belly up for her. It would have been great to have a terrific career *and* the guy of her dreams but possibly hoping for that winning combination had been downright greedy. In actuality she had fallen madly in love with the wrong guy and had taken her life apart to make it dovetail with his. All the lessons she had learned growing up had been forgotten, her ambitions put on hold, while she chased her dream lover.

And ever since then, Erin had been beating herself up for her mistakes. When she couldn't afford to buy something for the twins, when she had to listen in tolerant silence to her mother's regrets for the youthful freedom she had thrown away by becoming a single parent, she was painfully aware that she could only blame herself. She had precious little excuse for her foolishness and lack of foresight. After all, Erin had grown up in a poor home listening to her father talk endlessly and impressively about how he was going to make his fortune. Over and over and over again she had listened and the fortune had never come. Worse still, on many occasions money that could not be spared had been frittered away on crazy schemes and had dragged her family down into debt. By the time she was ten years old and watching her poorly educated mother work in a succession of dead-end jobs to keep her family solvent, she had realised that her father was just a dreamer, full of money-making ideas but lacking the work ethic required to bring any of those ideas to fruition. His vain belief that he was set on earth to shine as brightly as a star had precluded him from seeking an ordinary job. In any case working to increase someone else's profit had been what her idle father called 'a mug's game'. He had died in a train crash when she was twelve and from that point on life in her home had become less of a roller-coaster ride.

In short, Erin had learned at a young age that she needed to learn how best to keep herself and that it would be very risky to look to any man to take care of her. As a result, she had studied hard at school, ignored those who called her a nerd and gone on to university, also ignoring her mother's protestations that she should have moved straight into a job to earn a wage. Boyfriends had come and gone, mostly unremarked, for Erin had been wary of getting too involved, of compromising her ambitions to match someone else's. Having set her sights on a career with prospects, she had emerged from university with a top-flight business management degree. To help to finance her years as a student she had also worked every spare hour as a personal trainer, a vocation that had gained her a raft of more practical skills, not least on how best to please in a service industry.

Later that afternoon, when she returned from her visit to Black's Inn, the Stanwick receptionist informed Erin that Sam wanted to see her immediately. Realising in dismay that she had forgotten to switch her mobile phone back on after the interviews were finished, Erin knocked lightly on the door of her boss's office and walked straight in with the lack of ceremony that Sam preferred.

'Ah, Erin, at last. Where have you been all afternoon? There's someone here I want you to meet,' Sam informed her with just a hint of impatience.

'Sorry, I forgot to remind you that I'd be over at Black's doing interviews with Owen,' Erin explained, smiling apologetically until a movement by the window removed her attention from the older man. She turned her head and began to move forward, visually tracking the emergence of a tall powerful male from the shadows. Then she froze as though a glass wall had suddenly sprung into being around her, imprisoning her and shutting her off from her companions.

'Miss Turner?' a sleek cultured drawl with the suggestion of an accent purred. 'I've been looking forward to meeting you. Your boss speaks very highly of you.'

Erin flinched as though a thunderclap had sounded within the room without warning, that dark-timbred voice unleashing an instant 'fight or flight instinct she had to struggle to keep under control. She would have known that distinctive intonation laced with command had she heard it even at a crowded party. It was as unforgettable as the male himself.

'This is—' Sam began.

'Cristophe Donakis…' Cristo extended a lean brown hand to greet her as if they had never met before.

And Erin just stared in consternation at that wicked fallen-angel face as if she couldn't believe her eyes. And she *couldn't*. Cropped black hair spiky with the short curls that not even the closest cut could eradicate entirely, ebony brows level above stunning dark deep-set eyes that could turn as golden as the sunset, high cheekbones and, as though all the rest was not enough to over-endow him with beauty, a mouth that was the all-male sensual equivalent of pure temptation. The passage of time since their final encounter had left no physical mark on those lean dark features. In a split second it was as if she had turned her head and stepped back in time. He remained defiantly drop-dead gorgeous. Something low down in her body that she hadn't felt in years clenched tightly and uncomfortably, making her press her slender thighs together in dismay.

'Mr Donakis,' Erin pronounced woodenly, lifting her chin and very briefly touching his hand, determined to betray no reaction that Sam might question. Sam's 'big appointment' was with Cristo? She was horrified, fighting to conceal her reactions, could feel a soul-deep trembling begin somewhere in the region of her wobbly knees. That fast she was being bombarded by unwelcome images from their mutual past. Cristo grinning with triumph and punching the air when he finally beat her in a swimming race; Cristo serving her breakfast in bed when she was unwell and making a production of feeding her grapes one by one, long brown fingers caressing her lips at every opportunity, teaching her that no part of her was impervious to his touch. Cristo, sex personified night or day with an unashamedly one-track mind. He had taught her so much, *hurt* her so much she could hardly bear to look at him.

'Make it Cristo. I'm not a big fan of formality,' Cristo murmured levelly and even the air around him seemed cool as frost.

Just as suddenly Erin was angry, craving the power to knock him into the middle of next week for not being surprised by her appearance. Evidently he had known in advance that she worked for Sam and he was not prepared to own up to their previous relationship, which suited Erin perfectly. Indeed she was grateful that he had pretended she was a stranger, for she cringed at the idea of Sam and her colleagues learning what an idiot she had once been. One of Cristo Donakis' ex-girlfriends, *what*? That guy who changed women as he changed socks? *Really*? Inside her head she could already imagine the jeers and scornful amusement that that revelation would unleash, for Erin already knew that she had the reputation of being standoffish with the staff for keeping her private life private while others happily told all. Was Cristo the prospective buyer of Sam's hotels? For what other reason would he be visiting the Stanwick hotel? Cristo owned an international hotel and leisure empire.

'Erin…I'd like you to give Cristo a tour of our facilities here and at the other spas. His particular interest lies with them,' Sam told her equably. 'You can give him the most recent breakdown of figures. Believe me when I tell you that this girl has a mind like a computer for the important details.'

Erin went pink in receipt of that compliment.

'Looks *and* brains—I'm impressed,' Cristo pronounced with a slow smile that somehow contrived to freeze her to the marrow.

'You own the Donakis group,' Erin remarked tightly, trying to combat the shocked blankness of her mind with a shrewd take on what Cristo's source of interest could be in a trio of comparatively small hotels, which while luxurious could not seriously compare to the opulence of the elite Donakis hotel standards. 'I thought you specialised in city hotels.'

'My client base also enjoy country breaks. In any business there's always room for expansion in a new direction. I want to provide my clients with a choice of custom-made outlets so that they no longer have to patronise my competitors,' Cristo drawled smoothly.

'The beauty market is up-and-coming. What was once a treat for special occasions is now seen as a necessity by many women and by men as well,' Erin commented, earning an appreciative glance from her boss.

'You surprise me. I've never used a spa in my life,' Cristo proclaimed without hesitation.

'But your nails are filed and your brows are phenomenally well groomed,' Erin commented softly, earning a startled appraisal from Sam, who clearly feared that she was getting much too personal about his guest's grooming habits.

'You're very observant,' Cristo remarked silkily.

'Well, I have to be. One third of our customer base is male,' Erin fielded smoothly.

CHAPTER TWO

ERIN escorted Cristo to the fitness suite that connected with the spa.

'You *can't* buy Sam's hotels,' she said tightly in an undertone, the words framed by gritted teeth. 'I don't want to work for you again.'

'Believe me, I don't want you on my payroll either,' Cristo declared with succinct bite.

Well, she knew how she could take that. If he took over, she would be out in the cold as soon as the law allowed such a move and, appalling as the prospect of unemployment was, it was a welcome warning at a moment when she was feeling far too hot and bothered to think straight. What was it about Cristophe Donakis? That insidious power of his that got to her every time? Sheathed in a charcoal grey pinstripe suit, fitted to his lean powerful body with the flare that only perfect tailoring could offer, Cristo looked spectacular and, although she very much wanted to be, she was not indifferent to his high-voltage sexual charge. Cristo was a very beautiful man with the sleek dark good looks of a Greek god. As she turned to look at him, eyes as blank as she could make them, there was a lowdown buzz already feeding through her every limb like poison. She

knew what that buzz was and feared it deeply. It was the
burn of excitement, gut-deep, breathtaking *excitement*.

'I wasn't expecting to find a gym here,' Cristo remarked, eying the banks of machines and their sweat-
ing occupants, swivelling his handsome head to glance
through the glass partition to where a couple of men
were training with heavy weights. He returned his attention to her just as Erin slicked her tongue across her
white teeth as if she was seeking to eradicate a stray
smudge of lipstick. She wasn't wearing very much, just
a hint of pale pearlised gloss that added unnecessary
voluptuousness to the full swell of that sultry mouth,
which he was working very hard not to imagine moving
against his... Don't go there, his cool intelligence cau-
tioned him, acting to suppress the kind of promptings
that would interfere with his concentration.

'An exercise suite dovetails perfectly with the spa.
The customers come here to train and attend classes,
treat themselves to a massage or a beauty treatment and
go home feeling spoiled and refreshed.' As Erin talked
she led the way into the spa and gave him a brief look at
those facilities that were free for his appraisal. 'People
have less free time these days. It makes sense to offer a
complete package at the right price. The profits speak
for themselves.'

'So, how much are you creaming off in reward
for your great moneymaking ideas?' Cristo enquired
smoothly.

Her brow furrowed, amethyst eyes flickering in confusion across his strong bronzed face. 'I don't get commission for bringing in more business,' she responded
uncertainly.

'That wasn't what I meant and you know it. I've seen

enough of the premises here. We'll move on to Blacks now and fit in the last place before dinner,' he told her arrogantly.

Cristo strode out to the front of the hotel and the silver Bugatti Veyron sports car that was his pride and joy. Erin followed more slowly, her agile brain struggling to work out what he had meant. 'I'll take my own car,' she called in his wake, crossing to the BMW. 'Then I can go home without needing a lift.'

Cristo wheeled back in his tracks, brilliant dark eyes gleaming between lush curling lashes. He was quick to note the premium model that she drove and he wondered with derision just how she afforded such a vehicle. 'No, I'll take you. We have business to discuss.'

Erin could think of nothing she wanted to discuss with him and she wanted him nowhere near the home she shared with her mother but, as Sam's right-hand woman, keeping Cristo happy was paramount. She wanted Cristo to vanish in a puff of black smoke like the fallen angel he resembled but she did not want Sam to lose out because she hadn't done her job right: she owed the older man too much for his faith in her and could not have looked him in the eye again if she scared off Cristo to suit her own personal preferences. Yet was she capable of scaring him off? There was an air of purpose about Cristo that said otherwise. To be fair, Sam's busy hotels would make a good investment. She pulled out her phone to ring Owen, the manager at Black's, to give him notice of their intended visit.

With pronounced reluctance she climbed into Cristo's boy-toy car, trying not to recall the time she had attended the Motor Show with him where the beautiful models draped over the latest luxury cars had salivated every time Cristo came within touching distance. Women always *always* noticed Cristo, ensnared by his six-foot-four-inch height and breadth and the intensity of dark eyes that could glitter like black diamonds.

Out of the corner of his gaze, Cristo watched her clasp her hands on her lap and instantly he knew she was on edge, composing herself into the little concentrated pool of calm and silence she invariably embraced when she was upset. She was so damn small, a perfect little package at five feet two inches calculated to appeal to the average testosterone-driven male as a vulnerable female in need of masculine protection. His shapely mouth took on a sardonic slant as he accelerated down the drive. She could look after herself. He had once enjoyed her independent streak, the fact she didn't always come when he called. Like most men he preferred a challenge to a clinging vine but he knew how tricky she could be and had no intention of forgetting it.

Erin wanted to keep her tongue pinned to the roof of her mouth but she couldn't. 'What you said back there—that phrase you used, "creaming off," —I didn't like the connotations—'

'I didn't think you would,' Cristo fielded softly, his dark accented drawl vibrating low in his throat.

Gooseflesh covered the backs of her hands and suddenly she felt chilled. 'Were you getting at something?'

'What do you think?'

'Don't play games with me,' she urged, breathing in deep and slow, nostrils flaring in dismay at the familiar spicy scent of his designer aftershave.

The smell of him, so familiar, so *achingly* familiar, unleashed a tide of memories. When he was away from her she used to sleep in one of his shirts but she would never have done anything so naff and revealing when he was around. Sometimes when she was at his city apartment she used to wash his shirts as well, she recalled numbly, eager to take on any little homely task that could made her feel more like one half of a committed couple. But Cristo had *not* made a commitment to her, had not done anything to make her feel secure and had never once mentioned love or the future. Recalling those hard facts, she wondered why she had once looked back on that phase as being the happiest of her life. Admittedly that year with Cristo had been the most exciting, varied and challenging of her twenty-five years of existence but the moments of happiness had often been fleeting and she had passed a great deal more time worrying about where their affair was going and never daring to ask. She had worked so hard at playing it cool with him, on not attaching strings or expectations that might irritate him. Her soft full mouth turned down at the recollection—much good all that anxious stressing and striving had done her! At the end of the day, in spite of all her precautions, he had still walked away untouched while she had been crushed in the process. She had had to accept that all along she had only been a Miss All-Right-For-Now on his terms, not a woman he was likely to stay with. No, she was just one more in a long line of women who had contrived to catch his eye and entertain him for a while until the time came for him to choose a suitable wife. The knowledge that she had meant so little to him that he had ditched her to marry another woman still burned like acid inside her.

'Maybe I'm hoping you'll finally come clean,' Cristo murmured levelly.

Erin turned her head, smooth brow indented with a

frown as she struggled to recall the conversation and get back into it again. 'Come clean about what?'

Cristo pulled off the road into a layby before he responded. 'I found out what you were up to while you were working for me at the Mobila spa.'

Erin twisted her entire body round to look at him, crystalline eyes flaring bright, her rising tension etched in the taut set of her heart-shaped face. 'What do you mean, what I was up to?'

Cristo flexed long brown fingers round the steering wheel and then turned to look at her levelly, ebony dark eyes cool and opaque as frosted glass. 'You were helping yourself to the profits in a variety of inventive ways but I employ a forensic accounting team, who have seen it all before, and they traced the transactions back to you. You were *stealing* from me.'

For a split second, Erin was pinned to the seat by the sheer weight of her incredulity and her eyes were huge. 'That's an outrageous and disgusting lie!' she slammed back at him, her voice rising half an octave with a volume stirred by simple shock.

'I have the proof and witnesses,' Cristo breathed in a tone of cutting finality that brooked no argument, igniting the engine again and filtering the car back onto the main road without batting an eyelash.

'You can't have proof and witnesses for something that never happened!' Erin launched at him furiously. 'I can't believe that you can accuse me of something like that—I've never stolen anything in my life!'

'You *stole* from me,' Cristo shot back at her with simmering emphasis, his bold bronzed profile hard as iron. 'You can't argue with hard evidence.'

Erin was stunned, not only by the accusation coming

so long after the event and out of nowhere at her, but by the rock-solid assurance of his conviction in her guilt.

'I don't care what evidence you think you've got. As it never happened, as I never helped myself to anything I wasn't entitled to, the evidence can only have been manufactured!'

'Nothing was manufactured. Face facts. You got greedy and you got caught,' Cristo asserted grittily. 'I'd have had you charged with theft if I'd known where to find you but by the time I found out you were long gone.'

Trembling with frustrated fury, every nerve jangling with adrenalin, Erin waited impatiently for him to park outside the nineteen-thirties black and white frontage of the Black's Inn hotel. Then she wrenched at the handle on the passenger door and leapt out. Cristo watched her through the windscreen, bleakly amused by the angry heat in her shaken face. She was shocked that he had found her out and not surprisingly frantic to convince him that she was as innocent as a newborn lamb of the charges. Naturally she wouldn't want him to label her a thief with her current employer. Even if she *had* resisted temptation this time around, mud stuck and no boss could have a faith in a member of staff with such a fatal weakness.

Slowly and with the easy moving fluidity of a natural athlete, Cristo climbed out of the car and locked it.

Erin's small hands clenched into fists at her side as she squared up to him. 'We're going to have this out!'

Infuriatingly in control, Cristo cast her a slumberous glance from below his ridiculously long lashes. 'Not a good idea in a public place—'

'We'll borrow Owen's office.' Erin stalked into the hotel and saw the lanky blond manager already on his way out to welcome them. She hurried over to him. 'We'll do the tour in ten minutes. Right now we need somewhere private to talk. Could we use your office?'

'Of course.' Owen spread the door wide and as she passed him smiled down at her and whispered, 'By the way, thanks for the heads-up.'

Cristo noticed that friendly little exchange but not its content and wondered at the precise nature of Erin's relationship with the handsome young manager. Generally she liked older men, Cristo reflected until he recalled the youth barely, if even, into his twenties that he had surprised in her hotel bed and his expressive mouth clenched hard. He recalled Sam Morton's gushing praise of his beautiful area manager and his derision rose even higher. He doubted that he'd ever met a man more in a woman's thrall. Sam thought the sun, the moon and the stars rose on Erin Turner.

Erin closed the door on Cristo's entry and spun back to him, amethyst eyes dark with anger. 'I am not a thief, so naturally I want to know exactly why you're making these allegations.'

He studied her with narrowed eyes. She was breathing fast, her silky top sliding tantalisingly against the rounded bulge of her breasts. Creamy lickable mounds topped by succulent strawberry nipples, he remembered lasciviously, his desire firing at that imagery as a bolt of lust shot through him in a flash, leaving him hard as a rock. What she lacked in height she more than made up for with wonderfully feminine curves. He had loved her body. Even worse, he had dreamt of her passion when he was away from her, craving the unparalleled sexual satisfaction he had yet to find with anyone else.

'I'm not an idiot,' Cristo informed her coldly, forcing

his keen mind back to a safer pathway. 'At the Mobila spa, you sold products out of the beauty store on your own behalf, falsified invoices and paid therapists who didn't exist. Your fraudulent acts netted you something in the region of twenty grand in a comparatively short time frame. How could you think that that level of deceit would go unnoticed?'

'I am not a thief,' Erin repeated doggedly although an alarm bell had gone off in her head the instant he mentioned the theft and sale of products from the store.

She knew someone who had done that for she herself had actually caught the woman putting a box of products into her car. Sally, her administrative assistant in the office, whom she had relied on heavily at the time, had been stealing and selling the exclusive items online. Unfortunately Erin had no proof of that fact because she had neither called in the police to handle the matter nor shared the truth that Sally had been stealing with another member of staff. Instead she had sat a distraught Sally down to talk to her. Together the two women had then done a stocktake and Erin had ended up replacing the missing products out of her own pocket. Why? She had felt desperately sorry for the older woman, struggling to cope alone with two autistic children after her husband had walked out on her. But had she only scraped the tip of the iceberg when it came to Sally's dishonesty? Had Sally even then been engaged in rather more imaginative methods of gaining money by duplicitous means?

'I have the proof,' Cristo retorted crisply.

'And witnesses, you said,' Erin recalled. 'Would one of those witnesses be Sally Jennings?'

His lean strong face tightened and she knew she had

hit a nerve. 'You can't talk or charm your way out of this, Erin—'

'I'm not interested in charming you. I'm not the same woman I was when we were together,' Erin countered curtly, for what he had done to her had toughened her. There was nothing like surviving an unhappy love affair to build self-knowledge and character, she reckoned painfully. He had broken her heart, taught her how fragile she was, left her bitter and humiliated. But she had had to pick herself up again fast once she discovered that she was pregnant. Choice and self-pity hadn't come into that challenging equation.

Erin stared back at him, pale amethyst eyes searching his darkly handsome features, blocking her instinctive response to that beautiful bone structure. Had he truly not read a single one of her letters? What had happened to human curiosity? Her phone calls had gone unanswered and his PA had told her she was wasting her time phoning because Cristo wouldn't accept a call from her. Even when she had got desperate enough to call his family home in Greece she had run into a brick wall erected by his spiteful foster mother, who had proudly told her that Cristo was getting married and wanted nothing more to do with, 'a woman like her'. As if she were some trollop Cristo had picked up in the street for a night of sex, rather than the woman who had been his constant companion for a year.

Although, perhaps it hadn't been his foster mother's fault. After all, while she might have seen herself in the light of a serious relationship, it was clear that Cristo had seen her entirely differently. He had never let her meet his family and, even though he'd known that she wanted him to meet her mother, he had found it inconvenient every time she'd tried to set up even a casual encounter. She might have been part of his private life but he had walled her off from everyone else in it, for she had only occasionally met his friends and never again after the evening when one of his mates had made a point of commenting on how long he had been with Erin.

'I think you'll change your tune once you appreciate how few choices you have,' Cristo responded softly. 'Now let's view the facilities here. I have a tight schedule.'

Her mouth tightening, she followed him out of the office. How did he expect her to change her tune? Certainly, he hadn't listened to a word she'd said. Had Sally Jennings lied about her? What else could she think? Had her abrupt departure from her job at the Mobila spa played right into the older woman's hands when the irregularities were exposed by the accounting team? Change her tune? What had he meant by that comment? Her brain engaged in working out what she could possibly do to combat such allegations, Erin realised that she would have to see the evidence he had mentioned to work out her own defence and how to nail the real culprit. Had she been a total idiot to let Sally off the hook when she caught her stealing? She was appalled that her sympathetic and supportive treatment of the older woman might have been repaid with lies calculated to make Erin look guilty in her place. Confronting Sally, appealing to her conscience—if she had one—might well be the only course she could take. But what had Cristo meant about choices?

Owen brimmed with enthusiasm as he showed them round the spa, describing the latest improvements and special offers as well as the upsurge in custom that had resulted. He finished by offering them coffee but Cristo demurred, pleading time constraints as he whisked Erin back out to the car and angled it back out onto the road to make their last call. Brackens was Sam's most exclusive property. A Victorian house set in wooded surroundings, it was very popular with couples in search of a romantic weekend and the spa was run as a member's only club.

Erin watched Mia, the elegant brunette in her thirties who managed Brackens, melt at Cristo's first smile and allowed the knowledgeable manager to do most of the talking as she showed them round her impressive domain. Erin was struggling to concentrate on the job at hand. There was too much else on her bemused mind. So, for almost three years, Cristo had been under the impression that she had stolen a fat wad of cash from him. Why hadn't he contacted her? Why had he virtually let it go instead of informing the police? Cristo never let people get away with doing the dirty on him. He was a man few would wish to cross but he did reward loyal, hardworking staff with generous bonuses and opportunities.

Watching Mia laugh flirtatiously with Cristo made Erin feel slightly nauseous. She could recall when she had been even more impressionable. One glance at that lean dark face of sharp angles and creative hollows and those stunning black diamond eyes and she had been enamoured, her interest caught, her body humming with unfamiliar thrills. Her wariness with men, her long hours of study while others partied, had made her more than usually vulnerable for a young woman of twenty-one. She slammed down hard on the memory, award-

ing Cristo a veiled glance when he ushered her back
to his Bugatti with a fleeting remark on her quietness.

'May I go home now?' she enquired as he turned
the sports car.

'We're having dinner together at my hotel,' Cristo
informed her. 'We have things to talk about.'

'I have nothing to talk to you about. Sam does his
own negotiating,' Erin volunteered drily. 'I'm just the
hired help.'

'If rumour is to be believed, you're not *just* anything
when it comes to Sam Morton.'

Erin went rigid in the passenger seat at the suggestion. 'Do you listen to rumours?'

'You slept with me while I was employing you,'
Cristo reminded her without heat.

Her teeth ground together. For two pins she would
have slapped him. 'That's different. We were already
involved when I began working for you.'

Cristo compressed his beautifully shaped mouth, his
thoughts taking him back even though he didn't want
to go there. He had never had to work so hard to get a
woman into bed. Her elusiveness, her surprising inhi-
bitions had heightened his desire, persuaded him that
she was different. Yes, she *had* been different, she had
lined her pockets at his expense throughout their affair,
he recalled grimly. She had taken him for a fool just as
she was taking Morton.

'Sam and I are only friends—'

His eloquent mouth quirked. 'The same sort of
friendship you had with that other friend of yours, Tom?'

Erin stiffened, remembering how suspicious Cristo
had become of her fondness for Tom's company towards

the end of their affair. 'Not as familiar. Sam's from a different generation.'

Tom was a mate from her university days, more like a brother than anything else and still an appreciated part of Erin's life. Unfortunately Cristo didn't believe that platonic friendships could exist and Erin had eventually given up trying to convince him otherwise, reasoning that she was entitled to her own friends regardless of his opinions.

'Morton's old enough to be your grandfather—'

'Which is why there's nothing else between us,' Erin slotted in flatly. 'I'm not sleeping with Sam.'

'He's besotted with you. I don't believe you,' Cristo framed succinctly.

'That's your prerogative.' Erin dug out her mobile phone and tapped out her home number.

Her mother answered. In the background she could hear a child crying. Lorcan, she guessed. Her son sounded tired and cross and her heart clenched, for she felt guilty that she couldn't be there with him. It hurt that she got to spend so little time with her children during the week and she cherished her weekends with the twins when she tried to make up for her absence during working hours.

'I'm sorry but I'll be late home tonight,' she told Deidre Turner.

'Why? What are you doing?' the older woman asked.

'I have some work to deal with before I can leave.'

Tight-lipped and knowing she still had a maternal interrogation to face, Erin put her phone back in her bag. The very last thing she could afford to tell her parent was that Cristo had reappeared in her life. She would never hear the end of it, much as she had yet to hear the end of the reproaches about bringing two children into the world without first having acquired a wedding ring on her finger. But she didn't blame her mother for her attitude. Educated in a convent school by nuns and deeply devout, Deidre had somewhat rigid views. At the same time, however, she was a very loving and caring grandmother and Erin could not have coped as a single parent without the older woman's support.

'I still don't know what this is about,' Erin complained as Cristo parked outside the foremost hotel in the area. 'I didn't steal from you three years ago but until you give me more facts I can't defend myself.'

'One of the transactions was traced right back to your bank account. Don't waste your time trying to plead innocence,' Cristo shot back at her very drily.

'I don't want to have dinner with you. It's not like we parted on good terms,' Erin reminded him doggedly.

Cristo climbed gracefully out of the car. 'It's like this. Either you dine with me and we talk or I go straight to your boss with my file on your thefts.'

He spoke so levelly, so unemotionally that for several taut seconds Erin could not quite accept that he had threatened her without turning a hair. The blood drained from below her fair skin and she froze until she recognised that he had given her a choice. She could tell him to take his precious file of supposed evidence and put it where the sun didn't shine. She could call his bluff. But, unhappily for her, she *knew* Cristophe Donakis and she knew what he was capable of.

He didn't bluff and he was very determined. He would push to the limits and beyond to gain a desired result. He was tough, sufficiently volatile to be downright dangerous and a merciless enemy. If Cristo truly believed that she had stolen from him, he would not settle until he had punished her for her offence.

For the first time in a very long time, Erin felt utterly helpless. She had too much at stake to risk her children's future. She had worked very hard to get to where she was and she would fight just as hard to retain it...

CHAPTER THREE

ERIN walked into the cloakroom of the hotel and ran her wrists below the cold water tap until the panicked thump of her heartbeat seemed to slow to a tolerable level. Get a grip on yourself, she told her tense reflection as she dried her hands. Why should Cristo come back into her life now and try to wreck it? On his part it would be a pointless exercise...

Unless he *was* after revenge. At the vanity counter she tidied her hair and noticed with annoyance that her hands were no longer steady. He had already contrived to wind her up like a clockwork toy, firing all her self-defence mechanisms into override. And she needed to watch out because panic would make her stupid and careless. She breathed in slow and deep, fighting to stay calm. He didn't know about the children so evidently he had not read a single one of her letters. Had she known about the twins he would have left her in peace, she was convinced of it. What man went out of his way to dig up trouble?

Cristo did, a little voice piped up warningly at the back of her head, and all of a sudden time was taking her back to their first encounter.

At the time Erin was employed in her first job as a

deputy manager at a council leisure centre. Elaine, one of her university friends, was from a wealthy home and her father had bought her an apartment in an exclusive building. When Elaine realised what a struggle Erin was having trying to find decent accommodation on a budget, she had offered Erin her box room, a space barely large enough for a single bed with storage beneath. But Erin hadn't cared how small the room was, she had enjoyed having Elaine's company, not to mention daily access to the residents' fancy leisure complex on the ground floor.

Erin had always been a keen swimmer and had won so many trophies for her school that she could have aspired to an athletic career had her parents been of a different ilk. Regretfully, in spite of her coach's efforts at persuasion, Erin's parents had been unwilling to commit to the time and cost of supporting a serious training schedule for their talented daughter. However, Erin still loved the sport and swam as often as she could.

The first time she had seen Cristo he had been scything up and down the pool with the sleek flow of a shark. His technique had been lazy, his speed moderate, she had noted, overtaking him without effort as she pursued her usual vigorous workout.

'Race me!' he had challenged when he caught up with her.

And she still recalled those dark deep-set gorgeous eyes, gleaming like polished bronze, electrifying in his lean, darkly handsome features.

'I'll beat you,' she warned him ruefully. 'Can you take that?'

The dark golden eyes had flashed as though she had lit a fire inside him. 'Bring it on…' he had urged.

And just like him, she had loved the challenge, skimming through the water with the firing power of a bullet, beating him to the finish line and turning to cherish his look of disbelief. Afterwards she had hauled herself out of the water and he had followed suit, straightening his lean powerful length to tower over her diminutive frame, water streaming down over his six-pack abs, drawing her attention to his superb muscular development. It was possibly the very first time that she had ever *seriously* noticed a man's body.

'You're tiny. How the hell did you beat me?' he demanded incredulously.

'I'm a good swimmer.'

'We have to have a retrial, *koukla mou*.'

'OK, same time Wednesday night but I warn you I train every day and your technique is sloppy—'

'Sloppy…' Cristo repeated in accented disbelief, an ebony brow quirking. 'If I wasn't tired, I'd have beaten you hollow!'

Erin laughed. 'Sure you would,' she agreed peaceably, knowing what the male ego was like.

He extended a lean brown hand. 'I'm Cristophe Donakis…I'll see you Wednesday and I'll whip your hide.'

'I don't think so,' she told him cheerfully.

'Cristophe Donakis? You met Cristophe in the residents' pool where us ordinary people swim?' Elaine later gasped in consternation. 'What on earth was he doing there? He owns the penthouse and he has a private pool on the roof.'

'Well, he was slumming this evening. Who is he?'

'A spoilt rotten Greek tycoon and playboy with pots of money and a different woman on the go every week. I've seen him taking them up there in the lift. He's very fond of decorative beauties. Stay clear. He'd gobble you up like a mid-morning snack,' Elaine warned her drily.

But that same night the recollection of Cristo's flawless male perfection got Erin all hot and bothered in her dreams and she marvelled that he could have that effect on her, for her strict upbringing had made her reserved and wary about all things sexual. Even at a glance she had recognised that Cristophe Donakis was a very sexual animal. On the Wednesday she beat him a second time, albeit with a little more effort on her part.

'Join me for a drink,' he suggested afterwards, his hungry gaze wandering at leisure over her slim curves in the plain black and red suit she wore, rising to linger on her soft full mouth, the sexual charge of his interest blatant and bringing self-conscious colour to her cheeks.

'No, thanks.' Fear of getting out of her depth and of somehow making a fool of herself made Erin especially cautious

'A rematch, then…third time lucky?' he prompted, amusement dancing in his stunning eyes below the fringe of black curling lashes.

'My flatmate tells me you have your own pool.'

'It's in the process of being replaced. Rematch?' he pressed again, pure challenge gleaming in those bronzed eyes. 'The next time the loser buys dinner. Give me your phone number and we'll arrange a date for it. I'm about to leave for the US for a week.'

She admired his persistence and had never been able to resist a dare. The third time he beat her, punching the air with uninhibited triumph. And that was also the moment she fell for Cristo, loving the naturally dramatic streak that he kept concealed below the surface in favour of cool assurance and the gloriously wicked grin that could burnish his hard dark features with adorably boyish enthusiasm.

She fed him in an American-style diner down the street in the sort of basic unsophisticated setting that she could tell was unfamiliar to him, but he proved a good sport and an entertaining raconteur, who drew her out about her job and her ambitions. He assumed that she would accompany him back to his apartment after the meal, looked at her in frank surprise when she refused, for he was very much a male accustomed to easy conquests. After that rebuff it took him two whole weeks to phone her again.

'He'll hurt you,' Elaine forecast. 'He's too handsome, too rich, too arrogant. You're very down to earth. What have you got in common with a guy like that?'

And the answer was…*nothing*. But like a moth drawn to a candle flame she had refused to acknowledge the obvious and eventually she had got burned, badly enough burned to avoid getting involved ever since. From time to time other men had made a play for her but she had resisted, reluctant to entertain such a complication in her life. In any case living under the same roof as her mother was almost as good as wearing a chastity belt, she reflected with sheepish amusement.

Cristo was already seated in the elegant restaurant. He levered upright as she approached, his keen dark gaze welded to her delicate features. She looked like an angel, fragile, pure, amethyst eyes luminous as jewels in her heart-shaped face. He noticed the other men following her progress and the seductive image of her spread across his silk sheets flashed through his head, instantly hardening him. He marvelled at the effect she had on him even though he knew that she was both dishonest and untrustworthy, a thoughtless, foolish little slut below the patina of that perfection. No truly clever woman would have tossed him and what he could buy her away for the cheap thrill of a casual encounter and what he considered to be a paltry sum of money.

Erin felt the heat of his appraisal and flushed, her spine stiffening, her bone structure tightening as she exerted fierce self-discipline. Willing herself not to react, she sat down and immediately lifted the menu to peruse it. She picked a single course, told him that she didn't want any wine and sat as straight as a child told to sit properly at table.

'So, tell me what you want and get it over with,' she suggested, eager to take charge of the conversation rather than sit there quailing like a victim.

His dark golden eyes rested on the hands she had clasped together on the table top and his beautiful mouth took on a sardonic twist. 'I want you,' he countered levelly.

Her smooth brow indented. 'In what way?'

Cristo laughed, raw amusement lightening his stunning eyes to a shade somewhere between amber and honey. 'In the most obvious way that a man wants a woman.'

But she couldn't credit that, for hadn't he ditched her and moved on to marry an exceptionally beautiful Greek woman, a socialite called Lisandra, within weeks of their split? She hadn't been able to hold him then, hadn't been important enough to him to retain his interest. He had moved on with his life without her at breathtaking speed. Now he was divorced and it was mean of her to reflect that his marriage had barely lasted long enough for the ink to dry on the licence. Maybe he had got bored with his wife and being married in the same way that he had got bored with Erin. Maybe he didn't have what it took to really *care* about any woman.

'That's the price of my silence,' Cristo drawled smooth as silk.

Blackmail? Erin was shocked, so shocked that her teeth settled into the soft underside of her lower lip and she tasted the faint coppery tang of blood in her mouth. 'The silence relating to this supposed thieving you believe me to be guilty of—'

'*Know* you to be guilty of,' Cristo traded.

'You can't possibly be serious,' Erin breathed tightly.

Lean bronzed face radiating raw assurance, Cristo ran a lean brown forefinger down over the back of her hand and every skin cell in her body leapt into tingling awareness. 'Why would you think that? We had a very good time between the sheets.'

Assailed by unwelcome memories, Erin went rigid but that fast, still shockingly attuned to a certain dark intimate note in his deep drawl, her body reacted. Inside her bra, her breasts swelled, her nipples tightening into prominent points, and her breath rasped in her tight throat. She blinked, lashes lowering, shutting out the hot dark golden gaze pinned to her. He could still get to her and that shocked her but was it so surprising? She had lived like a nun since her children were born, grateful just to have a job and a roof over her head in the wake of the struggle to survive while she was pregnant and unemployed. *A good time.* That phrase cheapened her, made light of what she had once believed they had shared. Was a good time all she had been? Or was the very fact that he was back in her life, trying to force her to give him her time and her body again, proof that she had actually meant something more to him? It was a heady suspicion. Not that she still cared about him, she reflected, but like any woman she had her pride.

'So what are you suggesting?' Erin queried, resolving to play him along for a while until she better understood her position. 'Are you asking me to come back to you?'

'*Na pas sto dialo*...go to hell!' Cristo growled, incredulity flashing across his spectacular bone structure at that explosive suggestion. 'I'm talking about one weekend.'

Her delicate face froze tight. She felt the painful sting of that contempt right down to her marrow bone and inwardly swore that somehow, some way, some day he would pay for insulting her like that. Had the waiter not arrived with their meals she could not have trusted herself not to say something unwise. Forced to hold her tongue, she studied her plate fixedly, her hackles raised, bitterness poisoning her. How dared he? How dared he treat her like some hooker he could rent for an hour or two?

'A dirty weekend,' she framed through compressed lips. 'That does fit your MO.'

Those lustrous amber eyes shimmered below his thick sooty lashes, the leashed power of his strong personality and masculine virility creating an aggressive aura. Another punch of awareness slid through her. It was like poking a tiger through the bars of a cage and shockingly exciting, a welcome respite from the hard little knot of humiliation he had inflicted.

'One weekend in return for my silence and the twenty grand you stole...cheap at the price,' Cristo quipped cool as ice.

Erin wanted to thump him for that crack and restraining that natural urge made her slender hands clench into fists where she had placed them on her lap, out of view of his shrewd notice. The only way to play it with Cristo was cool. If she lost her temper she was lost and he would walk all over her.

'Stop playing the ice goddess. That may be a turn on for Morton but it doesn't rev my engine at all,' Cristo informed her drily. 'One weekend—that's the deal on the table—'

'Was this whole thing a set-up? Have you no intention of buying Sam out?' Erin pressed shakily.

'That is a question for me and my acquisitions team to decide. If it's a good investment your presence on the staff will not deter me, although obviously I'd be bringing back the forensic accounting team to run a check on your activities.'

Her chin came up. 'They'll find nothing because I have done nothing dishonest. Neither at Sam's company nor at yours. Furthermore I will not accept blackmail.'

'I think you'll end up eating those words,' Cristo forecast gently, spearing a chunk of succulent steak, primal male to the bone in his unspoilt appetite.

'You have to show me the evidence you say you have before I can make any kind of a decision.'

'After we've eaten. It's in my suite,' he responded equably.

His easy acquiescence on that score shook Erin. Clearly he was confident about the proof he had of her deceit. But, dismayed though she was by that suspicion, she brought her chin up, amethyst eyes glinting with challenge. 'We'll see.'

And she ate even though she wasn't hungry, for to push her food round her plate and leave it virtually untouched would only highlight the reality that she was sick with nerves.

'I have to go home for a week,' Cristo told her smoothly. 'My foster father's company is in trouble and he needs my advice. You must be aware of the state of the Greek economy.'

Erin nodded grudgingly. 'Aren't you suffering from the same effects?'

'My businesses are primarily here and in North America. I saw the way things were going a couple of years back but Vasos is stubborn. He dislikes change and he wouldn't listen to me when I tried to warn him.'

'And you are telling me this…*because*?'

'To help you to pen that weekend slot into your no doubt busy social calendar.'

Her teeth gritted behind her closed lips, her aggrieved sense of outrage building higher. He was so confident of winning that it was an affront. For a split second she was tempted to tell him that two young children took a heavy toll on what free time she had, but common sense kept her quiet, not to mention pride. She did not want him to know that a night out for her these days would most likely encompass a trip to the cinema or a modest meal with friends.

'So what is the state of play with Morton?' Cristo enquired quietly.

As Cristo was rarely quiet, she glanced up suspiciously. 'My relationship with Sam is none of your business.'

'I'm divorced,' he murmured flatly.

Erin shrugged a slim shoulder as if the information meant nothing to her. 'I read about it in the papers. Your marriage didn't last very long.'

He frowned, black brows drawing together. 'Long enough.'

And as his darkly handsome features shadowed and hardened Erin made a discovery that stung her. His broken marriage was still a source of discomfort to him. She sensed his regret and his reserve and the latter was nothing new. Cristo had always played his cards close to his chest, keeping his feelings under cover, and he had played it that way right to the end of their affair when he had told her it had run its course without drama or remorse. The recollection stiffened her backbone because she had been so shocked and unprepared for that development. This time around, she knew who and what she was dealing with: if he wanted a fight, one way or another, she would give him one!

They travelled up in the lift in a tense silence. She could not credit the situation she found herself in. Was she to be the equivalent of a rebound affair in the wake of his divorce? It occurred to her that a sleazy one-off weekend scarcely qualified for that lofty description and mortified pink highlighted her cheeks. Cristo studied her, picturing her silver gilt hair loose, a party dress to replace the business suit, high heels to show off those shapely legs. His body quickened to the image and was swiftly encouraged by far more X-rated images from the past. When he had her in his bed again, she would disappoint him, of course she would. It would not be as good as he remembered, he told himself urgently. That was the whole point of the game, that and, of course, a well-deserved dose of retribution. She had changed though. Those amethyst eyes no longer telegraphed every reaction making her easily read and she was more controlled than he recalled. Once she saw that he had definitive evidence of her thefts, she would surely study to please...

Erin had not quite bargained on the silent isolation of a hotel suite and she hovered in the centre of the reception room, having refused a drink. She watched him stride into the bedroom to retrieve whatever he was after, that long, lean, powerful body that had once haunted her dreams and ensured that other men could not compare so graceful in movement that she compressed her lips into a tight line, infuriated by the fact that she had noticed. But Cristo was a very noticeable guy. Every female head turned when he walked by and their attention lingered. But, Elaine had been right about him, he was a predator to the backbone and she was now simply a target with an X marked on her back. She wondered what his wife had done to him. Did Cristo have a score to settle against the female sex? And why, after almost three years had passed, was she on the menu again?

Cristo extended a file. 'Go ahead and take a look.'

Once again his self-assurance ignited her anxiety level. She took the file over to a sofa and sat down, determined not to be hurried or harassed. There were copies of many documents she had signed off while she worked for him, payments to suppliers and therapists, invoices attached to other copies that differed to show altered figures on the base lines. Her heart sank like lead in her chest and she felt as though someone were sitting on her lungs. It was very comprehensive stuff and shatteringly straightforward in its presentation.

Her knees developed an irritating tremor below the file on her lap but she still fought for a clear head. 'And according to your investigation these particular thera-pists didn't exist?'

'You know they didn't,' Cristo responded flatly.

Erin came to the final document and stared down at the evidence of a single large payment of a thousand pounds heading into a bank account in her name and nausea stirred in her stomach. Had she ever bothered to close that old bank account? She had intended to but couldn't remember. Only one payment but one was enough to damn her. In her opinion only Sally Jennings could be responsible for such duplicity. She had pretty much automatically signed anything that the older woman put on her desk. With hindsight she knew she had been too trusting. Unhappily managing the spa had been her first serious job and she had had no deputy to stand in for her when Cristo wanted her to make time for him. Torn between too much work, hostile staff, who loathed working for the owner's girlfriend, and a deep driving desire to impress Cristo with her efficiency, she had relied a lot on Sally, who had worked at the spa since it had opened ten years earlier and knew the business inside out. No such thing as a free ride, Erin told herself heavily now. Even Sam would doubt her innocence in the face of such damning proof as the file contained.

Erin stood up and dropped the file down with a distasteful clunk of dismissal on the coffee table. 'Very impressive, but I didn't *do* it! You gave me a great opportunity when you put me in that job and I wouldn't have gone behind your back to steal from you.'

Cristo continued to stare at her, eyes like chips of bright gold below his luxuriant lashes, and all of a sudden she was struggling to breathe evenly and something inside her seemed to speed up as if her blood were racing through her veins and the buzz of forbidden excitement in the pit of her tummy were spreading like contagion to her entire body.

'You still want me, *koukla mou*,' Cristo purred, revelling in the charge in the atmosphere, the awareness in her clear gaze. It was the first time he had been able to read her again and it satisfied him.

'No! That is absolutely not true!' Erin shot back at him vehemently, wishing she had not asked to see that evidence in his presence as she recognised how much it had unnerved her and damaged her self-discipline. Now she was all shaken and stirred, a state to be avoided in a predator's radius.

Cristo reached out a hand and curled his fingers around her slender wrist, edging her out from behind the table. The storm of reaction inside her rose to hurricane force, suppressing her caution and defensiveness.

'No...' she said in a small choked voice, fighting just to get air back into her lungs.

Nevertheless he drew her close, banding strong arms round her like a prison, and the heat and strength of him acted like an aphrodisiac on her disturbed senses. She tried to keep distance between them, her slender body rigid as a rock, but he closed the gap with inexorable purpose.

'It's OK,' he rasped in the most frighteningly soothing tone. 'I want you too.'

And Erin did not want to hear that from the male who had dumped her and gone straight off to marry another woman. He had never wanted her enough to love her or keep her and that was the only wanting she had ever needed from him. He meant sex, only sex, she told herself feverishly while the reassuring warmth of him filtered through their clothing to warm her chilled limbs. But far more insidious was the insanely familiar smell of him that close, her nostrils flaring on the faint aroma of the same designer cologne he had always worn, never forgotten, and she was breathing him headily in as though he were a forbidden drug.

'Stop it, Cristo!' she told him tartly. 'I am not going there again. I am never going there again with you!'

'We'll see…' And, golden eyes blazing down at the fiercely conflicted expression on her heart-shaped face, his beautiful mouth swooped down on hers to claim the kiss she would have done almost anything to deny him.

And the taste of him was instantly addictive even as her hands swept up to strike in fists against his broad shoulders while he hauled her closer. Hot, hungry need roared through her in a storm that made her knees shake and she didn't know whether it was her or him behind it, or if, indeed, both of them were equally responsible. His tongue delved and she shuddered, so awake and defenceless against his every seductive move that it hurt, hurt to feel anything so strongly after so long without it. She wanted that kiss then with a sudden ferocity that terrified her. Nothing else mattered but the forceful power of that lean strong body against her own, the pulsing prominence of her nipples and the liquid burn between her thighs driving her on. His mouth bore down on hers with a seething, sizzling urgency that zinged through her slight length like an electric shock, stunning every sense into reaction. Nothing had ever tasted so good, nothing had ever felt so necessary and answering the shrill shriek of warning firing at the back of her brain took every atom of her inner strength.

'No!' she said in fierce rebuttal, thrusting him away

from her with an abruptness that almost made him lose that famous catlike balance of his as he backed into a chair.

In a daze, Cristo blinked. She packed a punch like a world-class boxer. He shook his handsome dark head, dark eyes instantly veiling as he fought the bite of unsated hunger clawing through his big powerful frame. 'You're right...this is not the moment. I have a flight to catch,' he retorted thickly.

Erin's breasts heaved as she frantically breathed in deep in an effort to emulate his fast recovery. Her amethyst eyes were dark with strong emotion as she studied his lean, darkly handsome features with a loathing she couldn't hide. 'I meant no as in *never*,' she contradicted shakily. 'Leave me alone, stay out of my life and stop threatening me.'

His black diamond eyes flared brilliant gold again, for there was nothing in life that Cristo enjoyed so much as a challenge. 'I won't go away.'

'You're going to get burned if you keep pushing me,' Erin warned him angrily, her small face set like a stone, all emotion but anger repressed. 'Get back out of my life or you'll regret it.'

'No, I won't. I rarely regret anything that I do,' Cristo fielded, visibly savouring the admission. 'Are you worried that I'll screw up your future with Morton? Sorry, *koukla mou*. I'll be doing him a favour. You're toxic.'

Her hands clenched into tight fists. 'I think you'll feel the toxic effect more strongly by the time this is over.'

Cristo shot her a grimly amused appraisal. 'I could handle you with one hand tied behind my back.'

'You always did like to believe your own publicity,' Erin countered tightly, her spine as straight as an arrow as she walked to the door. 'I'll catch a taxi back to Stanwick.'

In the lift, she had what felt like a panic attack, her heart beating too fast for comfort, cold clamminess filming her skin. That kiss? Total dynamite! How could that be? How had that happened? She was not in love with him any more, had believed she was fully cured of all that foolishness…until the instant she laid eyes on him again and his mesmerising attraction gripped her as tightly as steel handcuffs.

Maybe she'd succumbed to that kiss because she had been upset after reading that file. Is that the best excuse you can find? a little voice sneered inside her brain. She reddened, hating herself almost as much as she now hated him. Her response to him had qualified as weak and that was something she could not accept.

CHAPTER FOUR

In the early hours of the following morning, Erin rocked her son, Lorcan, on her lap. A nightmare had wakened him and it always took a while to comfort him and soothe him back to sleep.

'Mum…' he framed drowsily, fixing big dark eyes on her as she smoothed his short tousled curls back from his brow, lashes lowering again as tiredness swept him away again.

Much like her son, Erin was utterly exhausted. When she had arrived back at Stanwick to collect her car Sam had wanted a briefing on Cristo's impressions, which had stretched into a meeting that lasted a couple of hours. Sam was keen for his properties to join the Donakis empire because he sincerely believed that a businessman of Cristo's standing could take his three hotels—his life's work—to a higher level. For the first time Erin had felt uncomfortable with the older man, too aware that she was not being entirely honest with him. He didn't know she had had a previous relationship with Cristo Donakis and she did not want him to know. If Sam were to realise that Cristo was the guy who had ditched her and ignored her letters and calls for assistance when she found herself pregnant, he would automatically distrust the younger man. And why should her messy personal life interfere with Sam's plans for retirement? Letting that happen, she felt, would be more wrong than continuing to keep her secrets.

Lorcan shifted against her shoulder, his curly black hair tickling her chin, a warm weight of solid sleeping toddler.

'Tuck him back into bed quickly,' a voice advised quietly from the doorway.

As Deidre Turner, a small blonde woman, moved past to hastily flip back the bedding and assist her daughter in settling the little boy back into his cot, Erin sighed and stood up. 'I'm sorry Lorcan wakened you again.'

'Don't be silly. I don't have to get up as early as you do in the morning,' her mother replied. 'Go back to bed. You look like you're sleepwalking. I don't know what Sam's thinking of, keeping you at work so late. He has no appreciation of the fact that you want to spend time with your family in the evening.'

'Why should he have? He's never had children to worry about,' Erin murmured soothingly, twitching the covers back over her son's small prone body. 'Sam always likes to wind down with a chat at the end of the day and he's very excited about the possibility of selling up.'

'That's all right for him, but if he does sell up where's it going to leave you and the rest of the employees?' Deidre questioned worriedly. 'We couldn't possibly manage on my pension.'

Erin patted her mother's tense shoulder gently. 'We'll survive. Apparently the law protects our jobs in a takeover. But I'll find work somewhere else if need be.'

'It won't be easy with the state the economy's in.

There aren't many jobs out there to find,' the older woman protested.

'We'll be all right,' Erin pronounced with a confidence that she didn't feel and a guilty conscience that she had not felt able to tell her mother that Cristo Donakis was Sam's potential buyer.

But that news would only inflame Deidre Turner, who would also demand to know why her daughter had not made instant use of her access to Cristo to finally tell him that he was a father. In addition her mother was a constant worrier, always in search of the next black cloud on the horizon, and Erin only shared bad news with the older woman if she had no other choice. Checking that her daughter, Nuala, Lorcan's twin sister, was still soundly asleep, curled up in a little round cosy ball inside her cot, Erin returned to bed and lay there in the darkness feeling every bit as anxious as her mother, if not more, as she struggled to count blessings rather than worries.

They lived in a comfortable terraced house. It was rented, not owned. Deidre, predictably imagining less prosperous times ahead, had decided that Erin borrowing money to buy a property for them was far too risky a venture. Her mother's attitude had irritated Erin at the time, but now, with the future danger of unemployment on her mind again she was relieved to be a tenant living in modest accommodation. Sam had reassured her about her job, reminding her that the current legislation would protect his staff with guaranteed employment under the new ownership. But there was often a way round such rules, Erin ruminated worriedly, and, when she was already aware that Cristo didn't want her on his staff, it would only be sensible to immediately begin looking for a new position. Unhappily that might take months to achieve but it was doable, wasn't it? She had to be more positive, stronger, fired up and ready to meet the challenges ahead.

But, Cristo was not a challenge. He was like a great big massive rock set squarely in her path and she didn't know how to get round such an obstacle. He believed she had stolen from him. But why hadn't he pursued that at the time? Why hadn't he called in the police? Erin was thinking back hard, reckoning that by the time Cristo received proof of her supposed theft he would have been married. Had he put the police on her, the fact that she was his ex would soon have emerged and perhaps got into the newspapers. Would that have embarrassed him? She didn't think that the Cristo she recalled would have embarrassed that easily. But that publicity might have embarrassed or annoyed his bride. Was it even possible that Lisandra and Erin had both been in a relationship with Cristo *at the same time*? And that he had feared having that fact exposed? After all, Cristo had got married barely three months after ditching Erin and few couples went from first meeting to marrying that fast. Had he been two-timing both of them? She had never had cause to believe that he was unfaithful to her but refused to believe that he would be incapable of such behaviour. After all, what had she ever really known about Cristo when she had not even suspected that he was about to dump her?

Erin had always liked things safe and certain and she never took risks. The one time she had—Cristo—it had gone badly wrong. On that level she and Cristo were total opposites because nothing thrilled Cristo more than taking a risk or meeting a challenge. So when he had started calling her to ask her out after finally beating her at swimming she had said no, sorry, again and again and again until he had finally manoeuvred her into attending a party at his apartment, urging her to bring friends as her guests.

Her presence bolstered by the presence of Elaine and Tom, it had proved a strangely magical evening with Cristo, she later appreciated, on his very best behaviour. At the end of the night Cristo had kissed her for the first time and that single kiss had been so explosive, it had blown the lid off her wildest dreams…and terrified her. She had known straight off that Cristo Donakis was a high-risk venture: lethally dangerous to her peace of mind.

'I like you…I do like you,' she had told Cristo lamely while still shaking like a leaf in the aftermath of the intense passion that had flared up between them. 'Why can't we just be friends?'

'Friends?' Cristo had echoed as though that word had never come his way before.

'That's what I'd prefer,' she had said brightly.

'I don't do that,' he had told her drily.

With those reservations she'd had more sense at the outset of their affair than she had shown later on, she acknowledged painfully. And once she had had the twins, her life had been turned upside down. She was ashamed to realise that she had been so angry with Cristo in that hotel suite that she had actually been threatening to tell him she was the mother of his children. What aberration had almost driven her to that insane brink? He would not want her children, would never agree to take on the role of father, would only angrily resent the position she put her in and make her feel small and humiliated, a burden he resented. Surely she was entitled to retain some pride when there was no perceptible advantage to telling him the truth?

Cristo had, after all, once confided in her that one of his friends' girlfriends had had a termination. 'It broke them up,' he had commented flatly. 'Few couples survive that sort of stress. I'm not sure I'll ever be ready for children. I prefer my life without baggage.'

And she had got the not exactly subtle message he had taken the trouble to put across, his so clever dark eyes pinned to hers: *Don't do that to me!* Revealingly, it had been the one and only time he ever chose to make her a party to confidential information about someone he knew for Cristo was, by instinct, very discreet. She had taken it as a warning that if she fell pregnant, he would want her to have a termination and their relationship would be over. It still infuriated her that it had actually been entirely his fault that she had conceived and, although she had later grown desperate enough to try and contact him to ask for financial help, she had known even then that the announcement she had to make of his impending fatherhood would infuriate him. Cristo was too arrogant and controlling to appreciate surprises from any source. That a woman could give birth to a baby without a man's prior agreement to accept the responsibility would no doubt strike him as very unfair. No, she saw no point whatsoever in telling Cristo that he was the father of two young children.

Even so, what was she planning to do about his threat to reveal that file of impressive evidence? Cristo was threatening the security of her entire family. Everything she had worked to achieve could vanish overnight. Not only Erin, but her mother and her children would pay the cost of her losing her job and salary. On the other hand, if she could sink her pride enough to play Cristo's cruel game, that file would never see the light of day and at the very least she would have another year of safe employment and plenty of time in which to search for an alternative position. What was one weekend out of the rest of her life, really? She pictured her mother's face earlier, drawn and troubled as she fretted about the hotel group even changing hands. Life had taught Deidre Turner to fear the unknown and the unexpected. She did not deserve to be caught up in the upheaval that was gathering on her daughter's horizon and there was little Erin would not have done to protect her children from the instability she had suffered growing up.

Unhappily, Erin believed that the entire situation was her own fault. Hadn't she ignored everybody's advice in getting involved with Cristo in the first place? Nobody had had a good word to say about Cristo, pointing out that his reputation as a womaniser spoke for him. And why had she made herself even more dependent by agreeing to go and work for him? Was that wise? her friends had asked worriedly. And no, nothing she had done that year with Cristo had been wise. Hadn't she hung on in there even when the going got rough and her lover's lack of commitment was blatantly obvious? He had not even managed to make it back into the UK to celebrate her last birthday with her. She had asked for trouble and now trouble had well and truly come home to roost. Cristo was not going to agree to play nice. Cristo had had over two years to fester over the conviction that she had dared to steal from him. Cristo was out for blood.

* * *

As the sun went down in a blaze of glory, Cristo was staring out at the shaded gardens of his foster parents' much-loved second home away from the smog and heavy traffic in Athens. On his terms, it was homely rather than impressive and it might be situated on the private island of Thesos, which Cristo had inherited at the age of twenty-one, but that was its sole claim to exclusivity.

Vasos and Appollonia Denes had always been extremely scrupulous when it came to enriching themselves in any way through their custodianship of a very wealthy little boy. Both his parents saw life in black and white with no shades of grey, which made them difficult to deal with, Cristo reflected in intense frustration. He had spent three very trying days locked in an office with Vasos, struggling to pull his father's company back from the edge of bankruptcy without the escape route of even being able to offer the firm a cheap loan. They would not touch his money in any form. Yet his father was suffering from so much stress that he had fallen asleep in the middle of dinner and his mother was still worryingly quiet and troubled, in spite of all her protestations to the contrary. She had never quite recovered from the nervous breakdown she had gone through eighteen months earlier.

Had they had any idea what he was engaged in with Erin Turner they would have been sincerely appalled, Cristo acknowledged grudgingly. They adored him, always thought the best of him, and firmly believed that with the conservative upbringing they had given him he must have absorbed their values, their decent principles. But even as a child Cristo had understood what it took to please his parents and he had learned how to pretend as well as accept that it wasn't always within his power to cure the evils of the world for them… His lean strong face hardened fiercely as a particularly unpleasant instance of that impossibility twanged deep in his conscience. He poured himself another drink and shook the memory off again fast.

When life was full of eighteen-hour days and the constant demands of his business empire, Erin was a wonderful distraction to toy with, that was *all*. If she didn't phone him within the next twenty-four hours, however, they would be entering round two of their battle of wits and he would play hardball. He was already figuring out his next move, no regrets whatsoever. Plainly he lacked the forgiving gene. That was becoming obvious even to him and he was not a man given to self-examination. But the lust driving him was on another plane altogether. One kiss…hell, what was he, a teenager to have got so hot and bothered?

And why did it disturb him that right this very minute she might be lying in a bed with Sam Morton, ensuring his continuing devotion in the easiest and most basic way a woman could? Why should that matter to him? Why, in fact, did that mental vision make him seethe? It should turn him off, douse the fire she roused…*disgust* him. But all Cristo could think about just then, indeed the only blindingly blue stretch of sky in his immediate future, was the prospect of that weekend. A weekend of the most perfect fantasy. Of course, it went without saying that fantasy would inevitably turn out to be dross, he pondered cynically. And then it would be over and he would be cured of this inconvenient, incomprehensible craving for her cheating little carcass for all time.

Done and dusted. He savoured that ideal prospect, increasingly keen to reach that moment of equilibrium.

Erin picked up the phone, her blood solidifying like ice in her veins. Caving in *hurt;* it was something she didn't do any more. Show weakness and people often fell on you like vultures. She was not the woman she had been three years earlier. But while she might be tougher, it was useless because Cristo had put her in the no-win corner, giving her no choice other than to try and protect those that she loved by whatever means were within her power.

'Yes, Miss Turner,' some faceless PA trilled at the end of the line. 'Mr Donakis mentioned that you would be calling. I'll put you through.'

His sheer certainty that she would surrender struck another blow to her already battered pride while she thought painfully of all the other times she had tried to speak to Cristo two and a half years earlier and had run into an endless brick wall of refusals. Of course, a call from an ex would not have been welcome to a newly engaged male but the potential offer of sex, it seemed, occupied a whole other plane of acceptability.

'Erin,' Cristo drawled smoothly. 'How may I help you?'

'Will the weekend of the fifth suit?' Her voice was breathless with strain and something very like anguish was rising inside her, for she had lost control of the situation. In the back of her mind something was shrieking that she just could not be doing this, could not possibly be contemplating such a sleazy arrangement, but her brain was mercifully in control as she pictured her children and her mother and once again acknowledged what was most important.

'That's two weeks away,' Cristo growled.

'And it's the soonest I can manage,' Erin said as coolly as if it were a business appointment she was setting up.

'Agreed. Someone will be in touch about the arrangements. Have a current passport available.'

'Why? Where on earth are you planning to go?' she gasped.

'Somewhere discreet. I'll see you on the fifth,' he murmured, the guarded quality in his tone letting her know that he was not alone.

Dry-mouthed, she replaced the phone, pure hatred strong and immovable as a concrete block forming inside her. What had she ever done to him that he should seek her out and threaten to destroy her life? So, he thought she was a thief. *Get over it*, she wanted to shriek at him. When they had been together she had refused to accept expensive gifts and clothes from him—did that telling fact count for nothing? In every way possible she had tried to make their relationship one of equals and her mind slid back into the past...

Surprisingly, he had banished her reluctance to enter a relationship with him with the use of romantic gestures. He had sent her flowers, occasional witty texts to keep her up to date with his life and on Valentine's Day he had sent her the most exquisite card and invited her out to dinner again. As there had not been a glimmer of him showing any interest in any other female during that period, Erin didn't know a woman alive who would have not succumbed to so persuasive an onslaught from a very handsome male. So, she had finally gone out with

him, just the two of them, thoroughly enjoyed herself
and that was how it had begun: date after date but just
kissing, nothing more because she wouldn't agree to
anything more. And, no fan of the celibate life, Cristo
had protested, persisting with his need for an explanation until she finally admitted that he would be her first
lover. Disconcerted by that admission, he had surprised
her by agreeing to wait until *she* felt that the moment
was right and she had loved him all the more for not
putting pressure on her.

And in the end she had slept with him because she
couldn't say no to her own craving any longer and the
experience, the connection she had felt with him from
the outset of true intimacy, had been unutterably wonderful. Four months into their affair, probably tiring of
the number of times she was not available through work
or the extra hours she put in as a personal trainer to a
few select clients, he had offered her the job of manager at the Mobila spa in his flagship London hotel. She
had thought long and hard before she accepted but as
she was already working as a deputy manager she had
believed that the position was well within her capabili-
ties. She had been more afraid that working for Cristo
might change their relationship but it had not occurred
to her that her new colleagues might resent her inescap-
ably personal ties to their employer.

At the time she had been taking the contraceptive pill
but, in spite of trying several different brands, she had
suffered mood changes that made her feel like a stranger
inside her own skin. Ultimately, Cristo had suggested
that he take care of precautions and soon after had come
that disturbing little chat about the friend's girlfriend,
who had had a termination, that same possibility ob-

viously having awakened Cristo's concern on his own
account. After six months she had virtually lived in
Cristo's apartment when he was there and he had begun
asking her to join him on his travels. She had pointed
out that she couldn't just walk out on her job and expect her staff to take her seriously. He had understood
that but he hadn't *liked* it and around the same time he
had started to question the amount of time she spent
with Tom while he was abroad. Tom Harcourt was the
closest thing Erin had ever had to a brother. They had
met on the same university course and had stayed close
friends when Tom also found work in London. There
had never been a sexual spark between Erin and Tom
but they got on like a house on fire, something Cristo
had witnessed on several occasions and had evidently
resented or found suspicious. Eight months into their
relationship Cristo and Erin had had a huge, horrible
row about Tom and Erin had stormed home in a temper.

'How would you like it if I had a female friend that
close?' Cristo had demanded.

And in truth she wouldn't have liked it at all, but she
loved Tom like a brother and refused to give him up.

'You're too possessive for me,' she had told Cristo,
inflaming him as he furiously denied the charge.

'You're a very beautiful woman—Tom has to be
aware of that. Truly platonic relationships don't exist,'
Cristo had insisted. 'One party or the other always feels
something more.'

'Either you trust me or you don't,' Erin had reasoned,
stripping the dispute back to the bare bones while resisting the dangerous temptation to inform him that he
had a shockingly jealous streak.

'Cristo is in love with you,' her more experienced

flatmate, Elaine, had pronounced with amusement. 'I didn't think it would happen but in my opinion men only get that possessive when they're keen.'

And that heartening forecast was why Erin had extended an olive branch to Cristo after a two-week silence while they both smouldered after that argument. In any case, by that stage Tom was already taking a back seat in her life because he had met the woman, Melissa, whom he would eventually marry. She had then waited hopefully for Cristo to demonstrate a more serious attitude towards her but it had never happened. They had spent Christmas and even his birthday apart while he went home to Greece without even dropping a hint that he might consider asking her to accompany him. Only one element of their affair had stayed the same: his passion for her body had never ebbed right to the very last night they had ever spent together and that same night was the one during which she was convinced she had fallen pregnant.

One week later, after bailing on her birthday party at his hotel, he had dumped her. He had had no qualms about the way he did it either, for he had walked into the spa, asked for a moment alone with her in her office and strolled away five minutes later, the deed done.

'You and I?' he had said drily. 'We've run our course and I'd like to move on.'

And he had moved on at supersonic speed to a wife, Erin recalled, settling back into the present with a dazed look on her delicate face. What she couldn't grasp was why, after that emotion-free affront of a dismissal almost three years ago, he should want to revisit the past. It didn't make sense to her. Yes, he might want to pun-

ish her for supposedly thieving from him, but how did
the act of sex, anything but retribution with a guy like
Cristo Donakis, encompass that ambition?

CHAPTER FIVE

Two weeks later, Erin stepped out of the car that had collected her at the airport and breathed in slow and deep. Italy, Tuscany in fact, not at all the setting that she had dimly expected Cristo to provide. In truth she had assumed the weekend would take place in London at his apartment, if he still lived there in the city, or even in one of his hotels. A grand fortified house presiding over an incredibly scenic hidden Italian valley had not featured at all.

Even with the sun starting to set in a golden blaze, the views of grape terraces, arrow-shaped cypresses, pine-forested slopes and silver-grey olive trees were magnificent; almost as much so as the wide graceful house with its shallow terracotta red roof and twin lines of tall elegant windows. Bells tinkled while sheep grazed on stretches of lush green grass in a timeless pastoral scene. It was not the backdrop she would have given to Cristo, whom she had once believed could only thrive on the often insane pace of city life.

A small balding manservant was already grasping the small case she had travelled with and with an expansive wave of one hand he welcomed her in English, introduced himself as Vincenzo and invited her to follow him indoors to an imposing marble hall that echoed with their footsteps. He escorted her straight up the sweeping marble staircase to a beautifully furnished bedroom decorated in masculine shades of gold and green. Her cheeks flared as she gazed at the wide gold-draped bed and hastily she glanced away again, preceding Vincenzo into the superb modern bathroom and politely smiling in admiration.

Did the wretched man know what she was here for? Or did he simply assume that she was yet another one of Cristo's women? And whatever he thought, what did it matter? She studied her taut reflection with self-loathing. Get over yourself, she told herself urgently. It might feel like a lifetime since she had had sex but at the end of the day sex was just sex even with Cristo and not worth risking her security over. She was being practical, choosing the safest option...

Over the past two weeks negotiations over the buyout of Sam's hotels had speeded up to reach agreement. The deal was signed, sealed and delivered and, whether she liked it or not, she was going to be working for Cristo Donakis again, although presumably only after that forensic accounting team he had mentioned had convinced him that she was to be trusted after all. The sting of his conviction that she was a thief still lingered though, not to mention the necessity of having had to lie outright to her trusting mother to travel to Italy. That latter act sat like a giant stone on her conscience.

Her face and her heart troubled, Erin doffed her light raincoat and agreed to come downstairs to enjoy the coffee that Vincenzo was offering. She had told her mother that she was catching the train up to Scotland to stay with Tom and his wife, Melissa, and their new baby, Karen. What else could she have told the older woman? Deidre Turner would have had a heart attack had she known the truth of what her wayward daughter was about to do and guilt nagged at Erin. Surely sometimes a lie was kinder than the truth, she reasoned uncertainly. But that was of little comfort to a young woman raised to 'tell the truth and shame the devil'.

Coffee was served on the terrace in the warmth of early evening and she thought about Lorcan and Nuala, resenting the loss of a weekend that she had expected to spend with her twins. As she abstractedly took in the fabulous view shadowing into dark hills and tree tops her phone buzzed and she drew it from her bag.

Wear your hair loose, the text told her.

Cristo was reducing her to the level of a toy with a starring role in *his* fantasy. The taste of her coffee soured in her mouth. She was sick with nerves. Cristophe Donakis was the man she had once loved beyond belief. Although she had worked hard to hide it, she had absolutely adored him and their intimacy had only added another dimension to that love. This demeaning emotion-free encounter would destroy even the good memories. Though perhaps that would be a godsend? Was Cristo getting a kick out of having her at his disposal? Cristo enjoyed power. Teeth gritting, she finished the coffee and went back upstairs to change. Was she supposed to dress as if this were a date or await his arrival in that vast bed? Tears stung her eyes and she blinked them away furiously as she headed for a shower. No, absolutely no way was she going to wait in the bed! Swathed in a towel, she tugged a silky blue dress from her case.

Cristo leapt out of the helicopter and strode up to the

villa, impatience and hunger burning through him. He hadn't been worth a damn all day, all week for that matter! Just the thought of Erin being there had wiped out his wits, Vincenzo's call to confirm her arrival catching him in the middle of a board meeting. How many times had he told himself he shouldn't be doing this? What the hell, he reasoned furiously, why shouldn't he be a bastard for a change? He had let her off the hook too lightly three years ago. This— being with her one more time—was an indulgence but it was also an exorcism, and when it was done he would be done with her as well.

The pulse in Erin's neck was beating like crazy as she hovered by the bedroom window, refusing to look outside while her tummy twisted into knots. She had heard the helicopter landing, knew Cristo liked to fly himself, and knew it would be him and that within minutes he would walk through the bedroom door. She clasped her hands tightly together, willing back her nerves, striving for calm and cool.

And then the door flew open, rocking back on its hinges to frame Cristo, brilliant black diamond eyes snaking across the room to rest on her, his tall well-built body casting a long shadow in the lamp light. And there she was, silvery pale hair tumbling round her shoulders, something pretty and blue swirling round her petite little body, *waiting* for him just as he remembered from times gone by. *Erin*. He savoured her, noting the glow of self-consciousness that coloured the beautiful delicacy of her features. He experienced such a charge of hunger at the first glance that a predatory smile crossed his mobile male mouth.

'Cristo…' Erin contrived to enunciate with admirable clarity, only the breathy quietness of her voice letting her down.

'Erin,' he breathed thickly, closing the distance between them and hauling her straight into his arms.

He said something in Greek as he gazed down at her and she would have given anything to know what it was. 'What—?'

'Don't want to talk, *koukla mou,*' Cristo husked, his breath fanning her cheek as he bent his handsome dark head.

His eyes, those beautiful beautiful eyes, lion gold surrounded by spiky black lashes, held hers fast and she literally stopped breathing because the clean designer scent of him was drenching her with every mouthful of air. He looked so good, so irretrievably, undeniably good that his pure impact overwhelmed her. He kissed the corner of her mouth in a tiny teasing caress and she shivered, her thoughts blanking out, her body taking over and she wanted more, wanted more so badly that it hurt. His mouth found hers with a sudden urgency that she welcomed. Her tongue slid against his and the pressure of his lips increased in a deep hot kiss that blew her away. In the midst of it he wrenched free of his jacket and dropped it, yanked at his tie and she trailed it free, her fingers releasing the shirt button at his strong brown throat.

And it took no thought to do any of those things and she was shaken by the instinct driving her at a level she didn't understand. Her fingers curved to one high cheekbone as she struggled to stay upright with her heart slamming against her breastbone as hard as though she were in race. Her legs felt weak, insufficient to support her and she was fiercely aware of the empty ache

in her pelvis and the swelling tightness of her breasts as
he spread his big hands over her buttocks and crushed
her into his hard erection.

'I'm burning alive for you,' Cristo growled almost
accusingly, spinning her round to find the zip on her
dress and taking care of it with efficiency.

'Me too,' Erin admitted with a bitterness she couldn't
hide, her whole body throbbing with uncontrollable desire as deft fingers brushed the straps of her dress off
her slight shoulders and the garment pooled in a silky
heap round her feet.

Breathing audibly, Cristo spun her back to him and
bent to curve his hands round her slim thighs, hitch-
ing her up against him and bringing her down on the
bed with a sound of satisfaction that started deep in
his broad chest. It's just sex, *amazing* sex, he adjusted
helplessly, but the burn, the burn of excitement was in-
describable. He slid a hand beneath her to unclasp her
bra and stared down into her amethyst eyes, purple blue
like precious gems. Thief, he told himself, liar, *cheat* but
that little mantra of reminders didn't work its desired
magic. He ripped off his shirt, felt her hands sweeping
up, up over his chest and honestly wondered if he could
hold it together long enough to get inside her.

'How can you still do this to me?' he demanded in a
fierce undertone, shimmering hot golden eyes pinned to
the flushed triangle of her face and then sinking down
a level to concentrate on the pale breasts he had uncovered, firm little mounds adorned with large pink nipples
that magnetised his attention.

Claiming a straining bud with his mouth, Cristo
suckled strongly, using his hands, his lips and the edge
of his teeth because he knew how sensitive she was

there. As her slim length jackknifed under him, spine arching on a strangled moan, his sense of achievement increased and he let his lips rove hungrily over her dainty breasts, lingering on the swollen straining peaks to torment them with pleasure. His attention glued to her prone body, he backed off the bed again and unzipped his trousers.

Her face hot pink with shame and discomfiture, Erin sat up and clasped her knees. She didn't want to enjoy anything they did. She wanted to lie there like a stone statue and stay inwardly untouched and detached from him. But Cristo was far too expert a lover to allow her that kind of escape route and he was seducing a response out of her resistant body.

'I didn't intend to fall on you like a wild animal the minute I came through the door,' he volunteered impatiently. 'I was planning on having dinner first.'

Erin averted her gaze, the victim of unwelcome memories of a passion that had never gone off the boil. 'You were never very good at waiting. It was always like this for us—'

'There is no "us" any more.'

Erin lowered her lashes. He was wrong. Lorcan and Nuala were a wonderful combination of their respective genes and unless she was very much mistaken her toddlers had inherited his volatile nature. Lorcan was wilful and hot-tempered and Nuala was sharp as paint and mercurial, neither of them demonstrating an iota of their mother's quieter, more settled personality. But she was grateful that Cristo didn't know about them. Lorcan and Nuala would never get the chance to emulate their father's tough cynical outlook on the world, where what he wanted always came ahead of what was best for other people. He would not get the chance to turn them into spoilt, selfish children and, after the manner in which he had corralled her back into his bed, she refused to feel guilty about the fact.

She glanced up in the silence.

'You look like you're plotting,' Cristo remarked thoughtfully.

He towered over her, naked and aroused, gazing down at her with hot golden eyes of appreciation. She was appalled when her body reacted deep down inside, her nipples tingling as dampness formed at the heart of her.

'What on earth would I be plotting?'

'I don't know.' He stroked the tight set of her sultry mouth with a considering fingertip. 'But you're wearing the same face you wore when you found out I'd taken business associates to a lap-dancing club, *koukla mou*.'

Erin flushed as he came down beside her. 'Not one of my better memories.'

Cristo unclasped the hands she had tightened round her knees and pulled her back against his warm, hair-roughened torso. 'Nor mine, but unfortunately that kind of venue is par for the course with certain men.'

Her breath scissored in her throat as he found her breasts again, gently, surely shaping and tugging at the swollen tips. He pressed her back against the pillows, long brown fingers dipping below the waistband of her knickers, moving across bare smooth skin to stroke her clitoris. As the ache between her thighs intensified, she shut her eyes tight. He kissed her with hot driving force, skimmed off that last garment and pressed his lips to the smooth slope of her belly. Her eyes flew wide because she had silvery stretchmarks there from her pregnancy and she quivered as he trailed his expert mouth over her abdomen and then lower, startling her with that move. He found her with his mouth and his fingers, delving into the honeyed heat of her until she moaned, hips squirming as the pleasure built. He tipped her back, drowning her in sweet sensation that sent her out of control. Her breath sounded in audible gasps as she shifted helplessly up to him, wanting, *needing* and then response took over to send her racing into an explosive climax.

'I love watching you come…it must be the only time in your life that you let go of control,' Cristo husked, looking down at her with an unusually reflective light in his keen gaze. 'You're so different from me.'

Emerging dizzily from the tremors of ecstasy still rocking her body, Erin looked up into his lean dark face and the stunning eyes engaged in tracking her every change of expression. She felt exposed, vulnerable, shaken that he had already seduced her so thoroughly that she could barely recall what day it was, never mind how they had ended up in a bed at such indecent speed. 'I don't want to be here doing this with you,' she said fiercely.

'Liar.' He brought his mouth down on hers and her tongue slid against his again and that single kiss was so passionate she shivered.

Cristo donned a condom and came over her like a one-man invasion force, tipping her legs over his shoulders and driving into her so hard and deep that her head fell back in a curtain of shiny silver blonde hair, neck arching feverishly in reaction. It was good, hell it was *amazing*, she thought furiously, angry with herself, enraged that she hadn't found it possible to lie there without responding and destroy his desire for her. She knew him well enough to know that if she had held back and failed to respond he wouldn't have persisted. He shifted position and ground into her faster with hungry pounding strokes that made her heart race as though she were in a marathon. He groaned with unashamed pleasure as she cried out, bucking up to him, reacting helplessly to the delicious friction of his fluid rhythm. And she felt the heat mushrooming up from her pelvis again until an explosion of light shot through her like a flash of white-hot fire, shooting wild hot tension along every limb. He pulsed inside her and groaned as she came apart at the seams in another shattering orgasm.

By the time she came free of that shattering onslaught of raw pleasure, she was trembling and, surprisingly, he still had his arms round her, one hand splayed across her stomach as he pressed his sensual mouth to her damp cheek. 'You're amazing. That was *so* worth waiting for, *koukla mou*.'

But she hadn't made him wait; they had ended up in bed five minutes after his arrival. *I'm easy*, she decided painfully, marvelling that she was still lying in his arms and revelling in that unbelievable sense of closeness with him again. How could she possibly feel connected to Cristophe Donakis again? It felt as if almost three years had vanished in a time slip to deposit her back to when she had cherished such private and vulnerable moments with the man she loved. Only she didn't love him any more, she told herself bitterly, and he had never loved her and, what was more, he had ruthlessly blackmailed her back into his bed. As she began to reclaim her wits and pull away Cristo pulled away from her to disappear into the bathroom.

She listened to the shower running and wondered how she would live with the victory she had given him, how she would ever look in the mirror and like herself again. It was all right to tell herself that she had done what she had to do to protect her life and her children's, but what she had just allowed to happen went against her every principle. It was a punishment to appreciate that she had participated in and enjoyed her own downfall.

Lithe, bronzed and truly magnificent, Cristo reappeared with a towel wrapped round his lean hips just as a knock sounded on the bedroom door. 'I told Vincenzo to bring up dinner,' he remarked carelessly.

Erin scrambled out of bed naked and vanished into the bathroom to use the shower. She was on automatic pilot, desperate to escape his presence lest she lose what little distance she had contrived to achieve. Stepping out of the shower again, she saw the black towelling robe hanging on the back of the door and made use of it because she hadn't packed anything that practical. She rolled up the sleeves, tied the sash tight.

Cristo had donned close-fitting jeans and a black tee. A heated trolley now stood beside the small table in the corner.

'How did Vincenzo get all that food up here?' she asked stiffly.

'There's a lift. The last owner was an elderly lady with mobility problems.'

'When did you buy this place?'

'About a year ago. I wanted somewhere to relax between business trips,' Cristo said, sounding amazingly calm and distant after what they had just shared. 'What would you like to eat?'

'I'll see to myself.' Her tummy rumbled as, maintaining a scrupulous distance from his lean, powerful body, she studied the tempting array of dishes. She was surprised that she was so hungry but then nervous tension had pretty much killed her appetite over the previous forty-eight hours while she was forced to pretend to everyone around her that life was normal. She chose meat-stuffed *tortelloni* and *Panzanella* salad and lifted a slice of home baked bread.

His lean, darkly handsome face composed, Cristo poured wine for them both and sat down in a fluid movement. His assurance set her teeth on edge. He had blasted her pride and confidence out of existence because all of a sudden she didn't know who she was any more. She was not the mature, self-contained woman she had believed she was and that acknowledgement hurt.

'Doesn't it bother you that you blackmailed me into bed?' Erin shot at him abruptly.

'It might have started out that way, but that's not how it concluded,' Cristo fielded smooth as glass, his gaze welded to her. Gleaming silvery fair hair tumbled loose round her slight shoulders, accentuating her flawless features. He had burned for her from the first moment he saw her standing wet and tousled beside the swimming pool where they had met. He had burned the same way when he met her again in Sam Morton's office. He wasn't happy that she set him on fire. He wasn't happy that one wildly exciting taste of her had only primed him to want the next. *Toxic,* he reminded himself grimly.

Erin met cool, measuring, dark golden eyes that contained not an ounce of remorse and gritted her teeth, afraid to utter a word in her own defence, for what exactly could she say? They both knew that she had not played the part of an unwilling victim. 'I don't under-stand why you wanted me here,' she admitted tightly. 'After all, when we split up, you made it clear that you were bored with our relationship.'

Cristo became very still. 'I never said I was bored.'

Barely forgotten frustration invaded Erin afresh. It was a throwback to the bewilderment of the past when she had tormented herself for months in the aftermath of their breakup wondering what she had done or not done to make him want his freedom back. Suddenly that old curiosity was biting into her like a knife point. 'Then why did you ditch me?'

His lean, strong face was impassive. 'I doubt that you want the answer to that question.'

Erin stabbed a piece of juicy tomato with her fork. 'It's a long time ago, Cristo,' she said drily.

'Precisely,' he slotted in sardonically.

'But I would *still* like to know why,' Erin completed doggedly.

Cristo set down his wine glass, brilliant dark eyes pinned to her and she felt the chill like ice water spill-ing across her skin. 'You cheated on me...'

Erin stared back at him in astonishment. 'No. I didn't.'

'I caught the guy in your bed in your hotel room the night after your birthday bash,' Cristo countered flatly. 'You cheated on me.'

Erin was frowning. 'Who did you see in my hotel room?'

Cristo shrugged a broad shoulder and dealt her a sa-tiric glance. 'I have no idea who he was. I let myself into the room intending to surprise you and instead *I* got the surprise.'

Erin was stunned. 'But I wasn't there—you didn't see me.'

Cristo dealt her a scornful look. 'I saw the man, the discarded clothes, the wine glasses and I could hear the shower running in the bathroom. I didn't need to see you as well.'

Erin was so tense she was barely breathing. In a sudden movement she pushed back her chair and stood upright, her amethyst eyes bright with anger. 'Well, actually you did because that *wasn't* me in the bathroom! I didn't even stay in London that night.'

Cristo gave her an unimpressed look. 'It was your room and he was in your bed—'

Anger coursed through her in a torrent of incredulous rage. 'And you're only telling me this now, nearly three *years* later? Why didn't you mention it at the time?'

'I didn't see any point in staging a messy confrontation. I had seen all I needed to see,' Cristo derided with harsh assurance.

CHAPTER SIX

ERIN genuinely wanted to strangle Cristo at that moment. In the space of seconds she was reviewing the misery she had endured after their parting and finally grasping why he had dumped her with so little fanfare. Hostility at his latest misjudgement roared through her, her facial bones drawing taut below her fine skin. 'You had seen all you needed to see—is that a fact?' she snapped back furiously.

An ebony brow elevated with sardonic cool. 'What more evidence would I have required?'

'*Proper* evidence!' Erin fired back at him quick as a flash with more than a hint of his own intensity. 'Because that wasn't me in that bathroom. I didn't stay in London that night. I got a call from the hospital to tell me that my mother had been rushed to Casualty with a suspected heart attack. Tom and his girlfriend offered to run me home—Tom's kid brother, Dennis, asked if he could use my hotel room to stay in town with his girlfriend. I said yes, why wouldn't I have? I wasn't expecting you to turn up. When you told me you couldn't make it home to my party, you also said that you probably wouldn't make it back to London for at least another twenty-four hours.'

His darkly handsome features set like stone, Cristo gave her an unyielding look. 'I don't believe your explanation.'

At that inflammatory admission, Erin simply grabbed up the bottle of wine and poured it over his head, watching with satisfaction as the golden liquid cascaded down over his black hair and granite-hard masculine features. Startled by the assault, he leapt up with an irate Greek curse and wrenched the bottle from her grasp. 'Have you gone insane?' he raked back at her in ringing disbelief.

Untouched by any form of guilt, Erin grimly watched him dry his face with a napkin. 'I must've been when I got involved with you. How dare you assume that I slept with some other guy? How dare you just accept that and judge me for it? After the amount of time I was with you, I deserved more respect. How could you condemn me without a hearing?'

'I'm not having this conversation with you—I'm going for a second shower,' Cristo declared, striding towards the bathroom door.

Erin moved liked lightning to get there ahead of him and leant back in the doorway, daring him to shift her out of his path. 'You are so stubborn. But I could put my hand on a bible and *swear* that I wasn't in the Mobila hotel that night.'

'You were there!' Cristo breathed rawly, wrathful challenge scored into every hard angle and hollow of his breathtakingly handsome face.

'No, I wasn't!' Erin snapped back at him angrily. 'How could you even credit that I'd spent the night with another man?'

'Why not? I couldn't make it back in time for your birthday party and I knew you had to be furious with me—'

'Not so furious that I would have got into bed with someone else! I can't believe that you thought that of me and just walked away from it.'

His eyes hostile, his hard jaw line squared and he said nothing.

'Of course, I understand why now,' Erin continued thinly. 'You are so full of ego and pride. Walking away was the easiest thing to do—'

'That's not why I said nothing,' Cristo argued, his Greek accent roughening every vowel sound, anger glittering in the golden blaze of his eyes. 'I had had doubts about you for a while. There had been other…things that made me suspicious—'

'Name them,' she challenged.

'I will not discuss them with you—'

'You unreasonable, *arrogant*…' she slammed back, so enraged with him that she was trembling. 'In all the time we were together I never so much as looked at another man but that wasn't good enough for you, was it? You're jealous and possessive to the bone—you couldn't even stand me spending time with Tom!'

Eyes glowing like the heart of a fire between black spiky lashes, Cristo closed his hands to her waist and lifted her off her feet to set her to one side. 'I've told you. We're not having this discussion.'

Erin followed him into the bathroom. 'We definitely are, Cristo. You can't accuse me of infidelity and expect me to accept it in silence! What's wrong with you? You think I'm a thief as well but you said nothing about that either at the time. In retrospect don't you find all this muck being flung at me a little strange?'

Cristo was engaged in stripping off his wine-stained clothing. 'In what way strange?' he queried curtly.

'It's beginning to look to me like someone set out to deliberately discredit me in your eyes.'

His handsome mouth took on a sardonic curve as he peeled off his jeans and left them in a heap. 'That sounds like paranoia.'

Erin averted her attention as he stripped off his boxers and discovered that she was studying his long, powerful, hair-roughened thighs instead. The colour in her cheeks heightened as she lifted her head again, struggling to blot out the sight of the lean ropes of muscle banding his powerful torso. 'There's nothing paranoid about my suspicions—'

'You cheated on me and I found out…get over it,' Cristo advised witheringly as he switched on the shower and stepped in, utterly unconcerned by the nudity of his lean bronzed body. But then he had never been shy. 'It's ancient history. Don't try to resurrect it.'

'I wish I'd hit you with that bottle.'

Cristo rammed back the shower door and rested cold dark eyes of warning on her angry, defiant face. 'Don't you ever do anything like that again or I won't be responsible for what I do.'

Erin clashed with scorching golden eyes and her tummy lurched. Rage washed over her again because butterflies were leaping in her pelvis. Infuriatingly her body was reacting to him with all the control of an infatuated adolescent. 'I wish I had cheated on you…the way you treated me, I might as well have done!'

She stalked out of the bathroom. He had knocked her for six with that accusation. He had also taught her that she didn't know him as well as she had always believed she did. Although she had recognised his reserve she had never dreamt that he might have the capacity to keep such big secrets from her. What else didn't she know about Cristo? And what else had happened that had caused him to doubt her loyalty? What were those other 'things' he had grudgingly mentioned? Yanking the bedspread off the bed, and lifting a pillow, she made up the sofa on the far side of the room for her occupation.

'You're not sleeping over there,' Cristo told her tautly.

'I'm certainly not getting back into a bed with a man who thinks I'm a slut as well as a thief!' Erin replied with spirit, pale hair bouncing on her shoulders as she spun round to face him.

Stark naked, Cristo was hauling fresh clothing from drawers. He shot her a censorious appraisal from brilliant dark eyes. 'We have a deal—'

'But I intend to add my own conditions,' Erin declared thinly. 'I'll keep to our agreement *if*—'

'Too late—we already have a deal.'

'If that's your attitude I'm sleeping on the sofa.'

His thick sooty lashes lowered on stunning golden eyes while he surveyed her. 'Do you cheat at cards too?'

'You ought to know—you taught me to play,' she reminded him.

The silence buzzed like an angry wasp. Cristo continued to watch her, his attention locked to the sultry pink pout of her mouth. He wished he had kept his own shut and could not think why he had admitted that he knew of her betrayal. Everything had been going so well until she decided that honour demanded she now prove that she was pure as the driven snow. In exasperation he scored long brown fingers through his damp black hair. 'What conditions?' he demanded impatiently.

'I'll get back into that bed if—and only *if*—you agree to talk to Tom, who will verify that he passed the key card for the room to his brother and later dropped me off at the hospital a hundred miles away to be with my mother.'

Cristo looked pained. 'That's ridiculous.'

Erin tilted her chin. 'No, it's the least of what you owe me.'

'I owe you nothing.' He was poised there insolently, still half naked but for the jeans he had pulled on. Just looking at Cristo made her heartbeat pick up speed and her breathing quicken: he was so physically gorgeous. White-hot sex appeal was bred into his very bones. Even more disturbingly, the wilful line of his beautiful mouth was remarkably like her son, Lorcan's, she registered in dismay, rushing to suppress that unnerving sense of familiarity. Inside himself Cristo was seething with anger, she *did* know that, but Cristo rarely revealed anger on the surface, deeming that a weakness. And one thing Cristophe Donakis did not do was weakness.

'I deserve that you check out my side of the story,' Erin proclaimed as regally as a queen. 'You didn't give me the opportunity three years ago, so the least you can do is take care of the omission now.'

A winged ebony brow quirked. 'And if I agree, you'll get back into bed?'

'I have just one more thing to say.'

'You're pricing yourself out of the market.'

Erin gazed back at him, remembering when she had loved him, when she had simply lived for his quick easy smile and attention and shrinking from the recollection, fearful of ever laying her heart out again. 'No, I'm worth waiting for.'

Cristo dealt her a hungry appraisal that made her triangular face burn as though he had turned an open flame on her skin. 'Speak...'

'Ask yourself why I would commit fraud and put myself at risk of a prison sentence while refusing to accept the valuable diamond jewellery you tried to give me on several occasions,' she advised softly. 'If I wanted money that badly, keeping the diamonds and selling them would have been much more sensible.'

Cristo held her eyes coolly without reaction and then released his breath on a slow measured hiss. 'Get back in bed,' he breathed.

Erin retrieved her pillow and undid the tie on the robe, letting it fall as she scrambled onto the divan. Cristo watched, desire igniting almost simultaneously to raise his temperature. Surely there had never been any woman with paler, more perfect skin or more delicate yet highly feminine curves? He lay down on the bed beside her with a sense that all was right in his world for the first time in a long time. Erin studied the stark beauty of his features, knowing why no other man had tempted her, knowing why she was still heart whole. Nobody had ever come close to comparing to Cristo either in looks or passion. Eyes drowsy, she lifted a hand in the simmering silence and with her forefinger gently traced the volatile curve of his full lower lip. His gaze smouldered and his hand came up to entrap hers, long fingers wrapping round her smaller hand with precision.

'Go to sleep,' he breathed ruefully, noting the shadows that lay below her eyes like bruises. 'You're exhausted.'

Why should it bother him that she looked so tired? Why had he even noticed? His expressive mouth tightened. They were enjoying the equivalent of a two-night stand: finer feelings of any kind were not required. Nor had he any intention of getting caught up in discussing their previous relationship. There was nothing to discuss. But Erin had looked so shocked when he accused her of cheating on him. Perhaps she had been shocked that he had found her out. Clearly her partner that night had stayed silent about Cristo's entry to the hotel room. And Erin had always had a talent for playing innocent and naïve. Once that had charmed him, fooled him. Now it merely set his teeth on edge with suspicion.

What was Erin hoping to get out of this weekend? She was a survivor. As was he and he didn't like the fact that he was enjoying her company so much.

The next day they had breakfast on the terrace mid-morning. Erin had slept so late she was embarrassed. Sleeping in, after all, was a luxury she no longer enjoyed at home. The twins woke up at the crack of dawn demanding attention and since their birth Erin had learned to get by on short rations of sleep. Casually garbed in white cotton trousers teamed with a colourful silk top, she spread honey on her toast and enjoyed the picturesque landscape of rolling hills covered with mature chestnut and oak woods at the rear of the villa. It occurred to her that she might as well have been on a pleasure trip, for the accommodation and food were superb and even the company was acceptable.

Acceptable, jeered a little mocking voice in her head as she glanced at Cristo, lean and darkly magnificent in a black polo shirt and tailored chinos, predictably pacing the terrace as he ate and drank, the restive spirit that drove him unable to keep the lid on his sheer energy this early in the day. He had let her sleep undisturbed, had already been up and dressed when he finally wakened her. As his spectacular dark golden eyes surged her she went pink, something akin to panic assailing her as she felt her treacherous body's instant response to his powerful masculinity. There was an ache at the heart of her, a physical reminder of the wild passion they had shared. Yes, *shared*, she labelled, refusing to overlook her own behaviour. The sleazy weekend of her worst imaginings had come nowhere near reality and it had also proved surprisingly informative, she acknowledged wryly as she continued to think deeply about Cristo's admission that he had believed she had cheated on him. How could he not have confronted her about that? And yet she knew why not, she understood the bone-deep unforgiving pride that was so much a part of his nature. He had successfully hidden his anger from her at the time, refusing to vent it, something she could not have done in his place. He had accepted her supposed betrayal and, even now, his lack of faith in her when she had loved him appalled her. As Cristo had reminded her, though, it was the past and she thought it was wiser not to dwell on it.

He took her out for a drive in an open-topped sports car. Such freedom felt strange to her. She was accustomed to taking the twins to the park on Saturday mornings. Guilt weighed her down for she knew that her children would be missing out on that outing because Erin's mother found it difficult to watch over her grandchildren alone in a public place. Lorcan loved to explore and he wandered off, often followed by his sister. Erin had twice found her son standing up to his knees in the boating lake and had carried him kicking and scream-

ing back to dry land where Nuala waited to enrage him
with the toddler version of, 'I told you so.'

'How did you end up working for Sam Morton?'
Cristo prompted.

'Pure good luck. I was living at home and working
as a personal trainer again. My best client was a friend
of Sam's. That kind lady talked me up to him when he
was looking for a spa manager and he phoned me and
offered me an interview.'

'What made you leave London to return to Oxford?'

Erin shot him a taut glance and opted for honesty. 'I
couldn't afford city life when I was living on benefits.
I should never have resigned from my job at the Mobila
spa—that was rash and short-sighted of me.'

'I was surprised when you resigned,' Cristo admitted. 'Later I assumed it was because you'd been dipping
into the till and you thought it would be safer to stage
a vanishing act.'

Erin stiffened at that reminder but said nothing, resigned to the fact that she could not combat that charge
until she had, at least, tackled Sally Jennings. 'I left because I didn't want to keep running into you and I assumed you'd feel the same way but I was over-sensitive.
Leaving after working there such a short time blighted
my CV. It was also much harder to find another job than
I thought it would be.' Especially once she had realised
that she was pregnant and no longer feeling well, she
completed inwardly.

A hundred memories of their time together were assailing Cristo and lending a brooding edge to his mood.
He remembered her twirling in the rain with an um-
brella. She had preferred nights in watching DVDs to
nights out at a club but the horror movies, which she

loved, gave her nightmares. He had learned not to mind
being used as a security blanket in the middle of the
night. They had virtually lived together at weekends
when he was in London, his innate untidiness driving
her wild while her love of pizza had left him cold. Now
he asked himself how well he had ever known her.

The sun beat down on them as they walked around
a little hill village, packed with stone houses and narrow twisting alleys. In the cool quiet interior of the tiny
ancient church, she lit a candle and said a little prayer
for peace while Cristo waited outside for her. Around
him she couldn't think straight and the level of her emotional turmoil was starting to scare her. She needed to
hate him but what she was feeling was *not* hatred. That
she knew, but what she did feel beyond the pull of his
magnetic attraction was much harder to pin down and
she abandoned the challenge. In twenty-four hours she
would be heading home and this little episode would be
finished, she reasoned doggedly, keen to ground herself
to solid earth again. What was the point in tormenting
herself with regrets and foolish questions?

They had a simple lunch in the medieval piazza
where Cristo stretched like a lion basking in the midday heat while Erin sat back in the shade, aware that
without it her winter pale skin would burn. The wait-
ress, a young woman in her twenties, couldn't take her
eyes off the striking beauty of Cristo's classic features
or the sizzling effect of his honey-coloured gaze when
he smiled. With a sinking heart Erin recalled when she
had been even more impressionable.

Even now, she flushed beneath his disturbingly intent scrutiny. '*What*?'

'You look beautiful and you didn't even have to make an effort. It only took you ten minutes to get dressed.'

'You're accustomed to more decorative women… that's all.'

'You always turn aside compliments as though they're insincere,' Cristo murmured, his attention lodging revealingly on the voluptuous curve of her raspberry-tinted lips.

Erin knew that look, recognised his sexual hunger and *felt* the raw pull of it deep inside her body. Her nipples tingled and a pool of liquid heat formed in her pelvis, making her instantly ashamed of her lack of self-discipline. Breathing rapidly in the warm still air in an attempt to suppress those unwelcome reactions, she tensed but she remained insanely aware of his appreciative scrutiny. The atmosphere positively smouldered. Cristo laughed with husky satisfaction and her heart hammered like a trapped bird in her chest.

'Time for us to leave, *koukla mou*,' he murmured, silkily suggestive, sliding fluidly upright to take care of the bill.

Tomorrow could not come soon enough for her, Erin told herself. The weekend would be over and she could pretty much slip back into the comforting routine of her very ordinary life. But she would also be working for Cristo again and in the wake of this forty-eight-hour break from reality that would be no easy challenge.

They walked back downhill, Erin moving a few steps in Cristo's wake. It was the hottest hour of the day and even her light clothing was clinging to her damp skin but she loved the sunshine. He caught her hand as he drew level with the car and drew her closer, hot, hungry eyes with the pure lustre of gold connecting with hers.

He bent his dark head and claimed her lips in a searing kiss. Every response she had fought since leaving the villa bubbled up in a fountain of need. The erotic charge between them was delirious, devastating her defences as he fed hungrily from the sweetness of her mouth. She could feel the leashed demand in his lean, hard body as he bent her back against the car bonnet, the tremor in the long fingers clasping her cheek as her tongue tangled with his. She wanted to eat him alive. With a ragged groan, he stepped back from her.

'Let's go,' he rasped.

Her legs were as bendy and unreliable as twigs as she stumbled into the passenger seat. With her heart thundering and her head swimming after that lusty exchange her thoughts ran blood red with guilt and shame. This was not how she had expected the weekend to turn out: she had never counted on still being so attracted to Cristo that every barrier between them dropped.

Snatching in a steadying breath, Cristo drove off. He felt out of control and he didn't like that. When had 'just sex' become 'must-have sex'? And what had happened to the exorcism goal? *This* was getting her out of his system? He thought of his marriage, an infallible reminder of the danger of undisciplined impulses, and straight away the electrifying heat in his blood cooled, his arousal subsiding to a more bearable level.

Erin's mobile phone started ringing as she entered the villa. She snatched it out of her bag with a frown and answered it. 'Mum?' she queried into the excited barrage of her mother's too fast hail of words. 'Calm down. What is it?'

Cristo watched Erin begin to pace the hall in quick short steps. 'What sort of an accident?' she was asking urgently, her triangular face lint white with shock and dismay. 'Oh m-my…word…how bad is it?'

Erin pressed a concerned hand to her parted lips and turned in a clumsy uncoordinated circle. Nuala had had an accident at the playground and had broken her arm. It was a fracture and required surgery. Erin's heart was beating so fast with worry that she felt sick. Assuring her mother that she would be at the hospital as soon as possible, she ended the call.

'Bad news?' Cristo prompted.

'It's an emergency—you've got to get me home as fast as you can. I'm sorry. I'll go and pack.'

Erin fled upstairs, nothing in her head but the thought of her daughter suffering without her mother's support. She had never felt so guilty in her life. Nuala was hurt and about to have an operation and Erin couldn't be with her. It would never have happened if Erin had stayed at home. Deidre Turner had tried to take the twins to the park in her daughter's place. Nuela had squirmed to the top of the climbing frame and hung upside down in spite of her grandmother's pleas for her to come down. When the child fell she might have broken her arm but she was exceedingly lucky not to have broken her neck. Knowing that her daughter had to be in pain and frightened, Erin felt her tummy churn with nausea. She should have told Cristo that she couldn't make the weekend because she now had children, *responsibilities*. Staying silent on that score had been the act of an irresponsible parent.

'What's going on?' Cristo questioned from the bedroom doorway.

Erin paused in the act of flinging clothes back into her case and twisted her head round. 'How quickly can you get me back home?'

'Within a few hours—we'll leave as soon as you're ready, but I'd appreciate an explanation.'

Erin folded her lips, eyes refusing to meet his, and turned back to her packing. 'I can't give you one. A relative of mine has had an accident and I need to get home...urgently.'

Cristo released an impatient sigh. 'Why do you make such a song and dance about even simple things? Why can't you tell me the whole story?'

Erin dealt him a numb, distanced look. 'I don't have the words or enough time to explain.'

Within fifteen minutes they had left the house to travel to the airport. Erin was rigid with tension and silent, locked in her anxiety about her daughter, not to mention her guilt that her mother was being forced to deal with a very stressful situation alone. This was her punishment for deceiving her mother about where she was staying for the weekend, she thought painfully. Her children needed her but she was not within reach to come quickly to their aid. Instead their next-door neighbour, Tamsin, a young woman with kids of her own, had come to the hospital to collect Lorcan so that her mother could stay on there and wait for Nuala to come out of surgery.

They were walking through the airport when Cristo closed a hand to Erin's wrist and said curtly. 'We have to talk about this.'

'Talking isn't what you brought me here for,' Erin countered tartly. 'I appreciate that you feel short-changed but right now there's nothing I can do about it.'

'That's not what I meant,' Cristo said glacially, frustration brightening his black diamond gaze to brilliance in his lean, strong face. 'I'll get you back to Oxford as quick as I can but you have to tell me what's going on.'

Erin nodded agreement and bit her lip. 'Once we're airborne.'

Tell him—he made it sound so simple. She thought of those phone calls she had made, desperate to tell him, desperate for his support in a hostile world. When she'd realised she was pregnant she had reached out in panic, not thinking about what she would have to say or how he would react. Those kinds of fears would have been luxuries when she was struggling just to survive. Now she was older, wiser, aware she was about to open a can of worms with a blunt knife and make a mess. But why not? Why shouldn't Cristo know that he was a father? How he reacted no longer mattered: she already had a job, a roof over her head. She didn't *need* him any more.

Ensconced in the cream-leather-upholstered luxury of Cristo's private jet, Erin struggled to regain her composure but she was too worried about Nuala and her mother. Deidre Turner didn't deal well with the unexpected and suffered from panic attacks. How could she have left her mother with the burden of the twins for the weekend when the older woman had already looked after them all week long? Her mother would have been tired, tested by the daily challenge of caring for two lively toddlers, who didn't always do as they were told, a combination that was an accident waiting to happen.

Cristo released his seat belt and stood up, six feet four inches of well-groomed male, in a dark business suit that made the most of his lean, powerful physique. Shrewd dark golden eyes below sooty lashes welded to her, he dealt her an expectant look.

'I have children now,' Erin declared baldly, breaking the tense silence. 'Twins of two and a bit, a boy and a girl—'

Unsurprisingly, Cristo was stunned. '*Children*?' he repeated the plural designation in a tone of astonishment. 'How could you possibly have children?'

CHAPTER SEVEN

'THE usual way. I fell pregnant. I became a mother eight months later,' Erin told him flatly.

'Twins?' Cristo bit out a sardonic laugh to punctuate the word.

'Yes, born a little early. And my daughter, Nuala, got hurt in a playground accident this morning. She broke her arm and she has to have surgery on it. That's why I have to get home asap,' Erin completed in the same strained tone.

'And you didn't feel that you could mention the little fact that you're a mother before this point?' Cristo derided grimly.

Erin studied the carpet. 'I didn't think you'd be interested.'

'I'm more interested in finding out who the father of your twins might be,' Cristo admitted, his stubborn jaw line clenching hard. 'Is it Morton?'

'No,' Erin fielded without hesitation. 'My children were very young when I first met Sam.'

'Why is this like pulling teeth?' Cristo demanded with ringing impatience.

'Because you're going out of your way to avoid the most obvious connection.' Erin lifted her chin and studied him with cool amethyst eyes, an ocean of calm co-cooning her as she moved towards the final bar she had set herself to clear. 'Lorcan and Nuala are your children and don't you dare complain about only finding that out now! It's your fault that I made endless attempts to get in touch with you and failed.'

His stunning dark eyes widened, his beautiful mouth twisting. '*My* children —don't be ridiculous. How could they possibly be mine?'

'The traditional way, Cristo. You turned over in bed one night shortly before we broke up and made love to me without using a condom. Of course I can't be a hundred per cent certain about the exact timing, but certainly that's when I assume that I conceived,' she explained curtly.

Beneath his bronzed skin, Cristo had grown pale as if such nit-picking detail added a veracity to her claim that nothing else could have done. 'You're saying that I got you pregnant?'

'There wasn't anyone else in the picture, in spite of all your misconceptions about Tom's little brother.' Erin rose to her feet with determination. 'You are the father of my children. You can do DNA tests, whatever you like to satisfy yourself. I really don't care. That side of things is immaterial to me now.'

Cristo poured himself a drink from the built in bar. His hand wasn't quite steady as he raised the glass to his lips and drank deep. 'This is inconceivable.'

He wheeled back round to stare at her with cloaked intensity, momentarily stepping outside the dialogue while with every fibre of his being he relived that last sweet taste of her in sunlight as her tongue tangled with his. The burn of that hunger had electrified him. She was a sexual challenge that never waned. That was what she meant to him, a high of satisfaction he craved every time he looked at her. He hated what she was but he wanted to bed her over and over again. That was easier to think about than the fantastic idea that he might have accidentally got her pregnant in the past. Hadn't he only just emerged from a nightmare in that category? A nightmare that had comprehensively blown his marriage and his family apart? And now, the least likely mother of all was telling *him* that he was immaterial? He would never let another woman deny him his paternal rights.

'I'll take a soda and lime,' Erin told him pointedly.

Frowning, his black brows drawing together, Cristo turned back to the bar to prepare her drink. His movements were deft and precise. He handed her a tall moisture-beaded glass, turning his arrogant dark head to study her afresh as he did so. He was so deep in shock at the concept of being a father that he felt as if the passage of time had frozen him in his tracks. 'You said you made endless attempts to get in touch with me.'

'Your PA finally told me that she had instructions not to put my calls through to you and that I was wasting my time.'

Cristo set his glass down on the bar with a sharp little snap of protest. 'I never issued any such instruction!'

'Well, maybe it was the bad fairy who issued it.' Erin lifted and dropped a slight shoulder, unimpressed by his plea of innocence. All too well did she remember how humiliated she had felt having to make those repeated and clearly unwelcome phone calls. 'I also sent a couple of letters.'

'Which I never received.'

Erin ignored that comeback. 'You had changed your

private cell phone number. I had no choice but to try and contact you through your office. At the last, I even phoned your family home in Athens…'

'You contacted my…*parents*?' Cristo queried with frank incredulity.

'And your mother refused to pass on a message to you. She said you were getting married and that you wanted nothing more to do with "a woman like me",' Erin grimaced as she repeated that lowering description.

'I don't believe you. My foster mother is a kind, gentle woman. She would never be so offensive, particularly to a pregnant woman—'

'Oh, I didn't get as far as telling her that I was pregnant during our conversation. I could hardly get a word in edgeways once she realised who I was.'

'She would not have known who you were,' Cristo countered with conviction. 'I never once mentioned your existence to my parents.'

Erin tried not to wince. She had often wondered and he had just confirmed her deepest suspicions. While evidently his foster mother had known her son did have a relationship with a woman in London, she had not received that information from him. Evidently, Erin had never been important enough to her lover to warrant being discussed with his family 'I wrote to your office as well. The letters were returned to me unopened,' she confided doggedly. 'That's when I gave up trying to contact you.'

Cristo drained his glass, set it down, shook his head slightly. 'You say I'm the father of your children. I cannot accept that.'

Erin shrugged and sank back into her seat. At least he wasn't shouting at her or calling her a liar…*yet*. Time might well take care of that oversight. In truth, though, she had never seen him so shaken, for Cristo was strong as steel and given to rolling with the punches that life dealt out. But right now he was in a daze, visibly shattered by her revelation.

'It's OK if you can't accept it. I'll understand. But at least I've finally told you. How you feel about it, whether or not you believe me, isn't relevant any more.'

Cristo shot her an exasperated look that hinted at the darker, deeper emotions he was maintaining control over beneath his forbidding reserve. 'How can it not be relevant?'

'Because it doesn't matter any longer. When I first fell pregnant, life was tough. I needed your help then and I didn't get it,' Erin pointed out ruefully. 'Now, thanks to my mother's support, the kids and I are quite self-sufficient as long as I have a reasonable salary to rely on.'

In the strained silence, Cristo poured himself another drink. She watched the muscles work in his strong brown throat and then recalled how only hours earlier she had wanted to eat him alive and she cringed at that reminder of how weak she could be around him. On the other hand, he was a sophisticated man and he had the sexual experience to make her burn—that was *all*! It would be foolish to punish herself just because she had sunk low enough to enjoy their intimacy on his terms. She was a healthy, warm-blooded woman who had suppressed her natural needs for too long. In the end, if anything, too much self-control had made a victim of her. Of course she had never met a man she wanted as she wanted Cristo, never known a man who, even in the midst of the most emotional scene she had ever endured, could still make her mind wander down undisciplined paths. For there he stood, shocked but unbowed, gorgeous dark eyes smouldering with raw reaction in his even more gorgeous face.

'If this story of yours is true, why didn't you tell me the instant I came back into your life?' he pressed, lifting his proud dark head high, a tiny muscle pulling tight at one corner of his unsmiling mouth.

Erin compressed her lips, shook her head. 'I didn't want anyone to know that we'd even had a past relationship, never mind that you're the father of my kids.'

'I don't follow that reasoning. Would Morton have turned against you had he known the truth?'

'Stop dragging Sam into everything. He's nothing to do with any of this,' Erin said vehemently. 'I owe Sam. He took a risk on me. The job with his hotel group made it possible for me to survive. As for other people knowing about our…er…past connection, I would have found that embarrassing.'

Embarrassing? Cristo gritted his even white teeth while resisting the urge to bite back. Why would she lie now? After all, if he was the father of her twins, he had to owe her thousands of pounds in child support. Nor, until he had made checks, could he disprove her claim that she had tried to contact him to tell him that she was pregnant. If it was true and if she had continued with the pregnancy rather than seeking a way out of her predicament, he owed her a debt, didn't he? While his intelligence urged caution, he would be careful of uttering any disparaging comments.

'I'll accompany you home,' Cristo announced in a tone of finality.

Disconcerted, Erin frowned. 'But why would you do that?'

'Perhaps I would like to see these children whom you insist are my flesh and blood.'

Her triangular face froze, long lashes sweeping down over her eyes while she processed an idea that seemed to strike her as extraordinary.

'Surely you expected that?'

Erin glanced up and clashed with eyes that burned like a furnace in Cristo's hard masculine face. 'I hadn't thought that far ahead.'

'I'm coming to the hospital with you,' Cristo decreed.

Erin winced at the prospect, picturing her mother's astonishment, not to mention the prospect of explaining that she had lied about going to Scotland and had gone to Italy to be with Cristo instead.

'There's nothing else that I can do,' Cristo added grimly.

Erin was mystified. Was curiosity or a sense of duty driving him? But then how on earth had she expected him to react to her revelation? Had she really believed that he might just walk away untouched by the news that he was a father?

'I'm not expecting you to get involved with the twins,' Erin muttered uncomfortably.

'It is more a matter of what I expect of myself,' Cristo countered with a gravity she had never seen in him before.

Oh, my word, what have I done? Erin wondered feverishly. What did he expect from himself in the parenting stakes? His own upbringing, after all, had been unusual. And he was a non-conformist to the marrow of his bones, shrugging off convention if it made no sense to him.

It was nine in the evening before they made it to the hospital. Deidre Turner was seated in a bland little side ward next to a bed in which a small still form lay. The older woman, her face grey with exhaustion and her eyes marked pink by tears, scrambled upright when she saw her daughter. 'Erin, thank goodness! I was scared you mightn't make it back tonight and I was worried about leaving Lorcan with Tamsin,' she confided, only then noting the presence of the tall black-haired male behind Erin.

'Mum?' Erin murmured uncertainly. 'This is Cristo Donakis. He insisted on coming with me.'

For once shorn of his social aplomb, Cristo came to a dead halt at the foot of the bed to gaze down at the little girl with the white-blonde curls clustered round her small head. She looked like Erin but her skin was several shades darker than her mother's fair complexion. His attention rested on the small skinny arm bearing a colourful cast and he swallowed a sudden unfamiliar thickness in his throat. She was tiny as a doll and as he stared in growing wonderment her feathery lashes lifted to reveal eyes as dark a brown as his own.

'Mummy...' Nuala whispered drowsily.

'I'm here.' Erin hastily pulled up a seat and perched on the edge of it, leaning forward to pat Nuala's little hand soothingly. 'How did the surgery go, Mum?'

'Really well. The surgeon was very pleased,' Deidre confided. 'Nuala should regain the full use of her arm.'

'That's a relief,' Erin commented, turning her gaze back to her daughter's small flushed face. 'How are you feeling, pet?'

'My arm's sore.' The little girl sighed, her attention roaming away from her mother to lock to the tall powerful man stationed at the foot of her bed. 'Who is that man?'

'I'm Cristo,' Cristo muttered not quite steadily.

'He's your daddy,' Deidre Turner explained without hesitation, a broad smile of satisfaction chasing the exhaustion from her drawn face.

Shock at that announcement trapped Erin's breath in her throat and she shot the older woman a look of dismay.

'Honesty is the best policy,' Deidre remarked to noone in particular, rising from her seat to extend a hand to Cristo. 'I'm Erin's mother, Deidre.'

'Daddy?' Nuala repeated wide-eyed at the description. 'You're my daddy?'

In the simmering silence, Erin frowned. 'Yes. He's your daddy,' she confirmed. 'Mum? Could I have a word with you in private?'

A nurse came in just then to check on Nuala and, after mentioning that her daughter was complaining of pain, Erin stepped outside with her mother. 'You must be wondering what's going on,' Erin began awkwardly.

'What's there to wonder? Obviously you've finally told the man he's a father and that's not before time,' the older woman replied wryly.

Erin breathed in deep. 'I'm afraid I lied to you about where I was this weekend—I wasn't in Scotland with Tom and Melissa. I was with Cristo.'

'And you didn't know how to tell me, I suppose. Did you think I would interfere?' Deidre enquired astutely. 'He's the twins' father. Naturally you need to sort this situation out but you've taken the first step towards that and I'm proud of you.'

Surprised by that assurance, Erin gave her parent a quick embarrassed hug. 'I'm sorry I wasn't honest with you. Look, now I'm here, you should go home—'

'And collect Lorcan and put him to bed,' Deidre completed. 'He was upset about Nuala. Will you stay the night here with her or will you come home later?'

'I'll see how Nuala is before I decide.'

'She'll be fine. She's a tough little article,' Erin's mother pronounced fondly. 'Lorcan cried when she fell because he got a fright and she called him a baby. By the time I got Nuala to the hospital they were fighting—at least it took her mind off the pain of the break.'

Erin saw the older woman into the lift and returned to the side ward.

'What do daddies do?' Nuala was asking plaintively.

'They look after you.'

Erin's daughter was unimpressed. 'Mummy and Granny look after me.'

'And now you have me as well,' Cristo told his daughter quietly.

'You can fix my arm with magic,' Nuala told him in a tone of complaint.

'Daddy doesn't have his magic wand with him,' Erin chipped in from the foot of the bed.

Nuala's dark eyes rounded. 'Daddy has a magic wand?'

Cristo skimmed Erin a pained glance. 'I'm afraid I don't.'

'Never mind,' Nuala said drowsily. 'My arm hurts.'

'The medicine the nurse gave you will start working soon,' Cristo asserted soothingly.

Within minutes, Nuala had drifted off to sleep.

'I'm sorry Mum just leapt in with her big announcement,' Erin muttered uncomfortably.

'Obviously she believes the twins are mine and, if that's true, there are no regrets on my part,' Cristo responded with a quality of calm she had not expected to see in him after the bombshell she had dropped on him. 'It's a bad idea to lie to children.'

Erin fell asleep in her chair and only wakened when the nurses began their morning round. She was surprised that Cristo had remained through the night, for she had expected him to leave late and make use of a hotel. Instead he had stayed with them and she was grudgingly impressed by his tenacity. His black hair was tousled, his tie loose where he had undone the top button of his shirt. A heavy dark shadow of stubble covered his strong jaw line, accentuating the sensual perfection of his mobile mouth. It shook her to open her eyes and see him and for her first thought to be that he was absolutely gorgeous. Her face flamed as his stunning dark golden eyes assailed hers. Her skin prickled with awareness, her breasts swelling and making her bra feel too tight. She tore her attention from him with a sense of mortification that she had so little control over her reactions to him.

'Apparently the canteen opens soon. We'll go down for breakfast once Nuala has had hers,' Cristo said decisively.

The night had been long and his reflections deep and interminable, Cristo acknowledged heavily, fighting off the exhaustion dogging him. He had watched Erin and the child who might be his daughter sleep. He had remembered the early years of his own childhood with the fortitude of an adult, processing what he had learned from those unhappy memories, already knowing what he must do while striving to greet rather than flinch from the necessity.

Erin took Nuala into the bathroom to freshen up. She was stiff from spending the night in the chair and slow to respond to her daughter's innocent chatter. She did what little she could to tidy herself but her raincoat, silk top and linen trousers were creased beyond redemption and without make-up she could do nothing to brighten her pale face and tired, shadowed eyes.

'Obviously you'll want DNA tests done,' Erin said over breakfast, preferring to take that bull by the horns in preference to Cristo feeling that he had to make that demand. 'I'll agree to that.'

'It would make it easier to establish the twins as my legal heirs,' Cristo agreed, his expression grave. 'But I believe that that is the only reason I would have it done.'

'You're saying that you believe me now?' Erin prompted in a surprised undertone.

Cristo gave her a silent nod of confirmation and finished his coffee. By the time they returned to Nuala's bedside the doctors' round had been done and the ward sister informed them that they could take Nuala home as soon as they liked.

Lorcan, already prepared by his grandmother for the truth that he was about to meet his father, was in full livewire mode, behaving like a jumping bean from the instant Cristo entered the small sitting room of Deidre and Erin's terraced home. Lorcan scrambled onto a stool and stood up to get closer to the tall black-haired male but, dissatisfied with the height differential, leapt off the stool and clambered onto the coffee table instead.

'Get down, Lorcan,' Erin instructed, stooping to gather up the pile of magazines that her son had sent flying to the floor while her mother cooed over Nuala like a homing pigeon. 'Right now...'

When Cristo focused on the little boy he felt as if he had been punched in the stomach. With his coal-black curls and impish dark eyes, Lorcan was a dead ringer for every photograph Cristo had ever seen of himself at the same age. His stare darkened in intensity, shock reverberating through his big powerful length as he made that final step towards accepting what he was seeing as fact: he was a father.

'I'm going to count to five, Lorcan,' Erin warned, her tension level rising. 'One...two...'

Lorcan performed a handstand and grinned with delight at Cristo from upside down. 'Daddy do this?' he asked expectantly.

'*Don't*!' Erin gasped as Cristo bent down.

But, mercifully, Cristo had not been about to perform a handstand. He had merely bent to lift his son off the coffee table and turn him the right side up while Lorcan shrieked with excitement. 'Hello, Lorcan,' Cristo murmured evenly. 'Calm down.'

Unfortunately Lorcan was in no mood to calm down. When Cristo returned him to the floor, Lorcan began to scramble over every piece of furniture in the room at high speed while loudly urging Cristo to watch what he could do. Erin almost groaned out loud as Nuala bounded from her side to try and join in the ruckus. Cristo snatched his daughter out of harm's way. 'Show Lorcan your arm,' he instructed her.

Nuala showed off her cast, small mouth pouting.

'Hurts,' she informed her brother, who moved closer to inspect the injured arm.

Erin crouched down. 'And we have to be *very* careful with Nuala's sore arm,' she told her son.

Lorcan touched the cast enviously. 'Want it,' he said.

'You should take them out to the park to let off some steam,' Deidre Turner suggested, beaming at Cristo, who was returning the cushions Lorcan had knocked off the sofa. 'Oh, never mind about that—I'm used to tidying up every five minutes!'

Erin swallowed a yawn. 'The park? That's a good idea. I'll just go and get changed first.'

Hurtling upstairs to her small bedroom, Erin could not quite come to grips with the knowledge that Cristo was in her home. It felt like some crazy dream but there was something horribly realistic about the fact that both her children were acting up like mad and revealing their every wild and wonderful fault. What did Cristo really think about them? How did he really feel? And why did she care about that side of things? After all, naturally he wanted to see both children to satisfy his curiosity, but she doubted that his interest went much deeper than that. Respecting the cool temperature of a typical English spring, Erin donned straight-leg jeans, knee-length boots and a blue cable knit sweater. She brushed her hair, let it fall round her shoulders and made use of a little blusher and mascara before she felt presentable. Presentable enough for what? *For Cristo*? Shame engulfed her like a blanket. Why was she so predictable? Why was she always worrying about what Cristo thought of her? Only last month she had seen Cristo in a gossip column squiring a beautiful model with hair like gold silk and the glorious shape of a Miss World!

Cristo specialised in superstar women with the kind of looks that stopped traffic. His ex-wife, Lisandra, was an utterly ravishing brunette. Erin had never been in that class and had often wondered if that was why he had lost interest in her.

But now she knew different, she reminded herself wretchedly as she went downstairs. Now she knew that Cristo had dumped her because he believed she was a total slut who had gone behind his back and slept with another man. Was it better to know that or *worse*?

A twin apiece, they walked a hundred yards to the park. Cristo had sent his limo driver off to locate and buy car seats for the children. Lorcan took exaggerated big steps as he concentrated on stepping only on the lines between the flagstones. Nuala hummed a nursery rhyme and pulled handfuls of leaves off the shrubs they passed until Cristo told his daughter to, 'Stop it!'

Without hesitation, Nuala threw herself down on the pavement and began to kick and scream.

'You shouldn't have said that,' Erin hissed in frustration. 'She's tired and cross and her arm's hurting her. Of course she's not in a good mood.'

'You can't let her vandalise people's gardens,' Cristo replied drily and he bent down and picked Nuala up. Her daughter squirmed violently, flailed her fists and screamed full throttle.

Cristo took a couple of fists in the face before he restored order. 'No,' he said again.

'Yes!' Nuala shrieked back at him, unleashing the full tempest of her toddler temper.

Erin was trying not to cringe and cave in to her daughter's every demand as she saw faces appearing at windows overlooking the street.

'Want slide,' Lorcan whinged, tugging at his mother's jacket. 'Want swings.'

'So, this is what it feels like to be a parent,' Cristo commented, flexing his bruised jaw with a slight grimace, his stunning eyes pure black diamond brilliance as if on some weird level he was actually enjoying the challenge.

'They're a handful sometimes…not *all* the time,' Erin stressed, walking on, keen to reach the park where noisy childish outbursts commanded less attention.

Lower lip thrust out, Nuala told Cristo, 'Want down.'

'Say please,' Cristo traded.

'No!' Nuala roared.

'Then I'll carry you the rest of the way like a baby.'

Nuala lost her head again and screamed while her brother chanted delightedly, 'Nuala's a baby!' as he walked by his mother's side.

Silence fell only as they reached the gates of the park.

'Please,' Nuala framed as if every syllable hurt.

Cristo lowered his daughter slowly back onto her own feet.

'I hate you!' Nuala launched at him furiously, snatching her hand free of his and grabbing her mother's free hand in place of it. 'I don't want a daddy!'

As Cristo parted his lips to respond Erin cut in, 'Just ignore it…*please*.'

Once she sat down on the mercifully free bench in her accustomed spot, Erin murmured, 'The best way to handle the twins is with distraction and compromise. Going toe to toe with them simply provokes a tantrum.'

'Thanks for the heads-up. I'm going to need it. I believe I used to throw tantrums,' Cristo confided. 'According to my foster mother, I too was a challenging child.'

'Tell me something I couldn't have guessed.' Erin laughed, abstractedly watching the breeze ruffle his cropped hair into half curls, so very similar to his son's. As she met his spectacular amber and honey coloured eyes framed by sooty lashes, it was as if a hand grabbed her heart and squeezed and possibly that was the moment that she understood that she would never be entirely free of Cristo Donakis. That was not simply because she had given birth to children who had inherited his explosive personality. It was because she enjoyed his forceful character, his strength of purpose and persistence and the very fact he could sit on an old bench in a slightly overgrown and rundown park and seem entirely at home there in spite of his hand-stitched shoes, gold cufflinks and a superbly well-cut suit that still looked a million dollars even after he had sat up all night in it. He might be arrogant but he was hugely adaptable, resourceful and willing to learn from his mistakes.

'I should tell you about my marriage,' Cristo said flatly.

'You never mention your ex-wife,' she remarked helplessly, disconcerted by the sudden change of subject and the intimacy of the topic as she watched Lorcan play on the swings and Nuala head down to the sandpit, her cast protected by the cling film Erin had wrapped round it. It wasn't like Cristo to volunteer to talk about anything particularly private.

'Why would I? We were only married for five minutes and now we're divorced,' Cristo fielded coolly.

'Have you stayed friends?'

'We're not enemies,' Cristo stated after a moment's

thought on that score. 'But we move in different social circles and rarely see each other.'

'Was it a case of marry in haste and repent at leisure?' Erin pressed tautly. 'Did you know her well before you married her?'

'I thought I did.' Cristo bit out a sardonic laugh. 'I also thought it was time I got married. My foster parents, Vasos and Appollonia, had been urging me to marry for a couple of years. It was the only thing they had ever tried to influence in my life and I did want to please them,' he admitted gruffly. 'I met Lisandra at a dinner party at their home. I already knew her but not well. We seemed to be at the same stage in life, bored with the single scene. We got married three months later.'

'So what went wrong?' she almost whispered, recognising the shadow that crossed his lean, darkly handsome face.

'About a year after we married, Lisandra decided that she wanted a child. I agreed—it seemed like the natural next step.' His shapely mouth tightened and compressed. 'When she got pregnant, she was ecstatic and she threw a party to celebrate. Both our families were overjoyed at the prospect of a first grandchild.'

'And you—how did you feel about it?' Erin prompted hesitantly.

'I was pleased, happy Lisandra was happy, grateful she had something new to occupy her. She got bored easily,' Cristo admitted stonily. 'And a couple of months into the pregnancy Lisandra got cold feet.'

'Cold feet?' Erin queried with a frown, her attention locked to the air of harsh restraint etched in his lean strong face that indicated that, while his voice might sound mild, his inner feelings were the exact opposite.

'My wife decided she wasn't ready to have a child after all. She felt too young for the responsibility and trapped by her condition. She decided that the only solution to her regrets and fears was a termination.'

Erin released her pent up breath in a sudden audible hiss. 'Oh, Cristo—'

'I tried to talk her out of it, reminding her that we could afford domestic staff so that she need never feel tied down by our child.' He breathed in slow and deep and bitter regret clouded his dark eyes. 'But I failed to talk her round to my point of view. She had a termination while I was away on business. I was devastated. Our families had to be told. My foster mother, who was never able to have a child of her own, had a nervous breakdown when she found out—she just couldn't handle it. Lisandra's parents were distressed but they supported their daughter's decision because they had never in their entire lives told her that, no, she couldn't have everything and do anything she wanted...'

'And you?' Erin prodded sickly, feeling guilty that she had not even suspected that a truly heartbreaking story might lie behind his divorce.

Cristo linked lean brown hands and shrugged a fatalistic broad shoulder. 'I suppose I couldn't handle it either. Intellectually I don't know what Lisandra and I would have done with a child whose mother didn't want it and resented its very existence but I still couldn't forgive my wife for the abortion. I tried, she tried, we both *tried* but it was just there like an elephant in the room every time we were together. I made her feel guilty, she made me feel angry. I saw too much in her that I didn't like and I didn't think she would ever change, so I asked her for a divorce.'

'I'm so sorry, Cristo…really, very sincerely sorry,' Erin murmured shakily, a lump forming in her throat as she rested a slender hand briefly on his arm in a gesture of support. 'That must have been a shattering experience.'

'I only told you because I want you to understand why I can't walk away from Lorcan and Nuala. If that's what you're expecting or even hoping for, I'm afraid you're going to be disappointed.'

Erin paled, wondering what he was telling her and fearfully insecure about what his next move might be.

CHAPTER EIGHT

CRISTO wasn't accustomed to feeling powerless but that was exactly how he felt after his consultation with a top London lawyer.

An unmarried father, he learned at that crucial meeting, had virtually no rights over his children under English law and even a married father, lacking his wife's support and agreement, might well have to fight through the courts to gain any access to his offspring. Furthermore he had no grounds on which to complain about any aspect of the twins' upbringing. In spite of the fact that he had not contributed to his children's upkeep they were currently living within the security of their mother and grandmother's home with all their needs adequately provided for.

'Marrying the twins' mother is really the only remedy for a man in your position,' he was told succinctly.

It was not good news on Cristo's terms for he loathed any situation outside his control. The DNA testing, achieved and completed within ten days of his first meeting with Lorcan and Nuala had merely confirmed what Cristo already knew and accepted. He was a father and the twins were his flesh and blood, a connection he was incapable of ignoring or treating lightly. He could not move on with his life without them. While he knew that Erin had done her best he also recognised that the twins would require firmer boundaries before they got much older. Yet did that mean that he was to overlook the less acceptable elements in Erin's character? A woman who had stolen from him? For the first time ever he acknowledged grudgingly that that charge did not quite add up. If Erin was mercenary why hadn't she taken more advantage of his financial generosity while she was with him? Why on earth would a woman who craved more money have refused to accept valuable diamond jewellery from him? That made no sense whatsoever. He resolved to take a fresh look at the irregularities that had been found in the accounts of the Mobila spa during Erin's employment there. But before the press got hold of the story—as he was convinced they inevitably would—he required a decent solution, not only to his and Erin's current predicament but also for the future. Some arrangement that would endure for as long as the children needed their parents' support. Recognising the direction his thoughts were taking him in, Cristo felt anger kicking in again.

On the exact same day, Erin was tackling a difficult personal matter with Sam. They were standing in his temporary office, the larger original room having been taken over by a team from Donakis Hotels, who were working to ensure a smooth changeover of ownership. The sale was complete. Sam was only still making himself available for consultation out of loyalty to his hotel group and former employees.

The older man knitted his brows, a shocked look in his blue eyes. 'Cristo Donakis is the twins' father?' he repeated in astonishment.

'I felt I should mention it. My mother has been telling people and I wanted you to hear it from me, rather than as a piece of gossip,' Erin admitted stiffly.

'But when you met here neither of you even admitted that you knew each other.'

'I hadn't seen Cristo since we broke up and my natural inclination was to keep my personal life private.'

Sam Morton dealt her a hurt look that made her flush with discomfiture. 'Even from me?'

'When I walked into your office that day and saw Cristo standing there it was such a shock that I wasn't exactly thinking straight,' she said apologetically. 'I'm sorry. Maybe I should have come clean afterwards but it was very awkward.'

'No, you're quite right. Your private life should be private. I assume it was Cristo you were working for in London?'

Erin nodded. 'I resigned when we split up.'

'I should have made that connection from your original CV. But Donakis let you down badly when you were pregnant,' Sam completed drily.

'There was a misunderstanding,' Erin declared, her eyes evasive. 'Cristo had no idea I was pregnant and there was no further communication between us.'

'But you tried very hard to get in touch with him,' Sam reminded her.

'It was just one of those things, Sam.'

Sam's nostrils flared. 'So, he's forgiven for putting you through hell.'

'It's not like that. Cristo knows about the children now and we're trying to work through that as best we can.'

'Are you getting involved with him again? No, scratch that!' Sam advised abruptly. 'I have no right to pry.'

Erin thought about Italy and screened her expressive eyes. 'I don't know how to answer that question—it's complicated?' she joked uneasily.

'I hope it's the right thing for you. I'd *hate* to see you unhappy again,' Sam pronounced feelingly. 'You gave Donakis one chance. Who's to say he deserves another?'

Well, her mother for one thing, Erin reflected wryly as she caught up with her emails ten minutes later. In her mother's eyes, Cristo had gone from being the most reviled womanising male in Europe to being a positive favourite. And all within the unlikely space of a mere ten days! His regular visits, his interest in the twins, his good manners, his tactful ability to defer to her mother's greater knowledge when it came to the children, his insistence that Deidre Turner join them when they went out to eat had all had an effect. Cristo had shone like a star at every opportunity and was piling up brownie points like a miser with a barn full of treasure chests. Erin, on the other hand, was finding the new order confusing and hard to adapt to.

Cristo was no longer her lover. That weekend in Italy, that single night of passion, did in retrospect seem more like the product of her imagination than anything that had actually happened. Now Cristo visited their home to see Lorcan and Nuala and stayed in one of his newly acquired hotels when he was in the area. He was wary and deep down inside that fact hurt Erin. She could remember another Cristo, a guy who had raced through the door to greet her eagerly when he'd been away for a while, unashamedly passionate, openly demonstrative, not picking his words, not hiding behind caution. This new Cristo was older and much cooler. He was polite, even considerate, but reserved when it came to more personal stuff. Even the confidences he had unexpectedly shared with Erin in the park still troubled her.

His wife's termination had deeply wounded Cristo and possibly made him think more deeply than many men about what a child might mean to him. Now Erin was seeing the results of that more solicitous outlook in practice, for Cristo undoubtedly wanted to do as much as possible to help her with their children. When he visited, he played with them, took them out with Erin in tow and had even helped to bathe them one evening after Erin fell asleep on the sofa after work. He was demonstrating that he could be a hands-on father and the kids were already very partial to his more energetic presence. Erin was impressed but more than a little concerned as to where all this surprising attention was likely to lead.

What did Cristo really want from her? Acceptance of his role? Could it be that simple? Could Cristo, for possibly the very first time in his life, be playing it straight? Or was there a darker, more devious plan somewhere in the back of his mind? Cristo Donakis did not dance to other people's tunes. He always had an agenda. Unfortunately for Erin she was unable to work out what that agenda might be and what it might entail for her and her children. In addition she was especially worried that Cristo still harboured serious doubts about her honesty. It was time she tackled Sally Jennings, she reflected ruefully. Somehow she had to prove her innocence of theft. But would Sally even agree to speak to her? It occurred to her that it might well be wiser to arrive to see Sally at Cristo's flagship London spa without a prior announcement of her intent. She decided to take a day's leave and tackle Sally. Would she get anywhere? She didn't know but it was currently the only idea she could come up with.

The phone by her bed rang at six the following morning and, ruefully knuckling the sleep from her eyes, Erin sat up in bed. *'Yes*?'

It was Cristo. 'Erin?'

'Why are you waking me up at this time of the morning?'

'A deputy editor I'm friendly with has just called me with a tip-off. Apparently there's a story in the pipeline about you, me and the twins. The publication he named is particularly sleazy so I don't think the article will contain anything that your family or mine would want to read.'

Erin's face froze. 'But why? Who on earth would be interested in reading about us?'

'Erin…' Cristo sighed, mustering patience for he was more accustomed to dealing with people who took tabloid attention in their stride and even courted it for the sake of their careers or social status. 'I'm a very wealthy man, recently divorced…'

Lorcan darted through the bedroom door, scrambled under the duvet with his mother and tucked cold feet against her slim thighs. His sister was only a few steps behind him.

Erin was squashed up against the wall as Nuala joined them in the bed. 'If it's true, if there is going to be a story, there's nothing we can do to prevent it.'

'Yes, there is,' Cristo contradicted. 'I can get you and the children out of that house and put you somewhere the paparazzi can't get near you for a photo opportunity. Then I can organise a PR announcement concerning my new status as a father and, once that's done, the press will lose interest.'

Erin breathed in deep. She certainly didn't fancy the press on her doorstep, but she was much inclined to think that he was taking the matter too seriously. 'Cristo, I have a job. I can't just drop everything and disappear.'

'Of course you can. You work for me now,' he reminded her. 'Pack. I'll make the arrangements. A car will pick you up to take you to the airport.'

'But I haven't agreed yet.'

'I will do whatever it takes to protect you and the twins from adverse publicity,' Cristo cut in forcefully, exasperation lending his dark deep drawl a rougher edge. 'I don't want some innuendo-laden piece appearing in print about us.'

'We had an affair. I got pregnant. It's not that unusual—'

'Trust me,' Cristo breathed. 'You'll be accused of having been a married man's mistress and that is not a possibility I want to appear in print.'

A flash of temper and distaste at that prospect rippled through Erin because that was also a humiliating label that she did not want to be lumbered with. 'OK. Where are you planning to send us…assuming I agree, which I haven't yet,' she reminded him.

'Greece…specifically, my island.'

Erin rolled her eyes. 'Oh, so you now have an island all your own?'

'I inherited Thesos from my father when I was twenty-one.'

'Well, you never mentioned it before,' Erin remarked curtly, wondering how much else she didn't know about him while trying to think frantically fast. 'Look, I'll consider going to Greece for a few days if you really think it's necessary—'

'I do.'

'But before I leave I want the chance to speak to Sally Jennings. She does still work for you, doesn't she?'

There was a moment of silence before Cristo responded expressionlessly, 'She does. She's now the deputy manager at the spa. Why?'

'And I'm sure she's very efficient. She was when I was working there,' Erin commented stiffly. 'I'll call in on the way to the airport. I don't want her to know I'm coming. I'll drop the twins off with you at your office.'

'There's no need. I'll meet you in the hotel foyer. But I don't think this is a good idea, Erin. Very few people know about the money that went missing. I handled it very discreetly. I don't think it's wise to start making enquiries again this long after the event.'

'This is the price of me going to Greece,' Erin countered flatly. 'I see Sally in London before I go or I don't go at all.'

'But that's bl—' Cristo retorted in a seething undertone.

'Blackmail?' Erin slotted in with saccharine sweetness. 'You're preaching to the converted, Cristo. Guess who taught me the skill?'

'If I facilitate this meeting at the spa, you'll come to Greece with me?'

'Of course I will. I keep my promises.' Erin came off the phone a minute later, feeling re-energised, and swept the twins out of bed to get dressed. It was past time she began calling some of the shots. Cristo became unbearable when he got his own way too much.

But she was rather touched that he was willing to go to so much trouble to whisk them away from the perils of too much press interest. Honestly, Erin thought ruefully, sometimes Cristo could be naïve. Did he really think she couldn't cope with journalists on the doorstep or some nasty article that tried to make her sound more exciting and wicked than she was? She was not that vulnerable. Life had taught her to roll with the punches. In any case the idea of travelling to Cristo's private island intrigued her. He was *finally* going to take her to his real home and naturally she was curious.

Her mother got up while the twins were eating their breakfast and, when she realised that her daughter was to leave the house in little more than an hour to travel abroad, she urged Erin to go and start packing. Before she did so, Erin rang work and requested a week's leave.

'Do you think you'll meet Cristo's parents?' Deidre asked hopefully.

Erin grimaced, in no hurry to meet Appollonia Denes, who had cut her off on the phone while making it very clear that she did not think Erin was good enough for the little boy she had raised to adulthood. Cristo had been born into a substantial fortune, the only child of two young, rich and beautiful Greeks, both from socially prominent families. Vasos and Appollonia had become Cristo's guardians when he was orphaned at the age of five, after his birth parents died in a speedboat accident. Vasos had been a trusted employee in the Donakis empire and Cristo's godfather. The older couple had had no children of their own. Erin recalled that Cristo had mentioned Appollonia having a nervous breakdown and during that phone call she had decided that the older woman was more than a little off the wall.

So, she hoped she wouldn't be meeting the older couple. Things would be challenging enough without having to deal with people who had disliked and disapproved of her even before they had met her. No doubt Vasos and Appollonia would find the news that she was the mother of Cristo's twins a source of severe embarrassment and dissatisfaction.

The twins fell asleep in the limo that carried them to London, waking up with renewed energy to bounce up the steps of the Mobila hotel. Garbed in a grey pinstripe dress and jacket, her pale hair curving round her cheekbones, Erin was apprehensive as she walked into the opulent foyer.

'Daddy!' Lorcan cried, tearing his hand free of his mother's to pelt across the open space.

'Kisto!' Nuala exclaimed, for she would not call her father Daddy, even though he had asked her to do so.

Erin focused on Cristo, seeing the manager of the renowned hotel anchored to his side and reckoning that so public a greeting from his secret children could scarcely be welcome to him. But Cristo was grinning, that wide wonderful smile she had almost forgotten flashing across his lean bronzed features in a transformation that took her breath away as he swung Lorcan up into his arms and smoothed a comforting hand over Nuala's curly head as she clung to his trouser leg with toddler tenacity.

As Erin looked at the drop-dead gorgeous father of her children a tingle of heat pinched the peaks of her breasts to tightness and arrowed down into her pelvis to spread a sensation of melting warmth. All her hormones, she registered in dismay, were in top working order and threatening to go into overdrive.

'Miss Turner.' The hotel manager shook hands with every appearance of warmth. 'What beautiful children.'

'Erin, I've arranged for Jenny to look after the twins in the crèche while we're visiting the spa,' Cristo explained, and a young woman stepped forward with a smile and proceeded to chat to Nuala.

'So, you've opened a crèche here now,' Erin remarked, her professional interest caught by that idea because she had first floated it to Cristo.

'It's very popular with our clients,' the manger advanced with enthusiasm. 'Many of them have young children.'

'The facility pays for itself,' Cristo explained, a lean hand resting to Erin's taut spine to lead her in the direction of the spa. She was filled with dismay at the realisation that he intended to accompany her, for she had not thought that far ahead and she was convinced that his intimidating presence could only injure her chances of success.

Momentarily. Erin glanced back anxiously at the twins. Lorcan was making a phenomenal noise with the toy trumpet the wily Jenny had produced while Nuala was trying her hardest to get her hands on the same toy.

'Are you certain you want to go ahead with talking to Sally?' Cristo pressed in a discouraging undertone. 'I don't agree with it. What the hell can you expect to gain but embarrassment from such a meeting?'

'Sally is the only person who knows the whole story. I don't have a choice,' Erin replied tightly, her nervous tension rising as Cristo bent down to her level and the rich evocative smell of his cologne and him ensnared her on every level.

'Don't do this for me, *koukla mou*,' Cristo urged suddenly, staring down at her as they came to a halt outside the door that now bore Sally's nameplate. 'It doesn't matter to me now. A lot of water has gone under the bridge since then. You were young. You made a mistake and I'm sure you learned from it—'

'Don't you dare patronise me, you…you…you *toad*!' Erin finally selected in her spirited retort. 'And don't interfere.'

'Toad?' Cristo repeated blankly.

'I'd have called you something a good deal more blunt if I hadn't trained myself not to use bad words around the children!' she told him curtly, hastily depressing the door handle of the office before she could lose what little remained of her momentum.

Sally, a tall middle-aged woman with red hair and light blue eyes, was standing behind her desk talking on the phone. When she saw Erin, she froze, her previous animated expression ironed flat as she visibly lost colour.

'Erin, my goodness,' she breathed in astonishment, dropping the phone back on its cradle in haste and bustling round the desk. 'And Mr Donakis…'

'I would like your assurance that anything that is said in this room remains between these four walls,' Cristo said quietly.

Sally looked bewildered and then she smiled. 'Of course, Mr Donakis. Take a seat and tell me what I can help you with.'

Erin was so nervous that she could feel her knees trembling and she linked her hands tightly together as she sat down. 'I'm sure that you're aware that the audit two and a half years ago threw up certain anomalies in the spa accounts…'

If possible, Sally went paler than ever and she dropped rather heavily back down behind her desk. 'Mr Donakis did ask me to keep that problem confidential.'

'Sally,' Erin muttered, suddenly filled with a sense of utter hopelessness. What craziness had brought her here to this pointless encounter? There was no way Sally was going to offer up a belated confession of fraud with her employer present. 'Perhaps you could leave us alone, Cristo.'

'No, I have news to share first. I'm planning to have the account irregularities looked at again.'

The older woman's face went all tight. 'But, Mr Donakis, I thought that matter was done and dusted. You said you were satisfied.'

'I'm afraid I wasn't. And bearing in mind how helpful you were during the first investigation, I thought you should be informed before the experts arrive to go over the books again,' Cristo completed.

Sally had turned an unhealthy colour, her dazed eyes flickering between the two of them, and suddenly she spoke. 'You're a couple again, aren't you?' she exclaimed, her attention lodging almost accusingly on Erin. 'And you've told him about me, haven't you?'

'Told me what?' Cristo enquired lazily.

Taking on board the reality that Cristo was piling the pressure on Sally to admit that she had lied and offering Erin a level of support she had not expected to receive from him, Erin squared her shoulders in frustration. She had always fought her own battles.

Sally compressed her lips in mutinous silence as if daring Erin to answer that question.

'While I was working here I discovered that Sally had been taking products from the store and selling them on online auctions.' Erin turned her attention back to the older woman, who had once been a trusted colleague. 'I know I promised that that was our secret but sometimes promises have to be broken.'

'You were stealing?' Cristo prompted Sally forbiddingly.

Tears spilled from Sally's eyes and she knocked them away with her hand and fumbled for a tissue, which she clenched tightly in one hand.

'I guarantee that whatever you tell me there will be no prosecution now or in the future.' Lean, strong face taut, Cristo stood up, a lithe powerful figure of considerable command. 'I very much regret that you felt unable to be honest with me when this business was first discovered but I'm hoping that for Erin's sake you will now tell me the truth.'

'No prosecution?' Sally queried uncertainly.

'No prosecution. I only want the truth,' Cristo confirmed.

'One lunchtime shortly before Erin resigned a man came to see me,' Sally related in a flat voice. 'He said he was a private detective and he offered me a substantial amount of money if I could give him information that would damage Erin's reputation.'

'*What*?' Cristo positively erupted into speech, his disbelief unhidden.

'His name was Will Grimes. He worked at an agency in Camden. That's all I know about him. At first I said no to him. After all there wasn't any information to give!' Sally pointed out with a wry grimace. 'You hadn't done anything but work hard here, Erin, but then you suddenly resigned from your job and just like that I re-

alised how I could get myself out of the trouble that I
was in.'

'Will Grimes,' Cristo was repeating heavily.

'I was in a great deal more financial trouble than
I admitted when you found me helping myself to that
stuff from the store,' Sally told Erin tautly. 'I had set up
a couple of other scams in the books—'

'The payments to therapists that didn't exist, the altered invoices?' Cristo specified.

'Yes, and then you organised the audit and I started
to panic,' Sally confided tearfully. 'Erin had left the
spa by then.'

'And you decided to let me take the blame for it?'
Erin prompted while she wondered how on earth she
had ever attracted the attention of a private detective.

'I *wanted* to stop taking the money,' the older woman
stressed in open desperation.' I knew it was wrong but
I had got in too deep. Once the fraud was uncovered
and I set up things so that you got the blame I could go
back to a normal life again and, of course, I still had
my job. I knew you would be safe from prosecution
with Mr Donakis—he wasn't likely to trail his own
girlfriend into court!'

'You got me right on that score,' Cristo derided.

'Will you prosecute me now?' Sally asked him shakily.

'No. I gave you my word and I thank you for finally
telling me what really happened,' Cristo responded.

Clearly limp with relief, Sally braced her hands on
the desk to stand up. 'I'll clear my desk immediately
and leave—'

'No, work out your notice here as normal,' Cristo

urged, resting a hand on Erin's taut shoulder to ease her slowly upright.

'Erin?' Sally breathed stiltedly. 'I'm sorry. When you were so kind to me, you deserved better from me.'

Erin nodded, even tried to force her lips into a forgiving smile, but couldn't manage it for she was all too well aware how the false belief that she was a thief had affected Cristo's opinion of her. In any case, she was deeply shaken by what Sally had confessed and she couldn't hide the fact. She had been fond of the older woman, had only lost contact with her because she had fallen pregnant and on hard times. Pride had ensured that she did not pursue ongoing contact with anyone at her former workplace. She stole a veiled glance at Cristo's profile. He was pale, his facial muscles taut below his dark complexion.

Cristo paused at the door on his way out. 'Did you collect the reward money from the private detective and give him the supposed evidence of Erin's dishonesty?'

Sally winced and nodded slowly. 'It got me out of debt and gave me a fresh start.'

Erin gritted her teeth, disgusted by Sally's selfishness.

Cristo felt as if the walls of his tough shell were crumbling around him. Astonishingly, Erin's seemingly paranoid suspicion that she was being set up for a fall by persons unknown had been proven correct. He, who rarely got anything wrong, had been wrong. He had made an appalling error of judgement. But more than anything at that moment he wanted to know who could possibly have hired a detective to discredit Erin in his eyes by fair means or foul.

CHAPTER NINE

ERIN picked at the perfectly cooked lunch served on board Cristo's private jet without much appetite. She was still angry at Sally and bitter that the older woman had got away with destroying Erin's reputation rather than her own. How many other people were suffering from the mistaken assumption that she was a con woman, who had escaped her just deserts solely because she was the owner's ex-girlfriend? As someone who had always worked hard with scrupulous honesty and pride in her performance of her duties, she deeply resented the false impression that Sally had created to hide her own wrongdoing.

'We have to talk,' Cristo remarked flatly.

'I don't think I've ever heard that phrase from you before,' she parried waspishly, recalling that once upon a time Cristo had been the first out of he door when such a suggestion was laid before him. That had certainly been his all-too-masculine reaction on every occasion when she'd tried to corner him for a *serious* conversation.

From the cabin next door she could hear the sounds of the children playing and talking. Jenny, the charming young brunette nanny, had turned out not to work for the spa crèche after all. No, indeed, Jenny had been specifically hired by Cristo to take care of the twins while they were in Greece.

'That's so unnecessary and extravagant,' Erin had criticised when she found out about the arrangement at the airport.

'You can't look after them 24-7,' Cristo had informed her authoritatively.

'Why can't I?' she had asked.

'Why shouldn't you have a break?' he had responded arrogantly.

'If Jenny is your concept of responsible parenting you need to buy another handbook,' she had retorted curtly, annoyed that he had taken such a decision over her head. He was Lorcan and Nuala's father: all right, she accepted that, however that didn't mean that she would accept his interference in matters about which he was scarcely qualified to have an opinion. She was no more in need of a break than any other working mother, she thought thinly, which she supposed meant that, rail as she had at him, the prospect of the occasional hour in which she could relax and think of herself again was disturbingly appealing and made her feel quite appallingly guilty.

Returning to the present and the tense atmosphere currently stretching between them, Erin shot Cristo a glance from cool amethyst eyes. 'You think we should talk? I'll be frank—only if you crawled naked over broken glass would I think you had redeemed yourself.'

A wicked grin very briefly slashed Cristo's lean bronzed features, his dark eyes shot with golden amusement below his thick sooty lashes, making him spectacularly handsome. 'Not much chance of that,' he admitted.

'So, where's my apology?' Erin demanded truculently to mask the effect of her dry mouth and quickened heartbeat because, no matter how furious he made her, she could still not remain impervious to his stunning good looks, a reality that mortified her. 'It's taking you long enough!'

'I was trying to come up with the right words.'

'Even if you swallowed a dictionary, it wouldn't help you!'

Lean strong face taut, Cristo sprang out of his seat. 'I am sincerely sorry that I ever entertained the suspicion that you had stolen from me, *koukla mou*.'

'You didn't just entertain it,' she objected. 'You fell for it hook, line and sinker!'

'My security team are even at this moment checking into this Will Grimes angle. I can't understand why a private detective would have been interested in you.' Indeed, having thought deeply about that particular issue, Cristo could only think that someone *he* knew had hired a detective in an apparent effort to disgrace Erin. But who would have wasted their money on such a pursuit and what had been the motivation? It still made no sense to him. Erin had not been his wife or fiancée? Why would anyone have wanted to harm her and, through her, him?

Erin tilted her chin, eyes glinting pure lavender. 'Seems I wasn't paranoid, after all. I'm still waiting on that apology too.'

His strong jaw line hardened, dark eyes gleaming. 'And you'll be waiting a long time because you're not getting a second. If you hadn't been so direct about your expectations I might have soft-pedalled for the sake of peace, but now I'll be equally direct: you brought that theft accusation down on your own head!'

Erin stared at him aghast, totally wrong-footed by that condemnation coming at her out of the blue when she had expected a grovelling apology. *Really*? Well, possibly not of the grovelling variety, but, yes, she had assumed he would be embarrassed by his misjudgement and eager to soothe her wounded feelings. Now, deprived of that development and outraged by his attitude, Erin leapt out of her seat to face him. 'And how do you work that out?'

'As far as I was aware Sally Jennings was an exemplary long-term employee with no strikes against her and no reason to lie. Had I known she had already been caught thieving at work I would have known to take a closer look at her activities,' Cristo shot back at her levelly.

Erin stiffened, feeling she was on weaker ground when it came to the decision she had once made over Sally and defying the reflection. 'Sally was going through a divorce and she has two autistic sons. At the time, I believed she needed compassionate handling rather than punishment.'

Cristo expelled his breath in a hiss, his brilliant eyes cracking like whips. 'Compassion? If I'd known then how you mishandled her dishonesty I would have sacked you for incompetence!'

'*Incompetence*?' Erin bleated incredulously, rage jumping up and down inside her like a gushing fountain suddenly switched on.

'Yes, incompetence,' Cristo confirmed with succinct bite. 'How would you feel about a manager who left a thief in a position of power in your business and chose not to warn anyone about her dangerous little weakness?'

'I dealt with the situation as I saw fit back then. Looking back, I can see I was too trusting—'

'Correction…bloody naïve!' Cristo shot back at her witheringly. 'I didn't hire you to be compassionate. Plenty of people lead tough lives but few of them steal. I hired you to take care of part of my business and that was your sole responsibility. Listening to sob stories and letting a clever calculating woman get off scot-free with her crimes was no part of your job description!'

It took enormous will power but Erin managed to restrain her temper and the urge to snap back at him because she knew that he was making valid points. 'It's not a decision I would make now. Unfortunately I liked Sally and believed she was a wonderful worker. I was naïve—I'll admit that—'

'Why the hell didn't you consult me about it or at least approach someone with more experience for their opinion on what to do about her?' Cristo demanded angrily. 'At the very least, once you knew Sally was a thief, all her activities at work should have been checked out thoroughly and she should have been moved to a position where she had no access to products, account books or money.'

As he made those cogent decrees Erin lifted her head high, refusing to go into retreat. 'You're right but I thought I could deal with the situation on my own. I didn't want you to think that I couldn't cope. But I was hugely overworked and stressed at the time. I notice the current manager has a deputy and I saw at least two administrators in the general office. I didn't have anyone but Sally to rely on.'

'Then you should have asked for more help,' Cristo fielded without hesitation.

'My biggest mistake was accepting a position from someone I was involved with. I was too proud, too busy trying to impress you about what a great job I was doing. I didn't have enough experienced staff around me and those that were there kept their distance because I was too close to the boss. I was very focused on building the business, bringing in more custom, increasing productivity. It made me far too dependent on Sally for support. I can see that now,' Erin concluded that honest statement curtly.

'At least you can now see what that inappropriate decision cost you. Sally didn't hesitate when it came to setting you up to take the blame for her acts of fraud or when she got the chance to reap financial benefits from her disloyalty,' Cristo pointed out.

'Don't forget that Sally Jennings fooled you as well. The role she played was very convincing,' Erin reminded him tightly. 'You didn't smell a rat in her performance either.'

'But I would have done had you tipped me off about her stealing. Right, we've aired this for long enough, subject closed,' Cristo pronounced decisively.

'Now that you've had your say and blamed me for everything?' Erin countered tautly, amethyst eyes dark and unwittingly vulnerable, for that word, 'incompetence', had cut deep as a knife. 'Was it too much for me to expect that after knowing me for a year you would question the idea that I might have been filling my pockets at your expense?'

'After certain suspicions had been awakened and the man I saw in your hotel-room bed I will concede that I was predisposed to think the worst of you,' Cristo derided, compressing his wide sensual mouth into a tough line. 'What's that cliché about the easiest explanation usually being the right one? In this case, the easiest explanation was the wrong one.'

Erin sank back down in her seat. 'Am I finally getting a clean slate on the score of the one-night stand with the toy boy?' she asked grittily. 'Tom's brother, Dennis, was only nineteen back then.'

'That's not quite so clear cut. My suspicions in that quarter were first awakened by other indications, which I will discuss with you when we get to the island,' he added as her triangular face tensed into a frown of bemusement. 'I am sincerely sorry that I misjudged you and that I didn't dig a little deeper three years back.'

Erin said nothing. What other evidence of her infidelity did he imagine he had? She hadn't a clue what he was talking about and had no time for more mysteries. In addition her mind was being bombarded with thoughts after that heated exchange of views. He had shot her down in flames and it rankled and that was precisely why she had not approached him for advice after she had caught Sally stealing. She had known he would take the toughest stance and would call in the police. She had feared that he would blame her for the inadequate security in the products store, which had made Sally's thefts all too easy. If she was honest she had also worried about how she would cope without Sally at her elbow. My mistake, she acknowledged painfully. A wrong decision that had cost her more than she could ever have dreamt.

Cristo watched in frustration as Erin made a weak excuse and went off to join Jenny and the twins. It had been right to tell her the truth, he told himself angrily. He was damned if the fact that she was the mother of his children would make him start lying just to please her! Did shooting from the hip mean he had also shot himself in the foot? Almost three years ago, he had not talked to Erin about important issues and this time around he was determined not to repeat that mistake. Blunt speech had to be better than minimal communication and misunderstandings, he decided impatiently.

Shielded by the need to keep the twins occupied for what remained of a journey that entailed a final helicopter flight to the island of Thesos, Erin licked her wounds in private. From the air she had a fantastic view of Cristo's island. It was bigger than she had imagined and the southern end was heavily forested with pine trees. She spied a cluster of low-rise structures on what appeared to be a building site on the furthest coast and a picturesque little town by the harbour before the helicopter flew level again and began to swoop down over the tree tops to land.

Lorcan was asleep and Cristo hoisted his son out of Erin's arms and carried him off. They had landed about twenty yards from a magnificent ultra-modern villa surrounded by terraces and balconies to take advantage of the land and sea views.

'This all looks new,' Erin remarked.

'I demolished my parents' house and had this one designed about three years ago. It made more sense than trying to renovate the old place,' he commented casually.

Three years ago, while they had still been a couple, Erin had known nothing about his island or the new house he was having built. Not for the first time Erin appreciated that Cristo had shut her out of a large section of his life and she wondered why. Obviously he had never considered her important enough to include her in the Greek half of his existence, which encompassed home and family. And that, whether she liked it or not, *hurt*, most particularly when he had married a Greek woman within months of dumping Erin.

A short brunette with warm brown eyes was introduced as Androula, the housekeeper. Straight away Androula cooed over the children in their arms and hurried off to show Erin and Jenny to the rooms set aside for their use. Erin was taken aback to discover that Cristo had already had accommodation specially prepared for his son and daughter, each complete with small beds, appropriate decoration and an array of toys. Leaving the capable Jenny to put the drowsy children to bed, Erin explored her own room with its doors opening onto the terrace and superb view through the trees to a white beach and a turquoise sea over which the sun was sinking in a display of fiery splendour.

'Will you be comfortable here?'

Erin spun to find Cristo behind her, poised between the French windows. 'How could I fail to be? It's the height of luxury,' she said awkwardly.

Cristo searched her shuttered face and breathed almost roughly, 'I was tough on you on the plane. I was angry that you let that scheming woman make you pay the price for her crimes.'

'But at least that's sorted out now. The rooms organised for the children are beautiful,' she told him stiffly, suppressing the discomfiture she was still feeling. 'You must have organised that almost as soon as you found out about them.'

Cristo inclined his dark head. 'Yes, even before I asked you if they could visit Thesos. I still tend to act first and ask later.'

Not even questioning that arrogant assumption of power, Erin turned away and rested her elbows back on the low wall girding the terrace. She had intended to get her revenge on Cristo for what he had done to her in Italy, but it had gradually dawned on her that angering or hurting Cristo would most probably damage his relationship with their children. Their own relationship was irrevocably meshed with the ties and responsibilities of also being parents. And how, in conscience, could she take that risk of weakening those links?

'You never ever told me that this place existed,' she said.

'What would have been the point if I wasn't planning to bring you here?' he murmured wryly. 'When I was with you I wasn't quite ready to move our affair on to the next stage. I was simply enjoying the place we had reached until it blew up in both our faces. I'm sorry.'

'No need to apologise.' Erin fought the just-slapped-in-the-face sensation of humiliation that his piece of plain speaking inspired and wondered why on earth he was suddenly telling her such things. In the past she had loved him and longed for a secure future with him but he had not felt the same. Why did that news still make her feel so gutted? That time was gone and she didn't love him any longer. She just lusted after him, enjoyed his energising company, respected his business prowess, intelligence and strength of principle. Enumerating that unacceptably long list of his supposed attributes, Erin gritted her teeth together. Why was she doing this to herself? Dwelling on things that no longer had any place between them? She was the mother of his children and that was all.

'In those days…' Cristo, engaged in watching the tense muscles in her slender back and the vulnerable piece of pale nape exposed by her bent head, floundered. 'I wasn't exactly in touch with my feelings.'

'I'm not sure you had any…above your belt,' Erin specified shakily.

'That is *so* wrong!' Cristo growled, lean hands closing forcefully to her shoulders to tug her back round to face him. 'I was sick to the stomach when I thought you'd gone to bed with another man! It turned my whole life upside down!'

'Try being pregnant by a man you can't even get to speak to you on the phone!' Erin lanced back at him with unconcealed bitterness.

His dark golden eyes shone amber bright at the challenge. 'I would never have knowingly allowed that to happen. What reason would I have to treat you like some demented stalker? I intend to get the full story out of Amelia when I'm next in Athens where she works now.'

'I'll still never forgive you.'

His superb bone structure was taut and he gazed steadily back at her. 'Was being pregnant so bad?'

'I had to live on welfare benefits. It was a struggle I'll never forget,' Erin admitted truthfully. 'My home was a damp tenth-floor council flat barely fit for human habitation. It was only when my mother came to see me and realised how I was living that she invited me to go home with her. There was also the not so little matter of me being pregnant and unmarried, which really did upset Mum. She's an old-fashioned woman and as far as she's concerned decent girls don't have babies until

they have a ring on their wedding finger. We were es-
tranged for most of my pregnancy.'

His concern was unfeigned. 'You had no support at
all? What about your friend, Elaine? Did she ask you
to move out of her apartment?'

'No, I made that decision— I couldn't pay my way
any more,' Erin explained ruefully. 'But Tom and
Melissa helped out as best they could.'

'Melissa?'

'Now Tom's wife but at the time they were living
together and I couldn't have had better friends,' Erin
declared. 'They were very good to me.'

His keen gaze was screened by his luxuriant black
lashes, his eloquent mouth set in a forbidding line. 'I
owe them a debt for that.'

'Yes, you do,' Erin told him bluntly. 'They didn't have
much either but what they had they shared.'

His lashes swept up on breathtakingly beautiful
golden eyes from which all anger had vanished. 'But I
owe the biggest debt of all to you for bringing my children into the world. Don't think I don't appreciate that
and know how lucky I was that you chose not to have
a termination. I *do* know—I *do* appreciate it,' he completed in a rare display of unmistakable emotion.

Cristo took the wind out of Erin's sails with that
candid little speech, but her anger with him was not so
easily soothed. 'When I was pregnant I assumed that if
you had a choice you would have preferred me to have
a termination. You once told me about that friend of
yours whose girlfriend got pregnant,' she reminded him.

'I didn't say that I approved of what they chose to
do. Maybe it was right for them but I would not have
reacted the same way that he did.'

'Easy to say,' she needled. 'Hindsight is a wonderful device with which to rewrite the past. You also said that you preferred your life without baggage.'

'Don't judge me for what I did and didn't do almost three years ago. I've grown up a lot since then,' Cristo spelt out tautly.

His marriage to Lisandra, she thought ruefully, thinking it was sad that she apparently owed this rather less arrogant and reserved version of Cristo to the machinations of another woman. Even so, her heart could only be touched by his gratitude that she had given birth to Lorcan and Nuala. She had felt his sincerity and it meant a great deal to her. Cristo had, after all, taken to fatherhood with enthusiasm and energy. He seemed neither resentful of the responsibility he had had thrust on him, nor ill-at-ease with it. That awareness tore more than one brick out of Erin's defensive wall.

Walking back indoors, she noticed a trio of large envelopes lying on an occasional table. Already opened, they were addressed to Cristo at his London office. 'What are these?'

Cristo hesitated and then frowned, his restive pacing coming to a sudden halt. 'The evidence I promised to show you once we got here. Take a look at what's in those envelopes…'

'Why? What's in them?'

'Photos which were sent to me during the latter months we were together in London.'

Erin extracted a large, slightly blurred photograph of a couple walking hand in hand. The man was her friend, Tom Harcourt, and the face on the woman was hers. As she had never held hands with Tom in her life she was astonished until she studied the body and the clothing of the female depicted. In a frantic rush, she leafed through the other photos, one showing the same couple kissing and another of them hugging. 'That may be my face but it's not my body—it's Melissa's. These photos are all of Tom with his wife, Melissa, but they've been digitally altered to make it look as though the woman is me!' she murmured in disbelief.

'*Altered*?' Cristo stood by her side as she fanned out the photos and one by one proceeded to verbally pick them apart. 'How altered?'

'Whoever sent these photos to you grafted my face onto Melissa's body,' she told him angrily. 'All we have in common is that we're both blondes but I'd recognise that sweater from a mile away! How on earth could you think that was me, Cristo? Melissa is much smaller, well under five foot tall. Didn't you notice how small she seems beside Tom, who isn't that tall? And since when did I have a bust as big as that?'

Peering down at the photos, Cristo noted every point of comparison. 'None of them are of you with Tom,' he finally breathed in bewilderment. 'Why didn't I notice those differences for myself?'

It might as well have been a rhetorical question because Erin had no intention of pursuing that pointless line of enquiry. 'As you said, you act first and ask later. But I just don't believe how secretive you can be! You received these rotten lying photos on three separate occasions and didn't once mention them to me. No wonder you became so suspicious of my friendship with Tom!'

In retrospect she could recall the surprisingly sudden alteration in Cristo's attitude towards her spending time with Tom while he was away on business. Cristo had gone from accepting that friendship without comment to suddenly questioning her every meeting with the other man, but only now was she discovering that genuine disquiet had provoked that change of heart.

Erin was struggling to understand why he had remained silent in the face of such provocation and failing. It was cruel to realise that she had gone through so much pain just because some hateful individual had decided to destroy Cristo's trust in her, ensuring that he would reject her. He had walked away from her and almost straight away gone on to marry another woman. The wound inflicted by that decision of his had never left her. He had got over her so quickly and she believed that he must always have viewed her as not being good enough to marry. His choice of a rich Greek wife from a background similar to his own had been revealing.

'Why didn't you show these photos to me at the time?' Erin demanded.

Lean, strong face shuttered, Cristo clenched his jaw. He walked away a few paces, his long, lean body as fluid and graceful as running water, his black hair gleaming like polished jet in the fading daylight above his bold bronzed profile. Sometimes he looked so incredibly handsome that she couldn't take her eyes off him, she thought rawly, anguish for what they had lost engulfing her.

'I had too much pride,' Cristo grated the admission. 'I could not make my mind up about whether you were cheating on me or whether your relationship with Tom had simply become too close and affectionate. I didn't know what to think but it did make me doubt your loyalty—'

'And when you walked into that hotel room and saw a strange man in the bed, you were in exactly the right frame of mind to assume that I was cheating on you,' Erin completed with fierce resentment. 'How could you not give me a single chance to defend myself?'

'I will always regret it,' Cristo confessed in a driven undertone, piling the photos together and cramming them into a single envelope. 'We are now living with the consequences. I've missed more than two years of my children's lives as a result. I would not like to be in the shoes of whomever I find is responsible for deliberately setting out to destroy us.'

'But the hotel-room thing was just an unlucky coincidence,' Erin reasoned heavily, shaken that anyone could have gone to such lengths to discredit her in his eyes. 'I do understand after seeing those photos that you honestly believed you didn't need to see me in the flesh in the same room to believe that I was cheating on you. Do you have a bunny-boiling ex-girlfriend somewhere in your past? Jealous women can be vicious. Who else would take so much time and trouble and put so much money into trying to split us up?'

'I don't know but I have every intention of finding out,' he swore, a hostile expression stamped on his hard features. He cast the envelopes aside and drew her back to him with determined hands.

He lowered his head and caressed her parted lips slowly with his own in a move that completely disconcerted her. Her entire body tingled with electrified awareness. Coming alive to his sensual call, she was shamefully aware that the peaks of her breasts were straining into bullet points and her thighs pressing together to contain the ache of emptiness there. 'I want a fresh start with you,' he breathed in a raw undertone, his breath fanning her cheek. 'Let's get all the rubbish out of the way and leave it behind us.'

'A lot of what you call rubbish messed up my life,' Erin replied defensively, her eyes prickling with tears behind her eyelids, and she didn't even understand why she so suddenly felt screamingly vulnerable and unsure of herself. *I want a fresh start with you.* She hadn't seen that coming, didn't know what to say.

'We both screwed up,' Cristo contradicted, gravity hardening his high cheekbones to make him look tougher and stronger than ever. 'We can't change the past but we can begin again...'

Erin looked up into his lean, tense features. 'Can we?' she whispered.

Long brown fingers framed her cheekbone and intent dark golden eyes flamed over her troubled face. 'I say we can,' he declared, curving a hand to her hip to ease her closer.

She wanted to believe it; she wanted to believe it so badly. He wanted her back. He *still* wanted her. A powerful tide of relief rolled through her, closely followed by a flood of happiness. Dark eyes glinting sensually below his lashes, he melded her to his big powerful length and desire flared through her like a hungry fire ready to blaze out of control. The heat of him against her, the glorious scent of his skin and the hungry thrust of his erection were a potent inducement and when he crushed her sultry mouth beneath his she was with him every step of the way.

Cristo peeled off her blouse with wildly impatient hands and then released her bra to bury his mouth urgently in the sweet sloping swell of her breasts. 'You're so beautiful, so perfect—'

'Not perfect,' she protested as he gathered her up and lowered her down on the bed with a scantily leashed impatience she could not resist.

'You're perfect for me, *koukla mou,*' Cristo countered, determined to have the last word. 'You always were.'

The passionate kiss that followed as he explored the confines of her mouth with devouring heat silenced her. Her nipples were hard and swollen and he dallied there with his mouth and his fingers to reduce her to gasping compliance with the hot sensuality that was so much a part of him. The remainder of her clothes were discarded and Cristo undressed in haste, returning to claim her with his lean, strong body boldly aroused. Her heart raced as she stroked the long, hard thickness of his shaft and she rejoiced when he groaned and arched his hips up to her in supplication. He flipped her back against the pillows, searching out the slick sensitive folds and the tiny knot of nerve-endings above to stroke her with teasing, tender skill. The tide of pleasure swept her out of her control, each touch of his fingers making her burn and writhe and finally sob with anticipation and need. And only then did he reach for protection and sink deep into her damp sheath, telling her huskily of his pleasure as her inner muscles tightened convulsively around him. Excitement gripped her when he withdrew and then plunged deep into her again, ripples of delight rising higher and higher inside her as the fire in her pelvis burned hotter than ever. And when she finally reached a climax and he reached the same point with her, he lay sated and uncharacteristically silent in the protective circle of her arms afterwards and she felt gloriously happy.

'That was…wonderful, *koukla mou*,' Cristo husked, folding her slight damp body, to him with possessive arms. 'I don't know how I contrived to keep my hands off you for so long.'

'I should've said no,' Erin lamented, studying his lean, darkly handsome features with dazed eyes. 'You blackmailed me into bed in Italy—'

'You wanted me.' Cristo punctuated that claim with a soothing kiss on her reddened lips, smouldering golden eyes scanning her flushed face with unashamed satisfaction. 'I wanted you. I found a way round the difficulties so that we could be together again. Now that I have you back in my arms where you belong I would be a liar if I pretended to have regrets.'

'The end justifies the means?' Erin pressed drily.

'You know that you want me just as much,' he argued with unashamed assurance. 'When we burn, we burn together.'

It was true and even with that frantic need fulfilled she could not lie in contact with that compellingly masculine body of his without experiencing the first little quivers of yet another sensual awakening. As the liquid warmth at the heart of her began to melt he ran the edge of his teeth down the extended length of her neck and she shivered violently. He reached for another condom and then pulled her over to him, watching as her lashes dipped low in a cloaked expression of intense pleasure that he savoured.

'Will you marry me?' he murmured tautly.

Eyes flying wide, Erin stared down at him, wondering if she had imagined that question.

'It seemed like the right moment,' Cristo asserted, his hands clasping to her hips to rock her gently up on him and then down in a controlling rhythm that was impossibly exciting. 'Don't laugh—'

'I'm not going to laugh!' she riposted, offended by the suggestion and studying him with troubled amethyst eyes. 'Are you serious?'

'I want you and the twins to be a proper part of my life.' His breathing fractured as she made a subtle circling movement above him, pale silvery fair hair streaming down over her shoulders to allow tantalising glimpses of her small pert breasts. 'I don't think it can get better than this, *koukla mou*.'

And when only minutes later yet another orgasm took Erin by storm, she decided she agreed with him. She lay in the relaxed circle of his arms, breathing in the hot damp smell of him like a hopeless addict, too long deprived of the source of her fix. He wanted her. He wanted their children. What more was there? *Love*? Cristo hadn't offered her love the last time she was with him and he likely never would. It was wiser to focus on what she could have rather than what she couldn't. Wasn't it the question she had always wanted him to ask? And did it really matter that he hadn't made an occasion of the proposal? Aside of the few gestures he had made when in initial pursuit of her, Cristo didn't have a romantic bone in his body. He was probably being practical. They were very much attracted to each other and it made sense for them to marry and share the children, she conceded ruefully, but she was slightly amazed that he was willing to surrender his freedom again after his first unhappy marriage.

'Are you sure about this?'

His sooty lashes swept up on his level gaze. 'I know what I want.'

'But is it really us as a family unit?'

'Do I get to wake up to you almost every morning?' Cristo raised a mocking brow. 'That's my sole demand. That's what I want and need.'

Erin was not quite convinced of that when two little wriggling noisy bodies tried to get into bed with them at dawn the next morning. Aghast, Cristo snatched up his boxers to make himself presentable and looked on in disbelief as the twins cuddled up between them, providing as effective a barrier as a wall.

'What are you doing in Mummy's bed?' Lorcan demanded curiously.

'Your mother and I are getting married very soon,' Cristo announced instantly.

Erin stiffened in dismay. 'Cristo, I didn't say yes.'

Cristo sent her a shocked look, his eyes dancing with wicked amusement. 'Are you saying that you took repeated gross advantage of me last night without any intention of making an honest man of me and doing the decent thing?'

Erin reddened at his mockery, the ache of her well-used body reminding her that after the enthusiasm she had demonstrated between the sheets he naturally took her agreement to marry him somewhat for granted. 'No, I'm not saying that.'

'Then I can go ahead and make the wedding arrangements?'

Erin nodded uncertainly, thoroughly shaken by the concept of becoming his bride. 'Shouldn't we have a living-together trial first?'

'Nope. You might change your mind. I refuse to be put on trial. And on a more serious note, it's time I told my parents about you and the twins. I don't want them to hear from another source,' he imparted wryly. 'I'll go and see them after breakfast.'

'They live here on the island?' Now she grasped why he had never offered to bring her to Thesos for a visit.

'They have a second home here. They use it weekends, holidays.' He shrugged. 'They're here right now.'

'How do you think they'll react?'

'I suspect my foster mother will be overjoyed—she's crazy about children.'

'Just not so crazy about me?' Erin remarked uncomfortably as the twins scampered out of bed and she followed suit.

'Some misunderstanding must've lain behind the strange impression you received of my foster mother during that phone call you made while you were pregnant. Appollonia had no reason to think badly of you. She knew nothing about you.'

The four of them enjoyed breakfast on the terrace and then Cristo left to visit his parents and Erin changed into a swimsuit, packed a bag and took the children down to the beach As the morning ticked slowly past she wondered anxiously what sort of a reception Cristo was receiving from his parents. His foster parents, she reminded herself again, having studied a picture on the wall of a glamorous young couple standing on the deck of a yacht and guessed that the glossy pair were Cristo's birth parents. When she came back from the beach, she let Jenny take the exhausted twins and went for a shower, emerging to phone her mother and describe the island and the house and, finally, their plans to marry. Her parent was very pleased by her news.

Choosing a book from the well-stocked, handsome library to entertain her until lunchtime, Erin relaxed in a cushioned lounger in the shade below the trees. She was drowsing in the heat when a slight sound alerted her to the awareness that she was no longer alone. Taking off her sunglasses, she sat up and frowned at Cristo, who looked grim. Lines of strain were indented between his nose and mouth, his black hair was tousled and stubble darkened the revealing downward curve of his beautiful mouth.

'What's up?' Erin demanded worriedly, checking her watch. He had been gone for hours. It was two in the afternoon.

As he sank down heavily opposite her Erin leant a little closer and sniffed. 'Have you been drinking?'

'I might have had a couple while I was waiting on the doctor's arrival with Vasos,' he volunteered half under his breath. 'It's been such a ghastly morning that I don't really remember.'

'Who needed a doctor?' she exclaimed.

'My mother.'

'Appollonia's taken ill?'

Cristo dealt her a troubled appraisal. 'It was her…she was the one who hired the private detective. I wouldn't have believed it if she hadn't known enough to convince me. My father is in shock—he had no idea what was going on.'

Erin was bemused. 'What are you talking about?'

'My mother hired Will Grimes.'

Her eyes widened while she recognised how much that staggering discovery had upset him. There was enormous sorrow in his unshielded eyes that made her wince and long to hold him close, for she knew how deeply attached he was to the couple who had raised him. In fact it hurt her so much to see him wounded in such a way that she stopped lying to herself in that same moment: all her proud pretences and defences fell away and she was left to face the inescapable truth that she still loved Cristophe Donakis and had never stopped loving him.

CHAPTER TEN

'APPOLLONIA learned that you and I had been together for at least a year from one of my friends. She was always ridiculously eager for me to settle down and have a family and she became convinced that you were holding me back from that development. She was obsessed with the idea of me marrying another Greek and spending more time here in Greece,' Cristo explained with a heavy sigh as he sat opposite Erin, who was studying him fixedly. 'She paid a private detective to investigate you and eventually told him that she would pay him a bonus if he would use whatever means were within his power to break us up.'

'But that's crazy,' Erin whispered, reeling from the unexpected tale he was telling her. 'You're an adult. How could your mother interfere in your life like that?'

'Appollonia seems honestly to have believed that she was doing it for the sake of my future happiness, *koukla mou*. How I might feel about it or how much damage she might do in the process to me or you never seems to have entered her head until it was too late.'

'How on earth did you realise that it was your foster mother who had hired the detective?'

'I was telling her about you and the twins and she

suddenly made a rather scornful reference to the thefts from the spa. That immediately made me suspicious because she did not get that information from me. It could only have come from the detective she hired. Once she grasped that you were the mother of my children she was very shocked and guilty and in that state she blurted out the whole story. My father, Vasos, was appalled and he asked her what she had been thinking of...'

'Did you tell her that I wasn't the thief?' Erin asked ruefully.

'Of course. She didn't ask the detective what weapons he used to bring about our split, in fact she didn't want to know the dirty details, and once it was achieved she invited Lisandra to dinner and dangled her under my nose. I told her about the doctored photos and Sally being rewarded for identifying you as the thief. I also told her that it was her fault that Lorcan and Nuala were strangers until I met them two weeks ago. She remembered your phone call. She did honestly believe that you had been stealing from me and that was how she justified her interference—you were a wicked woman and I needed help to break free of your malign influence. That had become her excuse and when that excuse was taken from her she became extremely distressed. Vasos was shouting at her and it all got very hysterical and overheated.' Cristo groaned, luxuriant black lashes almost hitting his exotic cheekbones as he briefly closed his eyes in frustration. 'In the end we called the local doctor to administer a sedative to calm her down...'

'Oh, my goodness, is this the reason she had a nervous breakdown when your marriage went wrong?'

'Yes, although none of us appreciated that at the time.

But she felt hugely guilty at having encouraged me to marry Lisandra.'

'No offence intended, Cristo, but right now Appollonia sounds like the mother-in-law from hell,' Erin remarked with an apologetic grimace.

'I think it is good that the truth has come out at last.' Cristo was seemingly determined to find a positive angle. 'Possibly Appollonia's secret arrangement with the detective has been the burden on her conscience which damaged her recovery from the breakdown she suffered. She is still a fragile personality but she wasn't always like that.'

'Was your PA got to by the detective as well? Was that why my calls were never put through and my letters were returned unread?'

Cristo sighed, 'My foster mother told her you were stalking me and that she'd be grateful if Amelia shielded me from nuisance calls and letters. Amelia probably believed she was doing me a favour.'

'Bloody hell!' Erin erupted furiously, standing up and walking away, only to spin back. 'No wonder I couldn't get hold of you!'

Cristo appraised with appreciation her slim, pale, delicately curved body in the brief red bikini she wore. 'If it's any consolation, Appollonia is the party most punished by the fallout from all this.'

Turning pink at the intensity of the gaze resting on her heaving breasts, Erin crossed her arms to interrupt his view. She hated the way he could just look at her and her body would have an involuntary reaction while her brain fogged over. 'And how do you make that out?'

'You're the one in possession of grandchildren she has never seen. Had she known you were carrying my

child she would never have targeted you and she would
have supported you in every way possible. I told her
how alone you had been and she felt guiltier than ever,'
he completed wryly.

'So, what happens now?'

'We go down to the village and see the priest and fill
out the forms for our wedding.'

'You want to get married here on the island?' Erin
was taken aback by the idea.

'I'll fly out your mother along with any friends you
want to attend.' Seeing that that assurance had no visible effect, Cristo unfolded to his full impressive height,
adding, 'We've been apart a long time—I don't want to
wait long for the wedding.'

'I didn't realise it would be happening so soon,' Erin
responded tentatively. 'When I agreed to come here it
was only for a week to escape the press because you got
so hot and bothered about them.'

A faint smile softened the harsh curve of his shapely
mouth. 'Everything has changed between us since then,
koukla mou.'

It had changed in the bedroom, Erin reflected guilt-
ily, recalling how easily she had succumbed to his hot-
blooded hunger for her. She had said yes where she
should have said no and that was the only green light
that a male with Cristo's high voltage libido required.

'I barely remember my birth parents. They're just a
stylish photo on the wall,' Cristo remarked tautly. 'The
first five years of my life I was raised by nannies. I was
always being told not to *bother* my parents because they
were such *busy* people. They had no time for me and
little interest.'

Erin was frowning. 'Go on…'

'I didn't know what a normal home and parents were like until Vasos and Appollonia took charge of me. They spent time with me, talked to me, took an interest in my small achievements and gave me love. I owe everything I am today to them. I want to do the same thing for Lorcan and Nuala.'

She had not realised that his early years had been so bleak and she understood his attitude, for her own childhood had been almost as troubled and insecure. Marrying Cristo made sense, she reasoned ruefully. She wanted her children to have a full-time father and the chance of a happy family life. Cristo was offering her that option and she put as high a value on that lifestyle as he apparently did. But he would not have wanted to marry her had she not had the twins and that hurt. It hurt that he didn't love and want her with the same intensity that he wanted their children.

That evening Sam Morton phoned her. 'Your mother told me you were in Greece. I was shocked.'

'We're getting married, Sam.'

'Yes, she told me that as well. Of course that's the safest choice for Donakis if he wants access to his children. I understand that he consulted an expert in family law in London to find out exactly where he stood. Watch your step, Erin. In a Greek court, he could gain custody of the kids.'

Erin's blood ran cold at that forecast. 'Are you trying to scare me? We're getting married, not divorced.'

'I think it's very convenient for Donakis to marry you now but he wasn't interested in marrying you three years ago. Don't forget that.'

Sadly that was a fact that Erin never forgot and she

could have done without the second opinion. Had Cristo consulted a legal expert? How had Sam found that out? No doubt someone knew someone in the legal field who also knew Sam and word had got back to him in that way. Ought she to be worried? She supposed it was understandable that Cristo should have sought advice when he first found out that he was a father. That was not in itself wrong. Even so, the knowledge sent a little buzz of insecurity through her that she could not shake.

'Cristo,' she said towards the end of the evening while she worried about whether it was foolish of her to trust Cristo to such an extent. 'Would you mind very much if I slept on my own until the wedding?'

Cristo frowned. 'Not if it's important to you.'

'With Mum arriving a few days before the wedding, it would really be more comfortable for me,' she told him stiffly.

One week later, Cristo and Erin were married in the little church overlooking the town harbour. She wore a white lace dress, tight on the arms and fitted to make the most of her slender figure, obtained from a designer in Athens. Her mother had thought her daughter was being controversial buying into the whole white wedding fantasy when she already had two young children but Erin had seen no reason why her special day should not live up to her girlhood dreams. After all, she loved Cristo Donakis and preferred to be optimistic about their future.

The Greek Orthodox service presided over by the bearded priest in his long dark robe was traditional and meaningful. The church was crammed with well-wishers and filled with flowers. The scent of incense and the fresh-orange-blossom circlet placed on her head mingled headily and, strange as it all was to her, she loved it, loved Cristo's hand in hers, the steadiness of his lion-gold gaze and utter lack of nerves. For the first time she felt that they were meant to be together and she fought off downbeat thoughts about what his wedding to Lisandra might have been like as it was clearly not on his mind.

The days running up to their wedding had been exceptionally busy. She had had to take Nuala to an Athens hospital to have her cast checked. Mercifully everything had been in order and the little girl had not required a replacement. That appointment had been followed by a shopping trip to buy Erin's wedding gown. The next day she had first made the acquaintance of Cristo's father, Vasos Denes, when he came over to meet the twins. Initially appearing stern and quiet, Vasos had slowly shaken off his discomfiture over his wife's interference in Cristo's private life and its disastrous side effects to relax in his son's home and Erin had decided that he was a lovely man. She had been surprised when Cristo explained that his father's company was on the edge of bankruptcy but that the older man refused to accept his financial help. She had soon grasped from whom Cristo had learned his principles and even if his volatile nature warred against them and occasionally won—as in when he had blackmailed her into going to Italy with him—she knew Cristo did try to respect scruples and operate accordingly.

In a gesture made purely for Cristo and his foster father's sake, Erin had volunteered to take the children to visit Appollonia Denes at their villa on the outskirts of the town. Even on the medication her doctor had advised to help her with her low mood, the older woman had been stunned to see the twins and tears had trailed slowly down her cheeks while she attempted awkwardly to express her regret for the actions she had taken almost three years earlier. That she absolutely adored Cristo had shone out of her and her wondering delight in Lorcan and Nuala had inspired pity in Erin. She knew it would take time before she could forgive Appollonia for what she had done but she was willing to make the effort.

Cristo had thrown himself into spending every afternoon with the twins. Watching her children respond to his interest, noting the shocking similarity in their lively demanding personalities, Erin had known that marrying Cristo was the right step to take. Lorcan was already learning that when his father said no he meant it and Nuala's tantrums had become less frequent. The first time she condescended to call Cristo, 'Daddy', he admitted to Erin that he felt as if he had won the lottery.

Her mother had travelled to Thesos in the company of Tom and Melissa. Sam had turned down his invitation but had sent a lavish present. The day before the wedding, Cristo had taken them all out sailing. He was a wonderful host and had been in the very best of moods. Erin had taken that as a compliment: Cristo was happy that they were getting married. And she had during the week that had passed learned to regret her request that they sleep apart until the ceremony. Intimacy brought a special closeness to their relationship and she missed it, disliking the new distance that her demand had wrought in Cristo. He was too careful to give her space. A couple of times she had lain awake into the early hours, her body taut with frustration and longing, trying to summon up the courage to go and join Cristo in the opulent master suite at the top of the stairs. Why was she still punishing herself for wanting him? Why had she let Sam's sour suspicious comments make her doubt Cristo's sincerity?

Cristo lifted her hand in the car on the way back to the house from the church and touched the shiny new platinum ring on her finger with approval. 'Now you're mine.'

'That sounds exceedingly caveman-type basic,' Erin remarked.

'I suppose carrying you upstairs *before* we entertain our guests would be even more basic?' Cristo rested scorching golden eyes on her face as she turned fire-engine red with sexual awareness and embarrassment.

'You're scaring me because I know you're capable of behaving like that,' she admitted ruefully.

'I was pure caveman when I blackmailed you into meeting me in Italy,' Cristo conceded with a sardonic laugh. 'I do crazy things with you that I've never done with any other woman. Italy was supposed to be an exorcism—'

Erin gave him a blank look while trying not to picture how wickedly exciting it would be if Cristo was were to trail her straight off to his bedroom. That was the real problem. He might be pure caveman but on some level she liked that side of him and responded to it. There was something uniquely satisfying about knowing she was such an object of desire to him.

'An exorcism?' she repeated.

'I couldn't stop thinking about you and how incredible we were in bed. It infuriated me. I thought that if I saw you again, slept with you again I'd be disappointed and I could get you out of my system. My, didn't that work well?' he said with rich self-mockery. 'Here we are just three weeks later and we're married!'

'Did you and Lisandra get married in the same church?' Erin asked, no longer able to stifle her curiosity.

'Of course not. We had a massive society wedding staged in Athens. Lisandra likes to make a big splash in public.'

'But the church here and the simple service were lovely,' Erin commented softly.

His handsome mouth twisted. 'You and Lisandra are very different.'

Did he have regrets? A little ache set in somewhere in the region of Erin's heart. Erin had seen photos of his ex-wife in glossy magazines and Lisandra was much more sophisticated than she was. Most people would reckon that Cristo had married 'down' in choosing Erin and when they realised that the twins were his they would put another construction altogether on their marriage. Did that matter to her? Was she too sensitive? Expediency, rather than love, made the world go round. She didn't *need* him to love her. Evidently she didn't have that essential spark that would inspire such feelings in him or he would have fallen in love with her when they were first together and everything was all shiny and new.

'Visiting my mother in spite of what she did, allowing her to be present today and treating her like one of the family,' Cristo specified wryly. 'Lisandra would never have forgiven her.'

'I haven't forgiven Appollonia either.'

'But you're willing to *try*. I'm very grateful for that,'

Cristo told her quietly. 'You had the opportunity to get your own back by excluding her from our lives but you didn't take it. That was generous of you.'

'She truly regrets what she did. We all make mistakes.'

Cristo grasped her hand, curved lean fingers to the side of her face and brought his mouth down on hers with a hungry urgency that sent pure energy winging through her trembling body. 'I'm wrecking your make-up,' he groaned against her sultry mouth.

'Doesn't matter,' Erin proclaimed breathlessly, looking up at him with starry eyes and a thundering heartbeat.

Cristo handed her a tissue for the lipstick he had smeared. 'Our guests await us but first…I have a gift for you.'

He handed her a tiny jewellery box, which she flipped open. It contained a band of diamonds, an eternity ring. 'Cristo, it's beautiful but I haven't got you anything.'

'My gift is having you back in my bed again,' he murmured lazily.

The burning intensity of the look that accompanied that statement was like a blowtorch. She tottered out of the car on wobbling knees, struggling to pin a social smile to her lips. He really *really* wanted her and that was good, a healthy sign for a very practical marriage, she told herself earnestly, striving hard to be sensible while she admired the new rings sparkling on her finger. Cristo for eternity would be paradise, she thought dizzily, barely able to credit that he was finally hers. She watched as the twins ran to him and he scooped them up in both arms in a movement that made Lorcan and Nuala break into fits of laughter.

'He's so good with them,' her mother remarked approvingly from the front door that stood open. 'I expect you're planning on more children.'

'Not at the minute,' Erin told her mother frankly. 'I think we'll be getting used to being married for quite a while.'

'Cristo looks happier and more relaxed than I've seen him in years,' Vasos commented approvingly at her elbow. 'You're good for each other. I only wish that my wife's interference hadn't parted you when you should have stayed together.'

'It's water under the bridge now,' Erin said lightly as she looked up at the older man.

'I had an argument with my son when he said he couldn't possibly take a honeymoon while my company was failing. Don't worry,' Vasos urged comfortably. 'I soon talked sense into him. Of course you're having a honeymoon.'

Erin swallowed uncomfortably. She knew how hard Cristo had worked in his efforts to support his father's business, which had suffered badly in the difficult economic climate in Greece, but she also knew that Vasos' stubborn independent streak had made it an almost impossible challenge. 'He worries a lot about you.'

'He'll get over it,' Vasos replied staunchly.

'No, he won't actually,' she told him in a low voice. 'He'll feel like the worst failure if your business goes down. Why won't you let Cristo help you?'

'I could never accept money from Cristo.'

'But you're his family.'

'When he came to us as a child he was a fantastically rich little boy and I swore never to take advantage of that.'

'Times change. For a start, he's an adult, not a child any more. He loves you very much. Isn't it selfish to force him to stand by and do nothing while you go bankrupt? He'll be devastated.'

Vasos frowned.

'Please don't be offended with me,' Erin begged. 'I just wanted you to know what it's like for him not to be allowed to help when you're in trouble. In the same situation wouldn't you want to help him no matter what?'

'I will consider that angle,' Vasos replied after a long minute of silence, his stern face troubled. 'You can be very blunt, Erin...but you do understand Cristo.'

'Hopefully.' With a warm smile, Erin moved away to greet other guests, praying she hadn't said too much to Cristo's foster father. Cristo would probably be furious if he knew she had said anything, but negotiations between him and the older man were currently at a standstill and she had decided that she might as well speak up on Cristo's behalf.

Late afternoon, Cristo informed her that they were leaving. 'To go where?' she pressed.

'It's a surprise.'

'I haven't even packed—'

'There's no need. A new wardrobe awaits you at our destination. You don't need to worry about the twins either because your mother has agreed to stay on here until we return. Let's go—'

'Like...*right now*?' Erin exclaimed. 'I need to get changed—'

'No. I want to be the one to take off that dress,' Cristo confessed, gazing down into her eyes with a sensual look of anticipation that sparked fire in her bloodstream.

They flew to the airport in the helicopter and, having

presented their passports, boarded the jet straight away. By then, having been up at the crack of dawn, Erin was smothering yawns and the drone of the engines sent her into a sound sleep. When she wakened, she was embarrassed by the poor showing she was making as a bride and barely had time to tidy her mussed hair and repair her make-up before they landed.

'You've brought me back to Italy,' she registered in surprise, recognising the airport. 'Why Italy?'

'It's where we began again even if we didn't appreciate it that weekend.'

And alighting from the limo that brought them to the villa and struggling to walk in the high-heeled sandals that were now pinching horribly, she decided that he had made a good point. Her emotions had rekindled along with her desire for him. It had been time out of time and wonderful in the strangest way of happiness coming when you least expected it to do so.

'I gave the housekeeper the weekend off.'

Cristo swept her up in his arms to carry her through the door he had unlocked.

It was a romantic gesture she hadn't expected from him and, eyes widening, she smiled up at him, colliding with dark golden eyes that made her heart race. They walked up the stairs, though, hand in hand and she almost giggled, unfamiliar as she was with such signs from Cristo, who was usually cooler than cool in that department. In the bedroom doorway she stilled, scanning the room, which had been transformed with lush arrangements of white flowers and dozens of candles with little flames that leapt and glowed in the darkness: she was transfixed.

'Good heavens,' she murmured, totally stunned by the display. 'You organised this?'

'I wanted it to be perfect for you.'

Hugely impressed, Erin smiled again and walked on in, kicking off her tight shoes with a sigh of relief.

'Now you've shrunk,' Cristo teased, uncorking the bottle of champagne awaiting them and handing her an elegant flute bubbling with the pale golden liquid.

Erin sipped. 'Did you do something like this for Lisandra?'

He frowned. 'Why do you keep on asking about her?'

'Well, *did* you?' Erin persisted.

'No, I didn't. It wasn't that kind of marriage. I thought you would have worked out by now that I married Lisandra on the rebound,' Cristo imparted with a rueful twist of his mouth. 'I reeled away from the wreckage of our relationship and made the biggest mistake of all.'

On the rebound? She liked that news. She liked it even better that he was willing to admit that his first marriage had been a mistake. It soothed the hurt place inside her that had formed when she had realised he had taken a wife within months of their split. An extraordinary urge to move closer and hug him also assailed Erin. She might want to wrap that confession in fairy lights and laugh and smile over it but an aching sadness afflicted her at the same time. Three years back, he must have cared about her more than she had realised but she had still lost him through no fault of her own.

'You weren't in love with your wife?' she prompted stiffly.

'I thought I'd made that clear.'

'Why did you marry her, then?'

'After losing faith in you I had no heart for dating.

My marriage pleased my family, gave me something to focus on other than you, but it was a catastrophe.' Cristo shifted a broad shoulder in a fatalistic shrug and gave her a wry look. 'This is our wedding night. I don't want to talk about this now.'

Something to focus on other than you. And suddenly Erin understood something that she had never quite believed in before. When they broke up, he had been badly hurt too, he had suffered as well. He had rushed into a marriage that he had hoped would cure him of his unhappiness. But now she was suddenly reflecting on the eternity ring and the beautiful bower of flowers and candles he had had prepared for their arrival and her heart swelled with warmth and forgiveness. He was doing things he had never done before. He was trying to show her that he had feelings for her and naturally he didn't want her rabbiting on about Lisandra in the middle of it.

'I love you,' he told her in a roughened undertone, detaching the champagne glass from her nerveless fingers and setting it aside so that he could pull her close. His eyes were bright with emotion in the flickering candlelight. 'I was in love with you when we broke up but I didn't know it. You've haunted me ever since. When I saw you in that photo with Sam and his staff, all I could think about was seeing you again. I lied to myself. I told myself that it was only sex and that I wanted to get over the memory of you, but I was still in love with you when I brought you here that weekend. When I woke up beside you the next morning I knew I didn't ever want to let you go again.'

Tears welled up in Erin's amethyst eyes and any strand of lingering resentment over that weekend vanished, for they had found each other again in this peaceful house, re-establishing the connection they had forged years earlier. That he loved her meant so much that she could barely contain the huge surge of happiness spreading inside her. 'We've lost so much time when we could have been together,' she sighed.

'But we're still young enough to make up for that and maybe while we were apart we both learned stuff we needed to know,' Cristo countered more thoughtfully. 'But if we had stayed together I would have eventually married you. I just wasn't in a hurry.'

'And this time around you probably felt like you didn't have a choice,' Erin completed.

Cristo spun her round to run down the zip on her gown. 'No, I thought very carefully about that decision. I didn't have to live with you to play a part in the twins' lives and my financial support would have taken care of any problems you had. No, I asked you to marry me because I wanted *you* in my life every day.'

Smiling widely at that assurance, a glow of pleasure lighting up her eyes, Erin turned back to help him out of his jacket. 'And there I was thinking that you had only married me because you thought it was the *practical* thing to do!'

Cristo curved long fingers to her cheekbones and groaned. 'I know it was a useless proposal. I should never have asked you when we were in bed but I couldn't hold back any longer. Wives are a lot harder to lose than girlfriends and I needed to know that you were mine again for ever, *pethi mou.*'

'I like the sound of for ever,' Erin savoured, shimmying out of her lace gown and standing in her frivolous silk and lace bra and panties, a blue garter adorning one slim stocking-clad thigh.

'I like the underpinnings,' Cristo teased, fiery dark eyes welded to her scantily clad figure as he appraised her with lingering intensity. 'But I'll like you out of them even better and after a week of celibacy it's over-kill.'

'Is it?' Her brows lifted, her uncertainty visible.

Laughing, Cristo picked her up and dropped her down on the gloriously comfortable bed. 'You look gorgeous but I did notice that the separate bedrooms made your mother more comfortable in our home, *latria mou.*'

'I wanted tonight to be special,' Erin whispered, running a possessive hand up a shirt-clad arm.

He sat up and discarded his shirt with alacrity, revealing a hard brown torso taut and roped with muscle. She spread her fingers there instead, revelling in the solid reassuring beat of his heart. 'I forgot to tell you that I loved you.'

'And as punishment you have to tell me at least ten times every day,' Cristo delivered, lowering his head to claim a long passionate kiss that sent her hands up to clasp his head. 'You know, I thought it might take you much longer to forgive me for not being there when you needed me…and even worse marrying another woman.'

Erin smiled. 'No, I know you've been through tough times too. What I didn't understand is why you were suddenly doing all the romantic stuff you never did before. Do you remember what our first ever row was about?'

'I forgot Valentine's Day once we were dating. Well, actually I didn't. I'd always avoided the mushy stuff as it raises unfair expectations and I was embarrassed about the one I sent you before you agreed to go out with me.'

'A card?' Erin scorned. 'A *card* would rouse expectations?'

Cristo winced. 'I thought that sort of thing, like meeting each other's families, should be kept for someone you're serious about. We had only been together eleven months and twenty three days…'

Her eyes widened. 'You counted how long we were together?'

'I was always a maths whizz,' Cristo fielded deadpan.

Erin was impressed. She glanced around her candlelit flower-bedecked bower and smiled happily at what that display said: she had finally made the grade for the mushy stuff! He would never ignore Valentine's Day again. She gazed up at him, enthralled by his lean, darkly handsome features and the tender look in his beautiful dark eyes.

'I missed you *so* much!' he breathed suddenly. 'Something would remind me and then, boom, all these images would flood my head. And then I would remember what I thought you had done and get really angry that I was thinking about you again.'

Erin reached up and kissed him. 'That time is gone. Now we've got something better and stronger, something that will last—'

'For ever,' he slotted in with determination.

Her eyes slid shut as he claimed her parted lips in another hungry, demanding kiss. Heat spread inside her with tingling, burning energy and she gave herself up to desire and happiness without any sense of fear at all.

* * *

Two years later, Erin hosted the grand opening of Cristo's first spa hotel on Thesos. Built beside a secluded beach and surrounded by lush pine forest, it provided a back-to-nature retreat with luxury on tap for the discerning traveller, and as the latest must-have place to go it was already fully booked six months in advance. As Cristo had been held up, Vasos and Appollonia Denes were by her side.

A sea change had taken place in her relationship with the older couple. The passage of time had soothed the bad memories of the past and Erin's natural resentment. Appollonia had grown stronger and calmer and as she recovered from her excessive nervousness and fatal tendency to apologise for everything had confided that her greatest fear had always been that Cristo would discover what she had done and refuse to forgive her. Once the secret was out, Appollonia had had to deal with her guilt, and forging a healthy, normal relationship with Erin and the twins had gone a long way to achieving that.

Vasos had ultimately accepted a loan from Cristo to save his business but had insisted that Cristo accept a partnership in the firm, an arrangement that had left both men with their pride and principles intact. Cristo had been overjoyed that Erin's intervention had wrought a change in his foster father's stubborn outlook.

For the first year of her marriage Erin had spent a great deal of time checking out the spa facilities in her husband's hotel empire and travelling a great deal. Jenny and the twins had often accompanied her while her mother was a frequent visitor to Thesos. During the second year Erin had begun supervising the final touches to the new island spa, which was providing much needed

work for the locals and had already prompted the opening of several tourist-type businesses in the village.

Sheathed in a shimmering silver evening gown, she
posed for photographers and waved back as Sam and
his former secretary, Janice, raised their glasses to sa-
lute her from across the room. Sam Morton was about
to embark on a worldwide cruise with his recently acquired bride. Erin smiled warmly at the other couple,
currently engaged in chatting to her mother, Deidre,
thinking that she had been blind not to appreciate that
Janice cared about Sam and that her removal from the
scene would make it easier for Sam to see Janice in a
different light. Sam had had to retire before he could
appreciate how much he missed Janice's company and
a friendly dinner date to catch up on news had eventually resulted in his second marriage.

'You look amazing, Mrs Donakis,' a rich dark drawl
purred above her head as a possessive hand curved to
her hip.

Erin whirled round. 'Cristo, when did you get back?'

'Half an hour ago. I had the quickest shower and
change on record,' he confided. 'That's it, though. I
won't be off on another trip for at least six weeks.'

Erin feasted her eyes on her handsome husband. He
looked spectacular in his dark designer suit. The female photographer was watching him as though dinner
had just walked through the door, but Erin was accustomed to the buzz that Cristo brought to the women in
a room and it didn't bother her. Jenny came through the
door with Lorcan and Nuala. Nuala, adorable in a fancy
party dress, skipped over to show it off to her father,
little hands holding out the skirt as if she were about to
perform a curtsy.

Lorcan took his hands out of his pockets at his father's request and then ran off to try and climb the huge palm tree in the centre of the foyer.

'Lorcan!' Cristo yelled, and he strode over to lift his squirming son off the trunk and imprisoned him under one arm, talking to the little boy before setting him down again.

'Lorcan's such a boy,' Nuala pronounced, rolling her eyes with pained superiority.

Erin's mother held out her hands to the children and they latched onto her immediately, begging her to take them down to the beach.

'I wonder what the third one will be like,' Cristo commented, his dark golden gaze dipping briefly to the barely perceptible bump visible below Erin's dress.

'A mix of our genes, some good, some bad.'

'I can't wait to see our baby,' Cristo confessed.

A warm sense of tenderness filled Erin, and only their public location stopped her leaning in to hug him. She hadn't initially been sure about how another child would fit into their busy lives, but one of the main reasons she'd come round to the idea had been the awareness that Cristo had missed out on the experience of the twins as babies. While she had conceived faster than she had expected, she had thoroughly enjoyed having a supportive, interested male by her side to share every development in her pregnancy and the sight of Cristo with tears in his eyes when he saw the first scan of their child was one she would never forget.

The evening wore on in chats with influential people and business associates. The twins were whisked home to bed and Cristo, his attention consistently returning to his wife's lovely face and smile, was unashamedly relieved when they could finally take their leave of their guests.

'I hate being away from you now,' he confided, lifting her out of the four-wheel drive he had taken her home in.

'You're not away half as much as you used to be.'

'I can do a lot of my work at home.' At the foot of the stairs he swung her up in his arms and insisted on carrying her the rest of the way in spite of her protests. 'I know your feet are killing you, *latria mou*.'

She kicked her shoes off when he put her down, holding up the skirt of her gown so that she didn't trip on the trailing hem. 'But the shoes did look gorgeous,' she pointed out.

Cristo framed her laughing face with tender hands. 'You don't need to suffer to look beautiful.'

'Only a man could say that. I still can't believe that you were *born* with eyebrows that stay in shape,' Erin lamented. 'It's so unfair.'

'I would love you even without all the waxing,' Cristo intoned huskily.

Erin tried to imagine getting into bed with a pair of hairy legs and barely repressed a shudder. 'The things you say.'

'I'm trying to impress you with how crazy I am about you.' Cristo sighed with a long-suffering look belied by the amusement dancing in his dark golden eyes. 'It's an uphill challenge.'

'No, it's not. I love you too, naturally perfect brows included,' his wife informed him, gazing up at him with an appreciation she couldn't hide. *Mine*, every natural instinct said and she adored the fact.

He bent his handsome dark head and kissed her softly

with all the skill at his disposal, and her head swam and her knees wobbled and the glory of loving Cristo swept over her like a consuming tide, filled with happiness and acceptance and pure joy.

* * * * *

PAINTED THE OTHER WOMAN
JULIA JAMES

Julia James lives in England, and adores the peaceful verdant countryside and the wild shores of Cornwall. She also loves the Mediterranean—so rich in myth and history, with its sunbaked landscapes and olive groves, ancient ruins and azure seas. 'The perfect setting for romance!' she says. 'Rivalled only by the lush tropical heat of the Caribbean—palms swaying by a silver sand beach lapped by turquoise waters... What more could lovers want?'

PROLOGUE

MARISA gave a soft gasp as the man opposite her opened the slim case he'd just taken out of his jacket pocket.

'For you,' the man said. There was a fond look in his eyes as he slid the case towards her. 'I want you to have it.'·

Marisa gazed at him, open pleasure in her expression.

She ran a finger lightly over the stones, which sparkled in the light from the candle on the table. 'It's beautiful!' she breathed. Then a more troubled expression showed in her eyes. 'But are you sure…?'

The man gave a decisive nod of his head. 'Yes, quite sure.'

Marisa picked up the case, reluctantly shutting the lid, gazing across at the man who had given her such a wonderful token of what she meant to him. She dropped the jewellery case into her handbag—the beautiful, soft leather handbag with a designer logo that was yet another such token. Then she lifted her eyes to the man again. She had eyes only for him! Certainly not for the middle-aged man dining alone, a few tables away, engrossed in texting on his mobile phone, his face in shadow.

Now Ian was in her life Marisa had neither eyes nor thoughts for anyone else. From their first meeting to this precious moment he had transformed her life beyond all recognition, and the wonder of it still amazed her. She had had no idea—none at all—when she'd come to London those short months ago how totally her life would change. Oh, she'd had hopes, it was true, and ambitions and purpose—but that they had actually come about was still wonderful to her. And it was all embodied in the startlingly handsome man sitting opposite her, gazing at her with such devotion.

She bit her lip slightly. If only she didn't have to hide in the corners of Ian's life, be hidden away from a censorious world like a shameful secret. Yet that, she knew, was what she would be seen as. Someone who had to be hidden away, never acknowledged in public, to the world. That was why they could only meet like this, in places Ian did not usually frequent, where he was not known or recognised,where he could be sure he would not bump into someone who would question her dining with him—someone who knew both him and Eva.

Eva...

The name echoed in Marisa's head, haunting her like a ghost that could not be exorcised. Emotion darted in her eyes. Oh, she thought in anguish, if only Eva were not who she was. The emotion deepened, and she gazed helplessly across the table at the handsome, smiling face opposite. If only Eva were not the woman who was Ian's wife...

CHAPTER ONE

ATHAN Teodarkis's eyes moved over the photographs spread out on his desk. His sculpted mouth tightened to a tight line like a whip, and anger speared him.

So it had started! Just what he'd feared right from the beginning. From the moment his sister Eva had told him who she was in love with...

He felt the anger stab at him again, and with deliberate control made himself release the tension steeling his shoulders, his spine. He contoured his back against the leather moulding of the executive chair he was sitting in behind the mahogany desk in his office. Across the wide expanse of expensive carpet the vista of the City, over which the lavish London HQ of Teodarkis International had a panoramic view, went unattended.

His hard gaze went on studying the photos. Though taken by a camera phone, and from half a dozen metres' distance, their evidence was indisputable. They showed Ian Randall, his boyishly handsome face gazing devotedly, eagerly, at the woman opposite him.

With part of his mind Athan could see why.

She was blonde, like Ian, fair-skinned and heart-stoppingly lovely. Her pale hair fell like a waterfall either side of her face. Perfect features—full parted lips, delicate nose and luminous blue eyes—all made her a total peach of a female. No wonder she'd captivated the fool sitting opposite her.

It had been entirely predictable. Right from the start Athan had feared that Ian Randall was weak, self-indulgent, and born to be a philanderer.

Just like his father.

Martin Randall had been notorious—notorious for womanising, notorious for succumbing to every tempting female who passed in front of him. He had indulged his incontinent desire for her until the next one floated by. Then he'd dropped the present incumbent and gone after a new one.

Time and time again.

Disgust and contempt twisted Athan's mouth. If that was what Martin's son was going to be like, then—

Then I damn well should have stopped Eva marrying him! Whatever it took, I should have stopped it!

But he hadn't—he had given the son the benefit of the doubt, even though it had gone against all his instincts to do so. His mouth set. And now he'd been proved right all along. Ian was no better than his father.

Philanderer. Womaniser. Libertine.

Adulterer.

With an angry impulse Athan got to his feet, picking up the innocuous-looking buff folder that contained enough dynamite to blow apart Ian's marriage. Could it yet be saved?

Athan speculated. How far had his adultery progressed? Certainly his *inamorata* had been installed in a fancy apartment by Ian, and judging by her designer outfit and freshly styled hair—not to mention the diamond necklace she'd been presented with—she was clearly benefiting from his largesse already. His mouth thinned. But had she paid the bill for that largesse yet?

The expression on Ian's face caught by the camera phone was—no other word for it—besotted. It wasn't the expression of a lascivious lecher—it was the expression of a man caught in the toils of a woman he could not bring himself to resist. A woman he was showering his wealth upon. But not, as yet, very much of his time. That was the one cause for optimism Athan could see in this whole sordid business.

The surveillance reports had found no evidence that Ian Randall visited the girl in her fancy apartment—not yet, at any rate—and nor did he take her to hotels. So far the only time he spent with her was in restaurants, clearly chosen for their out-of-the-way locations, and his only visible adultery was his besotted expression.

Can I stop this in its tracks? Can I stop it in time?

That was the question in the forefront of Athan's brain. Ian Randall was, it seemed, playing it pretty cautiously—in that, at least, he was unlike his father, who had been totally blatant about *his* affairs. But if that look of slavish devotion on his face was anything to go by he would soon throw caution to the winds and make the girl his mistress in fact as well as intention.

It was inevitable.

He set the folder back on the desk with a sense of angry frustration.

What the hell am I going to do about this?

The question hung in his head like a dead weight. He had to do something—that was inescapable. He had a responsibility to do so. If he had done from the outset what he'd wanted to do—put his foot down and objected to Eva's marriage to Ian Randall—then he wouldn't be facing this infernal situation now. He should have gone with his instincts, stopped the marriage. Whatever it had taken to do so. Oh, Eva would have been heartbroken, he knew, but what was she going to be once she found out what Ian had done?

Athan's expression shadowed. He knew exactly what she was going to be—going to become—if her husband followed the same damnable path his father had so heedlessly and selfishly taken. She would end up just like Ian's unhappy, tormented mother.

Athan had grown up knowing all about just how unhappy Sheila Randall was in her marriage to Martin Randall, Ian's father. Sheila had been his mother's best friend since finishing school in Switzerland, and once Sheila's eyes had been painfully opened to her husband's ways she had poured out her unhappiness into his mother's ears.

'Poor Sheila' had become a permanent fixture in their lives during his youth, as his mother did her best to comfort and console her friend—whether by phone or on mutually exchanged visits between London and Athens. Athan's mother had spent, so it seemed to him, an interminable amount of time trying to mop up Sheila Randall's tears, but despite his own sense that the best course of action would have been to divorce Martin Randall and be done with him, Sheila, it seemed, was of a romantic disposition.

Despite all the evidence she'd gone on hoping that her husband would one day realise that his wife was the only woman who truly loved him and his adulterous lifestyle would be finally abandoned. In this unlikely hope she had been supported by Athan's mother, who had been equally romantically disposed—a disposition also shared by her daughter, Eva.

This was the crux of his concern for his sister. His expression darkened. His mother had discovered the full depths of Martin Randall's irredeemability in a manner that had very nearly proved disastrous to her own marriage—and to her friendship with Sheila. For Martin Randall had been unable to resist the temptation of stooping so low as to target the best friend of his wife with his pernicious attentions. His attempt at seduction during one of her visits to his wife had, Athan remembered, caused an unholy row in both families. His mother had had to do everything in her power to convince her husband that Martin Randall's assiduously insistent advances were neither invited nor welcome, and it had taken almost as much persuasion to convince Sheila Randall as well.

A hard, brooding emotion filled him. Men like Martin Randall caused misery and torment and trouble all round. He had very nearly succeeded in breaking up his parents' marriage. If his son were *anything* like him he would wreak the same kind of devastation all around him.

But there was no way—*no way*—he was going to let Ian do that kind of damage. No way Ian was going to repeat his father's misdeeds. Athan would stop him in his tracks.

Whatever it took.

An angry rasp escaped him. If only Eva weren't married to Martin Randall's son! If only she could see through him the way he could himself. But Ian Randall's dangerously easy charm had fooled Eva just as it had fooled his own mother—Sheila.

Ian Randall had grown up the apple of his mother's eye, indulged and petted—especially after his father's early death. And with his good looks and his supreme confidence in his own ability to attract females he'd cut a swathe through the population as a teenager and a young man.

Yet again Athan's expression darkened. Had he had the slightest idea of just how dangerously indulged and doted upon Ian Randall was by his mother, he would never have let Eva get anywhere near him. But when *his* mother had so tragically died, when his sister was only just eighteen, Sheila Randall's heartfelt invitation for Eva to go and live with her in London had seemed a godsend.

Having already lost her father to a heart attack only two years earlier, this second blow had been grievous indeed to Eva. Athan, who had had to take up the full running of his late father's business enterprise, had been worked off his feet, and his bachelor apartment in Athens was scarcely suitable for a teenage girl to make a home in. Nor could Eva be left alone in the family mansion, with none but the household staff to live with.

Moving to London, living with her beloved mother's best friend and changing her college to one of the London universities instead, had been a far, far better choice for Eva. In Sheila Eva had gained a surrogate mother who'd taken her under her wing, and in Eva, the now-widowed Sheila had gained a surrogate daughter to lavish her attention upon.

She had also, so it had proved, gained a daughter-in-law.

Eva had fallen head over heels in love with Sheila Randall's handsome, indulged son, and had set her sights on him.

Just why Ian Randall, with his predilection for playing the field, had responded to Eva's open ardour with a proposal of marriage Athan didn't know—but his suspicions were dark: Had Ian not been able to bed Eva without a marriage proposal? Had the prospect of marrying into the fabulously wealthy Teodarkis family been too overwhelming a lure for him?

Athan, however, was the only one to have such suspicions, he knew. Neither Eva, with romantic stars in her eyes, nor Sheila Randall, with her doting maternal devotion to her son, shared them. So in the face of his sister's ecstatic happiness Athan had, with deep reluctance, given the marriage his sanction, if not his blessing. He'd also provided Ian Randall with a plum post in the Teodarkis organisation. Partly to satisfy Eva, but mostly to ensure that whatever frailties lurked in Ian's make-up he, Athan, could keep a very, very close eye on his brother-in-law.

For two years, however, Ian seemed to have toed the line, giving every appearance of being a devoted husband. Now, it seemed, his true nature was coming to the fore. The evidence against his brother-in-law was damming. Ian was consorting, in secret, with a beautiful blonde whom he'd set up in a lavish luxury pad and upon whom he was bestowing diamonds.

His next move would inevitably be starting to visit her in her love-nest….the long-feared adultery would begin in earnest.

Restlessly, Athan twisted in his leather chair. He would not—*would not*—see his beloved sister reduced to the sobbing wreck that his mother's best friend had become during her marriage, hoping and hoping that the man she so unwisely loved would mend his ways. He would *not* see that happen! Somehow he had to stop Ian in his tracks. But how? That was the devil of it!

Oh, he could confront the wretched man with the evidence against him, but Ian would probably try and wriggle out of it—after all, no adultery had been committed as yet, and he would probably find some weasel way of explaining away the blonde's existence. And if Athan took the photos to Eva that would achieve the very thing he dreaded most—breaking her heart with proof of her husband's betrayal. He couldn't do that to her—not if he could help it.

That might have to happen—but not yet. Surely not yet?

Besides, shouldn't he at least give Ian a chance—*one* chance!—not to go the way of his father? If he could manage to nip this incipient affair in the bud, find a way of deflecting Ian from it, maybe—just maybe—Ian Randall would prove himself a worthy husband for Eva.

I can give him a chance—and if he falls a second time then I shall be merciless.

The question was how to give him that chance and prevent him succumbing to what had every indication of turning into a full-blown adulterous affair with the delectable blonde he was lining up for himself?

The brooding look returned to Athan's stormy expression. This required strategy—cold, logical strategy.

A hard light darkened in his eyes. Icy logic sliced down through his synapses. OK, so Ian wanted to start an affair with this blonde—and the blonde, from the photographic evidence, looked every bit as keen as he did. Whatever was motivating her—Ian's obvious wealth and generosity, or his golden-boy looks and seductive charm—she was clearly very, very responsive to him. It would surely take little more effort on Ian's part to get her into bed.

Unless…

Thoughts moved across Athan's mind. Dark, ruthless thoughts.

When it came to adultery it took two to tango. The adulterer and a willing mistress.

His thoughts coiled and uncoiled like a serpent in his mind. But what if the willing mistress were no longer so willing? What if Ian Randall were not the only good-looking, wealthy admirer in her orbit? What if a rival arrived on the scene?

Cut Ian out…?

Slowly Athan felt his taut muscles finally relax, for the first time since he'd ripped open the envelope and the damning photos had spilt out in front of him.

His mind raced ahead, trying to assess whether what had crossed his mind could work. The answer came through loud and clear.

Yes! Because it simply replaces Ian with someone else. Someone else who can take his place. Someone else who is rich and has a track record of successfully wooing beautiful women…

For a moment he hesitated. Was this really something he could go ahead with? For all he knew the girl was genuinely in love with Ian Randall—she certainly had a sufficiently devoted expression on her face.

He pushed aside his doubt.

Well, if she is, then I will be doing her a kindness in removing him, in providing her with a rival to him. What possible long-term happiness could she find loving a married man?

He gave a tight smile. If his plan worked, then Eva would not be the only woman spared unnecessary pain.

His eyes went back to the photo in front of him. He let his eyes wash over it. She really was very, very lovely…

Could he do it? Could he *really* do it?

Could he really seduce a woman—have an affair with her—for no other reason than to achieve his aim of parting her from a married man's attentions? He had had many affairs in his time, but never for such a purpose! Was it not just too, too cold-blooded to consider?

His thoughts circled in his head, seeking justification for his actions.

I don't intend her to be hurt or devastated by such an affair. I don't intend her harm. I only intend to get her away from Ian, with whom she cannot have an affair.

The logic was clear—irrefutable—yet still his expression was troubled. Sitting here, at his desk, it was easy enough to set in progress plots and machinations to try and save his sister's marriage—at least for now. But what would he feel like when he actually had to put his strategy into action?

Once more his eyes washed over the perfect oval face, the celestial blue of her wide eyes, the perfect curve of her tender mouth…

As before, he felt his senses stirred by her heart-stopping loveliness.

Resolution filled him. Oh, yes, he could do it. He most definitely could do it…

For one long moment Athan went on staring down at the image on his desk. The beautiful, blonde face gazed ingenuously at the camera, all unknowing of its presence. Then another image formed in his mind. Female too, but dark brunette, with deep, doe-like eyes—eyes filled with love for her husband, whose attention was all taken by the blonde in the photo.

I will protect my sister whatever I have to do.

He had reached his decision. Now he simply had to do it. Neither flinching, nor hesitating, nor doubting.

Decisively, he flicked the folder shut. Opening a locked drawer in his desk, he slid the incriminating folder into its depths, making sure he locked it again. Then he picked up his phone. He needed to make a phone call to an interior designer. His London apartment was very comfortable, very luxurious, and its décor suited him perfectly. But right now he knew it was time to have it redecorated. And while that was being done—well, he would need a temporary place to live.

And he knew exactly where it was going to be…

Marisa headed home through the chilly gathering dusk of a winter's day, walking along the wide pavement briskly, but with a lightness to her step that echoed the lightness in her heart. Although busy with traffic heading both east and west, Holland Park Road was such an affluent part of London that she didn't mind. In comparison with where she'd lived when she'd first got here it was a different world. A cramped, poky bedsit, with a cracked sink in the corner and a grimy, shared bathroom down an uncarpeted corridor, had been all she could afford on her meagre wages. London was *so* expensive! She'd known it would be, but the reality of it had hit harder than she'd anticipated.

The money she'd set aside to make the journey from Devon and tide her over had all gone, but she'd blithely— and completely wrongly—assumed that getting some kind of decently paid job would not be hard. Certainly a lot easier than it had been in Devon, where even if she had commuted— lengthily—into Plymouth, jobs were scarce and hourly rates poor in comparison. But she'd discovered, to her dismay, that living expenses in London were punitive—especially accommodation. She'd never had to pay for accommodation before. The cottage she'd grown up in might be tiny, and dreadfully ramshackle, but at least there was nothing to pay there except council tax and utility bills. London rents, even for really grim accommodation in run-down areas were terrifyingly high. It meant that even after she had found a day job she'd still been forced to take a second job in the evenings to make ends meet.

All that had changed completely now, though. Her life couldn't have become more different. And it was all thanks to Ian!

Meeting him had been amazing. And the transformation he'd wrought in her life had been total. A glow filled her as she thought about him. The moment he'd realised what a dump she lived in, he'd waved his magic wand over her and the next thing she knew he'd organised for her to move into a flat in a de luxe building in Holland Park, paying her rent and all her expenses.

And the flat wasn't the only thing he was paying for.

The manicured fingers of her left hand stroked the soft dark tan leather of her handbag as she walked, and she glanced down at the beautiful matching boots she was wearing, feeling deliciously svelte in the *faux* fur-trimmed jacket keeping her warm against the chill February air. The weather here in the east of the country was certainly colder and crisper than it was in the west, but in Devon—especially on the edges of Dartmoor, where the cottage nestled into the side of the moorland—midwinter Atlantic gales could lift the tiles off roofs and rip the stunted trees off their rocky perches. Lashing rain could penetrate the rotting window frames and spatter down the chimney onto the wood fires that were the only source of heating in the cottage.

Wood fires might seem romantic to holidaymakers, but they'd never have to forage for kindling in all weathers, or lug basketloads of logs in through the rain from outdoor sheds, let alone clean out the ashes morning after morning.

Not that holidaymakers would ever want to step foot into a cottage like *hers*. It was no chi-chi romantic rural getaway, thoughtfully fitted out with all mod-cons for city folk used to comfortable living. The cob-walled cottage was the real thing—a farm-worker's dwelling that had never been modernised other than being supplied with mains electricity. It still had the original stone sink in the kitchen lean-to, and although her mother had painted the cupboards and papered the walls, done her best to make the cottage homely and cosy, Marisa had always considered it old-fashioned and shabby.

Her mother hadn't minded, though. She'd been grateful. Grateful to have a place of her own—even a run-down one. Marisa had always known how tight money had been as she grew up. Her mother had had no one to look after her...

Unlike her daughter.

Again Marisa felt a lightness, a glow inside her. Ian was looking after her—so, so lavishly! She was overwhelmed by it all. Overwhelmed by his insistence on providing such a wonderful apartment for her to live in. Overwhelmed by his giving her money to put in the bank for her to spend on herself, telling her to go and get her hair done, her nails done, any number of pampering beauty treatments, and to go shopping for clothes—lots and lots of clothes. Beautiful, gorgeous clothes, the likes of which she'd only ever seen in fashion magazines, that had been bliss to buy and which now filled the wardrobe in her new apartment.

And overwhelmed, above all, by his insistence that she must be in his life from now on—he would hear of nothing else, as he had said over dinner the week before, when he'd given her that wonderful necklace that had taken her breath away.

Her eyes darkened. For all Ian's care of her, she could only exist on the periphery of his life. Could never be taken fully into his life—never be acknowledged or recognised or accepted.

Her throat tightened. She must always remain what she was now to Ian. Nothing more than that.

A secret never to be told...

* * *

Athan glanced at the laptop set on the coffee table in front of him. His mind was only half on the report displayed on the screen. The other half was on the mobile phone lying beside the laptop. Any moment now it would ring, he knew. The security operative deployed to track his target's movements had already reported her progress towards the apartment block. The next call would be to inform his employer that she had gone inside the lobby was heading for the lift.

Logging off, he closed the laptop lid with a snap, sliding it into its leather monogrammed carrier case and picking it up as he got to his feet. His car, he knew, was already hovering at the kerb.

He would have to get the timing exactly right. He headed for the front door, holding his mobile, waiting for the ring tone. He paused by the unopened door. Two minutes later the phone rang. The terse, disembodied voice spoke briefly.

'The target has just entered the building and the lift doors are opening. Ascent to her floor will be complete in nineteen seconds.'

Athan gave his acknowledgement of the message and hung up, counting down the seconds. At zero, he opened his apartment door. Exactly as he did so, the lift doors at the far end of the landing slid open.

Ian Randall's intended mistress walked out.

Involuntarily, Athan felt his stomach clench. *Damn*—in the flesh she was even more lovely than she'd looked in the covert photos. Slender, graceful, luminous skin, beautiful eyes, hair like silk—a breathtaking vision.

No wonder Ian can't resist her!

No man could.

Even as the thought formed in his head he felt its corollary shaping itself—ineluctable, inescapable.

And I don't have to. In fact not resisting her is exactly what I am here to do....

He could feel masculine reaction creaming through him.

Up to now he'd had repeated slivers of doubt as to whether he should actually go through with the course he'd planned—his swift, ruthless method of cutting the Gordian knot of Ian's disastrous dalliance. Oh, his head might tell him it was the most effective, time-efficient and all round painless way of separating her from Ian, but what was the rest of his body telling him? Could he *really* go through with what he was planning?

But now, seeing her in the flesh, he felt relief flood through him. Yes, he could do this—there was no reason not to, and every reason to do so.

More than reason...

No—that was something he needed to block right now. He had a task in hand—essential, critical—and that was what he had to focus on. Most definitely *not* on what his own desires might be. His desires—whatever they were—must be the servant of his purpose. That was what he must not allow himself to forget.

He walked forward, his pace businesslike and decisive, simply heading towards the lift. She'd stopped right there, in front of the doors which were now closing behind her. She seemed momentarily transfixed, and Athan could swear he saw her eyes widen as she watched him walking towards her.

She was reacting to him...reacting just the way he'd hoped she would. Without vanity, he knew it was the reaction he'd expected. The reaction he usually got from women. It would be hypocritical of him not to acknowledge it—not to accept that what women saw was six foot of lean male, with sable hair, and features which, as an accident of genetics—nothing more, and certainly no credit to him—got a resounding female thumbs up. Oh, he didn't have the kind of blond, boyish looks that Ian Randall had, with his blue eyes and ready smile, but he knew that his own strong, darkly planed features had an impact on women that got him the kind of reaction he was getting now. Just as he wanted...

OK, time to stop assessing the situation and make his next move.

'Could you hold the lift for me?'

His voice carried the short distance to where she was still standing, apparently immobilised. As he spoke she seemed to come to, and automatically her hand lifted as she half turned to press the call button. Athan continued to close the distance to her, and as the lift doors obediently slid open again he dropped her a slanting smile of appreciation for her courtesy.

'Thanks,' he murmured, letting his eyes wash swiftly over her.

Not that there was much 'letting' about it. He'd have done it automatically, he knew. Any man would. This close, she was even more stunning. Her wide-set eyes were gazing at him, and her lips were parted as though she were slightly breathless. A light, heady scent of perfume wafted from her, just as enticing as she was...

He stepped through into the lift, pressing the ground floor button. A moment later the doors had closed, shutting her from his field of vision. He felt the lift descend, and just for an instant he experienced a sense of regret.

Regret that he was heading in the opposite direction from her.

Or was it regret for something quite different? The thought flickered through his mind, as he stepped out of the lift and strode across the lobby to his car waiting at the kerb.

Why does she have to be mixed up with Ian Randall...?

The question, just like the image of her standing there so tantalisingly lovely, hovered like an unwelcome intruder. Ruthlessly he banished it, bestowing on his driver, holding open the passenger door of the sleek black saloon car, a brief nod and sliding himself into the leather seat, setting his laptop case down beside him. Such thoughts were pointless and irrelevant. The girl had to be removed from Ian's orbit, and the threat she presented to his sister liquidated. As swiftly as possible. That was all.

His mouth tightening, he extracted his laptop and resumed his work. He was a busy man—a *very* busy man. The multinational company he'd inherited from his father, which was one of the major plutocratic mercantile dynasties in Greece, allowed precious little time for R&R. Especially in the current economic climate.

But for all that, he knew he would have to make adequate time to accomplish his mission to save his sister's marriage—at least for the moment.

For just a moment, no more, he felt that repeated flicker of doubt skitter across his mind. It was one thing to plan such a cold-blooded strategy when gazing at a photograph. Another to execute it.

Impatiently, he banished his doubts. It had to be done, and that was that. Marisa Milburne would come to no harm by his seduction of her. She would have an enjoyable interlude in her life, as luxurious as the one Ian Randall was offering her, and she would be none the worse at the end of it. He had nothing at all to reproach himself with.

Besides, playing around with men who were married was always a dangerous business. If she learnt nothing else from the experience she was about to have, that would be enough. She should never have let herself get as deep as she had with Ian—even if nothing had happened between them yet.

I'll be doing her a favour, getting her away from Ian—and in a way she can enjoy...

And now that he had seen her in the flesh, knew that she was as lovely as her photo had told him, he knew he would too...

Again burning onto his retinas came the image of the way she'd stood there by the elevator doors, a vision of fair-haired, feature-perfect beauty. For a moment longer he held the image in his mind's eye, savouring it. Then, as the words of the document he'd loaded came up on the screen, he sliced it from his mind and got to work again.

Marisa let herself into her flat, her mind a daze. It had taken only moments—sliding open the lift doors, stepping out—and there he'd been, instantly in her vision. Walking towards her.

Or rather towards the lift. A swift, purposeful stride that went totally with the image forming itself in her consciousness. Making its impact felt instantly.

Tall, dark and just jaw-droppingly handsome...

But not in the way that Ian was handsome. Ian was fair-haired, like her, with light blue eyes, like her, and his features were boyish, with a smiling, inviting charm to them that had drawn her in immediately.

This man striding towards her had been completely different. A head taller than Ian easily, and far more powerfully built. But lean, not broad, with long legs. And much darker skin. European, yes, but with a clear Mediterranean stamp that went with the sable hair.

And the eyes.

Oh, yes, the eyes...

Dark as obsidian—not brilliant blue like Ian's—and dark-browed. They had seemed, just for a moment, to be spearing her.

Then he had spoken—only a few words—she'd felt the timbre resonate through her. Accented—she hadn't been able to tell what accent—yet obviously fluent in English. Asking her to hold the lift for him. Nodding and saying a brief thanks to her as he passed by and stepped into the lift, the closing doors shutting him from her sight.

It had taken moments—only moments—for the whole incident to play out, but now, standing inside her flat, she felt it replay in slow motion inside her head.

She made her way into her bedroom, dropping her bag down on the bed, taking off her jacket and mechanically shaking it out and hanging it in the capacious closet. She still seemed to be in a daze.

Who is he?

The question formed in her head, wanting to be answered. There were only three apartments on her floor, and one was occupied by a sprightly elderly couple who seemed to use it only as a London *pied-à-terre*. She'd talked briefly to them once as they'd come in from a night out, nothing more than mild social chit-chat, and they'd given her, she'd been slightly amused to note, a swift once-over in assessment.

They'd seemed reassured by her, when she'd made polite noises and said something about having come back from the theatre. The woman had disclosed that they had as well, which had led to a brief exchange over what each had seen and some anodyne views thereon. They'd seemed obviously well-heeled, and had spoken in the kind of accent that people of their background did, mentioning that they were mostly based in Hampshire, but came up to London regularly for theatre visits.

The other flat on her floor was occupied by a Far Eastern gentleman whom she'd seen only once, and that had been over a fortnight ago. He'd bowed politely to her, she'd nodded her head in return, and that had been that. Since then she'd heard and seen nothing of him or anyone else.

But the man she'd just seen now had clearly emerged from that flat.

Visitor? Guest? New tenant? She had no idea.

And it doesn't matter anyway! she reprimanded herself, shaking out of her daze. *People around here aren't exactly gossiping over the fences. Everyone keeps themselves to themselves, and even if he is a new tenant that's probably the only time you're going to see him.*

Into her head, hard on the heels of the reprimand, came a lingering response.

What a pity.

Impatiently she sat down on the bed and tugged off her boots, exchanging them for a pair of pumps more suited to being indoors. Time to stop mooning over a tall, dark stranger she'd seen for all of ninety seconds—if that—and remind herself that she was here for Ian's sake, not anything else. Ian was the sole focus of her life and she had better remember that. She had so little time with him as it was, and every stolen moment together was precious. Speaking of which...

She checked the voicemail on the landline phone beside her bed. To her pleasure it was indicating a new message. She pressed 'play' eagerly, but as she listened to the message her face fell.

'Marisa, I'm so, so sorry! I can't make tonight. I'm really gutted. But a pile of work's come my way—some deal that has to be signed off by ten tomorrow morning—and that means I'm going to have to burn the midnight oil, checking through everything. If all goes smoothly maybe—*maybe*—I can make lunch. I'll text you late morning—'

Ian's voice cut out, and she stared disconsolately at the handset. She hadn't seen Ian for three days, and she'd been so hoping that tonight would be on. She'd filled the three days as she filled all her days now—'doing' London. But what had seemed an exciting prospect when she'd first moved into this fabulous apartment a month ago was, she knew, beginning to pall.

She felt bad that she should feel that way. Up till a month ago, in her pre-Ian existence, she'd worked non-stop just to earn enough to stay in London. All the sights and entertainments of the capital had been far beyond her. Now, with the magic wand that Ian had waved over her life, she had both time and a lavish amount of money to see and do everything that London had to offer. For a girl raised in the wilds of Devon it was a cornucopia of wonders. Things she'd only ever seen on TV or read about were suddenly available to her.

At first it had been bliss. Armed with a miraculously full

wallet—thanks to Ian's generous largesse—she'd been able
to wander delightedly around top department stores and fashion shops, putting together a wardrobe the like of which had
only previously ever been in her fantasies. Ian had been delighted, and warmly encouraging, and she'd read approval in
his eyes whenever they were able to meet.

It wasn't only shopping that had beguiled her. London
held so much more than shops, and she'd been able to do
all the famous sights, take in the capital's great cultural and
historical heritage, immerse herself in its wonders—from a
breathtaking trip on the London Eye to a wide-eyed tour of
Buckingham Palace and everything in between. In the evenings she'd sampled London's glittering theatre life, with tickets to musicals and plays, live performances with famous stars
on stage, sitting not in the cheapest seats up in the gods but
in plush, top-price seats in the stalls and dress circle, coming back to the flat afterwards not on crowded buses or tube
trains but in comfortable taxis.

It had all been absolutely, totally wonderful!

But she had always been on her own…

Ian had never come with her. Never.

He'd felt bad, as had she. She knew that. He'd said so repeatedly.

'I just *wish* I could take you out and about, but I can't—
I just can't.'

His voice always sounded strained when he said it, and
Marisa knew how much he wished it were otherwise. But it
was impossible for them to be seen out together. It was risky
enough just meeting as they did, and she knew she could not
ask for more.

*I mustn't be greedy about him. I have to be glad for what
I do have of him. He's been so wonderful to me—and I'm so
incredibly glad that we met.*

She reprimanded herself sternly as she got up off the bed
and headed towards the kitchen. She must not be doleful and

depressed when he had to cancel their rare times of getting together. And as for feeling sorry for herself because she was so alone—well, that was just totally inexcusable.

Look at where I live now—what my life is now. How easy, how luxurious. And it's all thanks to Ian!

Yet for all her adjuration to herself as she set the kettle to boil and popped the Danish pastry she'd bought into the microwave to warm, making herself appreciate for the millionth time how blissful it was to have a spanking new luxury kitchen to herself instead of the sparse, tatty kitchenette in her bedsit, or even the kitchen in the cottage, with its ancient stone sink and rickety wooden cupboards, she could feel bleakness edging around her insides.

Determined to shake it, she went through to the living room, made herself look around at the pale grey three-piece suite, the darker grey deep pile woollen carpet, the rich silvery drapes framing the window that looked out over the roadway. She gazed down over the scene two storeys below. The road was quiet, lined with trees that would bear blossom in the spring but which now were bare.

Cars—expensive ones, for this was, as her luxury apartment testified, an expensive part of London, where only the rich and highly affluent could afford to live—lined the kerbs. She was grateful that Ian had chosen a flat in such a quiet location, and so near to Holland Park itself, for despite the charms of London she was used to the quietness of deep countryside. The winter's dusk was deepening, and few people were out and about. There was a chilly bleakness in the vista that seemed to reach tendrils around her.

She knew no one in London. Only Ian. The other women she'd worked with briefly had all been from abroad, and she had been an obvious outsider though they'd been perfectly pleasant to her. She'd known London was going to be a big, busy place, and that she would know no one to begin with, but she hadn't realised just how big and busy a place it was. How incredibly alone one could feel in a crowd.

How lonely she still felt, despite the luxury in which she lived.

Angry at her own self-pity, she turned away sharply, drawing the curtains and lighting one of the elegant table lamps. A cup of tea, something to watch on the huge television set in the corner, and later on she would make herself something to eat and have an early night. She had nothing to complain about—nothing to feel sorry for herself about.

And I'm used to being lonely...

Living alone with her mother on the edge of Dartmoor, she had become used to her own company. This last year in Devon, having withdrawn into grief at the loss of her mother, days had passed without her seeing another living soul. It had taken well over a year to come to terms with her mother's death, even though the end had come almost as a release. Since being knocked down by a car some four years earlier her mother had been confined to a wheelchair, and it had been torment for her. But the accident had weakened her heart, too, and the heart attack that had taken her eighteen months ago had at least ended that torment.

And though the devastation of her mother's loss had been total, Marisa knew that it had given her a chance to leave home that her mother's disability and emotional dependence on her daughter had not allowed her.

But it had not just been her practical and emotional one needs that had made her mother so fearful about her leaving home. Marisa was all too conscious of the cause of that deeper fear, and before she'd finally set off for the city she'd gone to pay a last anguished visit to her mother's grave in the parish churchyard.

'I'm going to London, Mum. I know you don't want me to—know you will worry about me. But I promise you I won't end up the way you did, with a broken heart and your hopes in ruins. I *promise* you.'

Then she'd packed her bag, bought her train ticket, and set off. Having no idea what would befall her.

Having no idea that Ian would walk into her life.

Would change it utterly.

The microwave was beeping in the kitchen, signalling that the Danish pastry was warm. Roused from her drear thoughts, she walked into the kitchen to make her tea. She would *not* feel sorry for herself. She would remember how short a time ago her life had been so completely different from what it was now. She would have a quiet, comfortable evening in and be totally self-indulgent.

Clicking the thermostat a degree higher, she revelled in the central heating that kept the flat beautifully warm. Two minutes later she was curled up on the sofa, biting into the soft, fragrant pastry and watching TV. It was a nature programme, set somewhere hot and on the beach, and Marisa gazed at the shallow azure waters as the presenter informed her about its marine life. But it wasn't the marine life that made her gaze—it was the vista of the beach, a tropical idyll framed by palm trees.

Imagine being somewhere like that…

If only Ian…

She cut short her imagining. Ian could not take her somewhere like that. Could not take a single day's holiday with her anywhere, period. That was the blunt reality of it. He could rent this flat for her, give her that wonderful diamond necklace, give her the wherewithal to dress beautifully, but what he could not give her was time.

She reached for her cup of tea, making herself focus on the programme. The presenter wasn't British. He had some kind of accent. Lilting and attractive. She found herself trying to identify it. French? Spanish? She wasn't sure. She frowned. Was it the same kind of accent that man who'd asked her to hold the lift had? She shut her eyes to hear it again in her head. The presenter's accent was stronger, but maybe it was the same type. His appearance in so far as hair colour and skin tone was similar too. Reaching for the remote, she clicked on info for the programme. The presenter's name was Greek.

Was that what the man in the corridor was? she found herself pondering. It could be—it fitted his air of foreignness. And the flat he'd come out of had previously been let to a non-Brit. Maybe it was some kind of international corporate let, with one businessman after another passing through.

I wonder who he is? He's just so jaw-droppingly good-looking.

With a rasp of irritation she pushed the question out of her head. What did it matter who he was, why he was there, or what nationality he was? She'd seen him for less than two minutes, if that, and he'd done nothing but nod and say a passing 'thanks' at her before disappearing. She'd stared at him gormlessly for the duration, unable to control her reaction to his startling dark good looks. Given the way everyone kept to themselves in the apartment block, she would probably never set eyes on him again.

And if she did it would be utterly irrelevant to her anyway.

Clicking on the remote again, she changed channels and finished off the pastry. The evening stretched ahead of her...

Two hours later there was less of it left to stretch, but she was still feeling bored and restless. She couldn't decide what to do next—go to bed or watch a movie on TV. It was one she was only marginally interested in, and it did not particularly appeal. On the other hand neither did going to bed at nine o'clock, either. All around her the hushed silence of the flat enveloped her, as if she were the only person for miles.

She reached for the remote. It was stupid, wasting time watching something she didn't want to. She would head for bed and read something useful—like the newly published hardback history of London she'd splashed out on last week.

Buying new hardbacks was such a previously unknown luxury she should make the most of it. Besides, since leaving college she'd hardly used her brain at all—which was a waste.

And you really don't want to come across as some kind of country bumpkin to Ian, either. Even if he's not a raging intellectual, he obviously knows business, and current affairs and so on.

She clicked off the TV and gathered herself to get to her feet. But even as she did so, she froze. A sound she had never heard had penetrated from the hallway. The doorbell.

Who on earth…? Puzzled and apprehensive, she made her way to the little entrance hall. The door was on a security chain, and there was a spyhole too. She peered through it, but could only take in a distorted impression of a dark suit. Nothing else. Well, it didn't look like a burglar paying a call, at any rate.

Cautiously, she open the door on the chain, which restricted it to a couple of inches, bracing herself ready to flatten herself against it if someone put an intruding foot through.

Instead a voice spoke. A deep, accented voice that had the timbre of familiarity.

'I'm extremely sorry to disturb you…'

Without volition, she felt her insides give a little flutter.

'Just a moment.' She slid the security chain off and opened the door wider.

It was the man who'd asked her to hold the lift for him earlier.

'I do apologise,' he said, 'but I wonder if I might ask you a favour.'

There was a faint smile on his face, a slightly quizzical look. Marisa found it did strange things to her. Things that made her lips part and her eyes rest as if helplessly on his face. She tried to gather her composure.

'Of…of course,' she answered, trying to sound polite but cool.

The faint smile deepened. So did the sensation of fluttering inside her. Her hand tightened on the doorframe.

'I've just moved into the apartment next to you, and I've only just realised that I've made no arrangements for any groceries to be delivered. This may sound the most stupid request you've heard, but if you could possibly let me have some milk and a couple of teaspoons of instant coffee I would be in your debt.'

Dark eyes—ludicrously long-lashed, she realised as her brain spun idiotically in her head—rested on her, their quizzical expression at odds with the formidable air of command about him. Whoever he was, he was most definitely not one of life's minions.

He's the guy that gives the orders...others do his bidding. Snap to his command...

And respond to his faintly smiling requests as if he's turned a key in their backs.

Especially if they were female...

The fluttering inside her, the tightness of her hand on the doorframe, intensified.

She swallowed, managed to speak. 'Yes—yes, of course. No problem.' Her voice sounded husky, as if her throat had constricted.

The faint smile deepened, indenting lines around his mouth. Marisa's throat constricted again. Oh, good grief, when they'd been handing it out this guy got a double helping.

'It's really very good of you,' the deep, accented voice responded, its timbre doing things to her she could not prevent. Didn't have the slightest interest in preventing...

Jerkily, she pulled the door wider and turned away. 'I'll just—um—go and fetch them,' she managed to say.

She headed for the kitchen. Her feet felt clumsy, and she was sure she bumped into the corner of the sofa as she made her way through the living room to the kitchen beyond. She felt like an idiot, bumping into her own furniture. In the kitchen she fumbled with the fridge door, yanking it open and grabbing a pint of milk. It was semi-skimmed. She hoped he'd be OK with that. She hoped he'd be OK with her brand of instant coffee, as well. Not that he looked like an instant coffee type of man. Her eyes went to the terrifyingly complicated coffee machine that stood completely unused by the microwave. She'd bought coffee beans, hoping to try it out, but one glance at the instruction booklet had quashed her ambition instantly.

Oh, stop dithering, girl—just give him the milk and the coffee jar.

She hurried out of the kitchen, carefully avoiding bumping into the furniture. He'd stepped inside the hall, though the front door was still ajar.

'Here you are,' she said breathlessly, holding out the requested items.

'It's very good of you,' he said.

That faint smile was still doing its work. His height was making the small hallway even smaller. So was his dark suit and black cashmere overcoat. His presence seemed overpowering suddenly.

A thought struck her. 'I've got coffee beans, if you prefer. The packet's unopened. I can't operate my machine.'

Oh, hell, she was burbling inanely. What did he care whether she could operate the machine or not. Yet it seemed he did—a dark eyebrow had quirked.

'Would you like me to show you how? They can be fiendishly difficult.'

Immediately she stiffened. 'Oh, no, thank you. That's fine. I wouldn't dream of troubling you.'

His lashes dipped over his eyes. 'It would be no trouble, I promise you.'

His voice had changed. She didn't know how, but it had. And suddenly, with a piercing light, she knew why it had…

Knew it from the sudden glint in his eyes—his dark, deep eyes...

She took a breath—a steadying one that she needed. Needed in order to remind herself that a complete stranger— however much of an impact he was making on her—was standing inside her flat and signalling that he liked what he was seeing. Her brain seemed to split in two. One half—the half that was reducing her to a wittering idiot—reeled with the realisation. The other half was shouting a loud, strident warning to her. Time to pay heed to it.

She shook her head. A small but decisive gesture.

'Thank you, but no.' She held the milk and the coffee jar closer to him. Her smile was polite, but nothing more, her voice composed.

For just a second longer he kept that half-shut gaze on her, then abruptly reached out to relieve her of the proffered items, managing to take them both in a single hand. The other was holding a laptop case.

'Once again, thank you,' he said.

His voice had lost whatever it had so briefly held. So had his expression. He turned away, going back out into the corridor, pausing only to half turn his head towards her, standing ready to close the door.

'Goodnight,' he said.

She kept her face composed. 'Goodnight,' she answered back. Then closed the door.

Outside, Athan stood a moment, his eyes faintly narrowed. *Interesting,* he thought. She had responded to him—no doubt about that. Years of experience had taught him exactly when a woman found him attractive. But she had quite definitely drawn the line when he'd made his second gambit, offering to show her how to use the coffee machine.

And if she hadn't? If she'd let me into her flat, let me make fresh coffee—shared it with me. Let me move on to my third gambit—suggesting I order dinner to be delivered so we could dine together?

If she had, what would he have done?

Would I have stayed the night with her if she'd let me?

For one vivid instant, an image filled his head.

Pale golden hair spread loose across a white pillow. A slender, naked body offered to him. A lovely face alight with pleasure…pleasure that he could give her.

Abruptly, he started to walk to his apartment door, juggling with the damn milk and coffee that threatened to tumble to the ground in order to extract his keys. As he stepped inside he felt another stab of hunger. But this time for the more mundane fare of food. Well, he'd make coffee—even if only instant—and consult the internet to get some food delivered. There must be a catering company around that would oblige.

It was a nuisance, he mused, that the apartment block had no concierge who could take care of that sort of thing for him. But on the other hand a concierge was the last thing he needed—they were the kind of individuals who swiftly discovered too much about their tenants. And if there was one overriding necessity right now it was that his beautiful blonde fellow tenant should not have any source of information about him that he did not care to impart to her.

Least of all that he knew about her relationship with Ian Randall.

And why he was going to end it.

Marisa didn't sleep well. She tossed and turned restlessly. She might wish it was because she was disappointed not to have met up with Ian last night but she knew it wasn't because of that.

It was because of that man—that tall, dark, ludicrously handsome man—who had appeared at her door that evening.

With the corniest chat-up line in the book! That's what I've got to remember!

Good grief, couldn't he have come up with something more original than borrowing a pint of milk? And coffee, she reminded herself waspishly. The problem was, try as she might to be derisive about it and label it nothing more than a transparent ploy, another thought kept intruding.

That any man with those devastating looks wouldn't even have to crook his little finger to have every female for miles around come running.

Pick up lines, let alone corny ones, wouldn't even be in his ball park. He'd never be reduced to resorting to something so clichéd. Besides, she reasoned, he'd seen her come out of the lift and might well have assumed she had a flat on this floor, but for all he'd have known she might have had the flat the elderly couple occupied. As a new tenant he wouldn't know, would he? Which meant that his ring on her doorbell and his request had been genuine, and not a pick-up routine.

Anyway, what did it matter?

But he did do that bit offering to show me how the coffee machine worked.

No, that didn't prove anything except that he was a man and men thought it inexplicable that women found machinery complicated. He'd probably thought he was being polite in offering—that the reason she'd mentioned she couldn't get it to work was a ploy in order to get him to offer help.

Oh, help, maybe he thought I *was trying to pick* him *up! Trying to inveigle him to come in...*

She squirmed with embarrassment at the thought. Still, at least she'd immediately said no, which was something to be grateful for. He couldn't possibly think she was giving him the come on, could he?

You behaved like a gormless idiot, though, don't forget— stammering and staring bug-eyed at him.

Yes, well, he was doubtless used to that kind of reaction from women. A man with looks like his would be.

And it wasn't just his looks, was it? Nor that to-die-for

foreign accent of his. If she were brutally honest—and she had better be at this time of night—it was the whole package that made such an impact. The looks, the cashmere overcoat, the bespoke suit, the whole Mr Rich thing definitely contributed.

And more than that there had been a kind of *aura* around him. That was the only word she could come up with. A kind of self-assurance, an air of being someone who gave orders, moved in the corridors of power, made things happen that he wanted to happen.

It was curious, she found herself musing. Ian was wealthy, and he sported the trappings of wealth from flash pad to gold watch. But he didn't possess that aura of power, that sense of being someone not to mess with.

A little shiver went down her spine. Disturbing. Disquieting. For a moment longer she gazed into the darkness of her bedroom. She shouldn't think about the incident tonight. Should put it out of her mind.

Should go to sleep.

But her dreams, when they came, were filled with the same disquiet.

And a strange, disturbing sense of anticipation…

Athan left for his office early. He always did, finding the first couple of hours of the morning the most productive before his heavy schedule of meetings started. This morning, however, he found his usual high level of productivity diminished. It annoyed him. Annoyed him to realise that he was finding himself replaying the little scene he'd created last night. Letting his memory toy with recalled images—images of the way her long hair had framed her face, tumbling down over her shoulders, the way she'd gazed at him, wide-eyed, the way her voice had been breathy and husky. The way she'd walked away from him towards the kitchen on long, slender legs, the fall of her hair waving down her back.

She really was very, very lovely.

Yes, well, he knew that—had already acknowledged that—and other than her beauty making it easier for him to carry out his plan there wasn't any point in dwelling on it. He had a mountain of work to get through, and it wasn't going to go away of its accord.

He also had to decide on a pretext for getting Ian Randall out of the country. The upcoming West Coast contract would fit the bill well. He could say it required input from the UK. He could even—his eyes narrowed in speculation—mention the trip to Eva. Suggest it would be an ideal opportunity to go with Ian, and then to take a holiday afterwards—fly on to Hawaii, for instance. Eva would snap at it, he was sure.

That would ensure he kept Ian well away from London for a couple of weeks, if not longer.

That's all the time I need with Marisa Milburne.

He had no doubts about his ability to achieve his goal. It was experience, not vanity, that told him women didn't say no to him, and there was no reason to suppose this one would be different.

Especially after last night. Any speculation that her attachment to Ian was based on love had been set aside. No woman devotedly in love with another man would have reacted the way she had to him when he'd paid her attention. No woman would have started the way she had, gazed at him the way she had, displaying that telltale dilating of the pupils.

Yet she was not giving him the come-on, either. That was clear too.

His brows drew together. How would she react to his next move? he wondered. He clicked on to the internet and made a rapid search, made a purchase online, clicking on 'deliver before noon'. Then, job done, he cleared the screen and put his mind into work mode. There was a lot to get done if he wanted to be free by the evening.

* * *

Marisa was hand-washing one of her beautiful new sweaters when the intercom rang. Frowning, she picked up the phone.

'Delivery for Ms Milburne,' said a disembodied voice.

Puzzled, she went downstairs. As she walked out into the lobby and saw a man standing on the pavement with a bouquet of white lilies she smiled. *Oh, Ian,* she thought fondly, *how sweet. Just because you couldn't meet me last night.*

But when she took the beautiful bouquet into her kitchen to find a suitable receptacle for it, and opened the small gilt-edged envelope attached to the wrapping, the card inside held an unexpected message.

Thank you for the milk and coffee—it was much appreciated.

It was simply signed 'Your grateful neighbour.'

For a moment she stared. As a token of gratitude a bouquet of lilies that must have cost at least thirty pounds, if not more, was a bit overdone. On the other hand...well, since being with Ian she had come to realise that the rich really were different. Anyone who could afford the rents on these apartments could definitely afford to drop thirty pounds on a bunch of flowers without even noticing.

Yet for all her rationalising, as she arranged the glorious blooms with their intense, heady fragrance in a huge glass vase she'd found in a cupboard, she could not help wishing they *had* been from Ian.

Not some stranger who meant absolutely nothing to her.

However much of an impact he'd made on her.

She'd been doing her best to put the incident last night out of her head. Dwelling on it was stupid. So was moping. She'd definitely started to mope yesterday, and it was time to nip that in the bud. Of *course* Ian found it hard to meet her—she knew why and accepted it, even if she wished it otherwise. Well, it wasn't otherwise, and that was that. And if she were feeling lonely without him—well, considering the luxury of her life now, it was ungrateful and spoilt to be anything other than blissful.

Doing the hand-washing helped improve her mood, and so did a resolve to go for a brisk walk in Holland Park. The weather wasn't attractive—mizzling with rain today—but that wasn't the point. She should get out, breathe fresh air— even if London air could never really be fresh—and get some exercise.

I ought to find a gym, or take some dance classes of some kind.

That would definitely be a good idea. She would ask in some of the shops on Holland Park Road when she went to buy groceries. If she did start exercise classes it might be a way of meeting people—other women she could chat to, have coffee with. Make friends with, maybe.

She wasn't very good at making friends, she knew. It was because she'd always felt different, felt out of things. Though she and her mother had lived in their small village off Dartmoor they hadn't really belonged—they'd always been incomers. Outsiders. And her mother's introverted temperament, and circumstance of being a single mother, had added to their social isolation. Even as school Marisa had always felt remote from her peer group, finding it difficult to make friends, get on with others. She felt a little glow start up inside her. That was why it was so lovely being with Ian. They got on so well. His charm, his sense of humour, his liveliness— all drew her out of herself, made her feel relaxed and confident for the first time in her life.

It made it all the more frustrating that she had to be a secret part of his life.

If only he could acknowledge me openly—not keep me tucked away here...

Yes, well, that was impossible. No point going over it again. No point starting to mope.

Grabbing her jacket, and slipping a waterproof around her, she picked up her keys and set off for a walk. She'd find a café and have some lunch, then pick up some shopping. That would pass the time.

Guilt plucked at her. *Pass the time.* Was that what she was doing with her life now? Finding things to do to while away the hours?

As she walked along the park's pathways, heading vaguely towards the remains of Holland House and the beautiful glass Orangery, she started to think critically. Wonderful as it was to live in so beautiful a flat, with no money worries and a life of luxury that she'd never dreamt of, she could *not* live her life like that.

She should find another job, she knew—but doing what? Ian had insisted she give up the low-paid cleaning jobs she'd been doing when she'd met him. A thought struck her, and she stopped and stared at a leafless bush dripping water droplets along its branches. Why not take up some kind of charity work? Since Ian was insisting on paying her bills, why not take advantage of not having to earn a living by doing something to help others? What, precisely, she had no idea, but she could make a start, surely, by finding one of the many charity shops and volunteering her time—sorting out donated goods or working at the till. The charity shop could probably show her other pieces that needed volunteers, and she could take it from there.

Resolution filled her, and she could feel her spirits lift. Her mind ran on, wondering where the nearest charity shops were likely to be. Somewhere up at Notting Hill, probably, or down on Kensington High Street. And there would definitely be some around Shepherds Bush Green, surely?

She would start checking after lunch. She'd use her new laptop and the apartment's built-in broadband to search, and then start phoning round to see what was available. With a reviving sense of enthusiasm she headed back to her flat. As she walked in she was hit by an exotic fragrance—it was the bouquet of lilies, giving off their wonderful scent, filling the living room with it. As it caught her nostrils she had a vivid recollection of the man who'd sent them.

He really was extraordinarily good-looking...

When the doorbell sounded just after six she jumped. She'd been doing a web search of charities, had got immersed in reading about the work done by them, and the time had flown by. Reading about just how terrible some people's lives were had been a timely, sobering reminder. Yes, her life had had its challenges, no doubt about that, and every day she missed her mother, but what they'd been through had been nothing compared with the sufferings of so many in the world. It had certainly served to squash any resumption of her moping and self-pity because she could see so little of Ian.

The doorbell sounded again. With a mix of slight apprehension, slight irritation at being disturbed, and slight curiosity as to who it might be, she went to open the door.

'Did the flowers arrive?'

The deep, accented voice did exactly to her insides what it had done the night before. So did the six-foot frame and the incredible looks and the way his dark eyes were resting on her...

She took a breath. It seemed very slightly strangulated, much to her annoyance.

'Yes. Thank you. Though they were completely unnecessary.' Her voice sounded staccato. Even brusque. She didn't want to appear rude, but on the other hand there was no way she was going to be all over him for his over-the-top gesture of thanks for her very slight gesture of neighbourliness.

He seemed unrebuffed by her response.

'Not at all,' he contradicted her.

That faint smile was quirking at his mouth and doing,

just as his voice and his looks had, what it had done to her yesterday.

'The kindness of strangers should never go unappreciated.' His eyes glinted with a hint of humour in their dark, gold-flecked depths. 'You've no idea how badly I needed some coffee. It just never dawned on me that although these apartments come furnished there wouldn't actually be any provisions in stock unless they'd been ordered beforehand.' He paused. 'Tell me,' he went on, and now there was a quizzical enquiry in his voice, 'have you succeeded in getting your coffee machine to obey you yet?'

Marisa swallowed. She knew exactly what she should do. She should say, *No, and it doesn't matter, thank you very much. Thank you for the flowers, but they really were quite unnecessary, I promise you.* And then, politely but firmly, she should wish him good evening and close the door.

That was definitely what she should do. Anything else was madness. Asking for trouble. For complications. For something that she could do without and what was more to the point *should* do without.

I don't need a tall, dark, handsome stranger in my life! And certainly not this one!

A little chill went through her. Besides, he could be anyone. Just because he wore a cashmere overcoat and a bespoke suit and Italian shoes, and lived in a luxury apartment, it didn't mean that he wasn't a serial killer...

Yet even as she entertained the possibility she knew it must surely be impossible. Whatever serial killers looked like, it was not someone who quite obviously spent most of his day ordering minions around and doubtless cutting deals with a string of zeroes in them.

Had he read the disquiet in her eyes? Interpreted her momentary hesitation as understandable reluctance to engage in conversation on her doorstep with a man she didn't know? He must have, because before she could answer him he started speaking again.

'I apologise,' he said. 'I'm being intrusive, and presuming on far too slight an acquaintance.'

If he hadn't apologised she might well have made the answer to him that as she'd intended—she really might, she thought distractedly. But there was something about the open apology, the air of quizzical ruefulness, the slight backing off and withdrawal she sensed in his body language, that stopped her. Or was it, she thought with a kind of hollowing inside her stomach, the way those gold-flecked eyes were resting on her? As if they could reach deep inside her, hold her mesmerised until she gazed back at him.

'No, not at all,' she said awkwardly. She sounded very English, very stilted, she knew. 'It was kind of you to offer to help with the coffee machine. But instant coffee is absolutely fine, and anyway I drink tea mostly.'

Oh, Lord, she thought, why on earth had she said that? Why had she spoken at all? Why hadn't she just smiled and shut the door. Why—?

'Quite right. Just what an English rose *should* drink,' he replied.

And now, completely openly, there was amusement in his voice. It did even more to her than his accent did.

'We Greeks, however,' he went on, 'drink our coffee like mud. A legacy from our Turkish overlords.'

'So you *are* Greek!'

The words fell from her lips before she could stop them.

The glint came again. 'Is that good or bad?' he said, humour clear in his voice.

'I don't know,' she said candidly. 'I don't know anyone who is Greek, and I've never been to Greece.'

His eyes glinted again. 'Well, I hope I will put you off neither my compatriots, nor my country,' he responded, with humour still in his voice, that smile in his eyes.

Marisa swallowed. No, whoever this guy was, he definitely did not put her off either Greeks or Greece…

He was speaking again, she realised with a start, and made herself pay attention.

'Having asked one favour of you already,' he was saying, and his eyes were washing over her again, to the same devastating effect, 'I am going to push my luck and ask another.' He paused and looked down at her, a look of speculative questioning in his expression. 'Are you at all interested in the theatre? I've come into possession of two tickets for a preview performance tonight of the Chekov that's opening next week. Can I persuade you to keep me company?'

He was taking a gamble here. Athan knew that. Chekov might be the last thing to persuade her. But his surveillance records indicated that she had spent numerous evenings at the theatre, and that included any number of high brow plays. Tickets for the upcoming Chekov were like gold dust, and might be sufficient temptation for her.

Marisa could only stand there. Her heart rate seemed to have quickened, and thoughts were racing through her head.

He's trying to pick me up—he's definitely trying to pick me up. Asking me to the theatre is a pick-up—no question about it! No ambiguity or misunderstanding like it was about the coffee machine—just a plain straightforward date to go to the theatre together…

A strange kind of thrill went through her, but there was a tremor in it too. Thanks to the remoteness of her childhood home, the difficulties of her upbringing with her lonely, isolated mother, she had little experience of men. She knew she had the kind of looks they liked, but her mother had considered her beauty more of a danger than a blessing—just as her mother's looks had proved a danger to her when she'd been young, Marisa thought sadly. It had taken Ian's open admiration for her to let her blossom finally. His insistence that she indulge herself in beautiful clothes and lavish beauty treatments had finally convinced her that it was OK for men to find her attractive.

Even, she accepted, with another little thrill, this devastatingly gorgeous man, standing here inviting her out for the evening.

Of course it was unquestionably out of the question. It had to be. She couldn't go on a date with a strange man just because he happened to live—very temporarily—next door to her. Good grief, she didn't even know his name. Only that he was rich. And Greek.

And irresistibly good-looking…

And that combination makes a male that assumes he's going to get his own way, my girl! So you know perfectly well what you're going to say, don't you? You're going to smile, a small, tight little smile and step backwards, to convey the right body language, then say, politely but adamantly, No, thank you. And you are going to close the door and not have anything more to do with him. That's what you're going to do.

She opened her mouth to do just that. Which meant that it was incredibly, unbelievably annoying when what she heard her voice saying was, 'Is that that new production of *Three Sisters* that I've read about in the papers?'

'That's the one. Would you be interested?'

Marisa swallowed. Yes, she would be interested. Anyone who loved the theatre would be. She'd seen it advertised and it had a stellar cast, including a Hollywood star keen to make her mark as a classical actress.

But was that any reason to accept what this complete stranger had just offered?

She must have made her hesitation apparent, because before she could say anything more, he spoke again.

'Perhaps,' he said, and his voice had changed slightly, as had the expression in his eyes, though she wasn't entirely sure how, 'it might be timely at this juncture to reassure you that I am not, as you may possibly be currently wondering, either a murderer, a burglar, a spy or wanted for questioning by Interpol. I am, for my pains, merely a businessman, and tediously respectable…'

There was a mix of humour and frankness in his voice, and as he spoke he reached a long-fingered hand inside his jacket pocket and withdrew a silver card case, flicking it open and withdrawing one of its contents, proffering it to her with another of those quick, quirking smiles that seemed to have such a powerful effect on her in disproportion to their duration.

She found herself taking the card, staring at it. It was written in Latin script and it said simply, 'Teodarkis Holdings'. There was a Mayfair address, and a discreet name in the corner: Athan Teodarkis.

Athan watched her peruse the card. There was a lot riding on her reaction. A whole, game-changing lot. He was taking the gamble that Ian had never mentioned the name of his wife's family to her, or the company that owned the one he worked for himself. As he studied her face he could see nothing that would indicate, even under high-focus scrutiny, that it meant anything to her at all. He could feel relief rippling through him.

He gave her a moment or two to study the business card, then addressed her again.

'Does that convince you I am totally harmless?' he asked.

There was a touch of light humour in his voice, and she let her eyes glance up at him from the white card in her fingers.

Harmless? The word reverberated in her head. *Harmless?* As she looked straight at him, at his breathtaking dark good-looks, the word seemed to mock her.

'So,' he was saying, 'will you come? I hate going to the theatre on my own.'

'Surely there must be someone you already know that you could invite?' she countered. There was just a trace of acidity in her voice, because a man like this, who was the very last man any female would ever describe as 'harmless', must have a very long list of women who would drop everything for a date with him.

'No one who likes Chekov,' he responded promptly. 'He's not to everyone's taste.'

Hmm, thought Marisa, for not 'everyone' read 'the kind of high-maintenance glossy woman whose idea of a hot date with a man like him would *not* be a play by a nineteenth century Russian dramatist about a bunch of gloomy, indecisive provincials who drifted about aimlessly and got depressed'.

'And you think I would?' she challenged, suddenly and illogically stung that he clearly did not consider *her* the kind of female he usually asked out. 'Is that your reason for asking me?' she said pointedly.

Long lashes dipped down over gold-flecked eyes. 'Part of it,' he agreed.

The dark eyes rested on her, conveying their message. A message that told her that whatever she might have thought about not being the kind of woman he usually asked out, she had, in fact, been mistaken...

There was something new in his voice—something that told Marisa this was a very experienced operator indeed. For a second panic beat in her throat. She was out of her depth—way, way out! Oh, he might be seeing a woman living in a luxury apartment, dressed in designer clothes and looking svelte and groomed, but she knew that beneath that glossy surface she was only a raw country girl. Even her short time with Ian couldn't eradicate that.

She suddenly realised he was speaking again.

'Well—have I persuaded you?' There was nothing more than the familiar quizzical enquiry in his voice, his expression.

Marisa swallowed. 'Um...I—I...'

He smiled. The full on smile that changed his face, turned her insides out, parted her lips and made her stare gormlessly at him.

'Great. OK—so, can you be ready by seven?'

'Um—'

'Good girl,' he said approvingly, as if she'd agreed to his invitation. He made as if to step away, then suddenly paused, as if something had just struck him. 'I've just realised,' he said, and there was self-reproof in his voice, 'I've absolutely no idea what your name is.'

He made the omission sound like a cause for humour, not an indication that she was a complete stranger to him. He looked at her expectantly.

There was a strange sensation in Marisa's head. As if everything that was going on was completely, totally unreal. Then, as if in a haze, she said slowly, 'It's Marisa— Marisa Milburne.'

The long lashes swept down again. Then, before she had the faintest inkling of what he was about to do, she felt, of all things, her hand being taken, and lifted.

'I'm delighted to make your acquaintance, Miss Milburne,' he murmured, holding her wide-eyed gaze.

Instantly she held her breath, and he inclined his head and kissed her hand.

It was fleeting, it was momentary, it was over in a second, but it left her bereft of rationality.

'To compensate for the informality of our acquaintance,' he murmured.

Then, with a final stomach-dissolving smile, he turned and headed down to the lift. Marisa stared, incapable of movement, until the doors had opened, then closed again, shutting him off from her view. Then, very slowly, in a total daze, she went back into her apartment.

Inside, she stood, staring at her hand for several seconds, bereft of both speech and all rational thought.

Least of all any sense of danger...

CHAPTER TWO

'WELL, what do you think? Should she stick to Hollywood?'

The curtain had fallen, and Marisa was making her slow way out of the stalls. Athan Teodarkis's tall presence behind her was almost tangible as he followed her. But then it had been tangible the entire evening. Tangible even when he'd been on the far side of a taxi seat from her on the way to the theatre, let alone when he'd been sitting right next to her in the plush stalls seat, his sleeve almost brushing hers, even though she'd tried to make sure she kept her hands in her lap, not resting on the chair arm like he had.

A hundred times she'd told herself that she should never have accepted his invitation. That it was completely unacceptable to have done so, and a big, big mistake.

She didn't know the man. Didn't know him from Adam. However prestigious a business card he possessed, he was a stranger—a stranger who had quite blatantly picked her up. Not quite off the street, but even so—being some random guy in the flat next to hers was not exactly a formal introduction, was it? But the moment she thought about the total absence of any kind of formal introduction the memory of that hand-kiss was there, and the fleeting sensation of his lips scarcely brushing her knuckles...

No wonder Victorian maidens swooned when men kissed their hands!

How, she wondered for the millionth time, could such a formal gesture be so incredibly...*intimate*? For intimate was the only word for it. And swooning the only word for the sensation it had created....

The sensation that permeated her still. Not quite as intense, but there all the same, like a very low-level fever that had been running in her veins constantly, all evening. She'd sought to ignore it, sought to make herself behave with this man as if he *weren't* having that effect on her, as if it were perfectly normal to make polite, anodyne conversation about the play, the theatre, the state of London traffic, sounding composed and unaffected and sensible.

She'd deliberately dressed in a style that was demure—there was no better word for it. No way was she going to give him the slightest reason to think she was coming on to him! Either by her manner or her appearance. So the grey light wool dress she'd chosen was smart, no doubt about that, and had a mid-range designer tag, but the neckline was not low and the cut was quite loose, its hemline touching her knee. Matching grey tights and grey low-heeled shoes went with it, and the only jewellery she wore was a metallic haematite necklace. Her hair was dressed in a plaited coil at the back of her head, and her make up was as discreet as the rest of her.

Had he looked very slightly surprised at the overall demureness of her appearance? She wasn't sure, but if he had the look had disappeared immediately, and his manner towards her had mirrored her own. He was courteous and conversational, but he was not coming on to her—to her relief.

It *was* to her relief, wasn't it? She was *glad* he was simply talking to her as if she were, say, the wife of a friend or a colleague, or even a middle-aged woman. Because of course she wouldn't want him to talk to her as if she were a female he found attractive or wanted to make up to, would she?

Of course not, she told herself firmly. So, keeping that clear in her mind, she answered now, as they made their way into the foyer, 'I thought she was pretty good all round. At first I kept only seeing her as a "star," but after a while I just saw her as her character, and I thought she did it better than one might have expected.'

'Interesting,' he commented, 'that she took the role of the oldest and dowdiest sister—when her Hollywood parts are always so glamorous.'

'I expect she thought it was the most challenging part,' she answered lightly. 'Playing against type.'

His response was 'Yes, very probably,' and then he made a comment about another of the cast. As they walked out onto the pavement, the chilly air hitting her, he guided her towards the left.

'I do hope,' she heard him say, 'that you will agree to having a post-theatre dinner with me? I find that an evening performance is never best timed to eat either before or after.'

She felt her arm being taken. Not in a possessive way, let alone in any kind of intimate way, but simply lightly, cupping her elbow to guide her along the pavement. Guiding her where he wanted her to go.

For a moment she felt she ought to refuse, then she gave a mental shrug. She was hungry, and since she'd already gone to the theatre with him what harm would there be in going on to a restaurant? Besides, she wanted to talk about the play, and if she just went home there would be no one to talk to.

There never was, apart from Ian.

A pang went through her but she thrust it aside. She was lucky—beyond lucky!—to have Ian in her life now, and as for making friends in London—well, that was entirely up to her. She would volunteer for a charity, start up exercise classes, possibly evening classes as well—why not? And she'd soon have friends here—of course she could. She had a brand-new life, courtesy of Ian, and she would make the very most of it.

The restaurant Athan Teodarkis took her to was only a short walk from the theatre. It wasn't, she was glad to see, either a very crowded, popular one, or a quiet, intimate one. There were a fair number of other diners there, but the lighting was not conducive to romantic dining *à deux*, and she felt reassured. Post-theatre seduction was evidently *not*, thank goodness, on her escort's mind.

All that *was* on his mind, it seemed, was ordering from the menu, choosing wine, and then being perfectly prepared to discuss the production they'd just seen.

'I have to admit,' he opined, having nodded to the sommelier to fill their glasses and taken an appreciative mouthful of the wine, 'that the play did irritate me in respect of the sisters' endless preoccupation with wanting to go to Moscow but never going. I kept finding myself wanting to shout *Just buy a train ticket!*'

Marisa gave the requisite smile in response, but then said ruminatively, 'But if you're not used to travel, and you've always lived in one place, then going to a big city can be very daunting.'

Athan's eyes rested on her a moment. 'You sound like you speak from experience?'

'Well, yes, I do. Up until recently I'd never left Devon. It sounds odd, in this day and age, but I'd never been to London.' It was an admission she suddenly felt unsure about making, as if revealing it might put him off her. But it didn't seem to.

'What made you come here?' His voice was neutral.

She gave a little shrug. 'Oh, wanting to see the bright lights and so on. Usual reasons, really.'

The nonchalance in her voice did not deceive him. Yet he found himself unable to decide what was the cause of it. On the most cynical interpretation it could be, a blithe glossing over of an ambition to come up to London and catch the attention of a wealthy man…just as she had with his brother-in-law. But he had to acknowledge it might also be, simply because she felt that being seen as a country girl didn't go with her sophisticated image.

Not that she was presenting a sophisticated image tonight, he also had to acknowledge. He'd been unable to suppress a flicker of slight surprise when he'd first set eyes on her and taken in her outfit for the evening. *Demure* had been the word that came to his mind, and it was an odd one for a female who was happy for a married man to lavish his money on her.

Once again he felt a flicker of emotion go through him. He was glad she hadn't taken the opportunity to dress to kill this evening, to attempt openly to wow him. Instead, the fact that she was playing down her natural beauty was, he realised, really quite appealing...

He made another comment about the performance, drawing another response in kind from her, and by the time their first course arrived he was aware that he was, against his expectations, enjoying talking to her. Her views were intelligent and informed, and she revealed a sensitivity to the play's characters' various dilemmas that showed she understood the complexities of their situations—even that of the sisters' feckless brother.

'I suppose the brother is the least sympathetic character,' she was saying, 'though I suppose one has to allow that he made a disastrous marriage and make some excuses for him.'

Athan stilled. 'Does an unhappy marriage excuse bad behaviour?' He knew there was nothing audible in his voice other than dispassionate enquiry. His mouth, however, had tightened. However insightful she might be about Chekov, it didn't blind him to the fact that she was still in the dock about the way she chose to live her private life.

'Sometimes, perhaps,' Marisa said slowly. 'The second sister, Masha, wouldn't have had an affair if she'd been happily married, would she?'

'And that exonerates her, does it?'

Now the edge was audible in his voice, and Marisa looked across at him.

'I think it depends on each individual situation,' she said.

There was a shadow in her eyes as she spoke, and Athan did not miss it.

So, was that what she was telling herself? he thought. That Ian Randall was unhappily married, so that gave him—and her—*carte blanche* to have an affair?

'Do you think Masha's husband was right to forgive her?' His question was blunt.

'Well, divorce was probably impossible in those days, wasn't it? He would just have to make the best of things, I guess.'

Athan reached for his wine. 'Ah, yes, divorce—a very convenient option.'

Marisa looked at him. 'But not one that's always taken,' she said.

She looked away again. This wasn't a subject she wanted to discuss. It was too close, too painful, and the arrival of their main course was a welcome interruption.

As the waiters departed she picked up her knife and fork and said, deliberately seeking a new topic, 'What brings *you* to London?'

Her voice was bright and enquiring. Glancing at her, realising she was deliberately steering him away from a subject that was obviously too close to the bone for her, Athan momentarily wondered how she would react if he told her the truth: *I'm here to stop you having an adulterous affair with Ian Randall...my brother-in-law.*

Instead, of course, he responded in a similar vein to her conversational opening.

'Unlike the three sisters, I travel extensively for my work. I'm primarily based in Athens, but the company is international and travel goes with the ticket.'

A wistful look entered her eyes. 'That must be wonderful,' she said.

He gave a mordant smile. 'It can get tedious,' he answered.

'One airport is very much like another in the end—and offices are very similar wherever in the world they are.'

'Yes, I suppose it palls after a while.'

He looked at her speculatively. 'Why don't you try it some time—travel? If you'll excuse me saying so, you have the means to do so, don't you?'

Living in a Holland Park flat as she did, wearing the expensive closthes she did, it was a reasonable assumption for him to make—assuming, of course, he didn't know that she was *not* a free agent and that her accommodation and wardrobe were provided by a lover who was London-based and would want to keep his mistress close by and not gadding about abroad.

Her response confirmed that assessment of her situation.

A hesitant expression flitted across her face. 'Oh, it would be a bit difficult at the moment. But, yes, perhaps one day—it would be wonderful to see other countries.'

'What would be your first choice?' he asked. An idea was forming in his mind, but he needed more information first.

She glanced out of the window at the wintry rain that had started to descend through the streetlights.

'Anywhere with a tropical beach!' she said with a laugh.

He gave a light, answering laugh. 'Yes, I can see the appeal.'

She looked at him. 'You must be used to hot weather?'

'Contrary to popular opinion, Athens can have very cold weather sometimes,' he said wryly. 'At this time of year you'd need to go a lot further south to find any warmth, let alone tropical beaches.'

Even as he spoke his mind was racing ahead. Would it be feasible, what he'd just thought of? It would take some reorganisation, but it could certainly be done. Best of all, a cold, cynical part of his brain told him, it would be something she could not lie about afterwards. If he had to he could demonstrably prove to Ian that the woman he wanted to make his mistress had preferred another man to him.

She was speaking again, saying something about dream holiday destinations, and he turned his attention back to her. Her expression was more animated now, as if she were losing the guard that she'd put up against him all evening.

Was it deliberate, this lightening up, or was she unconscious of it?

Whichever it is, animation only makes her yet more beautiful.

As she spoke his gaze rested on her. Sitting across a dining table from her like this, he could see exactly why Ian Randall was so smitten with her. She could have been wearing a sack, for all her appearance was seeking to mute her beauty. Hers was a beauty that shone like a star.

Can I really go through with this?

The unwelcome question uncoiled again in his mind, troubling him. It had seemed easy enough when he'd decided this was the best, fastest and most irreversible way of terminating her relationship with Ian. But now that he was only a few feet away from her, dining with her, talking with her...drinking in her blonde, perfect beauty...was it really such a good idea? Were there hidden dangers that he did not see ahead of him?

He pushed the thought aside ruthlessly. Of course there was no danger—not to him. He would do what he intended, achieve what he'd set out to do, and then walk away, his purpose accomplished. Unscathed. Of course unscathed.

Why would he even be thinking of anything else?

Not the way her cheekbones seem to be sculpted out of alabaster, or the blue of her eyes seems to catch the reflection of a tranquil sea, or her mouth seems as tender as a newly ripe peach...

He tore his mind away from cataloguing her physical attributes and back to what she was talking about. He realised he had no idea what she'd just said.

'I'm sorry—you were saying...?' he said.

She seemed to have faltered to a stop, and he wondered

at it. Then he realised she was simply looking at him. A faint colour was staining her cheekbones—*those cheekbones carved from alabaster*, he thought, then pushed it aside. Her eyelashes swept down over her eyes, veiling their expression. But it was too late—he'd seen it, recognised it…

Knew it for what it was.

Marisa felt heat flare in her face, dipped her gaze swiftly. But she knew it was too late. Knew that she hadn't been able to disguise her reaction to the way he'd just been looking at her. The power of his gaze, the message clear and unambiguous in his eyes. She felt hot, then shivery, as if one moment her blood was heating in her veins, and the next it had drained from her, pooling somewhere very deep inside her. She felt a breathlessness, a constriction in her throat, a hectic beating of her heart.

She fought for composure. It wasn't supposed to happen! This wasn't supposed to be anything like this. She was here with him only because he'd invited her to the theatre, then to dinner afterwards—it wasn't a date, not in the romance sense. Of course it wasn't!

He's a stranger! I don't know him!

But she knew enough.

Enough to tell her that when he looked at her he was looking at her not as someone to accompany him to a play or to talk to him about it afterwards.

All that stuff she'd told herself about how he was behaving like she was the wife of a friend, or a colleague, or a middle aged woman…it mocked her—made a fool of her self-pretence.

Jerkily, she got on with eating. That was what she must do—focus on the meal, on getting to the end of it. Making herself chit-chat about anything and nothing—it didn't really matter what.

And don't look at him—not like that. Ignore him—make myself ignore him—if he looks at me.

It took self-discipline and effort—a lot of effort—but she managed to stick to her resolve. For the rest of the meal she made light, bright conversation, doggedly not meeting his eyes, not gazing at him, not paying any attention at all to the way his eyes seemed to be flecked with gold, or the way lines formed around his mouth when he smiled, or the way his head turned, the way his strong, long-fingered hands curved around the stem of his wine glass, or the way his deep, accented voice played on her nerve-endings like the low bass notes of a song that pulsed slow and heavy in her veins…

But it was as if there were two of her. One that was doing the light, bright chit-chat and another, watching from inside, wanting to do what she was not allowing herself to do. To drink him in, feel the power of his physicality, his presence, his impact on her.

In the taxi back to Holland Park she was as jittery as a cat, sliding to the far side of the seat, deliberately putting her handbag down beside her, as if to form a barricade against him, and then leaping out of the cab as fast as she could when they alighted. She kept up the hectic, inconsequential chatter as they ascended in the lift, ignoring—doggedly ignoring!—the fact that they were enclosed in a small, six-by-six box with no one else, alone together, and the moment the lift doors opened she was out in the corridor and turning towards him.

'Thank you so much for a lovely evening,' she said, in the light, bright voice she had kept up so determinedly. 'It was so kind of you—I really enjoyed myself.' She put a bright social smile on her face. 'Goodnight,' she said airily.

Athan looked down at her. OK, so she was holding him off. Keeping him at bay. Well, he would go along with it—for now.

He gave her the faint half-smile he'd used before. 'Goodnight, Marisa—I'm glad you enjoyed yourself. So did I.'

There was nothing in his voice or his expression to show her that he was playing along with her, but he was sure he saw her colour deepen fractionally before she turned away and got her key out of her bag to open her front door. Did she fumble slightly as she did so? And was that for the reason he wanted it to be? He watched her open the door and step inside, her hand lifting in a little half-wave of farewell as she shut the door on him.

For a moment or two he stood looking at her closed apartment door, his own face closed as well. Eyes masked. Thoughts went through his head. Conflicting, disturbing thoughts that were a waste of his time. That interfered with his purpose.

Then, with an abrupt turn on his heel, he strode down to his own apartment, and went inside.

He had made it to first base with her, just as he'd planned. Now it was a question of taking it to the next stage.

The idea he'd had during dinner flared again in his head. It was attractive, simple, decisive—and it would sever her, unquestionably from Ian Randall, in the shortest possible time.

He was quite some distance from it yet—there was more preparation to do. A lot more. But when it was complete Marisa Milburne would never be available to his brother-in-law again.

'Aren't you going to open it?'

Athan's voice held its familiar note of faint amusement as she stared down at the envelope he'd placed in front of her at their table in the restaurant. Marisa knew that tone of voice by now. It made him sound as if he found her behaviour funny but he chose to indulge it. Chose to indulge the way she behaved with him.

As if what was happening wasn't happening at all. As if she hadn't for the past two weeks held him at arm's length. Not that he'd tried to close the distance. She had to allow him that—and be appreciative of it. Of course if he *had* tried to close the distance she would have bolted instantly. Of course she would! If he'd made a move on her, flirted with her, come on to her, she'd have backed away—retreated out of reach.

But he hadn't. For a start, for several days after their theatre date she hadn't even set eyes on him. Well, that was understandable. It had been the weekend, and he'd probably gone back to Athens. Or spent his time with someone else.

Who else?

The moment she'd asked the question, she had supplied the answer. A woman, of course—someone svelte, glamorous and gorgeous. A supermodel, a high-powered career woman, a glittering socialite…her mind had run through the possibilities. Not someone like her—a quiet, provincial girl who didn't move in the kind of circles a man like him would move in. She was someone he'd taken to the theatre on the spur of the moment because he'd had no one else to take to such a play, and that was all. Not that she was asking for more— of course she wasn't. But it was as well to face the facts— a female who lived on her own, didn't go out anywhere, and was new to London didn't usually get to hang out with sinfully good-looking Greek tycoons.

The theatre date had been a one-off. That was the obvious conclusion. And the one she'd wanted. Hadn't she? Of course she had—hadn't she spent the whole evening reminding herself he was a complete stranger?

Except when she'd got back home in her flat again she'd realised she'd enjoyed the evening. Not just because it had been so nice to go to the theatre with someone else, but because his company had been so good. Oh, not only because he was so ludicrously good looking, but because it had been interesting to talk to him, to exchange views on the play with him. It had been mentally stimulating, and the discussion they'd had still buzzed in her head.

Spending that weekend on her own—she had accepted she could never see Ian at the weekends, for that was the time he spent with his wife—had brought home to her just how isolated she felt here in London, however easy and luxurious her life. Her resolve to get some sort of voluntary work, try and make friends, had strengthened, and on the Monday she'd headed for the nearest charity shop and enquired about volunteering. Then she'd investigated dance classes nearby, and signed up for those as well. But her good mood had been dashed later that day, when Ian had phoned. Yet again he wouldn't be able to meet her. He hadn't even known when he could be free to see her again—maybe later that week, maybe not.

He'd been apologetic, she'd been understanding. Of course she had. His job was demanding, especially at the moment, and there were a lot more demands on his time than work—including from his wife. That was understandable. It was all understandable.

But as he'd rung off, having cancelled yet another lunchtime with her, she'd felt depression pluck at her. When the phone had rung again, a little while later, and a deep accented voice had spoken, she'd felt her spirits lift in reaction.

'This is completely on the off chance,' Athan Teodarkis's distinctively accented voice had said, 'but would you have any interest in seeing *Hamlet* at the National? Or have you already been?'

'I'd love to!' she said immediately.

His voice warmed. 'Excellent. Would Thursday suit?'

For a moment Marisa hesitated. Thursday was usually the evening that Ian was able to meet her without arousing his wife's suspicions. Eva went to her book club that day and wouldn't be aware he'd returned late, or would accept that he'd just been at the office. But his phone call earlier had already warned her that this week he really would be stuck at the office, burning the midnight oil on a complex deal he was closely involved with.

He'll probably be relieved if I make another arrange-

ment. He won't feel bad about not being able to see me, she reasoned.

A second later she gave Athan Teodarkis his answer.

The answer he wanted, the answer he'd intended to extract from her. He'd deliberately let her cool her heels over the weekend, knowing that Ian Randall never saw her at that time. For once—Athan's lip curled—he'd be playing the devoted husband.

But with the weekend over he'd known he needed to target Marisa Milburne again, and continue with his strategy to part her from her married swain.

As with the Chekov, *Hamlet* was followed by dinner, over which their discussion of the production predominated. Yet again Marisa made sure she was wearing the kind of outfit that wouldn't scream *Find me attractive!* and yet again Athan Teodarkis behaved scrupulously towards her, bidding her a chaste goodnight at her door once again.

Expecting another solitary weekend, Marisa was surprised when her doorbell sounded just before midday the following Sunday

'It's a glorious sunny day—can I persuade you to lunch at the Belvedere in Holland Park?' Athan Teodarkis invited.

Her face lit. 'Oh, that sounds wonderful! I've never been there.'

He smiled—that increasingly familiar quirking of his well-shaped mouth. 'Then I must definitely take you. It's memorable.'

She took a breath. 'This time it's on me. I insist you must be my guest for a change.'

His expression stilled. For a moment Marisa thought she had offended him. Then, his eyes still veiled, he gave a distinct shake of his head.

'That's not in the least necessary,' he said, and there was a clipped note to his voice.

Marisa looked at him uncertainly. There seemed to be a

shadow in his eyes. She couldn't quite see into them. A little chill went through her.

Then it was gone. 'Cook me a meal one evening,' he said. 'Simple fare will do me fine. Oh, and I can show you how to work that coffee machine of yours!'

'OK,' she said slowly, not sure whether it was still that momentary chill that disturbed her, or the prospect of Athan Teodarkis coming into her apartment, eating dinner there...

Had she really felt that chill? she wondered later, as they set off for Holland Park.

Athan set a brisk pace and she kept up with it—walking was one thing, after her rural upbringing, where transport was sparse and the wilds of Dartmoor were close at hand, she had become inured her to. It was, as he had said, a glorious day—but very cold. She was glad of her pure wool jacket and warm leather boots as they walked through the park towards the restaurant, which was situated in the ballroom that was almost all that was left of the grand Holland House that had once stood there.

She wished she'd brought a pair of sunglasses, as Athan had. As she glanced sideways at him she could feel her insides do a little somersault. What was it about dark glasses that made him look so...so even *more* than he already looked in spades!

She snapped her head away. He was glancing down at her, she was sure of it, and being caught gazing at him was *not* what she wanted. Did his mouth give that familiar quirk? she wondered. To cover herself, she started talking. 'I do love Holland Park, even at this time of year. It's a real haven. I come here all the time. It's such a shame that Holland House itself got bombed in the war—all that's left is enough for a youth hostel. And the Orangery, where the Belvedere restaurant is, of course. Apparently there's an opera season in the summer. All outdoors. It must be wonderful on a warm summer's night!'

She was babbling, but she couldn't help it. He didn't seem to mind, though, and made an appropriate response to what she'd said, and they continued chatting as they made their way towards the restaurant.

The setting was indeed memorable—an eighteenth century summer ballroom, with beautiful long windows all around that let the winter sunshine pour in. And lunch was superb. Marisa wondered again whether to offer to pay, for she felt bad eating at his expense a third time, but found she dared not mention it again. He would take offence, she was sure. It was probably something he just wasn't used to. Even so, she felt she ought to insist, and it made her feel very slightly uncomfortable.

Apart from that, however, Marisa found she was the most comfortable yet in his company. He was, she realised with a little start, no longer a stranger…

She didn't know much about him personally—but then they weren't really talking about personal things. She was glad. She obviously couldn't discuss Ian, but she also didn't want to talk about her life in Devon. It was behind her now—she would not be going back. She felt a little flush go through her. Besides, Athan Teodarkis clearly saw her as a young woman of independent means, who lived in a plush apartment and wore expensive clothes. What would he think of her if he knew she'd been brought up in a run down cottage by an impoverished single mother who'd struggled to keep their heads above water?

But all that was a universe away from the way she lived now. She looked about her at the beautiful, expensive restaurant serving the most exquisite food, looked at the man she was lunching with, who headed up his own personal international company and casually talked about going to places in private jets and chauffeur-driven cars, and having an army of minions at his disposal. His sunglasses had a famous logo on them and his gold wristwatch was, she knew, a priceless heirloom. Athan Teodarkis had *rich* written all over him...

Sleek, assured, cosmopolitan, sophisticated.

Devastating...

A little thrill went through her. A susurration of awareness that of all the women in the world he could be choosing to spend his Sunday with it was her.

This was no one-off, no convenient using up of a theatre ticket. This was, she knew with a flutter of butterflies in her stomach, a genuine invitation to her personally. Because he wanted her company.

It was the only conclusion she could come to—and she came to the same conclusion over the following week, when he took her to a concert at the Royal Festival Hall and a production of *Twelfth Night*.

And invited himself to dinner at her flat.

She could hardly refuse, since she'd tacitly agreed that it was to be the way she would return all the dining out she'd done with him—not to mention the theatre tickets. Even so, she was very nervous. And not just because she had no idea what to cook that a man like him could possibly want to eat. Her culinary skills were entirely basic.

She admitted as much to his face, and was relieved when he smiled.

'Actually, I was hoping you might see your way to a traditional English roast,' he said.

'I think I can stretch to that,' she said, adding hopefully, 'How do you feel about apple crumble for pudding?' Along with roast dinners, pies and pastries were the one thing her mother had taught her.

'Crumble?' he quizzed.

'Pastry without water!' she exclaimed. 'Loads easier!'

So it proved—and so did the rest of the meal, including the company. She'd done her best to provide a traditional English roast, and he certainly seemed very appreciative of it. For herself, though, her stomach was full of butterflies—and not because she was worried the meal was not up to his standards.

It was because he was sitting at the dining table in her apartment and there was no one else around. Oh, she could tell herself all she liked that she was behaving with him no differently than if he hadn't been a drop-dead gorgeous male who raised her heart-rate just by quirking his half-smile at her, but she knew it wasn't true. Knew that for all her deliberately dressing in a cowl-necked jumper and jeans, with minimal make-up and her hair in a casual ponytail, she was all too aware that Athan Teodarkis was having a powerful impact on her.

Knew that she was having an increasingly hard time in keeping that awareness at bay, and was wondering just why she had to...

By strength of will she managed to get through to the end of the meal, keeping up a semblance of unresponsiveness to him, behaving outwardly as if he *weren't* having the kind of impact on her that he was. She wasn't sure just why she felt it was so vital to do so, only knew that it was.

I can't lower my guard—I just can't!

But it was getting harder—much, much harder.

Out in the kitchen after the apple crumble—which she'd served with custard and clotted cream and had had the satisfaction of seeing him polish off up, though just where it had gone on his lean, powerful frame she had no idea—he tackled the fearsome coffee machine, calling her over to explain the mechanism to her.

She was far too close to him. Far too close, his hand was pointing out the controls, his shoulders were almost brushing hers, his hip jutting against hers. His face was far too close as he turned to explain something to her. She jerked away, pulse leaping.

Had he noticed? Noticed the way she had drawn away and started to gabble something to cover her nerves? Something about how she loved cappuccino but hated espresso. She didn't think he had—or at any rate, he didn't show that he had, and that was what was important. That he didn't think she was getting ideas about him.

Flustered, she busied herself retrieving coffee cups from one of the cupboards and setting the tray. She carried the tray through and set it down on the coffee table, sat herself squarely on the armchair, leaving the whole expanse of the sofa opposite for him. No way was she going to let him think she wanted him up close and personal beside her.

Did he smile faintly as he saw where she'd sat herself? She wasn't sure and didn't want to think about it. Wanted only, as they drank coffee accompanied by music of her choice— some brisk, scintillating Vivaldi, definitely nothing soft and romantic—to get to a point where she could smother a yawn, thank him for coming and wait for him to take his leave.

Because that was what she wanted, wasn't it? Of course it was! Anything else was unthinkable—quite unthinkable. Unthinkable to covertly watch him drinking his coffee— rich and fragrant now that it was no longer instant—with one long leg crossed casually over another, his light blue cashmere sweater stretched across his chest so that she could almost discern the outline of his honed pecs and broad shoulders, his sable hair glinting in the lamplight, and the faintest dark shadow along his jawline that made her out of nowhere wonder what it would feel like to ease her fingertips along its chiselled line...

She blinked, horrified at herself.

This had to stop, right now! She mustn't start getting ideas—ideas that involved her and Athan Teodarkis up close and personal. The trouble was, that was exactly what was happening as they sat there, chatting about this and that, with him so obviously relaxed, like a cat that had dined well, and her curled up on the wide armchair opposite, with good red Burgundy coursing slowly through her veins and the low light

from the table lamps, and the Vivaldi now changing to something a lot slower, more meditative and soothing…

Seductive…

He was looking at her, his dark, opaque eyes resting on
her, with a veiled expression in them. Conversation seemed
to have died away, desultory as it was, and Marisa tried to
make a show of listening to the music.

Not looking at Athan.

Not taking in the way the light and shadow played with
the planes of his features, the way his broad shoulders were
moulding to the deep cushions of the sofa, or the way his
long, jeans-clad legs seemed lean and lithe, how his fingers
were curled around the coffee cup, shaping it as if they were
cupping her face…

There was a knot inside her. A knot of intense feeling
like a physical sensation. As if she couldn't move. Couldn't
do anything except sit there, her hands splayed on the wide
arms of the chair, her breathing shallow, her heart tumbling
around inside her.

His eyes held hers, and her own eyes widened—dilated.
Something changed in his. Flared with sudden light.

She jack-knifed to her feet.

'Oh, my goodness!' she exclaimed, her voice slightly too
high-pitched. 'I…I think I left the oven on. I can't remember
turning it off when I took out the apple crumble. What an
idiot I am! I'd better go and check—'

She hurried out to the kitchen. She hadn't left the oven on.
She knew she hadn't. But she'd had to break the moment. Had
to stop what was starting to happen. Because…

Because—

Because if he stays…

But she mustn't think about what would happen if he
stayed. Must only head back into the sitting room, smile
brightly and say how late it was.

Which she did. And she stayed standing, making it pointedly obvious that she expected Athan to stand likewise. Which he did. But she was all too aware he did so with a kind of suppressed amusement, as if he knew perfectly well why she'd suddenly become so animated and hyper. He strolled towards the door, pausing when he got there. She trotted after him, mouthing politenesses which he replied to with an appropriate murmur. But when he turned back to her she could see, quite disastrously, that glint in his eye.

'Sleep well,' he said.

His voice was low, and his accent more pronounced. Or maybe she was just more sensitive to it.

'Yes. Thank you.' Her reply was staccato. More high pitched than her normal voice. She felt wired, with adrenaline coursing through her. Why didn't he go? Walk out the door?

Stop looking at her like that.

For one long, endless moment he seemed to be just letting his gaze rest on her. She couldn't tell what he was thinking—knew only that if it was what she thought he was thinking he could just *un*-think it. Because—well, just *because,* that was all.

She'd think about why afterwards. But not now. Definitely not now when, as if in slow motion, she saw his hand reach out towards her, felt his fingers graze her cheek, so lightly, so incredibly and devastatingly lightly. It was a moment only—scarcely there, hardly enough time to register it. But it made her skin glow, and even after his hand had dropped away it was as if he was still touching her.

He smiled. A deep, amused smile. Still holding her helpless gaze.

Almost she went to him—almost she took that tiny fatal half-step towards him. She knew with absolute, searing certainty that he would draw her to him and lower his mouth to hers...

Almost—

But not quite.

Summoning all her failing strength, she stepped away. 'Goodnight,' she said.

Long lashes swept down over his eyes, veiling his regard. The glint was gone. Vanished. 'Goodnight,' he answered. His voice was nothing more than polite now—cool, even. Then, with a brief nod of his head, he was gone.

Outside in the corridor, with her apartment door firmly shut, he strode down towards his own flat. His face was closed. Troubled.

He wanted her. He knew that. Impossible to deny it. He desired the beautiful, demurely alluring woman who was Marisa Milburne. Desired her whether or not she was anything at all to do with his brother-in-law's lamentable weakness of character.

Oh, he'd known from the first moment of seeing her photo that it would be no hardship to him to seduce her for his own purposes. But with every encounter with her, every date, he'd come to know more and more that he was wishing she had never got herself mixed up with Ian. And not just for his sister's sake.

It was for his own.

I want her for myself—with no other complications, no strategy or plots or machinations or ulterior motives.

Heaviness filled him. It didn't matter what he wanted for himself, he thought savagely. What he did he did for Eva. That was what he had to remember. That was all he had to remember.

And time was running out. He would have only a brief window while Ian and Eva were away together in the USA to achieve his aim of seducing Marisa Milburne and taking her away from his brother-in-law.

Which was why he was now, two days after the Sunday roast in her apartment, sitting here in a restaurant off Holland Park Avenue, waiting for her to open the white envelope he'd proffered.

Marisa was still gazing down at it. She'd accepted the dinner invitation only with reluctance. She had to stop this. She really did. She was getting in too deep.

She had managed the previous day, right after her dangerous dinner *à deux* with Athan Teodarkis in her apartment, finally to meet up with Ian for lunch. His face had told her what she'd dreaded hearing.

'I have to go to San Francisco. I can't get out of it. There's no one else that can handle it, and I've had my marching orders from the top.'

Her face had fallen. 'How long for, do you think?'

'I'm not sure—at least a week, probably more,' he'd said apologetically. 'The thing is…' He took a breath, looked even more apologetic. 'Eva's got the idea of turning it into a holiday—flying on from SF to Hawaii. So I could easily be away three weeks or more.'

Even as he'd said 'Hawaii' she'd felt a pang of envy dart through her.

Hawaii…tropical beaches…palm trees…silver sand…

But it would not be *her* there. She was stuck in London—where the weather had turned vicious. The bright but cold sunshine that had filled the Holland Park Orangery had given way to a miserable, dull and biting cold, with a low cloud base and an icy wind. Spring seemed a long way off. Even just getting out of the cab when she and Athan had arrived at the restaurant had set the wind whipping around her stockinged legs. Now she sat with her legs slanted against the radiator against which their table was situated.

'Well?' prompted Athan, indicating the envelope. There was an expression in his eyes she could not read.

It looked, she thought curiously, like anticipation.

She turned her attention back to the envelope he so wanted her to open. Carefully she slit it with a table knife and shook out the contents. As she did so, her eyes widened.

'You said you wanted a tropical beach,' she heard him murmur.

But she was gazing, rapt, at the leaflet that was lying there. A palm tree, an azure sea, a silvered beach, and in the background a low-rise, thatch-roofed resort, fronted by a vast swimming pool even more azure than the lapping sea.

Projecting from the leaflet were two airline tickets.

'Come with me,' said Athan.

His voice was soft. Intimate. Persuasive.

Marisa lifted her head to look at him—and drowned.

Drowned in what she saw in his eyes, unmasked, unveiled…

Her lips parted, the breath stilling in her throat.

Her hand was taken, folded into his. It was the first time he'd touched her so deliberately—only in that first, formal raising of her hand to his lips, that faint, brief grazing of his fingertips against her cheek, had he ever made contact with her. But this—this warm, strong hand-clasp—seemed to envelop her whole being, not just her hand lying there inert, helpless in his grasp.

'Come with me,' he said again. 'Be with me.'

Emotion rushed through her like heady wine in her veins. Like a cloud of butterflies suddenly taking flight inside her. His clasp strengthened and his thumb stroked along the edge of her palm. Intimately. Possessively.

His eyes poured into hers. So dark, so deep, flecked with gold that glinted in the candlelight, that drowned her, sweeping her away.

His thumb indented into the soft flesh of her palm. She could feel its pressure, feel the power of his touch—its persuasion.

'Say yes—it's all I ask.'

Hadn't she always known this must happen? Hadn't she felt it from the moment she'd set eyes on him? Hadn't her heart skipped and her blood pulsed, her breath caught? Hadn't she known every time she'd been with him that this was what she wanted—dreamt of—desired?

He saw her yielding. Saw her features soften, her eyes fill with a lambent lustre that told him everything he wanted to know. Triumph filled him. He had got her—finally. She would not refuse him now. She would not continue to hold him at bay, to treat him as if he were forbidden fruit. Now she would yield to him—taste the fruit he offered her.

And he—oh, he would do likewise. He would take this time with her and make her his own. Put aside, even if only for a brief few weeks, all his worries about his sister and her troubled marriage, put aside all his fears for her, his doubts about her fickle husband.

For now—just for now—he would do what every moment with Marisa had confirmed to him. That what he wanted was her—all to himself.

Away from everything that cast a damning shadow over her.

Just the two of them—together.

Only that.

CHAPTER THREE

'WHAT do you think? Worth the long-haul flight?'

The familiar note of amusement was in Athan's voice as he posed his question. He knew what the answer would be. Had known it from the moment they'd landed, stepped out into the balmy, tropical heat seven thousand miles south west from bleak, icy London. Knew it now, as they stood side by side on the little wooden veranda of their beachside cabana.

Marisa turned to gaze at him. 'How can you ask?' she breathed. Then she turned back again. Back to look at the scene in front of her.

It was exactly like the photo in the brochure—but real. And she was *here*—here in the middle of it all! Like a dream—a wonderful, exotic dream.

And the Caribbean beach—silver sanded, backed with palms swaying in the gentle calypso breeze that rustled the scarlet hibiscus and the fragrant frangipani blooms—was not the only dream come true.

So was the man at her side.

She could feel her breath catch as it had caught over and over again during their journey here, cocooned in first class seats. Her eyes had been wide with the excitement not just of travelling abroad for the first time, or because it was first class, with all the pandering and luxury that came with it, but most of all because of the man sitting beside her.

She had made the right decision in accepting his invitation to come here. She knew it—felt it. For how could it be otherwise? How could she possibly have resisted what he'd offered her? The question was rhetorical; her answer was a given. It was impossible to resist Athan Teodarkis! Impossible to resist his invitation—both to this wonderful holiday with him and, she thought, with a shiver of quivering awareness, to what else he was inviting.

There had been, it was true, a momentary pang when she'd thought of Ian—but it had been swiftly quenched. Ian was far away—and if her alternative was to stay languishing in London, without him, what was to hold her there when she might be here...on this palm-fringed tropical beach?

With Athan.

Day after day, every time she met with him, her response to him intensified. She became more and more vividly aware of the effect he could have on her. It might be foolish, it might be rash—but it was so powerful this rush that came whenever she thought of him, whenever she was with him.

I can't resist him—can't resist what he's offering me. I can't...

And for this brief idyllic time, here in this tropical paradise he'd brought her to, she would resist nothing of what he offered her.

She gave a little sigh of pleasure at the view ahead of her—the time with Athan ahead of her. Happiness filled her, and a wonderful sense of carefreeness. Whatever else was complicated or difficult or troubling in her life this time was not going to be part of. This time was for her—and for the man she was with so willingly.

'I'm glad not to disappoint,' he said.

For a long, bewitching moment his eyes caressed her. Then, as if reluctantly, his expression changed.

'What would you like to do first?' he asked.

She had no hesitation as she answered, 'I can't resist that sea! It's calling out to me!'

He gave a laugh. 'And to me. OK—let's hit the beach, then.'

He ushered her indoors and she stepped through into the shady interior of the cabana. It was designed as if it were a simple, palm-roofed hut, but it was a simplicity that belied a level of luxury that went with the whole ambience of the resort.

On the flight over Athan had regaled her about the island and what awaited them there.

'St Cecile has been fortunate to escape mass tourism,' he'd told her. 'It's a little too off the beaten track, so until recently it's been something of a backwater. But to my mind that's all to the good. In the last ten years or so there has been some very careful development for tourism, but at the most upmarket end, so the handful of resorts are well separated from each other, and beautifully sited and landscaped. It's a little gem of an island, to my mind.'

Even without anything to compare it with, having seen it, Marisa could only wholeheartedly agree. It was like stepping into one of those luxury travel magazines, she thought. A place most people could never visit.

And I am! she thought, with another little rush of excitement.

With a companion anyone would swoon over...

She slipped into the bedroom. As they had followed the bellhop from the main resort building along sandy, shell-lined paths amongst the palm trees and entered their cabana she had felt a little flutter of nerves on seeing the one bedroom. Somehow it had made very real just what this holiday would entail.

So was it nerves she had felt, or a flutter of excitement? Anticipation?

She felt it again now, as she searched through her suitcase for her bikini. She had bought it in a mad hectic rush spent raiding the West End stores the day before flying out, and now, as she looked at it lying on the counterpane, she felt another flurry of nerves. In the changing room she had felt brave about it—its brevity had seemed entirely right for such an exotic destination. But now, realising that she was about to don it and emerge in it, displaying herself to a man who up till now had only seen her in high-coverage winter clothes, it was unnerving to say the least.

Nevertheless, she had bought it to be worn and to be seen in it. Even so, before she emerged on to the veranda she draped a matching voile sarong around her, which gave her a layer of veiling she was thankful for when, some moments later, Athan emerged as well.

His eyes went to her immediately, visibly drinking her in. For all the fine voile veiling her, she still felt acutely revealed. But if Athan were drinking *her* in, she had to acknowledge she was doing exactly the same to him. He was wearing a pair of hip-hugging dark blue boardies, and his torso was completely exposed. Marisa felt her eyes widen automatically.

Bare-chested, Athan was everything she'd imagined him to be—and more. Lean packed, with not an ounce of spare flesh on him, yet not overtly muscular. His smooth, tanned skin moulded over taut muscle, planed down over perfect pecs and delineated abs to arrow towards the low-slung waistband of his board shorts.

She dragged her gaze away.

'Race you to the sea!' she exclaimed, with slightly forced gaiety.

She turned to descend the wide shallow steps that led down to a path to the sea, a dozen metres or so beyond, set between palm trees framing the vista. But a hand stayed her, catching her shoulder.

'Wait—have you got sunblock on?'

She twisted her head back. 'Yes—loads.'

He nodded. 'Good. It's essential in this latitude. My skin

can take more exposure than yours, being naturally darker, but even so I have to use it copiously. You—' his eyes washed over her '—with your English rose complexion, must be totally protected. It would be sacrilege,' he told her, his voice changing suddenly so that it seemed to caress her as much as his eyes, 'to burn such pale, tender skin.'

As he spoke his touch at her shoulder softened, echoing the caress of his eyes and voice. She felt her pulse skip a beat, butterflies flutter in her stomach.

'OK, let's race!' He dropped his hand and surged forward, vaulting down the steps to the sandy pathway.

'Cheat!' she called out indignantly, and unfastening her wrap started after him.

Inevitably he reached the sea first and plunged in, diving headfirst into the aqua water as soon as he was barely waist-deep. Moments later she followed suit, feeling the water close like liquid silk over her. She surfaced, hair streaming down her bare back, water droplets glistening like diamonds all over her body.

Athan could only stare. It was impossible not to. *Thee mou*, but she was glorious. Like a sea nymph, a nereid foam-born as the translucent water washed around her—and as divinely beautiful as such a creature of ancient myth.

He had known right from the first that she was beautiful, and had seen with his own eyes that her figure was perfect, but to see it all now, so gloriously displayed in only the skimpiest of coverings, veiled only by the water itself, was breath stopping.

But even as he stood and gazed he could feel conflict writhing within him. How beautiful she was—how he desired her…. He wanted only to catch her in a rush of diamond water and feel her body close to his. Yet, like a flicker across his synapses, seeking to block the vivid visual image before him, came a whisper of warning.

Take care. She is beautiful, yes, and you desire her—how

could you not? But do not forget—do not allow yourself to forget—just why you are here. For what purpose...

Impatiently, he pushed the warning aside. There would be time for that later, when they returned to England, but for now he could set aside all that and focus only on the glorious fact that he was here with Marisa.

A sense of well-being descended on him as if from the hot, bright sun overhead. This was good—more than good. He was here, in this beautiful place, and the rest of the world with all its cares and worries, was an ocean away. This beautiful, breath-catching woman was for him—for him alone! Anticipation creamed through him.

'This is heavenly!' Marisa's voice was full. She lay back, giving herself to the water, letting the buoyancy of the sea support her as she bobbed gently in the gentle swell.

The sun poured down its blessing on her, and she had to close her eyes fully against its strength. Her arms drifted out as she rested on the bosom of the sea. How long she floated she wasn't sure, because time was drifting now, just as her body was. Until she felt two hands lightly on her shoulders, slowly starting to turn her like a starfish.

'I don't like to wake you, but I think, for the first time in this climate, you should probably come out now,' Athan told her. 'Your body feels cool, but the sun's rays still do their work, and more, even reflected off the sea.'

Reluctantly she let her feet sink down to the soft sand and stood up. Sunlight was glancing off Athan's tanned body, turning him to bronze, a sculpted work of art. She could not tear her eyes away, and he gave her his slanting smile.

'It's the same for me,' he said, his voice low, his meaning clear.

She felt her cheeks flush and dipped under the water again, making a show of smoothing out her hair as she re-emerged.

She waded towards the shore and as she gained the beach could feel the sun baking down on her back.

'Time for a shower,' Athan said, and immediately Marisa wished he hadn't. It conjured images that she had to banish straight away.

'Me first,' she said laughingly, and ran up the steps of the cabana, gaining the tiled bathroom before him.

The water sluicing down on her was not tepid and brackish, but beautifully refreshing, and she quickly gave her hair a light shampoo with the courtesy bottle provided. Feeling naked, she wrapped herself in one of the generous soft fleecy towels and emerged, wringing out her hair, and then her skimpy bikini, and wandered out on to their veranda to drape the wet bikini over the rail. It would dry fast, she knew, even in the shade.

The sun was lowering in the sky. Facing westwards, towards the sheltered Caribbean shore, the beach would be a fabulous place to watch it set, she realised. A little to the left of their cabana was a structure like a fixed palanquin, with a huge bleached canvas mattress and a matching awning. Generous cushions tumbled on the surface, and the edges turned into a kind of tabletop—to put drinks on, she reckoned.

Combing out her hair, she gazed out at the peaceful scene. She could tell there were other cabanas along the shoreline, but such was the distribution of vegetation and palms that each seemed to have its own portion of beach. It was designed, she realised, to be totally private.

Intimate.

Another of those electric flutterings skittered across her nerve endings. How would the evening end? she wondered.

But she knew—of course she knew! There could be only one way to end such an evening. Only one outcome beneath the tropical stars.

She would be in Athan's arms… She felt her heart give a little skip, her lungs a little squeeze.

How wonderful life was! To grant her this—so idyllic a place—and such a man as Athan to experience it with.

To experience far more than this beautiful island…

With a delicious shiver of anticipation she headed indoors to get dressed. It was too early yet to change for dinner, so instead she put on one of the lovely loose fine cotton sundresses she'd bought, with narrow straps and almost ankle length. Not bothering to put on a bra—it was too hot for that!—she slipped her feet into a pair of flip-flops, shook out her hair the better to dry it, and wandered into the little lounge-diner that the front of the cabana opened into.

She could hear the shower running, indicating that Athan had taken her place there, and she wandered across to the fridge set into the mahogany sideboard. She took out a carton of mango and orange juice, diluting it with chilled water before heading outdoors again. The shaded palanquin looked so inviting that she drifted in its direction, settling herself back with a comfortable sigh against the piled-up cushions.

'So this is where you are.' A deep voice sounded lazily behind her.

Marisa half crooked her neck and saw Athan approaching. He had changed into a pair of long cotton shorts and a pale blue short sleeved shirt, open at the neck. He looked cool, casual, and completely devastating.

He, too, had a glass in his hand.

'It's a little too early for a sundowner, but the moment that sun hits the deck I'm going to crack open the bottle of champagne that's in the fridge,' he told her with a grin. 'Till then, it's fruit juice only.'

'Me too,' she answered with a smile.

He climbed lightly up onto the mattress, but lounged back at the far end. Marisa was grateful. It was so overwhelming, this whole experience of being here with Athan, knowing what was to come, wanting to savour ever step of the journey.

I don't want to rush things, she thought. *I want them to be perfect.*

Unforgettable!

So for now it was perfect just to sit there, comfortably in her own space, with Athan unpressurised company, relaxed and carefree.

'I can't really believe I'm here,' she mused. 'It is just *so* unbearably gorgeous. Like being in a dream.'

'Oh, it's real all right.' Athan's voice was dryly amused.

But there was something else in it—some note she couldn't identify. She glanced at him.

He was looking at her, but just as in his voice there was something in his eyes she could not see—as if he were holding something back from her. Then, a moment later, it was gone as he leant forward to clink glasses with her.

'To a holiday we'll never forget,' he said. His eyes were warm, caressing.

'I'll never forget this!' she breathed.

For the briefest second that strange, half-hidden look was back in his eyes.

'No, you won't,' he agreed.

Then it was gone, and he was taking a long draft from his glass, turning his head to look out over the sea, where the sun was lowering its golden orb towards the waiting embrace of the ocean.

Just like I am waiting for Athan's embrace...thought Marisa dreamily.

They sat half in silence, half in companionable chit-chat, listening to the warm wind soughing in the tops of the palms, the gentle susurration of the wavelets breaking on the silver shore. It was so incredibly quiet and peaceful they might have been the only people on the beach or even the island, Marisa thought.

'Is that actually a coconut?' she asked, her gaze drifting to the top of one of the nearby palms.

Athan gave a laugh. 'Do you think it's a fake one, then?' he challenged, amused.

'Maybe the hotel ties fake ones to the tops of the palm trees to impress the visitors,' she responded, entering into the spirit of the banter.

'We'll ask one of the garden staff to get it down for us, if you like,' Athan said. 'You should see them climb palm trees. It's quite ingenious—they use a short length of rope which they hook around the trunk, then use it to lever themselves up to the top—it's quite a skill!'

'You sound like you've seen it before,' she said.

'Well, not here,' he admitted. 'I've never been to this resort before.'

That, of course, was why he'd chosen it. He wasn't known here, and he was unlikely to bump into anyone who knew him. Or his sister. Besides, this resort was specifically aimed at couples who wanted to get totally away from it all—including any other couples.

That was what made it so ideal a place for him to bring Marisa Milburne.

Remote, luxurious, discreet. Perfect for his intentions.

A shadow of a flicker fleeted across his face. She was so trusting of him—lounging there, sipping her juice, gazing out over the vista ahead, her pose relaxed and graceful.

Should I really do this?

The question he didn't want to hear came from nowhere—sliding like a needle under his consciousness.

His conscience?

You've brought her here to make her want you instead of him.

And she did want him! Wanted him as much as he wanted her—all his senses told him so. And for that reason he crushed down his disquiet.

England, his sister, his philandering brother-in-law—all seemed very, very far away.

And Marisa…ah, she was blissfully close.

He raised his glass to her again. 'To us,' he said softly.

And her eyes glowed like jewels in the golden light of the setting sun.

Marisa narrowed her eyes in concentration, listening intently. One of the serving staff was talking to another islander, and she was trying to make out what they were saying.

She abandoned the attempt, turning her attention back to Athan, sitting opposite her at the table.

'Do you know, I can't make out a single word?' she said. 'It doesn't even sound like English.'

'It isn't,' he told her, amused. 'The island Creole is French-based, dating from the time when St Cecile was ruled by France, but it also includes fragments of African languages, as well as the original Carib languages. Don't worry if you can't understand it—outsiders seldom do. All the island Creoles across the Caribbean have virtually evolved into their own languages. They have their own literature as well, and these days there's a real effort to preserve them for future genera-tions of islanders.'

Marisa shook her head. 'It doesn't sound like French, either,' she admitted.

She glanced across at Athan. He was looking, as the habit-ual little catch in her throat informed her, lethally attract-ive. Since lolling on the palanquin—where they had, as he had promised, toasted each other in champagne as the sun set— he'd changed into tan chinos and another short-sleeved open-necked shirt, and he looked disgustingly, casually gorgeous. His sable hair was slightly feathered, and his relaxed pose seemed to emphasise the lean, muscled power of his body.

What she wanted to do, she knew, was simply sit there and gaze at him. But what she had to do, she also knew, was keep chatting to him to stop herself being reduced to such a gormless level. It was hard, though—and not just because of her own sharpened awareness of him. It was also because he had the devastating habit of relaxing back in his chair and letting his gaze wash over her, making no bones about showing that he liked what he was seeing.

That he liked it very much…

Again that flutter in her stomach came, and she knew that the effort she'd made to look her absolute best tonight was paying off. After the champagne on the beach she'd disappeared into the bathroom, taking excruciating care over her make-up—not too much for the climate and setting, but enough to enhance her eyes to the maximum—glossing her lips with dew, and styling her hair so that it looked artlessly tumbled. Her choice of clothes was equally careful. A long dress in a swirling mix of vermilions and gold, with spaghetti straps and a high waist that made her seem taller and more slender. She'd wrapped a piece of filmy gauze picked out in the same vermilion and gold thread around her shoulders. The temperature had dropped, but by very little—the night was sweet and balmy, as caressing as a silken touch to her skin.

Now, as she lifted her wine glass to her lips, the golden sheen from her narrow gilt bangles catching the candlelight, she knew that she had got the look just right. Other couples were dining in the main restaurant as well, though each table was afforded privacy by potted palms and brilliant bougainvillaea, and the whole dining area formed almost a semicircle around the resort pool which glowed, unearthly, with underwater lights.

All my life, she thought hazily, I'll remember this. This wonderful, magical place, this wonderful, magical evening.

This wonderful, magical man who had made it all come true for her…

But she couldn't just go on staring helplessly at him.

'So, when did the island become English, then?' she asked, infusing interest into her voice.

'I believe it swapped hands several times—depending on the fortunes of war and various treaties between France and England during the eighteenth century. But it ended up being definitely English after the Napoleonic Wars. One of the perks of victory,' Athan said dryly. 'The French owners of the plantations kept their property, however, so they didn't mind too much. As for the slaves—well, I guess they benefited in the end by being emancipated in 1834, which was earlier than in the remaining French colonies.'

A troubled expression lit Marisa's eyes. 'It casts a long shadow, doesn't it, slavery? Over such a beautiful place?'

Athan reached for his wine glass, taking a reflective mouthful. 'It's long been one of the ironies of Greek civilisation,' he observed, 'that whilst the modern world pays tribute to ancient Greek democracy their economy relied entirely on slave labour.'

She frowned. 'It seems dreadful that slavery was able to flourish again after Europeans discovered the Americas. It was so obviously an evil thing.'

'Oh, it's easy enough to persuade yourself that your behaviour is justified when it benefits you materially,' Athan replied.

His eyes rested on her, and he saw a momentarily discomfited expression in her face. Was she thinking about how she herself was perfectly happy to let Ian Randall house and keep her?

Yet even as he speculated he felt his own thoughts prick at him.

And you—what about you? You say you are doing all this to help save your sister's marriage—yet you are benefiting from it yourself, aren't you? Having this beautiful, desirable woman for yourself!

But he didn't want to think about being back in England.

Didn't want to think about what he would have to say to Marisa then, and why. Didn't want to think about his sister, let alone his pernicious brother-in-law. Didn't want to do anything at all, except savour this moment to the full—enjoy the time he had here, the days and nights he would have with Marisa.

All to himself, without the outside world to trouble him with its disquieting, uncomfortable imperatives.

And that was just what he would do! Enjoy this time, relish it and experience it to the full.

He set down his glass, resumed his meal. It was exquisitely cooked—a concoction of grilled fish, caught that day, flavoured with sweet spices. Marisa was eating breaded prawns, each on a separate skewer, with a rich coconut dipping sauce.

She'd picked up another skewer a moment or two after he'd made his pointed observation, and now busied herself swirling it into the sauce.

'Are they good?' he enquired. The amused, lazy note was back in his voice. The mordant expression in his face gone completely. He would keep it that way. Why spoil what this evening would bring? What each golden day here would bring? Each velvet night…

'Fabulous!' she said. 'Though I think each one's about a million calories.'

'You can atone by only having fruit for dessert,' he said smilingly.

She glanced at him again as she took a delicate mouthful of the sauce-swathed prawn. That sudden austerity in his face had gone, and she was relieved. She wondered what had caused it. But it was gone now, and that was good enough for her peace of mind. She didn't want anything to spoil this idyll…

Atoning for her rich main course by eating fruit for dessert certainly didn't spoil things—the slices of luscious tropical fruit, served on crushed ice, were as delicious as the most calorific pudding. Athan dipped in and out of the heaped mound sporadically, lounging back in his chair, swirling a glass of brandy in his fingers. For herself, she wanted no more alcohol. The earlier champagne, together with wine over dinner, had made the world a sweet, hazy place.

A sense of absolute well-being filled her. Absolute happiness…That was the thought coiling in and out of her synapses. Because how could she be happier than to be here, in this warm, balmy paradise, with a man like Athan Teodarkis? Who was looking at her now with such an expression in his incredibly gorgeous eyes…

She gave a little inward shiver of excitement—anticipation, feelings that only mounted as, coffee consumed, Athan got to his feet.

'Shall we?' he said, and held his hand out to her.

She took it, and he drew her up, not relinquishing her hand. They strolled around the pool, and it seemed, Marisa thought, so absolutely right to be doing so hand in hand. He made casual conversation and she answered in kind, keeping the note easy and relaxed, even though inside her she could feel her blood pulsing.

Beyond the pool the landscaped gardens gave way to more sandy ground, with low green vegetation, and the tiled paved area dispersed into multiple little pathways, each one marked by shelled edges and lit at strategic intervals by lights set either low at the base of palm trees or hung high on ornamental stands. As they neared their cabana she could hear the gentle shooshing of the sea, the endless chitter of the cicadas in the bushes, and the insistent chirruping of the tree frogs.

They strolled down on to the beach that fronted their cabana. A moon was hanging low over the sea, and there was a sheen of moonlight on the water. A mild breeze teased, but the night was warm. She could feel the humidity in it like an embracing net around her.

She gazed upwards. Stars as brilliant as golden lamps

blazed in the heavens. She felt dizzy just gazing upwards—dizzy on champagne, on the sweet tropical air, on the blood pulsing in her veins. She seemed to sway...

Hands came around her waist, steadying her. Her gaze dropped down to mingle with his. Even in the moonlight she could see his expression. What he was telling her. She felt his hands at her waist, light and warm, fingers splayed. The pulse in her blood strengthened.

He murmured her name, and then came what she had been waiting for, yearning for all evening. From the moment she'd first seen him and felt her heart flutter at the sight of him, at the impact he made on her. Slowly, exquisitely, agonisingly slowly, his mouth descended.

His kiss was light, like a feather, teasing at her lips, playing with them, playing with her desire for him, with his for her. Only when it seemed to her she could bear it no longer did she feel the sudden impress of his splayed fingertips and the simultaneous deepening of his kiss—as if he, too, had been unable to resist longer.

Sensation made her swoon, and she could feel her heart turning over and over as his mouth took hers richly, deeply, with a warm, insistent passion that dominated every sense in her body. There was only this moment, only this kiss, in all the world...

It lasted an eternity—it lasted only the briefest moment of time. He drew back from her, his gaze pouring into hers. She felt liquid, boneless.

'I want you so much...' His voice was a low husk.

She could only sway in his clasp, lifting her mouth to his again, aching and yearning for his touch.

'I am yours,' she whispered.

Triumph glistened in his eyes and he gave a low rasp in his throat as he kissed her again, hungrily, voraciously, sweeping her up into his arms and carrying her off the beach, up on to the veranda and into their cabana.

The air was warm inside, for they had not put the air-conditioning on, and in the bedroom, as he lowered her to the turned-down bed, the heat was a cocoon around them.

Her body seemed aflame—all her senses aflame. Swiftly, skilfully, he slid her dress from her body, baring her to his view in the dim light. She slipped her arms up above her head, so that her breasts lifted. His eyes were hungry for them, his lips hungrier. She could hear him murmur something in Greek, but her whole being was focussed only on the sensations he was arousing.

Dear God, but it was blissful—blissful! Like softest velvet, finest silk, laving and teasing and arousing her, until her body was flickering with unseen fire, her head twisting, her stomach taut. Then his mouth closed over the crested coral peaks, suckling and caressing with his lips, his tongue. A sound came from her throat—primitive, powerful. His mouth slipped from her breasts, easing down over the smooth, taut line of her abdomen. His hands shaped her slender waist, splaying upwards so that the tips of his fingers could continue to tease her straining nipples, squeezing and nipping them so that eddy after eddy of sensation shimmered through her, each setting up a wave that was growing in power as he drew from her the response he sought.

Restless hunger started to fill her. She wanted more—so much more! She wanted *him*. Her hands reached for him, clutching over his shoulders, tugging his shirt from him in movements that became increasingly hurried and impatient. He paused in his ministrations, shrugging the garment from him, and while he was at it shedding the rest of his clothes as well. With a gasp, she realised that he was completely naked now—completely hers!

With a little moan she drew him down on her, feeling the warm, hard length of his body—feeling, too, with a thrill, the full power of his masculinity. Her reaction was instinctive. Her hips lifted to his as he responded, one iron hard thigh slipping between hers. His mouth was on hers now, and her hands were running along the sculpted lines of his back, eagerly tracing its moulded contours. His skin was like cool satin, and she gloried in the sensations she was clearly able to arouse in him as she trailed her fingertips delicately along his spine.

Urgency filled him. Desire was peaking in him and he wanted…needed…to fulfil it. She was afire for him, and he for her. The sweet softness of her body, yielding to his, was all he craved. He sought her, shifting his weight until he found what he desired. He arched over her, his hands shaping her shoulders as her hips arched questingly to his. For one long, endless moment he gazed down into her face, transfixed by what he was arousing in her.

Theos, but she was so, so beautiful! Her hair streaming across the pillows. Her face alight with an unearthly beauty. Her slender body aroused and yearning for his. It was a yearning that he matched, met…surpassed in every aching part of him.

Now, *now* he needed fulfilment—needed to be fused with her, melded to her core, to become one with her.

He heard her murmur his name, sounding urgent, so urgent in her need for him. Felt her hands press at his back to close him to her, to fuse herself against him.

With a surge he was there, filling her deeply, fully, feeling her close around him, hearing her cry out, hearing his own voice soothing her even as every synapse in his brain started an insistent, driving firing that swept across his consciousness.

His body started to move in an age-old, primeval rhythm, possessing him even as he now possessed her. She was threshing against him and it drove him wild, crazy for her, for what she was doing to him, for the way her incredible body was lifting to his, fusing to his, with a hunger, an insistence that he was answering. He was taking her with him on his urgent, storming journey to more and ever more peaks of sensation that heated every portion of his flesh to a white heat.

Her eyes were fluttering, their pupils so distended they seemed to flood her eyes even as sensation flooded her body—sensation such as she had never felt before. A storm of quickening that was sweeping her higher, always higher, higher—

Time stopped—it had no meaning. There was only this moment, this endless, incredible *now* of sensation, rippling through her body, melting her, fusing her. Her hands clung to him, her throat arched back, her hips pressed against his to take him within her, catching at him again and yet again. And with each stroke he was taking her further and higher and deeper. And the pleasure, the bliss, was so intense, so incredible, so absolute that when the storm broke within her she seemed to be consumed by it, as the storm drove through her, buckling and convulsing her.

She cried out. She could hear it. And it was a cry that went on and on, just as the storm within her went on and on, and it was another world, another existence, another *her*...one she had never known, never dreamt existed.

Then another voice joined hers—deep-throated, hoarse, as urgent as hers, as insistent. She felt his body fill her, felt the culmination of that endless driving rhythm, felt him soaring with her into that other world that was consuming her, so that her whole body had become a living, burning flame.

For long moments she was bathed in the fire, as if its flickering heat enveloped them both, making them one, making them unified, melded together. Then, when their sated, exhausted bodies could take no more, she felt the burning begin to ebb, the throbbing of her core lessen, die slowly to stillness. Ease. Leaving in its wake not ashes, but a sweetness—a sense of wellbeing so absolute that it bathed her in a profound wonder.

She could only let her fingers drift across his back, feeling the exhaustion of every limb as they lay wound about each other and the last lingering flickers of the consuming flames died gently away.

How long she lay there, entwined with him, she did not know. Knew only that she had found a place to be that she never wanted to leave. Here in Athan's arms, in his enveloping embrace, was world enough for her. Drifting in and out of sleep, she lay holding him close against her breast.

Close against her heart…

Marisa swam lazily towards the pool's swim-up bar. As she neared it the pool shallowed, and she waded the rest of the way before perching herself on one of the little half submerged stone stools. The barman sauntered along to her from his side, and asked in the lilting island accent what she would like. Opting for a virgin strawberry margarita, Marisa sat sipping through the crushed scarlet-coloured ice and gazed peacefully out over the turquoise water of the pool and the azure sea beyond.

Even after nearly two weeks here she still could not get enough of the vista before her. She gave a little sigh of happiness. Just as she could not get enough of Athan.

Not that she had to do without him. She was with him just about twenty-four-seven. There was only a brief daily interval when, as he was doing now, he checked into the resort business centre and communicated, as briefly as he could get away with, his direct reports, and received any unavoidable updates. But he was seldom gone for more than half an hour. Other than that they were together all the time.

A ripple of wonder went through her. She had known from the moment she'd yielded to his invitation to come here with him that this time with him would be unforgettable, but never had she realised just how much so.

And it wasn't just the sex—although even saying 'just the sex' was a universe away from describing the incredible, transforming experience it was every time. No, it wasn't 'just sex' at all. How could it be when it seemed to her that her very being caught fire, was consumed like a phoenix, to be reborn in that moment of ecstasy, enveloped in his arms? Surely it wasn't 'just sex' to be so consumed by passion for him—to want him and crave him not only in the fires of consummation but in the peaceful, languorous aftermath that wrapped them in its sweet, honeyed balm, when they simply lay together, softly caressing each other, all passion spent, their eyes entwining with each other, drowsy with satiation. To sleep in his arms, cradled by him, holding him close to her, only to wake later, in the long reaches of the tropical night, when he would start to make love to her again, as if he could not get enough of her.

Yet even as her eyes softened with the memory of his ardent, transforming lovemaking a haunted look fleeted therein. This idyll here on St Cecile was nearly over. Soon, in a day or two, they would be headed for home—back to London. Back to their normal lives.

What would happen then?

Disquiet plucked at her, disturbing her contentment. What would happen when they were back in England, away from here?

Could the idyll continue?

That was the question that coiled and uncoiled inside her head. She had shut it out, not let herself think about it, but over the last few days, as their second week had started to ebb away, day by precious day, she had felt it plucking at her consciousness, wanting to be answered.

But she didn't want to answer it. Didn't want to think what the answer might be—what she feared it would be.

This *was* an idyll—a blissful, unforgettable *intermezzo*— in a tropical paradise where reality seemed as distant as the British winter. But what would happen when the *intermezzo* was over?

Oh, Athan was as passionate, as ardent as any woman could want—could dream of—but that was here. What would happen back in London?

Doubts fed her disquiet. Yes, Athan was hers *here,* but even here, these last days, she had felt him withdraw from her sometimes—only briefly, but distinctly. It was not a physical withdrawal but much more disquieting than that. It was a kind of mental withdrawal, as though their casual intimacy was draining away. Sometimes there was a look in his eye, she was sure of it, when he seemed to be looking at her with a stranger's gaze. Then, a moment later, it would be gone and he would be his normal self again—and she would wonder if she had merely imagined it.

She could reason so well, she knew. He was a man of affairs who had a business empire to run—how could he possibly be confined only to focussing on her? She had to accept that his mind would go from time to time to matters of greater import.

Greater import than herself.

An ache started within her. A flickering of fear. A fear she didn't want to face.

Fear of a time she did not want to face.

But it would come, for all that. The hours were ticking inexorably towards that time. The sun's passage in the sky was arcing towards that time. It would come, fear it as she might—dread it as she did.

He says words of passion to me—but only passion. He smiles at me, and holds my hand, and walks at my side, and takes me in his arms—but what does he feel for me? Is it only passion? Only desire?

She could not answer—dared not answer. And dared not answer an even more fearful question.

What do I feel for him? Only passion? Only desire?

Yes! It had to be. It had to be only that and nothing more. She must allow it to be nothing else. Because when this idyll here was over, when the island was only a faint invisible sliver of land half a world away, and their reality was once more the busy wintry streets of London, then she would discover a truth she dared not know yet—a truth she feared.

What if he is done with me?

She took a heavy breath, staring sightlessly out over the blindingly bright water.

I have to prepare for that. I have to prepare for when he turns to me and tells me what I fear to hear.

That he was done with her.

No! She would not think ahead to that moment. She would not spoil these last precious days with Athan by dwelling on what might come. She would not cast the shadow of such fear over what she had now.

Resolute, she finished her fruit juice and got out of the pool. Athan would have finished at the business centre soon and be heading back to the cabana. Marisa wanted to be there waiting for him. As hungry for him as he always was for her. Mid-morning passion was so very, very enjoyable…

Putting her dark thoughts firmly aside, she set off, her steps eager.

Athan smoothed the silken hair, holding Marisa's slender body against his. They were both drowsy in the aftermath of lovemaking. The low swirl of the overhead fan was the only noise. Soon they would rouse themselves and shower, and then dress for lunch. Not that lunch was in the slightest bit formal. Everyone wore beach clothes, possibly with the lightest cover-up and nothing more.

Lunch was a leisurely, relaxed affair, mostly salads and fruits, served from a huge buffet in the open air dining room shaded by wide awnings from the heat of the noonday sun. The constant gentle breeze gave a welcome cooling, and the lap of the pool water added to the lazy, easy atmosphere.

But then the whole resort exuded a lazy, easy atmosphere. Relaxation was inevitable.

Except that right now Athan was not feeling relaxed in the slightest. It was not because of their recent passionate consummation—it had another cause. An unwelcome one.

There were only two more days left of the holiday, and then they would be flying back to London.

He could feel his muscles tense momentarily. And in London he would have to confront Marisa—tell her just why he had taken her on holiday here, and what that reason meant for her. And for his brother-in-law. It would mean the impossibility of any relationship between her and Ian.

But even as he reminded himself of the reason he'd brought her here he could feel his mind rebelling. Maybe there was no need to spell it out to her. After all, surely if she'd just spent two weeks with another man she couldn't possibly think of going back to Ian? Surely she would take it for granted that her time with Ian was over, and that was that.

So maybe I don't have to confront her.

One thing was for sure: he didn't want to. Right from the start he'd known it wasn't going to be easy—that it was going to be unpleasant and uncomfortable. But now, after all that they had here, together, it was going to be a whole lot more than just 'unpleasant'....

I can't do it.

Revulsion filled him. How could he? How could he go from holding her in his arms to denouncing her as a marriage breaker? How could he make love to her and then accuse her?

He'd known, of course—he'd known all along—that that was what he was going to have to do, but it was one thing to plan cold-bloodedly to seduce the woman who was threatening his sister's marriage and quite another, he thought hollowly, to spend two weeks with her and then have to face the ugly denouement that he'd envisaged delivering.

I must have been mad to think of such a scheme!

Mad to think that he could carry it out.

Madness to think that I could hold her in my arms like this and still be planning such a denunciation of her.

His eyes stared up at the rotating fan. Its movement echoed his thoughts, going round and endlessly round in his head. He knew what he had set out to do—what was coming closer and closer with every passing hour—knew that the very thought of it was building to a mountain of impossibility inside him.

An impossibility because of Marisa herself.

Even as he said her name silently in his head he could feel his response to it. Felt his arm tighten around her waist as she slept against him. Felt the rightness of her being there, in his arms…

I didn't know it was going to be like this. I knew I wanted her, desired her—but I never dreamt that the possession would be so…incredible!

Everything had seemed to come together. The passion flaring between them, their hunger for each other, the perfection of their union—and not just that, he thought wonderingly, if 'just' could ever be a word applied to what they'd experienced in their intimate exploration of each other. No, 'more' was what he'd never foreseen.

The little things—the time we spend together when we are not making love. The ease of being with her. The laughter. The silences that are a tranquillity, not a strain. The companionship.

Whatever they were doing—whether it was eating under the stars or lazily lounging on the beach, or by the pool, or taking a boat out on the water, watching the sun set in a blaze of glory, or watching the moon rise through the palm trees— it was all just so…so *easy*…

And as for the sex—

His eyes flared and he felt his body tauten despite its satiation.

How could he want her so much? How could he feel what

he did—such incredible intensity every time, reaching such an incredible peak? Feel afterwards as he did now, every time, as if there was nothing more in life that he could want except to lie here with Marisa in his arms?

And he was going to have to end it. Ruin it. Destroy it.

Denounce her as the woman threatening his sister's happiness. That would end it, he knew with biting certainty. Once he had told her what his intentions for her had been all along there would be nothing left of what they had here—now.

His eyes stared at the chopping fan blades, slicing through time, slicing up his thoughts, his emotions.

I don't want to do it. I don't want to tell her, confront her, denounce her, accuse her.

But if he didn't…

He hardened his heart against himself. How could he bottle out of it? How could he put himself in front of his own sister? Put his own desires, his own longings first?

I have to do it. I don't want to but I have to. If I don't I'm just a selfish, self-indulgent coward, who cares more about myself and what I want than about my sister.

That was the brutal truth of it. The truth he couldn't deny. Couldn't hide from. He had to do it—finish what he'd started.

In his arms Marisa stirred, waking from the drowsy sleep that came after physical fulfilment. He felt her body move against him, felt himself respond. Her eyes fluttered open, met his, entwined with his. She smiled slowly, sensuously at him.

Lifted her mouth to his…

He answered her invitation, and in the velvet pleasure of her mouth he banished the disquieting thoughts that beset him.

London was far away—an ocean away.

Here, now, was all his universe.

All he wanted…

CHAPTER FOUR

MARISA sat in the taxi heading from Heathrow into central London. She looked out of the window at the bleak view beyond of the outskirts of London encased in winter's drear grip. A million miles away from the caressing warmth of the Caribbean. The grim landscape echoed the feeling inside her. In her lap, her fingers clutched each other tightly. At her side Athan had got out his laptop and was frowning at the screen, his face closed. He was only a foot or two away from her—and yet much, much further.

Tightness gripped her. She knew what was coming. Knew it with a deep, stricken sense of dread—of impending loss. Knew exactly what was going to happen. It was what she had feared would happen. He was going to escort her back to her apartment and then, in whatever way he deemed appropriate, he was going to tell her that he wouldn't be seeing her again.

The knot in her stomach tightened and her heart slugged heavily in her chest. She tried to blot out her thoughts, tried only to stare out of the window, not thinking, not feeling.

But thoughts came all the same. Of *course* Athan had been all over her while they were on holiday! Of *course* she had been the entire focus of his attention, the intensity of his desire for her would be his whole purpose. But it was only a holiday—that was what she had to remember. Nothing more than a holiday. He'd seen her, wanted her—got her. Not in any kind of exploitative way—she could never accuse him of that—but his interest in her was temporary. Inherently so. They had had a fabulous time together—but now it was over.

Time to move on.

The knot in her stomach clenched. That was the thing—*he* wanted to move on. She…she only longed for him not to. Longed for him to want to keep her in his life.

I don't want to lose him, I don't want to never see him again. I don't want it to be over!

But her wants were not going to come into it.

That was what she had to face. What she dreaded facing.

The taxi came off the flyover, threading down into the streets of London, making its way towards Shepherd's Bush, Holland Park, the street she lived on. It drew up at the apartment block. The moment it stopped she got out, shivering in the sunless cold air, acrid with the scent of the city. Athan was paying the driver, picking up their suitcases. Politely he ushered her inside and they made for the lifts. She gave another little shiver.

'It's so cold after the Caribbean,' she said, as if attempting a light remark.

Athan only smiled briefly but said nothing, not looking at her.

He would be steeling himself for his speech, she knew. How many times had he given it before? How many other women had he whisked away to paradise and then returned to earth, bidding them farewell and walking away? She felt her emotions clench, her insides hollow.

Well, what did it matter how many times before he'd done it? This would be one more time. One more *It's been good but now it's over* declamation. She hoped against hope that he wouldn't try and give her some kind of parting gift. She hoped she wouldn't cry. Hoped she would find the strength, the courage, to simply smile agreement at him and thank him for such a fabulous time together.

Part as friends.

Or just passing acquaintances.

Not that she would see him again. With his own apartment ready to move back into now, the rented one next door to hers would not be necessary. He'd probably already had his things moved out. Easier that way—easier to make a clean break with her.

The lift doors opened and she got out her key, opening her door while he followed with her suitcase. He set his own down in the hallway.

'Could you just leave mine in my bedroom?' she asked. Her voice was steady. Light. Deliberately so.

She went into the living room. The air in the flat was stale and chill, and she moved to the wall to turn up the thermostat. She gave another shiver, but not from the cold. Temperature reset, she turned round.

Athan was standing in the centre of the room. His expression said it all. She waited tensely for him to speak. She would take it on the chin, and if nothing else behave with dignity.

I won't plead, I won't cry, I won't question. I'll just accept and move on—the way he will.

He still wasn't saying anything. He just stood there, tall, with a forbidding air about him. His face was like a mask—completely closed.

Then, abruptly, he spoke.

'I have something to say to you.'

A faint, puzzled look shadowed her eyes. His voice was so hard—so harsh. Surely he didn't have to be so hard? Wasn't there a…*civilised*…way of doing this? Of parting after a brief, incandescent affair that could not possibly last?

Did he see it in her eyes, her puzzlement, as if she were flinching a little from the severity of his tone? If he did, it only made his expression harden. The knot in Marisa's stomach suddenly tightened and adrenaline prickled in her veins. It was as if something bad…worse…were about to happen, and her body was steeling itself. For the first time she started to feel not just dread of him telling her it was over, but dread at something quite different…

Because what she could see in his closed, hard expression was something she had never seen there before.

It was anger.

Leashed, tightly gripped, but there. Like a force field emanating from him. She felt the dread change inside her—change into something else.

He was looking at her with eyes she'd never seen before. No flecks of gold—only bladed steel.

What is it? What's happening? Why is he being like this?

The questions flurried through her head. Bewildered apprehension showed in her eyes and her body tensed, flooded with adrenaline.

Then he struck.

'You will not be seeing Ian Randall again. You're out of his life for good.'

Shock detonated through her. He saw it in her face. Felt a savage pleasure in it. As savage as the anger that had been leashed tight within him. Now it was unleashed. He'd had to unleash it, to let it serve its purpose. An anger whose cause he would not name. Refused to name.

Because to name it would be to give it power. Power over *him*. Power he would not allow.

Could not allow…..

She clutched at the curved arm of the sofa, as if without its support she would crumple and fall. Shock was still etched across her face.

'You won't be seeing him again,' he told her. 'He's going to be working out of Athens from now on. I'm transferring him to my headquarters there.'

He'd finalised the transfer while they'd been on St Cecile—it had been the obvious thing to do, he'd realised. Get Ian out of London, keep him in Athens under his watchful and suspicious eyes. Ian Randall wouldn't be lining up any adulterous affairs under the nose of his wife's husband. Athan knew that for a certainty.

He watched how the news was going down with Marisa. His own face was still a mask. It had to be. He must not crack now—not when he'd achieved his goal. His purpose.

He had to focus on standing there, his muscles tensed. It was as if he had suddenly put on a suit of steel, banded tightly around him, keeping him motionless, immobile.

Because if he didn't—if he didn't keep his body leashed in steel—then he would surge forward, clip his arms around her, draw her to him, hold her close against him tightly, so tightly—

Marisa's expression worked—as if she were trying to cling to something, anything, that might make sense. Sense in a tidal wave of unreality…

'*You* have? But Ian doesn't work for you…'

It was a pointless thing to say—the least relevant—but the words fell from her lips all the same. Shock was ricocheting around inside her.

How does he know about Ian?

She heard him give a brief, hard laugh. There was no humour in it. Then it cut out abruptly.

'Of course he works for me.'

'No! He's marketing director of a company—'

'One of my subsidiaries.'

Her mouth opened, then closed. She had to make sense of this—somehow she had to make sense of this. She seized on the biggest thing she could not understand—out of all that she could not understand. Her mind was reeling.

'But why do you care about Ian and me? What does it matter to you, even if you do employ him indirectly? What harm is it to you?'

The questions tumbled from her—bewildered—accusatory. He felt his anger lash out again.

Anger at so much. Anger at Ian for what he was doing to Eva. Anger that he'd been landed in this mess to try and sort it out. Anger that sorting it out meant doing what he was doing now to Marisa.

I don't want to do this to her!

The thought burned across his brain. But there was no point to it. None. He had to do what he must—say what he had to. He lurched forward, his hands going around her elbows, his grip like steel.

'Because Eva Randall—' his voice was like steel wire '—Eva Randall is my sister!'

He watched her face whiten. Felt the steel bite into him, tighter yet.

'I didn't know.' Her voice was a whisper. Her eyes were distended.

He gave another harsh, humourless laugh. Because the universe was mocking him—mocking the scene he had to play out to the bitter, painful end. Because ending it was all he could do now.

'Why would he tell you?' he countered, forcing himself to speak. 'Why would he tell you what was no concern of yours? I knew he hadn't told you from the moment I introduced myself to you—the moment you saw my name on my business card. I'd gambled that he hadn't and it paid off.'

His voice changed suddenly, and as it did Marisa felt a new emotion slither through the disbelieving shock that was shaking her like an earthquake.

'Which left the field entirely clear for me. For my purpose.'

His eyes rested on her. Eyes that had once burned into her with a desire so intense she'd thought she must melt in the scorching heat of it...

Eyes that now were black like empty space. Desolate and devoid of all things.

'I sought you out,' he said, and his voice was as empty as his eyes. Saying the words he had to say. The words it would take to end it. Destroy it utterly. 'I took the apartment next door—timed my meeting with you. You'd been under my surveillance ever since I first suspected that Eva's husband was harbouring a secret. A sordid little secret. Once I'd met you I could simply put in place what had to be done. Put an end to things between you and Ian.' His voice twisted. 'After all, how could you possibly be part of his life after what you have been to me...?'

Faintness drummed at her.

From somewhere very deep inside her she found words. Each one was pulled from her like knives from wounded flesh. Costing her more than she could pay.

'It was all a set-up?'

Her eyes were huge, her face stark, skin stretched over bones, white as alabaster.

It gave her an unearthly beauty...

Anger rived through him again. Anger that she should look so beautiful.

It was a beauty he could never possess again...barred to him for ever.

'Yes,' he said. 'It was all a set-up.' He paused—a fatal pause. 'Nothing more than that.'

Nothing more than that...

The words tolled in his head like a funeral bell. Killing everything.

She was staring at him, still as a whitened corpse.

Nausea rose in her throat. 'Get out—' Her voice was a breath, a shaking rasp.

The steel bands bit into him, constricting like a crushing weight around him. He had more he had to say—must force himself to say.

'This is what you will do.' He spoke tersely, without emotion. Because emotion was far too dangerous. He had to crush it out of him. 'You will sever entirely all relations with Ian Randall. You will have nothing more to do with him. You will stay out of his life—permanently. Give him whatever reasons you want—but be aware that if you do not part from him—*permanently*—then I will give him a reason to sever relations.' He paused—another fatal pause. 'He will know what you have been to me.'

She swallowed. She could feel nausea—more than nausea—climbing in her throat. She fought it down—had to fight it down. Had to.

'Do you understand?' he demanded harshly. 'Is that clear?'

She nodded. He would not go, she knew, until he had obtained what he had come for.

What he had always planned to obtain...

No! She must not think of that—must not let the realisation of what he'd done to her explode in her brain. Not now—not yet. She stood very still, holding herself together. She was beyond speech, beyond everything.

He exhaled a sharp breath. He had done what he had set out to do. He had done it and now there was nothing else for him to do. Nothing but to do what she had told him to do—to go.

'I'll see myself out.' His voice was clipped, back in control.

He turned and walked towards the door, seizing up his suitcase from the hall beyond. His hand closed over the handle to the front door. For a moment, the barest moment, he seemed to freeze—as if...as if...

Then, abruptly, he yanked open the door and was gone.

Behind him, Marisa went on standing. Staring at where once he had been. Then slowly, very slowly, she sank down upon the sofa.

Burning with pain.

Athan strode down the corridor. His face was closed. His mind was closed. Every part of him was closed. Shut down like a nuclear reactor that had gone into meltdown and was now so dangerous only total closure could keep it from devastating all around it.

He must keep it that way. That was what was important. Essential. Keeping everything closed down.

As he descended in the lift, walked across the lobby, out into the road, reached for his mobile phone to summon a chauffeured company car to take him back to his own apartment, words went round in his head.

It's done.

That was all he had to remember.

Not Marisa at his side, his arm wrapped around her shoulder as they walked along the beach at sunset, the coral sand beneath their bare feet, the foaming wavelets washing them as they walked, and the majestic blaze of the sun sinking into the gilded azure sea.

Not Marisa beneath the stars, her beautiful swan neck stretched as she lifted her starlit face, her hair cascading like silk down her back, as he pointed out constellations to her. Not the sudden tightening in his loins as he framed her face with his hands, cupping her head, lowering his mouth to hers, lowering her body to the waiting sand beneath...

Not Marisa with her arms around him, her beauteous naked body pressed to his, crying out in ecstasy...

He wrenched his mind away, his hand around his suitcase handle clenching like steel.

He went on walking, with the biting winter all around him. Inside him.

Marisa was packing. One suitcase was packed already. She'd packed it on another continent, in another lifetime. The suitcase she was packing now was a new acquisition—one she'd bought that morning, from the nearest shop that sold luggage. Methodically, unthinkingly, she opened drawers, took out clothes, folded them into the suitcase. It didn't matter what order they went in—any order would do. It mattered only that she went on folding and packing. Folding and packing. Once the drawers were empty she moved on to the closet, performing the same office with its contents.

There were some other things as well as clothes, but those could follow later. She would box them up and have them sent on. Things like the pretty ornaments she'd acquired during her time in London, souvenirs, books, CDs. Bits and pieces.

Everything else stayed with the flat—all the kitchen goods, all the furniture, all the bedding. All she was taking were her clothes and her personal effects.

And memories.

She couldn't get rid of those. They were glued inside her head. With a glue that ate like acid into her brain.

But they were false memories. Every one of them. False because they had never happened. Because the man in the memories was not the man she had thought he was.

Her throat convulsed. Whatever her wariness over him, over what he wanted of her, she had thought she was at the least a romantic interlude for him—someone to while away a Caribbean idyll with, share a passionate affair with, enjoying their time together however transient. But she hadn't even been that. Not even that.

A lie—the whole thing had been a lie. A lie from the moment he'd asked her to keep the lift doors open for him. A set-up. Staged, managed, manipulated. Fake from the very first moment. With no purpose other than to bring her to the point she was now—cast out of Ian's life.

Because there was no going back—she knew that. She could never be any part of Ian's life now. Not even the fragile, insecure part that she had once so briefly been.

His wife is Athan's sister... Ian is his brother-in-law...

She hadn't known—hadn't guessed—hadn't suspected in a million years. And obviously Ian had not thought it necessary for her to know that his wife's brother was Athan Teodarkis, because it would mean nothing to her—why should it?

But it didn't matter, she thought tiredly. It didn't matter

who had known or not known who was what to whom. All that mattered now was that Athan Teodarkis—Ian's wife's brother—knew about her—knew what she was to Ian.

Anguish writhed inside her.

Why didn't Athan just confront me straight off? It was all he had to do. If he knew about Ian and me he could just have threatened to expose me. Why did he do what he had gone and done?

The answer was bleak and brutal. The method Athan Teodarkis had chosen was far more effective. Far more certain.

He'd been right about that. She was out of Ian's life now—and she would stay out. Nothing else was possible now. Nothing at all...

Unthinkingly, methodically, she went on with her packing.

The intercom on Athan's desk flashed repeatedly, and his secretary's voice, when she spoke, sounded flustered and apologetic.

'Kyrios Teodarkis—I am so sorry! It is Kyria Eva's husband! He insists on seeing you. I told him you had a board meeting in ten minutes, but—'

'It's all right,' Athan interrupted her. 'I'll see him.' His voice was grim. So was his expression. He had half expected this. Ian Randall would not lightly give up his intended mistress.

Who would give up Marisa Milburne? So beautiful, so passionate a woman.

The familiar guillotine sliced down over his thoughts. It had been much in use these past days. Slicing down ruthlessly on so many thoughts—so many memories. But he would allow himself none of them—not a single one. Their indulgence was forever barred to him. His eyes hardened. He would not allow his feckless, faithless brother-in-law to indulge himself any longer with his forbidden fruit.

I had to give her up—so must he!

His expression was still reflecting the savagery of his thoughts as Ian swept in. He looked agitated and launched straight in.

'Athan—what the hell is this about? Neil Mackay says it comes from you, but I don't understand why. Why do you want me at your HQ?'

Athan sat back. He appeared unperturbed by the outburst. 'It's time you moved on. And up. It's promotion, Ian—aren't you pleased?'

His tone was equable. He would keep this civil—or his sister would get wind of a fracas between him and her husband and get upset.

'Oh, come on,' Ian said disbelievingly. 'You've no call to promote me!' He paused, eyes narrowing. 'This is about Eva, isn't it? You think it will please her to be back in Athens.'

Athan's gaze levelled on him. 'Eva's happiness is paramount to me.' He paused. 'Never forget that.' He paused again, and when he spoke, it carried the message he intended it to. 'After all—' his voice was limpid '—it was because it made her happy that I let her marry you.'

Colour mounted in his brother in law's face. 'And you've never forgiven me for marrying her, have you?'

Athan's gaze never dropped. 'Providing you don't hurt her, or upset her, I…tolerate you.'

He watched glacially as the colour flared out across his brother-in-law's handsome face. The face of a man who helped himself to whatever he wanted in life—smiling, charming, selfish, self-indulgent. He'd charmed Eva, wooed her, and ended up persuading her to marry him.

And proved himself faithless within two years of their wedding.

Silently Athan cursed his unwanted brother-in-law. Cursed the life-long intimacy between their families— Sheila Randall's all-but-adoption of his then teenaged sister.

He cursed Sheila's son for getting anywhere near the impressionable, vulnerable Eva so disastrously eager to fall in love with his golden looks and easy charm.

Cursed him for having used those same golden looks and easy charm to work their damage on yet another woman—on Marisa...

'You...*tolerate* me?' Ian's voice cut through his litany of inner curses.

'That's very good of you, Athan. Very...generous. But maybe—' now there was something different in his voice that made Athan's eyes narrow '—maybe I'm tired of your tolerance. Tired of your generosity. Tired of it being known that as Athan Teodarkis's brother-in-law no wonder I'm a board director, no wonder I get sent off on plush secondments to the West Coast, with instructions to take holidays in Hawaii to keep my wife happy—my boss's sister.' He took a step forward. 'Maybe it's time to tell you I can live without your *tolerance,* your generosity!'

Athan's gaze skewered him. 'And maybe—' his voice cracked like a whip, all civility gone now '—you'll do *exactly* what I say you will. Or would you rather—' he bit out each word '—I tell Eva about Marisa Milburne.'

Ian Randall froze. Before Athan's eyes the other man's face paled. 'How the hell do you know about Marisa?' he demanded.

Athan spread his hands out on his desk. 'Don't take me for an idiot. You installed her in a flat in Holland Park.'

'You bastard,' Ian breathed. 'You spied on me.'

'Like I said—don't take me for an idiot.' Athan's voice was caustic.

'And you would actually be prepared to tell Eva about her?' Ian said in a hollow tone.

Athan's lasering gaze never left his brother-in-law's face. 'I won't have to. Marisa Milburne is no longer in your flat.'

'*What*?'

'You heard me. She's gone. Cleared out.' He paused. 'Presumably,' he said deliberately, his eyes like slate, 'she's selected another wealthy lover to beguile…?'

He saw Ian's face freeze again. But this time there was something in his frozen gaze that Athan could not identify. Then slowly, as if the ice was thawing, his brother-in-law turned and headed for the door. As he reached it, he turned. His face was like marble.

'You'll have my letter of resignation on your desk tomorrow morning.'

Then he was gone.

Almost, Athan charged after him. Charged after him to seize his shoulders and shake him like the rat he was. But he wouldn't soil himself on the man. As for his threatened resignation—he'd never do it. The position he had was far too cushy a number. And if he tried to go it alone, escape from Athan's scrutiny—*necessary* scrutiny, as he'd amply demonstrated—Eva would kick up. She wouldn't want any bad feeling between her husband and her brother.

Grimly, Athan made himself sit back in his chair, his face like thunder. Let Ian rush out and vent his spleen! Do whatever the hell he wanted. Anger bit through him. Damn the man—damn him and double damn him!

Angrily, he swung in his chair, his eyes stormy, unforgiving. If Eva's philandering husband had had the slightest moral backbone Marisa Milburne would never now be plaguing him the way she was.

Never haunting him the way she was.

Filling his memory. Tormenting him.

Tormenting him with wanting her. That was the damnation of it—the thing he was trying to crush out of his mind, his memory. Because what was the point of letting it torment him? There was nothing he could do about it—nothing. He had to accept that. He'd decided on his strategy to ensure that his wretched, faithless brother-in-law would be severed from the woman who had beguiled him, and now he had to abide by the consequences of that strategy.

But I didn't think it would be like this.

That was the devil of it. He'd never for a moment imagined that he'd be left feeling like this.

Cheated. That was the word. The emotion. Cheated of a woman who'd turned out to be someone not just easy to seduce but…memorable. Memorable in so many ways. All of them incredible.

Cheated… The word twisted in his head again. He knew it was a pointless word—a pointless emotion for him to feel. He'd gone into this with his eyes open, his mind made up, his strategy planned and flawlessly executed. He had succeeded completely, achieved his aim, finished his mission. It should be the end of the story. It was—for her and Ian. But not for him.

I still want her. I want her, and I don't want it to be the end. I want to have her back again

I can't. It's as simple as that—and as brutal. I seduced her to take her away from Ian—not for myself. It was never about her, it was only about Eva.

Moodily, he stared ahead of him, seeing not his plush office but the silver sand beach, the swaying palms, the turquoise sea. And Marisa.

Always Marisa.

Tormenting him.

Slowly, Marisa climbed out of the taxi and handed the driver the fare. It was a horribly large amount, and in her pre-Ian days she would never have dreamt of taking a taxi from the railway station some twenty miles away. She would have waited for the local bus, which ran four times a day and no more, and then got out at the village and walked the remaining mile up to the cottage. But now she could afford the luxury of a taxi from the station—all thanks to Ian.

But she mustn't think about Ian. Not now. Ian belonged to a world she had never been part of—not even on the fringes, where she had clung. Athan Teodarkis had prised her from where she had been so hopelessly clinging. She should be glad of it—glad that he had shown her with callous brutality just how much she was not any part of that world.

She looked about her as the taxi turned around and headed back down the narrow lane, out of sight. She shivered. Winter still clutched the land, making the air clammy with cold, and the bare trees shivered in the chill wind that blew off the moor. It was dank and drear, and the late afternoon was losing its light, closing down the day. In front of her the cottage looked forlorn and ramshackle. A slate had come loose, she could see, and water dripped from a leaf-blocked gutter. The garden looked sodden, with the remnants of last autumn's leaves turned a mushy brown on the pathway to the front door.

With a heavy sigh and a heavier heart she heaved up her suitcases and the bag of groceries she'd bought and opened the creaking wooden gate. She walked up to the front door. As it opened to her key the smell of damp assailed her. Inside was colder than outside. She gave another shiver, set down her cases, and went through to the kitchen with the carrier bag. The ancient range was stone-cold, not lit since the day she had left for London months before. The cob walls and small windows made it darker than ever, and she turned on the electric light—which only showed up the dust on the kitchen table, illuminated the dead flies on the windowsill.

Depression closed around her like a cold, tight blanket. Numbly, she went about the tasks required to make the cottage habitable: turning on the fridge and putting the fresh food away in it, relighting the range, wiping down the dusty surfaces, trying to keep her mind on the mundane tasks, not on anything else. Not on the empty dreariness of the cottage, on the bleakness in her heart.

The cottage was so empty—so absolutely and totally

empty. Grief filled her—grief for the mother no longer there, her absence palpable. Grief for Ian, whose life she could no longer be even the barest part of.

And grief for something else—something that she dared not allow lest it consume her.

Overwhelmed, she felt her throat tightening, the emotion welling up inside her, and she sank down on one of the kitchen chairs, her head sinking on her folded arms. Hot, shaking sobs filled her. She cried out all her loneliness, all her grief. And one more emotion too. Fiercer, sharper—like a needle flashing in and out of her, over and over again, weaving through her in a thousand piercings. Questions, accusations—self-accusations—tumbled about in her. Jumbled and jostled and fought for air.

How could he do that to me? How could I fall for it? How can it hurt so much? How can it matter so much? How could I mind so much?

How, how, how...?

Anguish consumed her. Why had he not simply confronted her and told her she must have nothing more to do with Ian? Been up-front, honest—brutal from the start?

Not at the end. Not after luring her with soft words, false smiles…

False kisses…

And more, far more than kisses.

She lifted her head, staring sightlessly out over the kitchen. Once so familiar to her, now it was like an alien landscape. In front of her was not the cottage with its thick cob walls, its old fashioned cupboards and furniture, the smell of damp and mustiness.

Heat and blazing sun, and the lapping of azure waters, the feel of the sand beneath her feet and her heart full.

She felt her lungs tighten as though they must burst.

How could he do it to me? How?

How was it possible that he should have been able to take

her in his arms, make love to her, and all the while it was just some cruel, calculating manoeuvre to get her out of his brother-in-law's life?

Her tears dried on her cheeks, leaving dampened runnels and her expression like stone.

He deceived me from the very first—fooled me and conned me and lied to me. Lied in word and deed.

Grimly she stared blindly ahead. Lies, lies, lies. Foul, deceiving lies. Smiling while he lied. Kissing her while he lied. Making love to her while he lied.

She jumped to her feet as if to banish all the hot, angry, anguished thoughts from her head. Nothing could change what had happened. It was as if she'd swallowed a snake— a poisonous snake that was now biting at her with its fangs inside, injecting its venom into her blood.

Angrily she strode through the narrow corridor to the front door, seizing up her suitcases, and heading up the creaking stairs to her old bedroom. It was freezing upstairs, and the smell of damp prevailed. But what did she care? What did she care about anything any more?

He can go to hell! Go to hell and stay there!

Hatred seared through her as venomous as the poison in her veins, seeking only one target—Athan Teodarkis. The man who had brought her to this. Taken her to paradise— and then smashed her into the ground.

CHAPTER FIVE

'ATHAN—what's happening? What's going on?'

Eva's voice down the phone line from London sounded strained. Athan could hear the anxiety in it, the worry, and cursed inwardly.

'Ian won't explain—won't tell me anything. But you and he have fallen out, haven't you? I know you have.'

He took a breath and put on his most calming voice—the one he used to try and reassure her when she got stressed over things. 'I don't want you worrying—' he began.

She cut across him, her voice rising in pitch. 'How can I possibly not worry? I'm worried sick! My husband comes home and announces he's resigned from his job! That he won't work for you any more. Athan, what have you said to him? Why is he doing this?'

Athan's hand around the phone receiver tightened. Ian had stormed out like a damn drama queen because he'd been shown up for the adulterous rat he was. But that was the last thing that Eva could ever know. Athan's teeth ground together angrily. And to protect her he had to protect her husband's dirty little secret.

'Eva, it isn't like that,' he said soothingly. 'It was a mutual decision,' he lied. 'Ian's made it clear to me for some time that he's restless, that he wants to quit.'

'But *why?* I was so thrilled that you trusted him enough to take him on board!'

Athan rolled his eyes, glad his sister couldn't see his expression. It wasn't because he trusted Ian Randall that he'd taken him on. The complete reverse! It was because he'd wanted to keep him where he could see him—where he would have to toe the line. His mouth thinned. And that was just what he hadn't done—and now Ian thought he could evade control by doing a runner.

Eva must not see it like that, though—that was essential. So he had to lie, to smooth it down, play it down.

'I guess he felt a bit overpowered, Eva,' he said. 'It's natural that he wants to try his wings out on his own—prove his own mettle. It could even be that he's been head-hunted,' he ventured placidly. 'After all, a stint at one of the Teodarkis companies makes Ian very employable.'

His efforts to placate his sister, to assure her that her husband's desertion was not a bad thing and did not indicate any falling out with his brother-in-law seemed to be working. Eva seemed to be calming down.

'Well, I suppose that's true,' she said, her voice steadying and losing the nervous tension that had racked it when she'd first spoken. 'But I was scared that he'd walked out because he'd quarrelled with you. You know he's in awe of you, Athan.' Her voice sounded sad. 'I just want you and him to get on well together, that's all.'

Athan said nothing. There were some things he couldn't lie about. Like the fact that nothing could make him 'get on well' with the man who had married his sister against all his instinctive disapproval of the match. His sister deserved so much better than a philandering lightweight like Ian Randall.

As for what the man would do now—Athan had no idea. He'd trotted out that line about Ian being highly employable but he had no great belief in it. He knew perfectly well that others assumed Ian Randall held his prestigious position as director of marketing at one of the key subsidiaries within the Teodarkis organisation purely because his brother-in-law owned the company. He wouldn't pick up another plum position like that out in the open market. No, without the shelter that he'd got from his brother-in-law Ian would find the corporate world a much harsher place. He might have enjoyed himself, storming out of his office, but reality would soon hit home. Athan's lip curled. He'd take pleasure in seeing Ian come crawling back for his old job.

He gave an exasperated sigh. He'd get it, too—because Eva would be upset otherwise. In the meantime—well, Ian Randall could just stay out of his hair or do anything else he damn well liked.

With one exception.

He would not go anywhere near Marisa Milburne.

So far he hadn't, and Athan intended it to stay that way. He didn't believe Ian would try, now that he knew that his brother-in-law knew about her, but he wasn't taking chances. On the other hand job-hunting should, Athan profoundly hoped, keep Ian's mind off his intended mistress—*former* intended mistress, he reminded himself grimly—at least for the time being.

He sighed heavily.

I have to get over her! I have to put her away, in the past, and not let myself think about her or remember her and the time we had together. It's over—gone, finished. She's out of Ian's life—out of mine.

For good.

But it was one thing to adjure himself to forget Marisa—to refuse to let himself go back down those tempting, dangerous pathways of his mind—quite another to achieve it. He stared out over the Athens skyline. Where was she now? he found himself thinking. She'd cleared out of London—out of the apartment Ian Randall had paid for—and gone. That was all he cared about—all he could allow himself to care about. The fact that she had disappeared. Disappeared as swiftly as she had appeared. Had she left London altogether? Or just gone to live somewhere else in the city?

Had she found another man? Another lover?

An image, hot and tormenting, leapt in his mind's eye.

Marisa in another man's arms—another man's bed...

He thrust it out of his head, refused to let it back in. It was nothing to him—*nothing!*—whether or not she'd found another man to fill her life with. That was all he must remember—all he must allow himself to think.

Grimly he crossed to his drinks cabinet, yanking open the doors. Maybe a shot of alcohol would banish the image from his head. Give him the peace he sought.

I need another woman.

The crudity of his thought shocked him, but that, he knew, was what it boiled down to. There was only one way to get Marisa Milburne out of his consciousness and that was by replacing her in it. He took a heavy intake of breath. OK, so how about starting right now? He could fill every evening with a hectic social life if he wanted—and right now that seemed like a good idea. A whole lot better than resorting to alcohol, for a start.

Shutting the drinks cabinet doors again, he strode from the room.

An hour later, changed from lounge suit to dinner jacket, he was mouthing polite nothings in a crowded salon at a cocktail party, wondering whether he needed his head examined. At least three women, each of them stunningly beautiful, were vying for his attention, and he was trying to give none of them reason to think he was favouring any of them. None of them, nor any of the other women at the party, had the slightest allure for him. Even after a second glass of vintage champagne.

Restlessly he looked about him, hoping against hope that someone, somewhere, would catch his eye. But as his gaze ran over the assembled females dispassionately not a single one made him look twice.

'…in the Caribbean…'

The fragment of speech brought him back. One of the women—a voluptuous brunette with lush lips and a traffic-stopping figure—was talking, it seemed, about a proposed cruise. She was pausing invitingly for him to say something.

But he wasn't seeing her…

He was seeing Marisa leaning against him, curled up beside him on the wide palanquin-style sun-shelter in front of their cabana, overlooking the beach, sipping a cocktail with him as they watched the sun go down in a blaze of gold and crimson. Her body so soft, so warm nestled against him. Her pale hair was like a golden rope down the backless sun-dress she was wearing. His mouth was brushing the satin of her hair, his hand cupped her shoulder, holding her close… so close.

The warmth of her body—the sweetness of its scent—the heady longing of desire, of possession, wrapping them together.

His mouth nuzzled at her cheekbone. She turned her face to his, caught his lips with hers, let him draw her down upon the soft, yielding surface…

'What do you think?'

The brightly voiced enquiry roused him painfully, and he had to refocus his eyes, his mind. 'Is a cruise around the Caribbean a good idea? Or is it better to be based on land?'

He gave an absent half smile. 'I guess it depends how vulnerable you are to seasickness,' he answered, hoping it was a suitable answer in a conversation he had paid no attention to.

'Oh, I get *horribly* seasick,' one of the other women contributed, and turned her eyes full-on to Athan. 'There are so many gorgeous islands. Which one do you recommend? St Bart's? Martinique? Barbados—though that is *so* over-popular now, alas!'

He answered at random. His thoughts were far away, across the ocean, on the only Caribbean island he cared about. St Cecile. The one that held all his memories of Marisa.

I want her back.

The words formed in his head before he could stop them. Burning and indelible.

He wanted Marisa back. That was all there was to it. Simple, and straight to the point.

I don't care who she is—what she was to Ian—why I did what I did. I just want her back. I don't care how impossible it is.

He had finally admitted it. Faced up to and acknowledged the truth he'd been trying to deny ever since he'd stalked out of her apartment, having told her that everything between them had been a set-up—a lie.

But he could deny the truth no longer. He wanted Marisa back again...

But I can't—it's impossible. Out of the question. It's the most damn out-of-the-question thing in the world!

He had to put it out of his head. Put *her* out. Whatever it took. He looked anew at the bevy of beautiful women dancing attendance on him. He had come here tonight to this glittering social gathering, to where he was a familiar face, the Athenian high society circuit, with the specific purpose of finding another woman to take his mind off the one he couldn't have. But the problem was he didn't want any of them. Not a single one.

Dispassionately he assessed them, and those around him in the ornate salon. Even those not blessed with natural beauty were wearing *haute couture* numbers, shimmering with expensive jewellery, coiffed and manicured to the nines, looking fabulous and elegant whatever their age. Yet not one of them appealed.

Marisa could float in with just with a towel wrapped round her, not a scrap of make up and her hair in a ponytail, and she would still be the only woman I want.

With a heavy, self-accusing sigh at his own hopeless weakness, he rejoined the conversation. It was not the fault of the women here that he didn't want them. At the very least he owed them courtesy and attention.

Somehow he got through the remainder of the evening until he felt he could bid his hostess goodbye and finally beat a retreat. Back in his own apartment, glad to be on his own again at last, he went out on to the balcony. Though it was still chilly, winter was over now. Spring would be blessing the land again soon, and then the heat of the Aegean summer. For now he welcomed the cool—welcomed looking out over the Athens skyline, polluted though the air was, and thinking his own thoughts.

OK, he reasoned, for a change marshalling his brainpower to a purpose, not of corporate affairs or the economic problems besetting the world, but to his own dilemma. He had to be blunt about this. He wanted a woman it was impossible to have. Impossible because it would damage his family, jeopardise his sister's shaky marriage. Having anything more to do with the woman who had nearly destroyed it was unthinkable.

Yet when he had tried to divert his attention to another woman—any woman!—he had found to his dismay that he might as well have been gazing at a cardboard cut-out.

There was, therefore, only one solution. It was staring him in the face, but it wasn't one he was particularly attracted to. But still there it was.

Celibacy.

Going without.

Abstinence.

He took a heavy breath. It would be hard, but it was his only option right now. Somehow he had to purge the last influences of Marisa Milburne from him, and living like a monk was his only effective method. And what he would have to do in order to ensure that he could achieve that purging was refuse to think about her, remember her, long for her. He'd fill his head up with other stuff.

Work would be good 'other stuff'...

He gazed out bleakly, glimpsing the ancient rock of the Acropolis crowned with the ruins of the Parthenon. A temple to Athena. The patroness of Athens. A virgin goddess. The goddess of wisdom and fortitude.

He would need both those qualities in quantity from now on.

Marisa watched the dark blue car wind its way slowly down the narrow lane from the cottage back towards the village and the road beyond that led out of Devon, back towards the motorway that headed for London. Her heart was heavy and torn, but she had done the right thing—she knew she had.

Ian had pleaded with her, but she had held firm—cost her though it had.

I had to do it—I had to convince him that I just can't be part of his life any more. Not now—not ever.

He had arrived, despite all her pleas to him by text and phone not to, that morning. He had been aghast that she had moved out of the flat in London he'd leased for her, begged her to reconsider, change her mind—come back.

But of course she couldn't. Wouldn't. Athan Teodarkis had made that impossible. Unthinkable.

Going back to her old home, her old life, was the only thing that was possible. Here at the very least she could hide. Hide from everything—and everyone. Ian insisting on confronting her here had been an ordeal, but draining though it had been, and upsetting, she knew that it had had to be done to convince him she'd made her decision and was going to stick to it. So now—painfully—he'd gone, leaving the knowledge that she could not possibly tell him what his brother-in-law had done to her burning inside her like acid.

As she watched Ian's car disappear around the curve of the lane she shut her eyes, feeling a kind of relief at his departure that was at odds with the wrench of watching him leave her life. She felt breathless and suffocated by all the emotion pressing down upon her. On an impulse she went back inside the cottage and changed her indoor shoes for a stout, well-worn pair of ankle boots, grabbed an anorak and the cottage keys, and headed out of the back door.

A pathway led from the garden up through the last of the fields below the moor, then broke free onto the moorland itself. It was a cloudy day, with a westerly wind sending the clouds scudding, and drops of rain shaking down from time to time. But the weather didn't matter—only getting out of the cottage. It was a familiar walk—she'd done it a thousand times in her youth. Sometimes with her mother, sometimes on her own. It had always given her refreshment. There was something about the moorland, up above the farmed fields, directly under the sky, that opened her up, let out the feelings and emotions that troubled and oppressed her—whatever those troubles and oppressions were.

And now she was walking here again, into the wild air, across the infertile land where only heather and gorse and rough grass flourished, up across the uneven, curving terrain towards the distant tor—the granite outcrop that loomed on the horizon.

It took an hour of brisk walking to get there, and she was out of condition after all her time in London, but she got there in the end and found her familiar nook amongst the rocks, sitting herself down on a horizontal shelf of granite, facing out over the vast expanse of moorland beyond. The westerly wind keened over the land and through the gaps in the rocks, winnowing her face. Rain blew in on the wind, but her cheeks were already wet—wet with the tears she was shedding.

Tears for so much. For her mother, who had been deprived of the love and happiness she'd sought, and who'd had to make do with a constricted, unfulfilled life here when she'd once hoped for so much more.

Just like I did—so short a time ago.

But those hopes had been crushed and brutally exposed for the folly they always had been.

I should have known that I could never be part of Ian's life—never be accepted, never tolerated.

She gazed bleakly over the bare landscape. Her mother had warned her—warned her about the world she sought—but she hadn't believed her, hadn't wanted to believe her. Her mother had been burnt, too, expelled and rejected, and that was why she'd sought refuge here, in this lonely place, accepting a life austere and alone, instead of the life she had once hoped for.

Her mother's hopes had been cruelly dashed.

So, now, had her own.

Marisa's eyes darkened. She had had days now to try and accept what Athan had done to her—to join together the two utterly different people he seemed to be, to accept that the man she'd thought she'd known, the man she'd come to trust, to give herself to, had been nothing like that at all.

Ruthless. Brutal. Lethal.

That was the true Athan Teodarkis. That was the man she had to see him as. No matter what dreams came in the night, beguiling her. No matter what memories tried to seep into her consciousness, tormenting her.

She lifted her face into the wind, the oncoming rain. Her hair was plastered to her head but she didn't care. She was used to the weather—glad of the punishing elements battering her. She deserved them to be lashing her.

I was a fool—a trusting, self-deceiving fool—who fell for a man who was all surface, all temptation...

Just as her mother had done.

The realisation hit her like an intake of breath. She shut

her eyes, rocking with the ugly, accusing truth of it. The pain of recognition scalded her.

Her mother had been a fool once, hoping for her dreams to come true—but she'd founded her hopes on a man who had made a fool of her.

Just as Athan has made a fool of me...

Pain seized her. Racking her body. She forced herself to be still, to wait it out, to let it pass. She'd been doing that for days now, every time the memory of that nightmare conversation in the apartment leapt to malevolent, vicious life in her head—his denouncement of her, telling her that he'd set up everything between them for the sole purpose of separating her from Ian.

The last of the louring clouds passed overhead and sunshine, bright through the rain-washed air, pooled over her. It was pale and had hardly any heat in it—a frail, fleeting lightening of the grim, bleak day.

Not like the hot, fierce sun of the Caribbean, beating down on my bare shoulders like a physical force, soaking into me as I lay on a sun lounger, idly chatting to Athan lying beside me. Filtering through the louvered windows when we retired to our cabana after lunch to make love...

The pain came again, but she quenched it. Quenched it by will power, by the power of the shame that she had fallen for such a ruthless, heartless masquerade. Because, whatever the rights and wrongs of it, he had lied to her from the very start, and nothing—not the slightest thing about him—had been true.

She got to her feet, scrambling down from her perch in the rocks of the tor and jumping down onto the wet ground. She paused to gaze around her at the vast expanse of open moor. On a rise a few hundred yards away she could see the low outline of stone-edged walls, almost obliterated by heather and time. It was a Bronze Age village, thousands of years old, and it was a familiar part of the landscape to her.

Now, as she looked across at it, she wondered at the people who had once, so very long ago, lived there, made their lives there. They had loved and lived and worked and died, each little life as important to its owner as hers was to her. Yet all there was left of them was a few stones.

My life will be like that one day. Leaving not even a shadow on the land. So what does it matter if I am hurt or humiliated or angry or anguished? Soon the pain I feel will pass—soon I will feel nothing.

It had been true for her mother, surely, that a time had come when the man who had treated her so badly no longer had the power to wound her?

I'll make it true of me, too. I have to.

Slowly, she made her way back down off the moor. The sunshine remained, thin and pale, but better than the rain. The wind was softer here, in the lee of the moor, and there was the scent of spring in it. Winter was nearly over.

All she needed was time. Time to let him fade like a bad dream, to let him go, to move on, forward into a life that she was yet to make. What that new life would be she didn't know—couldn't even envisage. She had thought when she'd left the cottage to go to London that her life was just starting—now she was stranded back here again, with no way forward that she could think of.

But I'll find one—I can. I must. And I can be strong—I have to!

Resolution filled her. With a firmer step she headed down the trackway that led off the moor, climbing the stile that gave on to the dead end of the lane that went back past her cottage to the village a mile or so beyond. The light was fading now, the sun sunk below the tor behind her, and she wanted to get back to the cottage before evening closed in. But as she rounded the final bend of the narrow lane she stopped short.

A car was parked in front of the cottage. For a moment she thought it must be Ian, returning despite her refusal to go back to London with him, but then she realised it was another make of car, and even in the dusk she could see the colour was different. It was an expensive car, though, as Ian's had been—sleek and powerful-looking. But it wasn't until the driver's door opened that she realised just who had come to call...

Athan unfolded his tall frame from the confines of the car he'd been sitting in since his arrival half an hour ago, and watched Marisa walk towards him. His emotions were tamped down—under strict control. They had been ever since he'd got the phone call from his security agency—the call he'd been steeling himself against, hoping he would never get it. But, as predictable as a greedy child stealing from the candy jar, Ian Randall had done exactly what Athan had feared he would do.

Icily he'd heard out the phone call, taking in the bare, bald details provided. Time, route, venue. It was all he'd needed to know. Now, though, he needed to know a hell of a lot more...

She walked up to him. She had nerve, he gave her that. Or perhaps it was her lover's presence that was giving her confidence. Not that there was any sign of Ian, or his car.

His voice, harsh and rough, cut through the chilly air.

'Where is he?' It was a curt demand, and he wanted an answer.

She stopped dead. Absently, Athan wondered at her appearance. She looked totally different from the way he was used to seeing her. She had a baggy pair of trousers on, mud-spattered boots, and a voluminous anorak that was as unflattering as it was obscuring of her figure. Her hair was sopping wet, and dragged back off her head with a clip. She looked a sodden mess.

But her face—her face was as breathtaking as ever. Her eyes, flashing with anger, were luminous, her mouth kissed by the rain...

'He's gone.' Her voice was as curt as his. She knew exactly who Athan meant. Knew exactly why he was here. Anger

spiked in her, because it was obvious that the only way Athan
Teodarkis could have known where his brother-in-law had
gone was if he'd had him tailed.

'Didn't your spies spot him heading back to London?' she
threw at him caustically.

Athan's face tightened. No, they hadn't—or at least he
hadn't had a report to that effect. He'd told them to keep a
discreet distance—presumably it had been too discreet. But
even so the point was clear. Despite everything he'd said to
Ian, the man had still come chasing after his mistress like a
dog on heat…

He strode towards her.

She flinched, but held her ground. Shock waves were detonating through her, but she had to ignore them. Had to ignore
more than just the shock of seeing Athan Teodarkis, tall, forbidding and grim-visaged, here outside her home. The juxta-
position was jarring. Athan Teodarkis didn't belong here in
this rural backwater, in this bleak, stark landscape dripping
with the dregs of winter. But, however jarring, it was not that
which was consuming her self-control.

Emotions were hurtling through her—tumbling and overwhelming her.

*Athan! Athan here—now! Right in front of her! So close…
his presence overpowering her senses.*

She almost reeled from the impact of it.

I didn't think I would ever see him again!

But he was here, and she could feel her treacherous blood
leaping in her veins, emotion pouring through her…

She had to subdue it—had to make herself realise that he
was here for one reason and one reason only. Because Ian
had come to her. That was all. That was why he was here—
angry. Accusing.

But this time her conscience was clear. His accusations
could reach no target—none.

'So whatever you think you're doing here—you can clear off!' she said. 'He isn't here.'

His eyes narrowed—eyes that had once looked at her with hot, melting desire...now filled only with cold anger.

'But he came here all the same.'

Her chin lifted. 'And now he's gone—for good.'

Athan stilled. 'Did you tell him about us?'

Marisa's lip curled in scorn. 'Of course I didn't.'

No, thought Athan, *of course you didn't. You wouldn't want him to know how easily I seduced you...took you away from him.*

He smiled in grim satisfaction. His anger was ebbing now. Anger fuelled by much more than fury at his philandering brother in law. Fuelled by a far more powerful impulse. The impulse that had brought him here, powering down the motorway relentlessly, as driven as the car bringing him here. Driven by a force he could no longer suppress—no longer wanted to suppress.

He nodded at the cottage. 'I need to talk to you—and not out here.' He stamped his feet. His Italian leather handmade shoes were fine for the city. Not fine for a cold evening in the wilds.

'I've got nothing to say to you.' Marisa's voice was still curt. Shock was still detonating through her.

He looked at her. In the dusk his expression was saturnine. 'But I,' he told her, 'have something to say to *you.*' His expression changed slightly. 'You look frozen,' he said.

For a moment the breath caught in her throat. There had been concern in his voice—caring.

The way he'd once sounded when he spoke to her...

Brutal truth sliced down, forcing open her throat. He'd lied to her from the beginning—lied with every caring, affectionate, casual word. That was what she must remember.

Not the way he used to look at her—the way his mouth

*would quirk with that half smile of his, the way his dark, lam-
bent eyes used to rest on her...*

She cut off the memory again. No, not that way at all.

She shivered under the anorak. He was right—she felt frozen. Stiffly she went up to the front door and opened it with
the key taken from the map pocket in her anorak. He followed
her in. Immediately the small cottage felt smaller. She didn't
want to let him in—didn't want him here. Didn't want him
anywhere near her within a thousand miles.

Liar! Liar—liar—liar!

The words in her head accused her, betrayed her. Again
she had to call on the cold, emotionless self-control she'd
faced him with outside the cottage. It didn't matter where he
was—he was nothing to her. The same nothing to her that
she was to him.

She would let him say whatever it was he had to say—another reinforcement about her staying out of Ian's life was all
it could be—and then she would send him packing. He could
find his own way back to the village, his own way back to the
motorway. What did she care? Nothing—that was what she
cared. All that was left of her feelings for him...

Nothing.

She went into the kitchen, feeling relief at the warmth from
the wood range enveloping her. Shrugging off her wet anorak,
she draped it around one of the chairs at the scrubbed wooden
kitchen table and opened the door to the range, restacking it
with wood. Then she filled the kettle and set it on one of the
rings to boil. Familiar tasks that gave her hands and brain
something to do while she tried to assimilate the fact—jolt-
ing, bizarre, impossible—that Athan Teodarkis had sat himself down at the kitchen table in a tiny cob-walled cottage
that had been a haven for her mother after the ruination of
her happiness.

Her gaze went to the man sitting at her kitchen table who
could reach out with a single finger and with a single touch

melt her like honey. Who could quirk a slanting smile at her and weaken her bones. Who could wind his hand around the nape of her neck and lower his mouth to hers, and take her to a paradise she had never dreamt of...

A man who had never—not once until that bitter, scathing denouement—said an honest word to her.

She took a breath. 'You said you had something to say—so say it. Say it and go.'

Gimlet eyes snapped to her. He'd been looking around him, taking in the room they were in. It had come as a shock to him, seeing how poor a place it was.

No wonder the world Ian moved in had seemed so tempting to her—no wonder she'd been so impressed by him, beguiled by him. Coming from a place like this, to her Ian's world must have seemed glittering and luxurious beyond anything she could have hoped for.

It sobered him. He couldn't deny it.

His gaze went back to her. His mind split instantly into two. One half was taking in just how shabby she looked—the other was simply drinking her in like a thirsty man in a desert. Even without a scrap of make-up, with wet, stringy hair and atrocious clothes, she still made his pulse leap!

'Well?'

Her voice refocused him. 'Do you need any money?' The question came out more bluntly than he'd intended. Nor was it the question he'd wanted to ask her—but after seeing this rundown place it had come out of his mouth without thinking.

'What?'

Athan looked slightly awkward. He really hadn't meant to sound that blunt, but it was too late now. He took a breath.

'Look, I've got eyes in my head. I can see there's one hell of a difference between your lifestyle in London and what you've got here. So, if you need something to tide you over I can easily—'

He got no further. She slammed the mug she'd been about to fill with coffee down on to the wooden table.

'No! I do *not* want your stinking money!' Her eyes were like lasers, and he had to shield himself from their glare.

'It was an offer—nothing more than that.' He had to mitigate. 'If Ian's seen you all right then you won't need anything from me.'

'You'll be glad to know,' she said, as sweetly as acid, 'that Ian does not continue to fund me.'

'I'm glad to hear it,' he said evenly, taking the fight back to her. 'And it's just as well—he is about to become unemployed. No,' he said, holding up a hand to silence her, 'it was not my doing. He's resigned from the company.' He paused. 'He didn't tell you?'

Marisa was looking pale. 'No. But…but why?'

Athan spelt it out, keeping his gaze on her to assess her reaction. 'He wishes to cut the apron strings from me. Assert his independence. Which is why,' he went on, his voice tinged with sarcasm, 'you will doubtless understand my concern that he has high-tailed it down to find you. I don't want him thinking he is now free to take up with you again.'

'Well, he isn't, is he?' she retorted. 'You've seen to that. How can I possibly look him in the face knowing what his own brother-in-law did to me?'

'Indeed,' Athan's voice was smooth now. 'So—' he took a breath '—he's accepted he cannot see you again? You told him that? Made it crystal-clear?'

'Yes.' Her monosyllabic reply was clipped, unemotional. But her emotions were running all the same—like a deep, underground river, cutting through the rocks and obstacles in her mind. Obstacles she had to keep in place. Absolutely had to…

'Good.'

He sounded satisfied. But there was something in his voice that alarmed her. It was not the satisfaction of a man who had disposed of an embarrassing and unwanted family problem.

'In which case...' he said, his eyes resting on her. 'In which case,' he repeated, 'I have something else to say to you.'

She stared. Her heart-rate had started to quicken, but she didn't want it to. As she didn't want to see what she was seeing in his eyes.

He's too close. This kitchen is too small. I can't breathe—can't find fresh air...

He was still sitting at the kitchen table, but his presence dominated the room—dominated her senses, her vision. She tried to think straight, but she couldn't. Everything about him focussed her on *him,* and deep within her still that powerful subterranean river of emotion was coursing, seeking its way upwards, out of the depths of her mind...

'It's this.'

He was speaking again, and she heard his words—heard the accent in them that had so worked on her, drawn her to him, just as everything about him had drawn her hopelessly, ineluctably, irresistibly...

His sloe-dark eyes were resting on her, delving into her, winding her gaze on his like a spool, so she could only look back at him, her eyes widening, melting...

'I want you back.'

His words fell into the space between them. The space that would soon no longer be between them...

Because it was quite clear in his head now. Crystal-clear. It had taken till this morning to crystallise—and it had done so instantly, irreversibly, when his phone had rung and he'd been told that Ian Randall was heading down to Devon.

In that instant he'd known—known with a spike of emotion that was like a punch to his guts—that he would never allow Ian or any other man to take Marisa from him. That whatever it cost he would take her back. However impossible, he would smash those problems to pieces and get what with every cell in his body over this punishing absence had grown more and more and more impossible to deny.

So he had let instinct—hot, overpowering instinct—take over. Take him from his desk, his office, London, and into his car, pressing pedal to the metal and storming his way westwards.

And now he was here—and so was Marisa, so was everything he wanted. Everything he was going to have.

No one and nothing was going to stop him. Not any more...

'You're out of Ian's life now, and that was what I had to achieve.' He looked at her, said what he knew he had to say. 'I didn't like what I was doing, Marisa, but I had to do it. Family is everything—and I had to protect my sister from the threat you represented to her. You can have no share in Ian's life. But,' he went on, 'you've accepted that, and I'm relieved to hear it—drastic though my method was. I acknowledge that.'

He held up a hand again, as if to brush aside the means he'd adopted to part his brother in law from her, and continued, getting to the most important part of his communication. The essential part. The part he'd driven over two hundred miles to deliver.

'Now we're free—both of us. Free to do what I have wanted to do since the moment I left you in your flat on our return.'

He got to his feet, crossed towards her. The narrow space between them disappeared. He reached out his hand, sliding it around the nape of her neck. The tendrils of damp hair were like silk on his fingertips. The scent of her body was like incense. The flush in her cheeks like roses. Her parted mouth was like honey waiting to be tasted...claimed...*reclaimed*...

'This,' he said, and his eyes poured down into hers like a golden haze, so that she was dizzy, blinded. Triumph surged in him—triumph and sweet, sweet possession...

He lowered his mouth to hers and bliss consumed her. She had dreamt of his kisses, yearned for them, craved them like an addict—and now it was happening. Here, now...

Bliss, sweet golden bliss.

He was drawing away from her again, but his hands were cupping her head, his body close against hers, his eyes still pouring down into hers.

'I've missed you so much,' he said. His voice was a husk. 'I can't do without you. And now, with you severed from Ian, I've realised I don't have to! I am free to take you back—to have again what I had before.'

His mouth started to lower again.

But, as if wires had jerked every muscle in her body, she yanked away. Stumbled around the corner of the table, getting it between them. Her eyes were wide and staring.

'Are you mad?' Her voice would hardly work and she had to swallow to make any sound come out. 'Are you *mad?*' she said again, louder now. Stronger.

Her mind was reeling. Reeling the way her body was. Her senses were aflame. But now water had been poured on them—an icy, frozen douche that doused them utterly. Emotion was knifing through her—but not the one she had just experienced, the bliss of his kiss. This was the one that had been coursing its way from deep, deep underground. That broke through now in a terrifying roar in her head.

'You lied to me from beginning to end! You lied to me and manipulated me and played me like a total idiot. How can you *possibly* think I would just take up with you again? That I would meekly go back to you after what you did to me? I'd have to be certifiable to do that.' She took a shuddering breath. 'Get out! Get out of here! I've done what you wanted me to do—given up Ian. So you've got no right—no right at all!—to come here and *dare* to say what you have.'

If he was reeling from her onslaught he didn't show it.

'You're angry with me—it's understandable,' he began. 'But—'

'Get out!' Her hands clenched the edge of the table. 'I don't ever want to see you again. I don't want anything to do with you ever again.'

His expression changed. 'Liar,' he said. 'You can't deny. It's impossible for you—just as it is for me, Marisa—to deny the effect we have on each other. Don't you think I curse the fact that I had to deceive you the way I did? I wish to God you'd never had anything to do with my damn brother-in-law in the first place. I wish I'd met you in any other circumstances. Because the effect you have on me would have been the same.'

He paused, his expression changing yet again. The molten, liquid lambency was back in his eyes, and his body language was charged with a voltage she would have to be blind, insensible not to recognise…to respond to.

'I might have lied to you about why I inveigled an acquaintance with you, lied about what purpose I had—but nothing else was a lie.' His eyes were resting on her, pouring into her. 'I never lied to you with my body…'

Breath rasped in her lungs, and her nails dug into the wood of the table's edge.

'Go!' she got out. 'I just want you to go.' She couldn't cope with this—she just couldn't. Ever since she'd seen him get out of his car she had been mentally shaking. But this—what he was saying…proposing…

'Marisa—listen to me.'

His voice sounded urgent. She couldn't bear it. Couldn't bear him being here, saying such things to her—asking such things of her.

She took another shuddering breath, not letting him speak as she cut across him. 'No! There's nothing on this earth that would ever make me even consider even for a single second what you are saying to me! How could you even think I would? Just how *stupid* do you think I am? After what you've done to me—said to me.'

He shook his head. Hell, this was all going wrong—totally wrong. He had to claw back somehow—anyhow. He had driven here with the devil on his tail, furious that Ian had dared to seek her out again, consumed with anger at his

brother-in-law, consumed even more by an emotion he knew
he had to name—could no longer deny.

Jealousy. Raw, open jealousy. Of Ian.

*He's not having her. Never again! She's mine—and I want
her back.*

That was the stark, strident message he'd had to face up
to as the miles had been eaten up by his foot on the accelera-
tor. He had to get to her so that Ian couldn't try and persuade
her back to him.

So that *he* could persuade her back to *him*.

So that she wouldn't haunt his dreams any more, or torment his memory, so that she could finally be to him what he
wanted her to be—not the woman he'd had to sever from his
brother-in-law but the woman he wanted for himself.

'Do you think I *wanted* to do what I did?' he demanded.
'But it's done now—finished. Over.'

Her eyes iced. 'Yes, that's exactly what it is. Finished. Over.
And I don't mean Ian—I mean you. So, like I said, go—just
go.'

'You don't mean that.' His voice was flat, disbelieving. 'If
you're waiting for me to apologise for doing what I did the
way I did it, then I can't. You had no business getting involved
with my brother-in-law, and nothing can change that.' Again
his voice changed. 'But having now seen where you come
from, seen the kind of background you have, I can understand
the temptation to inveigle yourself into his life. Gain from
him the affluence and comfort you certainly don't have here.'

He looked around disparagingly at the cramped, shabby
kitchen.

'I can make allowances,' he said. 'Understand *why* you
found Ian so tempting.' His gaze swept back to her. 'You don't
have to live like this, Marisa. Let me take you away from it
all. We were good together. We can have it again—honestly,
this time, with no more secrets.'

His eyes were blazing, rich and lambent, his voice deep, accented, sending vibrations through her.

'I want you to go.' Her voice was controlled. Very controlled over an emotion so strong that it might burst from her like an eruption. 'I don't want you here. I don't want anything more to do with you. And for your information, I don't want you to "take me away from it all". This happens to be my home. It may be poor, but it is mine, and it is where I live, and where I will go on living now.' She took a ragged breath. 'It's where I belong,' she finished.

Because this *was* where she belonged. She knew that now. Not in Ian's softly luxurious, pampering cocoon, kept secret from the world. And not—a jagged knife-thrust went through—dear God, *not* helplessly captive in Athan Teodarkis's cruel web of lies and deceit that had killed anything that she might once have felt for him.

Stony-faced, insistent, she stood her ground. 'So I want you to go,' she said again

Before she cracked, broke down, gave in—gave in to the desperate longing in her to throw herself into his arms, to pretend that nothing had come between them, to pretend that he'd never deliberately set out to seduce her and then denounce her the way he had. To pretend that what she'd thought was true *was*—he had never set her up, deceived her, lied to her…

But he had, and nothing could undo that

He wasn't saying anything. He was just standing there, tall and dark and so heart-stoppingly handsome that she could feel the power of it radiating like a force field. His face was a mask.

She'd seen it like that before when he'd confronted her on their return from St Cecile. When he'd closed himself to her, shut and locked the door, thrown away the key.

'I see,' he said. His voice was terse. Clipped. 'Well, you've made yourself very clear. So, yes, I'll go.'

Yet for a moment—a moment that seemed to hang in the

air like a weight—he remained motionless. She stood frozen, behind the table that divided her from him—behind everything that divided her from him and always would.

Always.

Then, 'I wish you well, Marisa. It would be…ungenerous of me to do less,' he said. His voice had no emotion, no depth. Nothing. Nothing at all.

His face still blank, still closed, he turned and walked out of the room.

She couldn't move. Could only wait while she heard his footsteps in the narrow corridor to the front door, and then the creaking door open and close behind him. For a few moments longer she waited. Only the crackling of the logs in the range was audible. Then another sound penetrated. A car engine gunning. Louder, then fading.

Fading completely.

He had gone.

Marisa went on standing there, quite motionless. Her eyes started to blink. Slowly, and then faster, tears began to run down her cheeks.

Along the narrow lane Athan drove—dangerously, recklessly fast. He had to. Had to gain as much distance from her as possible. He had arrived here a bare hour ago, driven by a demon he could not shake off his back. By the fear that she had succumbed to Ian Randall's forbidden blandishments, his begging to resume their affair. A demon had bitten him with the venom of savage jealousy.

Now a different demon drove him. Worse, much worse, than the first.

He wanted her—and she would not come to him.

I've lost her.

The words fell into his head like stones. Stones he could not shift. Stones that sat there crushing his thoughts, his emotions, everything.

All around him, pressing on the glass of the car windows, was darkness.

Darkness outside him.

Inside him.

He drove on into the winter's night.

CHAPTER SIX

MARISA dug carefully with the trowel. The garden her mother had loved so much had become overgrown, and she was trying to clear away the weeds from the new shoots sprouting up all over the flowerbeds. Spring had finally arrived, and as she knelt she could feel the sun warm on her back. It seemed like a blessing.

She was in need of blessings. Working hard to count them. To keep them in the forefront of her mind. Keep buried in the depths of her mind all remembrances of Athan Teodarkis—buried deep, buried safe.

She was humming to herself intermittently—some tune she'd heard on the radio. She listened to the radio a lot these days. It was companionship. Comforting. The cottage was so isolated she could play the radio out here in the garden knowing no one would be disturbed by it.

A robin was hopping around at the back of the flowerbed, tilting its head sideways and eyeing her hopefully. A small worm coiled itself under a clod of earth and she kept it buried. Fond as she was of the robin, who was a cheery visitor to the garden, she didn't feel up to deliberately feeding it a worm who was only trying to have a quiet life.

The way she was.

A quiet life. That was all she wanted right now. One that,

like the tiny earthworm could be spent buried deeply and safely. Sheltered and out of the way.

Where she belonged.

It had been weeks since Athan had been and gone. Weeks and weeks. How many, precisely, she hadn't counted. Hadn't wanted to. The days drifted by, one after another, marked only by the burgeoning spring. That followed a calendar that had its own schedule. One day it was a clump of primroses, unfurling their pale blossoms, another day the catkins showering her with golden pollen. Another the first flush of green on the once bare branches of the trees.

It was all she wanted right now.

She kept herself almost entirely to herself. She had set up a grocery delivery service with a supermarket in a large market town, and it suited her not to have to go there in person. The weekly delivery was good enough. Sometimes the local farmer's tractor rumbled past the cottage, but when she heard it coming she made sure she was not visible. She wasn't being deliberately stand-offish. She just didn't want to see anyone. Anyone at all. Whether local or stranger.

It was as if she was hibernating. Tucking herself away. Shutting down. Trying not to think. Trying not to feel. Trying to keep busy in the garden. While she worked she could feel her mother's presence, approving of her for what she was doing. Glad her daughter was back here again, safe in the haven she had found for herself—her refuge from a world that had rejected her, a man who had not wanted her.

Marisa's face twisted. Athan had wanted *her*.

That was the bitter, poisoned irony of it. After what he'd done to her, he wanted her.

Did he really think I would just totally ignore what he'd done? Why he'd done it? Just act like it had never happened?

But he had—obviously. That was what he'd assumed— that he could just pick her up again, carry on with her again. Take her back to his bed again...

No! She mustn't think like that—they were dangerous thoughts. Bringing in their wake memories that were even more dangerous. Lethal.

She dug deeper with the trowel, wrestling with a long, tenacious dandelion tap root to extract the last fragment. It wasn't the kind of root you could leave in the soil—a new weed would sprout even from the tiniest portion, seeking the air and the sun, thrusting up to grow and flourish.

Thoughts about Athan were like that. So were memories. She must get every last fragment of them out lest they seek to flourish once again.

She paused in her work, lifting her eyes to the hedge that bordered the garden, to the slope behind that led up onto open moorland. She would go for a walk later—blow away the cobwebs. Blow away the dangerous thoughts and memories that tried to get out.

Questions went through her mind and she wished she could have an answer to them, but knew she could not. Questions she had never asked but wished now she had. Questions of her mother.

How long did it take you to get over my father? To get him out of your head, your mind, your heart? To be free of him—free of what he'd done to you?

And the question that was most fearful of all: *Did you ever get over him?*

That was what she feared the most. That the wound was too deep, the scarring too brutal.

Because the problem was that despite all she was doing not to think about him, absorbing herself in this world, so familiar and so utterly different from the places she had been with Athan, it wasn't working. That was what she was scared of.

How long will it take to get over him?

That was the question that fretted at her, tormented her. She wanted not to think about not thinking about him. She wanted not to have to make this continual effort to turn her mind to other things. To immerse herself in this place she knew so well, surrounded by nature, by the wild landscape of the moors, the quiet fields and hedgerows.

But it didn't seem to be working—that was the problem. Surely by now she should at the very least be starting to forget him, to get over him. Not wanting to think about him, remember him. Surely she ought to be able to use her head to control her heart?

She froze. With one part of her brain she watched the robin hop closer to her. Bright-eyed. Red-breasted.

Predatory.

But the rest of her brain didn't see him. Didn't see the garden or the sunshine on the bushes, or the hedge behind the flowerbed.

The words that had sounded unconsciously in her mind came again.

Surely she ought to be able to use her head to control her heart?

No! She hadn't meant that—she hadn't. Panic filled her, choking in her throat.

It's not my heart—it's nothing to do with my heart.

Because if it was…

Before her eyes, the robin pounced. His sharp, deadly beak indented into the damp earth and in a flash, triumphantly, he tugged out the worm she'd tried to hide from him. With a flurry of wings he was gone, his prey consumed.

It's not my heart. I don't love him. I don't love him!

'Global economy…fiscal policy…employment levels…infrastructure investment…'

Athan let the words drone over his head. He wasn't listening. He gave the appearance of it, though—anything else would have been rude. But the speaker at the conference—a top economist at a major bank—had been going on for what seemed like for ever. And Athan had heard it all before—

several times now. This was the third day of the conference, and he had been here right from the start.

It mopped up time, this conference, and that was the most important aspect of it.

Time that he would otherwise have spent brooding.

Obsessing.

Because that was what it was, he knew. He could look it in the face and know it for what it was. Know *why* it was what it was.

He'd lost her. Plain and simple.

Devastating.

How had it happened? How had he screwed it up so badly? But he knew why—just didn't like accepting it. He'd high-tailed it down to the back of beyond where she'd holed up in that rundown hovel, seething with a raw, angry jealousy that he'd disguised to himself as outrage because Ian was daring to try and hook up with her again, and he'd hit a stone wall. Her point-blank refusal to have anything more to do with him.

Frustration warred with self-castigation. Frustration usually won—frustration that what he wanted so badly he wasn't going to get—but every now and then self-castigation managed to force itself through.

Did you really imagine that, having been manipulated and deceived, she was going to open her arms to you again? Take up with you again just where you left off—or rather, just before where you left off, at the bit where you hadn't yet denounced her as your brother-in-law's marriage-wrecker?

Of course she wasn't going to tamely come right back to him. Of course she was going to throw him out on his ear...

His eyes flashed darkly as he berated himself yet again.

You never stood a chance of getting her back. Not after what you did to her.

Then his expression hardened. Yes, well, she had no call to feel herself ill-used. *She* was the one who'd welcomed the attentions of a man she knew was married. That was what he

had to remember. Then another thought flickered uncomfortably across his consciousness—that cramped, dilapidated cottage she lived in, stark evidence of a penurious background
that would have meant Ian's lavish attentions being so very
tempting to her. No wonder a practised, suave philanderer
like his brother-in-law had been able to impress her, lead her
astray. She'd fallen head first for his superficial charms and
turned a conveniently blind eye to the wedding ring he wore.

That was what he had to remember. That was what justified what he'd done to her.

But another emotion slashed across his consciousness,
obliterating any others. What did it matter now whether he
was or was not justified in what he'd done? The fact that he'd
done it had destroyed his chances of getting her back—that
was all. Marisa had sent him packing and that was that. She
was gone. He'd lost her.

All that was left was frustration.

One more emotion. One he was trying hard not to admit
to. Because in comparison even the most obsessive frustration was easier to endure.

*We were good together—it worked. I don't know precisely
why, or how, but it did. It was easy being with her—natural.*

His mind went back to that idyllic fortnight in the
Caribbean, remembering how his mind had plucked so trou-
blingly at what he was doing, what he was going to have to
do when they went back to London, when he could no longer
shut his eyes to the purpose he'd set out with, when he'd have
to set aside what they were enjoying now and destroy it all…

*Well, I did destroy it—and I can hardly sit here and com-
plain that I can't get her back, can I? I did what I did for my
sister's sake, and now I have to accept the consequences.*

It was stern talk, and he knew he had to hand it out to
himself. But even as he did so, he could hear another voice,
deep inside.

Saving your sister's marriage has lost you something you will never recover...never...

His eyes gazed out unseeing over the conference hall.

His face as bleak as a winter wind.

Marisa turned down the radio and cocked her ears. It was a car approaching, she could tell. She frowned. It wasn't the day for her grocery delivery, and very little traffic other than heavy farm vehicles ventured this far along the dead-end lane. Setting down her paint roller and clambering off the chair she'd been standing on to reach the parlour ceiling she was busy painting, she made her way to the front door. As she got there an envelope came through the letterbox. Opening the door, she saw the postman getting back into his van and reversing. She gave him a half wave of acknowledgement and picked up the envelope. Her frown deepened. She got very little post, but the handwriting was familiar. She felt a knot start in her stomach.

It was from Ian.

Slowly, she took the envelope into the kitchen and slit it open, drawing out a handwritten letter.

My dearest Marisa—I have something I simply must say to you...

The knot tightened in her stomach, but she made herself read on. When she reached the end she stared for a moment, blinking.

Should she really do what Ian was asking?

It took her all day and all of a sleepless night to find the answer, but in the morning she dug out her mobile and texted him. It was the first time she'd contacted him since she'd sent him away—over a month ago now. He texted back almost instantly, cock-a-hoop, telling her he'd made the arrangements and all she had to do was get herself to Plymouth railway station. He would meet her at Paddington that afternoon.

His buoyancy did not elicit a similar response in her. Foreboding filled her. Should she really go ahead with this? She looked about her. The little cottage looked a lot better now than it had when she'd first fled back here. She'd subjected the whole place to a spring clean, and was now working her way round the rooms, brightening them with fresh paint. Outside, the garden was in full spring glory—daffodils thronging the beds, primroses nestling near the sun-warmed earth, the foliage in verdant green leaf. There was birdsong in the air, which was sweet and mild with the eventual promise of summer to come.

Could she really face leaving this remote, tranquil haven, where she had finally started to find some peace after all the torment she had been through? Could she really face going back up to London, doing what Ian wanted of her?

Becoming part of his life again…

Deep reluctance warred with longing.

But he was so adamant that now was the time. That he was finally brave enough to do what he knew with every fibre of his being he had to do. Tell the truth about them.

He said as much to her when he sat down with her over a drink in a pub close to Paddington station, where he had taken her after meeting the train.

'I've got to do it, Marisa,' he said, his expression full. 'I've got to tell Eva. And you have to be there when I tell her, so that she will believe how much you mean to me.'

Anxiety and doubt filled her eyes. 'Ian, I'm just not sure…'

'Well, I *am* sure,' he told her. He took her hand, squeezing it fondly. 'I won't live this lie any longer. I've tried to—God knows I've tried. I tried while you were here in London and I hated it—keeping you a secret the way I did. And I tried when you went back to Devon and buried yourself there. But

I hated it still—and I will go on hating it, Marisa, until we stop keeping this a secret.'

He took a breath and went on. 'Things are different now. It's not just that I've missed you like the devil since you went away, but things have changed for me, too. You know I chucked in the job at Eva's brother's company? Well, I'm glad I did. I've got another job, and it's one I really want to make something of.'

His expression changed, and Marisa could see the enthusiasm in it, hear the vigour in his voice.

'I've been taken on as marketing director of a third world fairtrade company that wants to tackle the supermarkets. I'm really fired up by it—it's a great cause, and I feel I can use my talents to do something important.' He made a rueful face. 'It also frees me from any sense of obligation or gratitude towards Eva's brother. In the circumstances—' he eyed Marisa meaningfully '—that's pretty much essential.'

He squeezed her hand again.

'Finally I feel I'm in a position to open up about you—to come clean. And that's what I want to do tonight.' He took one last decisive breath. 'We've got to do it, Marisa. You and me—telling the world about us.' He got to his feet, drawing her with him. Smiling down at her. 'Let's go and do it,' he said.

Still filled with anxiety, Marisa went with him.

Absently, Athan fingered a wine glass set out on the table in one of the hotel's private dining rooms. Eva was talking to the butler, telling him she'd changed her mind about what desserts to have.

For himself, Athan couldn't have cared less what she'd chosen for that evening. He had no appetite—none at all. Certainly not for this travesty of a 'family celebration' that Eva had said she was organising at her favourite Park Lane hotel.

'It was Ian's idea,' she'd said happily. 'He wants to tell you all about his new job. He's so excited by it—and so am I. It's as if there's a huge weight off his shoulders.'

Glancing at the vintage champagne on ice, the perfect damask napery, the silver service and the huge display of hothouse flowers, and knowing just what dinner in a private dining room cost at a place like this, it was just as well, Athan thought sourly, Ian had private means of his own—and that his wife was backed by the Teodarkis coffers. His new salary would not be nearly as generous as his old one had been.

Well, it was all to the good, he supposed. Not only did Eva seem very happy about it, but a demanding new job—even if poorly paid—had the notable benefit that it would keep his wayward brother's nose to the grindstone, with no time for dalliance. Athan's face hardened. At least there had been no sign of Ian trying to take up with Marisa again—nor was there any sign of him attempting to line up a replacement for her either. With luck, his sister's marriage might really be on the level again—at least for the time being.

His eyes shadowed. Something good had come out of the unholy mess that was Marisa Milburne's impact on his life. He'd better hang on to that. Find cold comfort in it.

He glanced out of the window over the rain-wet street beyond. He hadn't been to England since his fruitless pursuit of Marisa to the derelict dump she lived in. Hadn't been able to face it. Work, conferences—anything at all had kept him away—and he'd been glad of it. Coming here to London, now, for this dinner party his sister had organised, had not been on his itinerary, but Eva had pressed him so he'd reluctantly given in.

He was trying to be happy for her. Hell, it was to ensure *her* happiness that he'd gone and got himself into the mess he was now in with Marisa—so of course he had to be glad for his sister. Whether her happiness would last, of course, was a completely different thing.

He gave a heavy sigh. Well, at least he'd achieved his original purpose. He'd have to be content with that. Now he just had to get through this evening's dinner party, say whatever was appropriate in the circumstances by way of congratulating Ian on getting a new job, standing on his own feet, not cheating on his wife any more—not that he could mention that last, of course. At least not in front of Eva.

'Athan?' Eva had finished with the butler. 'I'm just going to go and check my make up in the powder room. Ian should be here any moment.'

She wafted by and Athan nodded at the butler, dismissing him for the moment. He wanted to be alone, even for a brief while. To steel himself for the ordeal ahead. Could he really get through an entire meal with Ian, knowing that he knew about the infidelity he'd planned, with both of them putting on a good front for Eva?

Well, he'd have to try—damn hard!—that was all.

The doors to the private dining room opened, and Athan turned back from gazing bleakly out of the window.

As he turned, he froze.

Ian had just walked in.

In his wake, stepping with obvious trepidation, was Marisa.

Athan's reaction was instant. 'You *dare* to bring her here!' he hurled at his brother-in-law.

Marisa could feel the breath congeal in her lungs. How could this be happening? She felt faint, clinging automatically to Ian's arm as if to keep herself upright. Oh, dear God, if she'd had the faintest idea Athan would be here...

Ian had stiffened. 'Where's Eva?' he demanded.

Athan ignored the question. His expression was a mask of fury. 'You have *one* second to get that woman out of here before—'

'Before what?' A light, feminine voice sounded from the doorway.

Athan whirled round. His sister stood poised in the doorway, looking at the tableau frozen in front of her. Her expression changed when her gaze took in the presence of a completely strange woman on her husband's arm.

'Ian?' she said enquiringly, a bemused but unsuspicious look on her face.

Marisa swallowed. So, finally, this was Ian's wife. She could feel her thoughts racing in her head, tried to get control of her emotions. Emotions that had been erratic enough ever since she'd read Ian's letter that morning. But when she'd felt the full force of her dismay at Athan's presence here she'd reeled.

Oh, God, she couldn't do this! She had to get out of here—now. Jerkily, she stumbled forward, heading for the door, and Eva automatically stepped aside. Her expression was changing from bemusement to astonishment. Marisa threw her an agonised look.

'I'm sorry. So sorry—I can't do this! I—'

Suddenly her arm was taken. A deep, harsh voice spoke—but not to her.

'Eva—I'll deal with this.'

Athan's hand around her forearm was like a steel clamp, hustling her out. Out of his sister's presence—before her worthless snake of a husband could inflict the blow he was so obviously, outrageously intending to. Rage consumed him.

What the hell is he thinking of—to bring Marisa here? To confront Eva with her?

It could mean only one thing—the very worst. Ian was going to tell Eva he was leaving her...

But not for Marisa Milburne—not for her!

Emotions seared within him—utterly disparate, but inextricably entwined. To protect his sister from her cheating rat of a husband—to stop Marisa going off with anyone, anyone at all.

Except himself.

Possessiveness scalded within him. Just seeing her there,

despite his anger at realising what Ian was intending, had been like a shockwave through his senses.

He thrust her out into the wide, deserted corridor beyond, yanking the dining room door shut behind him and dragging her down towards the elevator. His only thought was to get her out of the hotel—away from Eva. But was Ian already spilling his treacherous guts to her? Hell and damnation—he could slug him to kingdom come for this!

He jabbed furiously at the elevator button and rounded on Marisa.

'You despicable little bitch! How dare you? How dare you walk in, bold as brass, with Ian?'

Marisa paled, trying to drag herself away from him, but it was impossible. His hand was like steel around her arm.

'I'm sorry! I knew I shouldn't have gone along with Ian.'

Athan shook her like a rag, his face black. 'Then why the hell *did* you?'

'Because we've had enough of this endless secrecy!' she cried. 'He convinced me we couldn't hide it any longer. He refuses to hide me away any more. I won't be his sordid little secret.'

He dropped her arm. It fell to her side limply. She swallowed, just looking at him. His face was like granite. Emotion scythed through her.

'But whether Eva knows about you or not, you *are* the "sordid little secret", aren't you?' he said, his voice low and knifing. 'And telling her won't make you any less sordid.'

She shut her eyes. 'I know,' she said heavily. 'And I know that walking out now isn't going to mend anything. She'll be wondering who I am, why Ian brought me here tonight. So even if I walk out now it's too late—'

He swore in his own language, the Greek words harsh. 'Then there is only one thing to be done—only one way to hide it from her.'

She looked at him. He took her arm again. His mind

was working frantically, trying to work out how to salvage something from this unholy mess. This was a denouement he hadn't foreseen.

I thought Ian had let her go—and all along he was planning this.

Rage consumed him. Rage at Ian—and rage at himself for not realising what a treacherous little rat the man truly was.

He took a heavy breath, marshalled his thoughts.

'I'll tell Eva you're here on my account. That Ian was escorting you to the hotel for me as I've only just arrived from Athens. That I wanted to introduce you to her.' He finished heavily, his words biting and accusing, 'That way I might just manage to protect her from the sordid truth of your existence. After all—' his lip curled '—better that you are *my* mistress than her husband's.'

He made to steer her back towards the dining room..

But she wouldn't move.

She was looking at him. Staring at him. Just staring.

There was no emotion in her face. None whatsoever. Then slowly, very slowly, she peeled his fingers off her arm, and stepped away. He looked down at her, frowning. What the hell was she playing at now?

'Athan! Come back in!'

He slewed round sharply. Eva was in the dining room doorway, beckoning to him. Ian was standing beside her. Athan's head whipped back. Marisa had started to walk forward, towards the couple. There was purpose in her steps.

As they all went back inside the dining room and he closed the door on the four of them a sense of doom came over Athan. It was going to happen. The ugly, painful disclosure of the 'sordid little secret' that he'd gone to so much trouble to keep hidden from his sister. And all for nothing. For this— for his sister to be humiliated and her heart broken. Well, at least he would be there for her. Ready to let her sob on his shoulder after her husband had walked out on her with his mistress on his arm.

His mouth twisted, but there was no humour in it.

The mistress I want for myself...

But that wasn't going to happen. All that was going to happen was the destruction of his sister's fragile marriage. Well, better it ended now than later. Better never to love than to have love smashed to pieces...

He should know...

A blade like a vicious shard of ice slid into his side. He watched Marisa walk up to his sister. Watched Ian smile at her reassuringly.

Intimately.

Watched his sister frown wonderingly.

He went to stand beside her, opposite her husband. Opposite the woman who was never going to be anything more to do with him—who was going to take his sister's husband from her.

He should have felt rage. Fury. Black murderous anger for his sister's sake. For his own. But all there was inside him was an empty, bleak hollow. His eyes went to Marisa. She was looking so pale. So pale and so incredibly beautiful. She was standing beside Ian. They made a startlingly handsome couple—both so blond and blue-eyed, with their English complexions. A matched pair—a foil for his and his sister's dark, Mediterranean looks.

The blade slid into his guts, twisting its sharp, serrated edge as he gazed at Marisa.

Not mine. Never mine. Never—

'Eva—'

Ian's voice jolted him. It was thin, but resolute. Athan stood beside his sister, waiting for the axe to fall so he could pick up the pieces when it did. His face was still, like granite. Marisa's had no expression in it at all.

She would not meet his eyes. Well, that was understandable...

'Eva—' Ian said his wife's name again—stronger this time. He squared his shoulders. 'I've got something I have to say to you,' he said.

The puzzled look on Eva's face deepened.

'I've got to tell you something you will not like, that will be upsetting, but it has to be said. I asked Marisa here tonight for a particular reason. To tell you about her.'

Athan could keep silent no longer. He started forward, placing his hand on his sister's wrist, intending to speak Greek to her. He had to tell her himself—he could not let her bastard of a husband proclaim it.

'No!'

Marisa's sudden interjection silenced him before he had even started. His head swivelled to her. For a moment he reeled. The expression blazing from her eyes was like a hundred lasers.

'Ian will tell her,' she bit out. Her face snapped round to the man at her side. 'Go on! Tell her. Tell *him*.'

There was something wrong with her voice, Athan registered. She had never spoken like that before. Even when she'd been ordering him from that tumbledown cottage of hers. This was like ice—ice made from the coldest water.

Ian's expression flickered, as if he was taken aback by her tone. Then he looked straight at his wife again.

'There is no easy way to tell you this,' he said. 'So I'm just going to say it straight out. Marisa—' he said, and as he spoke he reached for her hand.

She let him take it, curled her fingers around it, warm and familiar, stepping forward slightly, aligning herself with him. A couple. Together.

Like a guillotine cutting down, Athan spoke. Contempt was in his voice, harsh and killing.

'Marisa is his mis—'

'—is my sister.'

The words fell like stones from a great height, crushing Athan dead.

Marisa looked at Athan, her face still completely, totally expressionless.

'I'm Ian's sister,' she said.

CHAPTER SEVEN

HAD the world stopped moving? It must have, thought Athan with what was still working in his brain, because everything else seemed to have stopped. Including his breathing. Then, explosively, it restarted.

'His *sister?*' Shock reverberated in his voice.

Marisa's gaze was levelled at him, still expressionless. Like a basilisk's gaze.

She might have laughed to see the shock on his face—but she wasn't in the mood for laughing. She was in the mood for killing.

Anger—dark, murderous anger—was leashing itself tighter and tighter around her. She had to hold it down—hold it tight down. Because it if escaped...

'Ian's *sister?*' The voice this time was Eva's, and all it held in it was complete bewilderment. 'But Ian hasn't got a sister.'

Marisa's eyes went to Ian, knowing that this was the moment they had dreaded but now had to face. She saw him draw breath, then open his mouth to speak.

'I didn't know—I didn't know about Marisa. Not until very recently.' He took another breath. 'Look, maybe we should all sit down. It's...it's complicated, and it's going to be... difficult,' he said.

He gestured towards the table and after a moment's hesitation Eva went and took her place.

Marisa did likewise. Her body felt very stiff. Immobile. She watched Athan stalk to the other side and sit himself down opposite her, while Ian took his place opposite his wife. Just like two couples settling down to a dinner party. As though a bombshell hadn't just exploded in the middle of them.

'I don't know about you, but I could do with a glass of wine,' Ian said in a shaky voice, trying, Marisa knew, to keep it light.

He reached for the bottle of white wine cooling in its chiller, and for the next few moments there was a hiatus while he poured four glasses and handed them round. Instinctively Marisa found herself taking a gulp.

She needed it.

As she set the glass back on the pristine white tablecloth she realised her hand was trembling slightly. Involuntarily, her eyes glanced across at the dark figure sitting opposite her. His face was like marble—showing absolutely nothing.

Emotion spiked in her, but she crushed it down. She mustn't let anything out—nothing at all. She was here to support Ian, that was all. And he, poor lamb, looked drawn. She watched him take a generous mouthful of wine, then he straightened his shoulders, looked straight across at his wife, and started.

'Marisa is my half-sister,' he said. 'We share the same father. But Marisa's mother—' He stopped.

Across the table, Marisa could see Athan tense. Her eyes went to his. For one brief moment they met, and in them she could see that he knew exactly what was going to be said next.

And it would have to be by her. It wasn't fair to get Ian to say it.

'My mother...' She swallowed, turning her gaze to include Eva. 'My mother was Ian's father's mistress.'

She dropped her gaze, unable to continue for a moment. Emotion welled in her like a huge, stifling balloon.

Eva said something. It was in Greek. Even to Marisa's untrained ears it sounded shocked.

But she dimly realised it didn't sound surprised...

Ian was talking again, and she could hear in his voice what she had heard before so often when they had talked about themselves and their backgrounds: a weary resignation.

'You both know what he was like—Eva, you of all people know because of your mother's long friendship with mine—how she supported my mother through so many unhappy years. Even when my father threatened your parents' marriage with his troublemaking.' He took another mouthful of wine, as though he still needed it. 'Marisa's mother wasn't the first of his mistresses and she certainly wasn't the last. But she was...' He paused, and now he reached his hand out and slipped it comfortingly around Marisa's wrist. 'She was the only one who made the terrible mistake of falling in love with him.'

Marisa spoke. Her voice was low, and she couldn't look at Eva—let alone Athan. Above all not Athan.

'I don't exonerate her. She knew he was married. But she told me that he always said it was a marriage wherein both partners understood—' her voice twisted '—understood that it was primarily about business and property, preserving wealth and inheritance and so on, and that he had never married for love.' Marisa took another breath, lifting her eyes this time and they were filled with a bleak, sad pity for her foolish, trusting, self-blinded mother. 'She chose to believe him. He pursued her relentlessly because she'd said no to him.' Her voice twisted again. 'He wasn't a man who liked women to say no to him, so he told her whatever he considered effective in getting her into bed. He told her his wife had met someone else and asked for a divorce.' Her voice became tight. 'When she had yielded to him, and subsequently found herself pregnant, he suddenly didn't want to know any more. And she realised far too late how stupid she had been.'

She took a heavy breath.

'He gave her a lump sum—enough to buy the cottage I was brought up in—and a small income to go with it. He got her to sign a document waiving all claims to official child support from him. She was too devastated to refuse, and she went along with being bundled out of his life and kept quiet. She moved to Devon and disappeared. I grew up having no idea who he was—only that he was "the great love of her life," as she used to say. After she died I came to London to try and find him. But I had no name and nothing to go on but a photograph my mother had kept—'

'Which is how she found me,' Ian interjected. 'It was total, absolute chance. Marisa took a job at a cleaning company and my office was one of their contracts. One evening I was working late. She saw me, stared at me—and that's how we found each other.'

'Of *course,*' Eva said slowly, comprehension dawning. 'Ian looks the image of his father…and presumably the photo was of a man around his age?'

Marisa nodded. She could say no more.

'It's extraordinary,' Eva breathed. 'To have absolutely no idea that you had a sibling.' She turned to her brother. 'Athan, imagine not knowing you even existed—it would be dreadful.'

He didn't respond. Then, abruptly, he got to his feet.

'Excuse me. I must—'

He stopped. There was nothing he 'must' do except get out of there.

'Athan?'

Eva's voice was bewildered, but he couldn't help it. He couldn't help anything right now. He just had to walk out.

Without another word he left the room, ignoring Eva's astonished rush of Greek at him, asking what on earth he was doing. Like an automaton he strode to the bank of lifts, jabbing at the button, willing the doors to open and let him escape. Leave. Get away. Away from her.

Away from what he'd done to her…

Inside the private dining room Eva was still staring, non-plussed, at her brother's empty place.

'What on earth—?' she began.

Her bewildered gaze came back to her husband, then moved on to Marisa. She started to speak, but Marisa spoke instead.

'I'm sorry—I have to—' Her voice was staccato and she couldn't finish. All she could do was get to her feet, roughly pushing back her chair, seize up her clutch bag and leave the room.

She could hear her half-brother call her name anxiously, but she ignored it.

Outside, the hotel corridor was deserted.

All except for the tall, dark figure standing by the elevator.

Sudden slicing memory knifed through her. Herself emerging from the elevator on her way back to the apartment Ian had leased for her, seeing the tall, dark figure striding towards her, asking her to keep the doors open for her.

A set up. That was all it had been. A calculating, carefully timed set-up with one purpose only.

To snare her. Captivate her.

Seduce her.

Seduce her away from the man he'd assumed she was having an affair with. A married man. His own brother-in-law.

Emotion buckled through her—hot and nauseating. Icy and punishing.

'Wait!'

Her voice carried the length of the deserted corridor, made him turn instantly. His expression froze. She strode up to him. The anger she'd kept leashed so tightly inside her while she'd sat at the table and told of her relationship with Ian, leapt in her throat. She stopped dead in front of him. Of its own volition her hand lifted, and she brought it across his face in a ringing slap.

'*That's* for what you thought I was!'

Then, in a whirl of skirts, she pushed past him into the lift that was opening its doors behind him, jabbed the 'close' button urgently.

But he made no attempt to follow her—made no movement at all. Only turned very slowly and watched her as the doors closed and the elevator swept her up to the bedroom floors. Her heart was pounding. In her vision seared the image of his face. Like a dead man's, with a weal forming across his cheekbone. Livid and ugly.

Marisa was walking. She did a lot of walking these days. Miles and miles. All over the moor. But however far she walked she never got away from what was eating her. Consuming her.

Destroying her.

Round and round the destructive thoughts went in her head. Over and over again she tumbled them.

How could she not have realised what it was that Athan thought about her? How could it not have penetrated through her thick, stupid skull that he had jumped to the conclusion about her that he had?

With hindsight—that most pointless and excruciating of all things—it was glaringly, blazingly obvious that that was what he had assumed all along

She'd replayed every line of that conversation—their ugly, utterly misbegotten conversation—where she had completely failed to understand just what he'd meant about her relationship with Ian.

I assumed he meant he'd discovered I was his sister. I never dreamt he thought anything so sleazy about me— anything so vile.

But that was exactly what he had done.

Right from the start.

She wanted to scream and yell and denounce him to the world. But there was no one she could tell. All she could do was swallow it down herself and keep it down. Keep totally out of everyone's way. Bury herself down her in Devon again—for ever this time.

The way she should have done first time around.

I should never have let Ian persuade me to go up to London to tell Eva about me. Because of what Athan did—because I can't tell Ian what he did—I can't have anything to do with him and Eva anyway. I can't ever look at Athan again— I can't bear to!

Emotion seared in her, hot and scalding.

How can I ever have anything more to do with a man like that? A man I hate with every fibre of my being.

Because of course she hated him. What else was it possible to feel about Athan Teodarkis now? Nothing. Only hatred. Black and venomous.

All consuming.

All destroying.

She trudged on. The rising slope had peaked, and now she was on the low crest looking down onto the half-buried remains of the Bronze Age village below the tor. Someone was standing in the middle of the site, which wasn't fenced off—there was very little damage walkers could do to such meagre remains.

At first when saw the solitary figure from the distance she was at she took no notice. On a warm day like this, in full Dartmoor spring, fellow walkers and ramblers on the moor were commonplace. But as she headed along the path that would take her past the site she stilled. There was something very familiar about the motionless figure.

He was looking towards her. Hands in his jacket pockets, legs slightly apart. The wind was ruffling his hair. His eyes were slightly narrowed against the sun behind her.

In a kind of daze—a mental suspension that kept one foot moving after another—she carried on down the slope towards the ancient village where once a whole community had thrived—living, loving, dying...

Now not even their ghosts remained to haunt the sunlit, windswept air.

He moved towards her, intersecting her path. Waiting for her.

She came up to him. Said nothing. Did nothing. Only stood there, her hands plunged into her anorak pockets, her face a mask.

Like his.

'Ian told me you were back here.' His voice was terse. Low. Strained.

'I gave you time,' he said. 'I gave us both time. But now we have to talk.'

She looked at him. Just looked at him. 'There is absolutely nothing to say,' she stated.

She was calm. Very calm. Amazingly calm, considering the seething tumult that had been inside her only moments ago, racking through her with all the unbearable impossibilities of the situation, the destructive morass of it all.

'You know that's not true,' he contradicted her.

Something flared in her eyes, then died again. Quenched.

'Well, what *is* there to say, then?' she threw at him, hands digging deeper into her pockets.

This was unreal—unreal to be standing here, beside a place where people had once lived and loved and died, nothing more than shards of bone in the earth now, who could feel no pain or loss any more, no emotions—nothing. Unreal to be standing in such a place and confronting the man who had driven her back here.

'What is there to say?' she demanded again. She stared at him, unblinking. Unflinching. 'You thought I was Ian's mistress, so you seduced me to take my mind off him while he went back to his wife—your sister. Now you've discovered that actually I wasn't his mistress after all. I'm his sister. And because I can't stomach having any more contact with *you,* it means I can't have anything to do with Ian or Eva, so telling Eva about me actually turns out to be have been a totally pointless exercise all round! There.' She took a sharp, incising breath, glaring at him. 'Does that just about sum up why there isn't the slightest thing more to be said on the subject?'

Expressions worked in his face and his jaw tightened. 'No, it doesn't.' He gave a heavy sigh. 'You know it doesn't. It doesn't even begin to get to the reason why we have to talk.'

He took her arm. She tried to shake it off, but he simply led her to a nearby lichen-covered drystone wall and sat her down on it, lowering himself beside her. She edged away and she knew he could see she'd done it, and she was coldly, savagely pleased. She was still calm—still amazingly, icily calm. It was like being inside an iceberg, and it suited her fine— just fine. She waited for him to drop his grip on her, but he didn't. She wouldn't flatter him by shaking herself free. She would just endure that tight, hard clasp. It would remind her of how much she hated him.

He turned to look at her. She closed her face. She wanted to close her eyes, but again that would have shown him that she was affected by him. And she wasn't affected—not at all.

She never would be. Never again.

He spoke abruptly. 'This is what I don't understand. That you didn't realise I'd thought Ian had set you up as his mistress. Surely to God you must have done?' His face worked. 'Why the hell else would I have done what I did—said what I said? Why else would I have done or said those things to you? Just because you were Ian's *sister?* Why the *hell* did you and Ian hide your relationship from everyone?'

Marisa's eyes widened. 'How can you even ask that? You know how close Eva is to Ian's mother—her godmother. How she's become like a second mother to her, taking her own mother's place. That's why we were so reluctant to tell Eva. Because it would have torn her loyalties in two. How could she have anything to do with her husband's sister when that sister was living proof of just how much Sheila Randall was hurt and betrayed by her husband?'

She swallowed. 'After I fled London, telling Ian it was because I couldn't go on hiding in the shadows, and he got a new job without your patronage, he became determined not to go on concealing such an important part of his life from his wife. It was a new start for him, and however difficult it was going to be he didn't want any secrets from Eva any more. Even the secret of my existence,' she finished bitterly.

Athan was silent a moment. Then he spoke. His voice was heavy—as heavy as the lead that seemed to be weighing him down, crushing him.

'I thought Ian was like his father. Incapable of fidelity. I've always thought it—feared it. I never approved of his marriage to Eva. Thought him lightweight. Superficial. Unworthy of my sister. And I thought that she was doomed to follow the same path as her mother-in-law, whose life was made a misery by her faithless husband.'

He paused, glancing briefly at Marisa and then away again, because it hurt too much to do otherwise. 'When my suspicions became aroused I took out surveillance on him. I found out about your existence—that you were living in an apartment he was paying for. There was no doubt about it. There were photos of you and him in a restaurant. Intimate photos that showed you and he billing and cooing over each other.' He paused again. 'And one of the photographs showed Ian giving you a diamond necklace.' Another pause, briefer this time, then words broke from him—harsh and hard. 'What the *hell* was I supposed to think? My brother-in-law was giving another woman a diamond necklace!'

Marisa stiffened.

'It was Ian's grandmother's. Our father's mother's necklace. He wanted me to have it. He wanted me to have all the things that our father had denied me—wanted to lift me out of the poverty that my father had condemned my mother to.' She looked away—far away—back into the past to her childhood. 'She knew she should never have given in to my father. Knew she was at fault. Knew she was a fool to love him. Knew she deserved what she got from him—rejection and short shrift. It was a lesson, she taught me well,' she said heavily. Her eyes came back to Athan. 'Which is why it was so unbearable to realise you thought I'd stoop to carrying on with a married man. Why I was so angry that evening Ian told Eva about me.'

Athan's face was drawn. 'You had every right to be.' His voice was sombre. 'I misjudged you totally. Thought the very worst of you.'

She could hear the self-laceration in his voice, and something twisted inside her.

'I hated you for it!' she burst out. 'I thought I hated you for what you did to me—deliberately seducing me. But when I realised…realised that what you thought of me was a million times worse than simply trying to latch on to my wealthy brother and mess up his family…oh, then I hated you a million times more than I did before.' She felt her hands fist in her pockets. 'When I threw in your face what I truly was to Ian—what our relationship actually is—oh, it felt so damn *good*. Wiping that condemning contempt off your face. And slapping you felt even *better*!'

She jerked to her feet, yanking her arm free of him. Standing there, buckling with emotion, she swayed in the wind, her face convulsed.

Why had he come here? To torment her again? What *for*?

It was over now—all over. Nothing more to be done, or said. It was all a mess—a hideous, insoluble mess. But she knew she had to accept that in the end, it wasn't his fault.

Heavily, she turned around to face him again. He hadn't moved. Was just sitting there immobile, looking at her.

His expression was...

Was what? she thought, finding thoughts skittering across her mind inchoately, incoherently.

Wary—that was what it was. But there was more than wariness in it. His eyes—his dark, gold-flecked eyes, whose glance had once turned her to jelly—were now regarding her with...

Such bleakness.

That was what was in his face. His eyes.

She took a scissoring breath. 'There isn't any point to this—there really isn't. It's just a mess—a total mess all round. I can see...understand...why you jumped to the conclusion you did. I can see why you wanted to protect your sister. You did what you thought best at the time. But now... now that it's all out in the open—the actual truth, not your assumption—it just makes it impossible for me to have anything more to do with you, or Eva—or even Ian, really. I can't ever see you again—you must see that. What you did to me will always be there, poisoning everything.' She looked at him. Looked into those dark, wary, bleak eyes. 'I can't get over what you did—I will never be able to get over what you did.'

For one long, unbearable moment they just gazed at each other across everything that divided them. An impossible divide.

A huge, crushing weariness pressed down on her. Her head bowed. She knew she should head for home, back to the sanctuary of her cottage. But her legs were suddenly like lead.

Then behind her she heard a movement. Hands lightly—so lightly—touched her hunched shoulders, then dropped away.

'And nor will I.'

Athan's voice was low. Conflict filled it. Filled his head. Was she right? Should he never have come here? Never have followed the crushing imperative to find her—talk to her? Because he *had* to talk to her. He couldn't just leave it the way it had been—with her denouncing, punishing slap ringing across his mind. His soul.

Punishing him for what he had thought about her. Punishing him for what he'd done to her. Punishing him for getting her totally, utterly wrong…

'It will be like a brand on me all my life,' he told her. 'What I did to you.'

She gave a little shrug. It was all she could manage. 'It doesn't matter. I understand why you did it. It was a… misunderstanding, that's all.' Her voice gave a little choke as she said the word that was so hideous an understatement. 'A mess up. But it doesn't matter. In the end it doesn't leave any of us worse off, does it? If anything, Ian and Eva's marriage is stronger than ever, so that's surely some good out of it. He finally has a job where he feels he can not only make a real contribution to the world, in a way he never could before, but he can stand on his own two feet—out from under your shadow. Plus, of course—' her voice twisted '—he has finally won your trust—convinced you he's not cut from the same corrupt cloth as our father. So that's all to the good, isn't it?'

She spoke negligently, carelessly. As if nothing mattered any more—just as she was saying.

'As for you and me—' She swallowed. There was a stone in her throat. Making it hard to speak. Impossible almost. But she had to force the words all the same.

She stared out ahead of her, towards the granite tor beyond. Rocks that had thrust up out of the burning earth so deep below, then cooled and congealed in the air. Hardened and set. Unchangeable now. Only the wind and the rain would weather them, wear them down over aeons of time. Aeons that mocked the brief, agonised flurry of human lives. Just as the vanished ghosts of the dead village they stood in haunted those who came after them.

'As for you and me,' she said again, 'what does it matter? What happened was…a mistake. An error. Regrettable, but understandable. It can't be mended, but—' The stone was harder now in her throat, but she had to get the words past it all the same. 'It can be ignored.'

She heard his intake of breath behind her. Then, carefully, he spoke.

'No—it can't. It can't be ignored. It has to be faced. I have to face it.'

The hands came again—lightly, briefly, on her shoulders. She could barely feel them, yet it was like electricity shivering within her as he turned her around to face him. Face what he was going to say.

His expression was sombre. The bleakness in his eyes was absolute.

'I wronged you. I wronged you and I will regret that all my life—however unintentioned it was, the wrong remains. But if you ask me to regret what happened, then…I won't. I can't. I came here to you afterwards wanting only one thing. Thinking that because you were now no longer a danger to my sister I could indulge myself—take from you what I wanted so, so badly. Have you back for myself again.'

He gazed down at her, and behind the bleakness in his eyes something else flared. Something that was dangerous to her. That threatened her. That sought to set aside the aeons of time that formed the moors, the millennia that separated them from the people who had once dwelt here in the shadow of the tors. That sought to mock the effect of time on human lives.

Something that was stronger than time. That would outlast all things.

'To have you back,' he said. 'To have you as you were in that brief, precious time we had—a time that enraptured me. And tormented me. Tormented me because I knew it was only a fleeting bubble—a bubble I would have to burst, cruelly and callously, when I denounced you.'

Emotion came to his eyes again, but it was stormy now. 'I hated what I had to do—hated what I thought you were. It made me even harsher to you than I had to be. And when I followed you down here, saw how you lived, I could see how Ian must have turned your head, beguiled you…led you astray.' He paused again, then said what needed to be said. 'Just as his father led your mother astray.'

Her eyes fell. She could not answer him. He answered for her.

'We're human, all of us, Marisa. We make mistakes. Your mother made hers. I made mine—misjudging you. Misjudging Ian.'

He paused and her gaze flickered back up to him. The bleakness was back in his eyes.

'We make mistakes and then we pay for them. Your mother paid for hers. I shall pay for mine.' He paused. 'Mine…my payment…will be doing without you.' He took a razored breath. 'I won't impose upon you by giving a name to why that will exact a price from me, but be assured it will be a heavier price than I ever imagined possible.' His mouth twisted. 'A price I didn't know existed until I started paying it.'

He lifted a hand as if to bid her farewell, as if to bid farewell to many things.

'I'll go now,' he said. 'I wish you well—it's all I can do, isn't it? All that you could possibly want me to do. I wish you well and leave you be.' He looked around him, across the wide, sunlit moorland, ablaze now with gorse and new growth, at the blue sky above arcing from east to west. A wild bird was singing somewhere as it rose on currents of air. Then his eyes came back to her.

Looked their last on her.

He felt the knife slide into his heart as he tore his gaze away again, and set it instead on the lofty tor beyond, piercing the sky with its dark, impenetrable mass. He started to walk towards it, following the path that led there, leaving her behind.

She watched him go. Watched his figure start to recede. Watched him walk out of her life.

There was a haze over the sun. Which was strange, because there were no clouds in the cerulean sky. Yet the haze was there, like a mist in her vision. She blinked, but it did not clear.

Only the wind stung her eyes, beading her lashes with a misty haze.

Thoughts crowded into her head. She could make no sense of them. They jumbled and jostled and each one cried for space. Then one—only one—stilled the others. Formed itself into words inside her head. She heard them, made herself hear them, even as she stood there, watching him walk away from her...

The words came again in her head. Athan's words.

'We make mistakes. Your mother made hers. I made mine...'

They came again, circling like a plane. Bringing more words in their wake.

What if I'm making my mistake now?

Her mother had ruined her life, giving her love to a man—a man who had proved utterly unworthy, totally deceitful and uncaring—instead of telling him to leave her alone, get out of her life before he could destroy it.

But what if my mistake is the opposite one?

The thought hung blazing in her mind.

What if my mistake is to let go of a man I should never let go? A man I should clutch to me and hold tight in my arms?

A man it would be—will be—an agony to lose?

Her eyes held to the figure striding away from her, getting further and further away. The air in her lungs seemed to turn to granite. Impossible to breathe. Impossible.

'Wait!' The word tore from her, freeing her breath. 'Athan! *Wait!*'

He stopped. Stopped dead. Froze. Then, as she stood, heart hammering in her chest, he turned.

She didn't speak, didn't cry out again. She had no thoughts, or words, or breath. She started forward, stumbling at first over the uneven ground, then found her balance, running now, faster and yet faster. The wind whipped the haze to her eyes, blinding her, but it didn't matter. She knew where she was going. Knew it with every fibre of her being. Knew the only place she would ever want to be.

He caught her as she reached him. Caught her in an embrace that swept her off the ground, swept her round and round as his arms wrapped her to him. She was crying, sobbing, but it didn't matter—nothing mattered. Nothing at all would ever matter—only this…this.

Being in his arms.

Loving him.

Loving him so, so much!

He was saying her name. Over and over again. Kissing her hair, clutching her to him. She was crying, and then she was laughing, and he was lowering her down so she could feel the ground beneath her feet again, but her arms were still wrapped around him so tightly, so close she would never let him go—*never* let him go….

'Oh, my darling—my darling one!'

Was that her speaking or him? It didn't matter—nothing mattered but this. The joy surging through her, the love…

Then he was loosening his arms around her, cupping her upturned face with his hands, his eyes blazing down into hers.

All bleakness was gone.

Only love—blazing.

And slowly, beneath the towering tor, which had no power to mock what stood so far beyond the power of time, circled by the ghosts of those who had lived and loved here so long ago, he lowered his mouth to hers and kissed her.

'This is love,' he said. 'This is my love for you. For all that

I did to you, this is why I cannot regret it. Because it gave you to me.' He took a painful breath, his eyes full. 'I didn't realise what it was…what was happening to me…until I lost you. Lost you, my dearest one, over and over again. So many times. I lost you when I said those cruel, denouncing words to you. Lost you when, eaten by jealousy of Ian, I chased you down here. I wanted to grab you back like a spoilt child deprived of what he wanted. I lost you when you threw the truth about yourself in my face at that nightmare dinner. Lost you when you walked up to me and vented all your anger for what I'd thought about you. Lost you over and over and over again.' His hands cupping her face pressed more urgently. 'And with each loss it hammered home to me more what was happening. That I was falling in love with you.'

He shuddered, and she felt his pain and clung to him more closely.

'Falling in love with you…even as I was losing you…over and over again…'

She gave a little cry, kissed him again to obliterate the pain she saw in him.

'I feared loving you,' she said 'Feared it so much. When I saw you sometimes on St Cecile, looking at me when you thought I couldn't see you, you looked so…so remote. I thought it was because you knew I was falling for you when you only wanted something passing that would end when we returned. That's what I thought when you said you needed to speak to me. I was steeled for it—ready for you to tell me it was over. I had the strength to bear that.'

Her expression changed. 'But when you threw at me what you did—oh, God, I didn't have the strength for that. How could I have? What you hurled at me—what I thought you were accusing me of—I could not defend myself against that. Because I knew…knew that what I'd wanted so much was to be taken into my father's family, not to be rejected by them any more. But you made me see it was impossible—that I was just a sordid little secret from Ian's father's past...'

Athan groaned and held her away from him, only the better to talk to her. His hands slipped to her shoulders.

'I would never have objected to you for that reason alone. Yes, Ian's mother suffered—but that was not your fault. How could it be? *Nothing* has been your fault. Only mine.' His voice was heavy. 'Only mine.'

She heard the self-accusation in his voice and hated it.

'No.' Her negation was fierce. 'I will not let you say that. I will not let you...or me...look backwards now. I let anger blind me—blind me into rejecting you.' She clutched him suddenly, clinging to him urgently. 'Oh, I so nearly let you walk away from me. Don't ever, *ever* let me be so blind again!'

'Every time you look at me,' he promised her, his voice warm and rich and full of all he felt for her, 'you'll see my love for you. It will be your mirror for all time. A true mirror. That I promise you.'

Her gaze was troubled suddenly. 'It *hurt*,' she said. 'It hurt so much to realise that all the time you knew me in London, all the time we had on holiday, it was just...fake. The whole thing. When I thought it was real...'

Now the negation was his—and fiercer.

'It *was*—it was real! That was the whole torment of it all! Knowing that if it weren't for Eva, for what I thought I was doing to save her marriage, I would be spending that time with you without that hanging over my head. That's why I so arrogantly thought I could get you back again—get that time back again. Oh, God, Marisa, to hold you in my arms again—to have you for myself this time, *only* myself. With no other reason to get in the way of us.' He gazed down at her, emotion pouring from him. 'And now...finally...after all this time...there truly is nothing to part us...to confuse and confound and blind us. Now—oh, my most beloved girl— there really is only this...'

He kissed her. Tenderly. Carefully. Lovingly.

'Only this,' he murmured.

He eased her away from him, changing his hold on her to put an arm around her shoulder, holding her hand in his across his body as he started to walk her along the path again. Side by side.

Peace filled her. Peace she had not felt for so long. A peace that she knew now would last for ever.

'What fools we've been,' she said dreamily, leaning her head against his shoulder.

He gave a low laugh. 'Me more than you.'

She shook her head. 'No, me more than you.'

He glanced down at her. 'You'll have to grant me the privilege of being right this time around.' He dropped a kiss on her hair.

'Uh-uh.'

He lanced the quirking smile at her that made her heart turn over—her tumbled, jangled heart that had finally found its resting place.

'An argumentative woman, are you?' he teased. 'Well, there is only one way to settle it. You shall be right, my darling, all the time henceforth. Will that keep you happy?'

She shook her head. 'Only one thing will keep me happy.'

'Oh?' he queried, his smile tugging deeper. 'And what will that be?'

'You,' she said. 'Only you. For all time.' Love blazed from her eyes. A fire that could never be quenched.

'Done,' he answered. 'And shall I seal the deal like this?'

Their kiss was long and deep and stronger than time.

Which stood still all around them and always would.

EPILOGUE

'READY?'

Athan's tone was a mix of encouragement and support. His arm, to which Marisa was clinging tightly, was steady as a rock. A rock she knew she could always lean on—all her life. Including this evening.

'OK, let's do it,' he said.

He started forward, opening the door and leading the way into the room beyond. Marisa was conscious of a slight increase in her heart rate, but that was only to be expected. She walked in, Athan at her side. Together they paused on the threshold.

'Marisa!' Ian's voice was warm and welcoming as he hurried up to them. He bestowed his golden smile on her, and kissed her lightly on the cheek.

His smile encompassed Athan as well, and Athan returned it. His regard for his brother-in-law had increased dramatically now that he was assured that nothing of Martin Randall's faithless nature was in him. Ian had proved increasingly loyal and steadfast, working hard to make his new job a success, and ensuring Eva was the happiest wife in the world.

Almost the happiest, he amended, and his glance down at Marisa at his side was rich and full with love. He felt his heart constrict. How very much he loved her! She was the centre of his world—the other half of his being...

'Marisa?'

Ian's voice interrupted Athan's reverie.

'This is a moment I have longed for. Will you take my hand?'

Still with an edge of tension inside her, Marisa placed her free hand in Ian's and he closed his fingers tightly over hers. The three of them walked forward to the figure standing by the ornate fireplace on the far side of the drawing room in Ian's family house. Though her vision was focussed on the figure standing there Marisa was conscious of Eva, sitting in the armchair beside the fire, smiling encouragingly at her.

For a moment as Marisa approached she thought she saw a tension in the features of the figure's face that equalled her own. She could understand its cause only too well. Then once more Ian was speaking. Not this time to Marisa, but to the older woman.

'This is Marisa,' he said. His voice was level, his gaze steady. 'My sister.'

For a moment time seemed to hang still. Then, with a little sound in her throat, Sheila Randall broke the tension. She held out her hands to Marisa.

'My dear,' she said. Her voice was rich with emotion.

As Marisa took the outstretched hands, dropping her hold on both Athan and her brother, she felt an answering emotion well up in her. In Sheila Randall's face was nothing but kindness—and the haunting of past sorrows.

Her hands pressed Marisa's. Her eyes looked deep into hers. 'I sincerely believe,' she said, 'that your poor mother suffered as greatly as I did, and for that reason I know I can never blame her or accuse her.' There was a choke in her voice now. 'I can only be glad that Ian found you. So glad that you are part of our family,' she said. Her gaze went to Athan. 'I can think of no happier ending,' she said.

Marisa's hands slipped from hers, took Athan's wait-

ing hands instead, and felt their warmth and strength flow
through her.

'Nor I,' she agreed.

And love, like a swelling tide, swept through her.

With eyes only for her, his beloved, Athan lifted Marisa's
hands to his mouth, kissing them one after another, holding
them close against his heart.

'Nor I,' he said.

For an endless, timeless moment their eyes poured into
each other's. Then a soft pop drew their attention back to
their surroundings.

'Time for champagne,' said Ian.

Eva was there in an instant, holding out glasses to be filled
with the gently fizzing liquid. When all the glasses were
charged, Ian lifted his first, to give the toast.

'To Athan and Marisa,' he said. 'And the triumph of true
love.'

It was a toast that no one there objected to.

* * * * *

BREAKING THE
GREEK'S RULES

ANNE McALLISTER

Best-selling two-time RITA® winner (with a further nine finalist titles) **Anne McAllister** has written nearly seventy books for Mills & Boon Modern, American Romance, Desire, Special Edition and single titles, which means she basically follows the characters no matter where they take her. She loves to travel, but at home she and her husband divide their time between Montana and Iowa. Anne loves to hear from readers. Contact her at: www.annemcallister.com.

CHAPTER ONE

ALEXANDROS Antonides studied the crumpled receipt, the one with the hastily scrawled name, address and phone number on the back, and was tempted to stuff it right back in his pocket.

Or better yet, throw it out.

He didn't need a matchmaker, for God's sake!

His fingers crushed the already frequently crumpled piece of paper and he stared out the window of the taxi as it headed north on Eighth Avenue. They weren't out of midtown Manhattan yet. It was nearly five-thirty. He should just tell the driver to forget it.

But he didn't. Instead he made himself lean back against the seat and, just as he had done a dozen or more times before, he smoothed out the paper against his palm.

Daisy Connolly. His cousin Lukas had scribbled down her name and address a month ago when he and Lukas had met up at the family reunion out at Lukas's parents' place in the Hamptons. "She'll find you the perfect wife."

"How do you know?" he'd asked Lukas, letting his voice carry his obvious doubt. He'd looked around pointedly, noting Lukas's complete lack of not only a wife, but even a date for their family reunion.

"Seen her do it," Lukas said frankly. "I went to college with her. She did it then. She does it now. She has some uncanny sense of who belongs together." He shrugged. "Who knows how she does it? Hocus-pocus? Tea leaves? Beats me. Give her a call or go see her."

Alex had grunted, not a sound meant to convey agreement.

"Unless you really don't want to get married." Lukas had cocked his head, considering Alex. Then, "Maybe he's chicken," he had said to his brothers.

One of them had made a clucking sound.

Alex had masked his irritation and rolled his eyes. "Fine," he'd said curtly. "If I get desperate enough, I'll look her up."

"I'd say you're already desperate," Lukas had said, grinning. "How many fiancées have you gone through?"

"Two," Alex said through his teeth. "But Imogene doesn't count."

Imogene had been perfect. She hadn't loved Alex any more than he'd loved her. When her long-time boyfriend had got cold feet faced with a lifetime commitment, Alex had grabbed her on the rebound. Unfortunately two days after she'd said yes to Alex, the love of her life had come to his senses and begged her to marry him.

"What can I do?" she'd wailed at Alex. "I still love him!"

The more fool she, Alex had thought. But he'd been polite and wished her good luck. He still did. If she was that besotted, she'd need it.

"I don't know," Lukas had said slowly, studying him. "Two fiancées in a little over a year…" He'd arched his brows in speculation, then looked over at his brothers. "Sounds pretty desperate to me."

His brothers, Elias and PJ, had nodded sagely.

Alex had merely snorted. He didn't want a perfect wife, anyway. He just wanted a suitable one. He was thirty-five years old. Time to get married.

Of course lots of men would disagree. But not Antonides men. Antonides men married. All of them.

Not young, as a rule. Most all of them sowed their wild oats before settling down. But in the end, every last one of them took the plunge.

As a young man Alex had turned his back on the notion. He'd figured to be the exception to the rule. Besides, then the thrill of the hunt and endless variety had enticed him.

Now it often seemed more trouble than it was worth.

Sex? Well, that wasn't too much trouble. But picking up women who wanted a one-night stand seemed tawdry to him now. And while it was fine to play the field when they were young, Alex understood what every Antonides male understood—that there came a time to turn into a responsible, steady, dependable, mature man.

And that meant having a wife.

Elias might have been born responsible. But even PJ, who had been a beach bum for years, was respectably married now. In fact he had been secretly married for years. And Lukas, the youngest of them and definitely a free spirit, would get married, too.

Even Lukas knew it. It was just a matter of time.

Alex's time was now.

He had made up his mind last year. The hunt had begun to bore him and he found he preferred spending his time designing buildings than enticing women into his bed. It wasn't all that difficult, honestly. The difficult part was when he had to convince them he didn't intend to fall in love with them.

It would be easier and more straightforward, he decided, to find a woman he liked, spell out the rules, marry her and get on with his life.

It wasn't as if he had a lot of rules. Basically all he wanted was an easy-to-get-along-with, undemanding woman who wanted an easy-to-get-along-with, undemanding husband. He wasn't looking for love and he wasn't looking for kids. He wasn't looking to complicate his life.

He and his wife would share bed and board when they were in the same country and would attend each other's duty functions when possible. Presently he lived in an apartment he'd restored in Brooklyn above his offices, but it was a bachelor's pad. He wouldn't expect his wife to live there. They could get another place close to her work. She could choose it. He didn't care. He was perfectly willing to be accommodating.

So, really, how difficult could it be to find a woman willing to agree to his terms?

Harder than he thought, Alex admitted now.

His last three dates had seemed promising—all of them were professional women in their thirties. He'd met them at business social functions. They all had high-powered careers, fast-track lives, and nearly as many demands on their time as he had on his.

They *should* have been perfect.

But the lawyer had treated their dinner date as a cross-examination about his determination not to have children. The dentist bored on about how much she hated her profession and could hardly wait to quit and start a family. And Melissa, the stock analyst with whom he'd had dinner with last night, told him point-blank that her biological clock was ticking and she wanted a baby within a year.

At least Alex had had the presence of mind to say just as firmly, "I don't."

But that date, like so many of the others he'd had since he'd decided that it was possible to marry without anything as messy as love complicating the relationship, had gone downhill from there.

Which brought him back to the receipt he held in his hand.

Daisy.

He stared at the name Lukas had scrawled on the crumpled paper. It brought with it flickers of memories, a frisson of awareness. Honey-blonde hair. Sparkling blue eyes. Laughter. Gentle, warm words. Soft sighs. Hot kisses. He shifted in the seat of the cab. Once upon a time, for one brief weekend, Alex had known a woman called Daisy.

So maybe this was fate.

The hot-kisses, soft-sighs Daisy had wanted to marry him. Maybe the matchmaking Daisy would find him a wife.

"Think of it as delegating," Elias had urged him pragmatically when he'd balked at Lukas's suggestion. "You do it all the time at work."

That was true. Alex had a whole staff at his architectural firm who did the things he didn't have time for. They did what he told them, checked availability, researched zoning and land use and materials, sorted and sifted through piles of information, then presented their findings and recommendations, and left him to make the final decision.

It was sensible. It was efficient. And Elias was right: a matchmaker could do the same thing. It would be smarter, in fact, than doing it himself.

He would be leaving less to chance if he deputized a disinterested employee to find appropriate candidates. And he'd be spared the awkwardness of future dinners like the one he'd shared with Melissa last night. With a matchmaker vetting the candidates, he would only have to meet the really suitable ones, then decide which one would make the best wife.

It suddenly sounded promising. He should have dropped in on Daisy Connolly before this. But Alex didn't ordinarily get to the Upper West Side. Today, though, he'd been working on a building project in the West Village and, finishing early, he'd had a bit of time to spare before he headed back to Brooklyn. So he'd plucked the paper out of his wallet and hopped in a cab.

Twenty minutes later he consulted it as he got out again on the corner of Amsterdam Avenue and the cross street on which Daisy Connolly had her office.

He hoped she hadn't gone home already. He hadn't made an appointment. It had seemed more sensible to leave himself the option of changing his mind if, when he saw the place, something about it made him want to walk straight on past.

But the street wore the New York City version of homey respectability. It was quiet, lined with four and five story brownstones, a few blocks north of the Museum of Natural History. The trees on either side of the street were all varying shades of gold and orange this early October afternoon,

making it look like a photo op for an urban lifestyle magazine. Alex took his time walking up the block, the architect
in him enjoying the view.

When he'd first bought a place to live in New York three
years ago, changing his base of operations from Europe to this
side of the Atlantic, he'd opted for an apartment in a high-rise
about a mile south on Central Park West. Twenty-odd stories
up, his aerie had given him a useful bird's-eye perspective of
the city, but it had literally kept him above it all. He hadn't
felt connected.

Two years ago, offered a chance to tear down a pre-war office building in Brooklyn not far from where his cousins Elias
and PJ lived with their families, he'd found a purpose and a
place where he was happy at the same time. He'd found another property on which to build what the owner wanted, and
seeing a chance to make a useful contribution to the gentrifi-
cation of a neighborhood in transition, he had snapped up the
pre-war building for himself. Now he had his offices downstairs and his apartment on the fourth floor. He felt more like
he belonged and less as if he were soaring above it.

He got the same feeling here on Daisy Connolly's street.
There was a laundry on one corner, a restaurant on the other.
Between two of the brownstones he passed an empty lot which
now held a small local playground with some climbing equip-
ment, a swing and slide. One brownstone had a small discreet
plaque by the door of the garden floor apartment offering
herbs and organic seedlings. Another had a small sign for a
chiropractor's office.

Did matchmakers have signs? He felt an unwelcome flicker
of awkwardness. When he found the address midblock, there
was no sign. It looked like a version of all the rest—a tall, narrow, five story building with three stories of bay windows and
another two stories above them of more modest windows—
where once servants had dwelt no doubt. It was the color of
warm honey, lighter than the traditional brownstone, and it

sported lace curtains at the first floor bay windows making it look pleasant and professional at the same time.

Besides the lack of signs, there were no astrology signs or crystal balls in sight. No tiny fairy lights flickering in the windows, either. None of the "hocus-pocus" Lukas had mentioned. Alex breathed a sigh of relief.

He straightened his tie, took a deep breath, strode up the steps and opened the outside door. In the tiny foyer, on the mailbox for apartment 1, he saw her name: *Daisy Connolly.* Resolutely he pressed the buzzer.

For half a minute there was no response at all. Alex shifted from one foot to the other and ground his teeth at the thought of wasting the end of an afternoon coming all the way to the Upper West Side for nothing.

But just as he was about to turn away, he heard the sound of a lock being turned. The door opened into the shadow-filled front hall and he could see the silhouette of a slim woman coming to push open the door to admit him.

She was smiling—until their gazes met. Then the smile faded and the color drained from her face.

She stared at him, stricken. "Alex?"

Honey-blonde hair. Deep blue eyes. A memory of scorching hot kisses. *"Daisy?"*

Alex? Here? No!

No. No. No.

But all the time the word was banging around inside Daisy's head, the truth—all six feet of his whipcord-lean, muscular, gorgeous male self—was staring at her in the face.

Why in heaven's name couldn't she have looked out the window before she'd answered the door?

The answer was simple: Alexandros Antonides was so far in her past she never ever considered that he might turn up on her doorstep.

She'd been expecting Philip Cannavarro.

She'd done a photo shoot with the Cannavarro family—

Phil, Lottie and their three children—last month at the beach.
A week and a half ago, they had chosen their photos, and
Philip had called at lunch to ask if he could drop by after work
and pick up their order.

So when the buzzer had sounded at twenty minutes to six,
Daisy had opened the door with a smile on her face and an
embossed portfolio of photos in her hand—a portfolio that the
sight of Alexandros Antonides had let slip from her nerveless fingers.

"Oh, hell."

Her heart hammering, Daisy stooped quickly and began
gathering up the photos. Focusing on that gave her a few moments of time and a little bit of space to get her bearings. Ha.
What was he doing here?

She hadn't seen Alex in years and she had never expected
to ever see him again. Only the fact that he seemed as surprised as she was allowed her to breathe at all.

She stopped doing that, though, when he crouched down
beside her and began to help pick up the photos.

"Don't do that. Leave them," she said, trying to snatch them
away from him. "I can do it!"

But Alex didn't let go. He simply kept right on. He only
said, "No."

And there it was—the same single word, delivered in the
same implacable tone that he'd said five years ago—that one
that had pulled the rug right out from under her hopes and
dreams.

Worse, though, was that his rough-edged, slightly accented,
unconsciously sexy baritone still resonated all the way to the
core of her exactly as it had from the moment she'd first heard
him speak. It was as if he had been her very own personal
pied piper of Hamelin. And foolishly, mindlessly, Daisy had
fallen under his spell.

Then she'd called it "love at first sight." *Then* she had believed in the foolishness of such fairy tales.

Now she knew better. Now she knew the danger of it, thank

God. There would be no falling under his spell again. She gathered the last of the photos, no longer in any shape to be presented to Philip Cannavarro, and got to her feet.

"What are you doing here?" she demanded, stepping away as he rose to his feet, too.

He shook his head, looking as dazed as she felt. "You're Daisy?" He glanced at a piece of paper he held in his hand, then frowned. "Well, of course you are, but...Connolly?"

Daisy lifted her chin. "That's right. Why?"

But before she got an answer, another man appeared outside on the stoop, just beyond the heavy front door and looked past Alex questioningly.

Daisy's knees went weak with relief. "Phil! Come on in!" He might as well have been the cavalry come to her rescue. She beamed at him.

Alex turned and stared over his shoulder, his brows drawing down. "Who's he?" he demanded as if he had more right there than her client.

Fortunately Phil was already pulling the door open, glancing in quick succession at Daisy's relieved face and Alex's scowl and finally at the photos in Daisy's hands. "Sorry. Didn't mean to interrupt—"

"You weren't," Daisy said quickly. "But I heard the bell. I thought it was you, not—" she gestured helplessly toward Alex who was standing so she could almost feel the heat of his body "—and I accidentally dropped your photos. I am so sorry." She gave Phil a hopeful smile. "I need to have them redone."

"Don't worry about it. They're probably just a little frayed at the edges," Phil said cheerfully. "No problem." He held out his hand and doubtless would have taken them from her, but Daisy shook her head and clutched them against her chest like a shield.

"No," she said. "I guarantee my work. And I don't give less than my best. You and Lottie deserve my best." He and Lottie had been one of the first matches she'd made. Lottie had been a makeup artist she'd met when she first began working as a photographer after college. Phil used to do her taxes. She felt almost like their mother even though they were older than she was. And she wasn't giving them less than her best.

"I'll put a rush on it," she promised. "You should have them in two days. I'll have them couriered directly to your house."

Phil looked doubtful. "We won't mind," he said. "Lottie will want…"

"Take these then." Daisy thrust them at him. "But tell her they're just until the new ones come in. Tell her I'm so sorry. Tell her—" She shut her mouth, the only way to stop babbling.

Phil fumbled with the photos, too, then stuffed them in his briefcase, shooting Daisy worried sidelong glances. "Are you sure you're okay?"

"I'm fine," she lied.

But she knew why he was asking. Phil and Lottie were used to the unflappable Daisy, the one who rolled with the punches, adjusted on the fly, never worried if life threw pitchforks in her path.

"Daisy always copes," Lottie said. It was like a mantra.

Daisy wasn't exactly coping now. Alex's mere presence created an electricity in the air, a force field of awareness she could never manage to be indifferent to. Damn it.

"She'll be fine," Alex said smoothly now. "She's just had a bit of a shock." He stepped even closer and looped an arm over her shoulders.

Daisy nearly jumped out of her skin. At the same time, though, her traitorous body clamored to sink into his embrace. Muscle memory was a dangerous thing. Daisy held herself rigid, resisting him, resisting her own inclination.

"She'll be all right. I'll take care of her." Alex's tone was all reassurance as he smiled and somehow put himself between her and Phil, edging the other man toward the door, making it clear that Phil didn't need to hang around.

Phil didn't hang around. He understood male territoriality as well as the next guy. "Right," he said, all smiles and cheerful bravado. "I'll tell Lottie."

And he was out the door and down the steps without glancing back.

"Thank you very much," Daisy said drily, slipping out from beneath his arm, which still managed to leave her with a sense that it was still there. She could feel the warm weight of it even though she'd stepped away. Instinctively she wrapped her own arms across her chest.

What was he doing here? The question pounded again in her brain.

"Daisy." The way he said her name was somewhere between musing and caressing. It sent the hairs on the back of her neck straight up. A slight smile played at the corners of his mouth. "It is fate," he murmured.

"What?" Daisy said sharply.

"I was just thinking about you." His tone was warm. He acted as if they were old friends. Well, maybe to him that was all they were.

"I can't imagine why," Daisy said, which was the absolute truth.

"I'm looking for a wife."

She stared at him, her jaw dropping.

He just smiled, expecting no doubt to hear her say, *Oh, yes, please! Pick me.*

Daisy hugged her arms more tightly across her chest. "Good luck with that." She could have said, *You don't want a wife. You made a huge point of telling me you didn't want a wife!*

Now Alex raised his brows. The smile still lurking. "I wasn't proposing," he said mildly.

Mortified, Daisy said stiffly, "Of course you weren't."

She wasn't going to bring up the past at all. It did her no credit. She'd been young and stupid and far too romantic for her own good when they'd met five years ago at a wedding reception.

Daisy had been one of her college roommate, Heather's, bridesmaids, and Alex had been pressed into service as a last-minute substitute for a sick groomsman. Their eyes had met—something wild and hot and amazing had sparked between them—and to Daisy's fevered romantic twenty-three-year-old brain, it had been one of those meant-to-be moments.

They had only had eyes for each other from the moment they'd met. They talked, they danced, they laughed, they touched. The electricity between them could have lit New York City day and night for a week.

So this was love at first sight. She remembered thinking that, stunned and delighted to finally experience it. She had, of course, always believed. Her parents had always told Daisy and her sister that they'd known from the moment they'd met that they were destined to be together.

Julie, Daisy's sister, had felt that way about Brent, the moment she'd met him in eighth grade. They'd married right out of high school. Twelve years later, they were still deeply in love.

Daisy had never felt that way—wasn't sure she believed it—until the day Alex had walked into her life.

That afternoon had been so extraordinary, so mind-numbingly, body-tinglingly perfect that she'd believed. It was just the way her parents had described it, the way Julie had described it—the sense of knowing, of a belief that all the planets were finally lined up, that the absolutely right man had come into her life.

Of course she hadn't said so. Not then. She'd just met Alex. But she hadn't wanted the day to end—and he hadn't, either. She was the bridesmaid who had been deputized to take Heather's car back to Manhattan after the reception.

"I'm coming, too," Alex had said in that rough sexy baritone, and his eyes had met hers. "If that's all right with you."

Of course it had been all right with her. It was just one more reason to believe he was feeling the same thing, too. Together they had driven back to Manhattan. And all the way there, they had talked.

He was an architect working for a multinational firm, but

eager to strike out on his own. He had his own ideas, a desire to blend old and new, to create both beauty and utility and to design buildings that made people more alive, that spoke to their hearts and souls. His eyes had lit up when he'd talked about his goals, and she had shared his enthusiasm.

He had shared hers about her own professional hopes and dreams. She was working for Finn MacCauley, one of the pre-eminent fashion and lifestyle photographers in the country. It was almost like an apprenticeship, she'd told him. She was learning so much from Finn, but was looking forward, like Alex was, to finding her own niche.

"People definitely," she'd told him. "Families, kids, people at work and play. I'd like to shoot you," she'd told him. She wanted to capture the moment, the man.

And Alex had simply said, "Whenever you want."

When they got to the city, she had left the car in the parking garage by Heather's Upper East Side apartment, then she'd taken Alex downtown on the subway to the Soho flat she was subleasing from a dental student on a semester's internship abroad.

On the subway, Alex had caught her hand in his, rubbing his thumb over her fingers, then dipping his head to touch his lips to hers. It was a light touch, the merest promise, but it set her blood on fire. And when he pulled back, she caught her breath because, looking into his eyes, she had seen a hunger there that was as deep and intense as her own.

It had never happened before. A desire so powerful, so intense just grabbed her—and it wouldn't let go. Daisy wasn't used to this sort of intensity. She didn't fall into bed at the drop of a hat, had only once before fallen into bed with a man at all. It had been fevered groping on his part and discomfort on hers.

With Alex, she'd tried telling herself, it would be more of the same.

But it wasn't.

His kisses were nothing like any she'd tasted before. They were heady, electric, bone-melting. They'd stood on the sidewalk nearly devouring each other. Not something Daisy had ever done!

She couldn't get him back to her apartment fast enough.

Once there, though, she'd felt suddenly awkward, almost shy. "Let me take your picture," she'd said.

And Alex had given her a lazy teasing smile and said, "If that's what you want."

Of course it wasn't what she wanted—or not entirely what she wanted. And it wasn't what he wanted, either. It was foreplay. Serious and smiling, goofing around, letting her direct him this way and that, all the way watching her—burning her up!—from beneath hooded lids.

He wanted her. He didn't have to say it. They circled each other, moved in, moved away. The temperature in the room rose. The temperature in Daisy's blood was close to boiling.

Then Alex had reached out and took the camera from her. He aimed, shot, posed her, caught the ferocity of her desire, as well. He stripped off his jacket, she unbuttoned his shirt. He skimmed down the zip of her dress. But before he could peel it off, she had taken the camera back, set the timer and wrapped her arms around him.

The photo of the two of them together, caught up in each other, had haunted her for years.

But at the time she hadn't been thinking about anything but the moment—the man. Within moments the camera was forgotten and in seconds more the rest of their clothing was gone.

And then there was nothing between them at all.

Alex bore her back onto her bed, settled beside her and bent his dark head, nuzzling her breasts, tasting, teasing, suckling, making her gasp and squirm.

And Daisy, shyness long gone, had been desperate to learn every inch of him. She'd prowled and played, made him suck in his breath and say raggedly, "You're killing me!"

But when she'd pulled back he'd drawn her close again. "Don't stop," he'd said.

They hadn't stopped—neither one of them. They'd driven

each other to the height of ecstasy. And it wasn't at all like that other time.

With Alex there was no discomfort, there was no second-guessing, no wondering if she was doing the right thing. It had been lovemaking at its most pure and elemental, and so perfect she could have cried.

After, lying wrapped in his arms, knowing the rightness of it, she had believed completely in her mother's assertion that there was a "right man"—and about knowing instinctively when you met him.

She'd met Alex and—just like her parents, just like her sister and Brent—she had fallen in love.

They'd talked into the wee hours of the morning, sharing stories of their childhood, of their memories, of the best and worst things that had ever happened to them.

She told him about the first camera she'd ever had—that her grandfather had given her when she was seven. He told her about the first time he'd climbed a mountain and thought he could do anything. She told him about her beloved father who had died earlier that winter and about the loss she felt. He understood. He told her about losing his only brother to leukemia when he was ten and his brother thirteen. They had talked and they had touched. They had stroked and smiled and kissed.

And they had made love again. And again.

It was always going to be like that, Daisy vowed. She had met the man of her dreams, the one who understood her down to the ground, the man she would love and marry and have children with and grow old with—

—until she'd said so.

She remembered that Sunday morning as if it had been yesterday.

They'd finally fallen asleep in each other's arms at dawn. When Daisy had awakened again it was nearly ten. Alex was still asleep, sprawled on his back in her bed, bare-chested, the duvet covering him below the waist. He was so beautiful. She could have just sat there and stared at him forever, tracing the strong lines of his features, the hollows made by his collarbone, the curve of muscle in his arms, the long, tapered fingers that had made her quiver with their touch. She remembered how he'd looked, naked and primal, rising above her when they'd made love.

She would have liked to do it again. She had wanted to slide back beneath the duvet and snuggle up against him, to rub the sole of her foot up and down his calf, then let her fingers walk up and down his thigh, and press kisses to the line of dark hair that bisected his abdomen.

But as much as she wanted to do that, she also wanted to feed him before he had to catch his plane. She knew he had an early evening flight to Paris where he would be spending the next month at the main office of the firm he worked for. She'd hated the thought of him leaving, but she consoled herself by hoping that when he started his own company he would bring it stateside. Or maybe she would follow him to Paris.

Daisy had tried to imagine what living in Paris—living in Paris with Alex—would be like while she made them eggs and bacon and toast for breakfast. The thoughts made her smile. They made her toes curl.

She'd been standing at the stove, toes curling as she turned the bacon when hard muscled arms had come around her and warm breath had touched her ear.

"Morning," Alex murmured, the burr of his voice sending a shiver of longing right through her.

"Morning yourself." She'd smiled as he had kissed her ear, her nape, her jaw, then turned her in his arms and took her mouth with a hunger that said, *The hell with breakfast. Let's go back to bed.*

But she'd fed him a piece of bacon, laughing as he'd nibbled her fingers. And she'd actually got him to eat eggs and toast as well before they'd rolled in the sheets once more.

Finally in the early afternoon he'd groaned as he sat up and swung his legs out of bed. "Got to grab a shower. Come with me?" He'd cocked his head, grinning an invitation that, despite feeling boneless already, Daisy hadn't been able to refuse.

The next half hour had been the most erotic experience of her life. Both of them had been wrung out, beyond boneless—and squeaky clean—by the time the hot water heater had begun to run cold.

"I need to go," he'd said, kissing her thoroughly once more as he pulled on a pair of cords and buttoned up his shirt.

"Yes," she agreed, kissing him back, but then turning away long enough to stuff her legs into a pair of jeans and pluck a sweater from the drawer. "I'll go out to the airport with you."

Alex had protested that it wasn't necessary, that he was perfectly capable of going off by himself, he did it all the time.

But Daisy was having none of it. She'd smiled saucily and said, "Yes, but now you have me."

She'd gone with him to the airport, had sat next to him in the back of the hired car and had shared long drugging kisses that she expected to live off until he returned.

"I'll miss you," she'd told him, nibbling his jaw. "I can't believe this has happened. That we found each other. I never really believed, but now I do."

"Believed?" Alex lifted his head from where he'd been kissing her neck long enough to gaze into her eyes. "In what?"

"This." She punctuated the word with a kiss, then looked deeply into his eyes. "You. Me. It's just like my mother said. Love at first sight." She smiled, then sighed. "I just hope we get more years than they did."

There was a sudden stillness in him. And then a slight movement as he pulled back. A small line appeared between his brows. "Years? They?"

"My parents. They fell in love like this. Took one look at each other and fell like a ton of bricks. There was never anyone else for either of them. They were two halves of the same soul. They should have had fifty years. Seventy-five," Daisy said recklessly. "Instead of twenty-six."

Alex didn't move. He barely seemed to breathe. The sparkle in his light green eyes seemed suddenly to fade.

Daisy looked at him, concerned. "What's wrong?"

He'd swallowed. She could remember the way she'd watched his Adam's apple move in his throat, then the way he'd shaken his head slowly and said, "You're talking a lifetime, aren't you?"

And ever honest, Daisy had nodded. "Yes."

There had been a split second before the world tilted. Then Alex had sucked in a harsh breath. "No." Just the one word. Hard, decisive, determined. Then, apparently seeing the look on her face, he'd been at pains to assure her. "Oh, not for you. I'm not saying you won't have a lifetime…with someone. But…not me."

She remembered staring at him, stunned at the change in him. He seemed to have pulled inside himself. Closed off. Turned into the Ice Man as she'd watched. "What?" Even to her own ears her voice had sounded faint, disbelieving.

Alex's jaw set. "I'm not getting married," he'd told her. "Ever."

"But—"

"I don't want to."

"But—"

"No." His tone was implacable. Yet despite the coldness of his tone, there was fire in his eyes. "No hostages to fortune," he'd said. "No wife. No kids. No falling in love. Too much pain. Never again."

"Because…because of your brother?" She had only barely understood that kind of pain. Her parents had been gloriously happily married until her father's death a month before. And she had witnessed what her mother was going through after. There was no doubt it was hard. It was hard on her and on her sister, too. But her parents had had a beautiful marriage. It had been worth the cost.

She'd tried to explain that to Alex in the car. He hadn't wanted to hear it.

"It's fine for you if that's what you want," he'd said firmly. "I don't."

"But last night…this morning…?" Daisy had been grasping desperately at straws.

"You were great," he'd said. Their gazes had met for a moment. Then deliberately Alex looked away.

By the time they'd arrived at the airport, there were no more kisses, only a silence as big and dark as the Atlantic that would soon stretch between them. Alex didn't look at her again. His fingers were fisted against his thighs as he stared resolutely out the window.

Daisy had stared at him, willed him to reconsider, to believe—to give them a chance!

"Maybe I was asking for too much too soon," she ventured at last as their hired car reached the airport departure lanes. "Maybe when you come back…"

Alex was shaking his head even as he turned and looked at her. "No," he said, his voice rough but adamant.

She blinked quickly, hoping he didn't notice the film of unshed tears in her eyes as she stared at him mutely.

"I won't be back, Daisy. A lifetime is what you want," he'd said. "I don't."

It was the last thing he'd said to her—the last time she'd seen him—until she'd opened the door a few minutes ago.

Now she dared to stare at him for just a moment as she tried to calm her galloping heart and mend her frayed nerves, tried to stuff Alexandros Antonides back into the box in the distant reaches of her mind where she'd done her best to keep him for the past five years.

It wasn't any easier to feel indifferent now than it ever had been. He was certainly every bit as gorgeous as he had been then. A shade over six feet tall, broad-shouldered in a pale blue dress shirt and a gray herringbone wool sport coat, his tie loosened at his throat, Alex looked like the consummate successful professional. His dark hair was cut a little shorter now, but it was still capable of being wind-tossed. His eyes were still that clear, light gray-green, arresting in his tanned face with its sharply defined cheekbones and blade-straight nose. And his sensuous mouth was, heaven help her, more appealing than ever with its hint of a smile.

"Why are you here?" she demanded now.

"Lukas sent me," he said.

"Lukas?"

Alex's cousin Lukas had been her official "other half" at the wedding where she'd met Alex. He'd insisted she stay by his side at the reception long enough so that his mother and aunts wouldn't fling hopeful Greek girls at his head. Once he'd established that he wasn't available, he'd given her a conspiratorial wink, a peck on the cheek and had ambled off to drink beer with his brothers and cousins, leaving her to fend for herself.

That was when she'd met Alex.

Now Alex pulled a piece of paper out of his pocket and poked it in front of her face. "He said I should talk to his friend Daisy the matchmaker."

Yes, there it was—her name, address and phone number—in Lukas's spiky handwriting. But she was more arrested by his words than what he was waving in front of her face. "You're looking for a matchmaker? *You?*"

Alex shrugged. "No doubt you're amazed," he said easily. "Thinking I've changed my mind."

She didn't know what to think.

"I haven't," he said firmly. "I'm not looking for hearts and flowers, kindred spirits, the melding of two souls any more than I ever was."

She wondered if he was being so adamant in case she decided to propose. No fear of that, she wanted to tell him. Instead she pressed her lips into a tight line.

"I want a marriage of convenience," Alex went on. "A woman with her own life, doing her own thing. She'll go her way, I'll go mine. But someone who will turn up if a business engagement calls for it. And who's there…at night."

"A sex buddy?" Daisy said drily.

Was that a line of color creeping above his shirt collar? "Friends," he said firmly. "We'll be friends. It's not just about sex."

"Hire a mistress."

"I don't want a mistress. That *is* just about sex."

"Whatever. I can't help you," she said flatly.

"Why not? You're a matchmaker."

"Yes, but I'm a matchmaker who does believe in hearts and flowers, kindred spirits, the melding of two souls." She echoed his words with a saccharine smile. "I believe in real marriages. Love matches. Soul mates. The kind you don't believe in." She met his gaze steadily, refusing to look away from those beautiful pale green eyes that she'd once hoped to drown in forever.

Alex's jaw tightened. "I believe in them," he said harshly. "I just don't want one."

"Right. So I repeat, I can't help you." She said the words again, meant them unequivocally. But even as she spoke in a calm steady tone, her heart was hammering so hard she could hear it.

Their gazes met. Locked. And with everything in her, Daisy resisted the magnetic pull that was still there. But even as she fought it, she felt the rise of desire within her, knew the feelings once more that she'd turned her back on the day he'd walked out of her life. It wasn't love, she told herself. It was something else—something as powerful and perverse and demanding as anything she'd ever felt.

But she was stronger now, and no longer an innocent. She had a life—and a love in it—that was worth resisting Alex Antonides.

"I hope you find what you're looking for," she said, holding his gaze. "It was nice to see you again."

It was, she hoped, a clear dismissal. It was also a blatant lie. She could have gone the rest of her life without seeing Alex again and died a happy woman. She didn't need a reminder of the stupidest thirty hours of her life. But in another way, she was aware of owing him her unending gratitude.

That single day had forever changed her life.

"Was it?" he asked. His words were as speculative as his gaze. He smiled. And resist as she would, she saw in that smile the man who once upon a time had melted her bones, her resolve, every shred of her common sense, then broken her heart.

She turned away. "Goodbye, Alex."

"Daisy." His voice stopped her.

She glanced back. "What?"

The smile grew rueful, crooked, far too appealing. "Have dinner with me."

CHAPTER TWO

"WHAT? *No!*" She looked panic-stricken. Horrified.

Not at all like the Daisy he remembered. And yet she was so much the Daisy he remembered that Alex couldn't just turn and walk away. Not now. Not when he'd finally found her again. "Why not?"

"Because…because I don't want to!" Her cheeks had grown red in the throes of passion. Her whole body had blushed when he'd made love to her. His body—right now—was already contemplating doing the same thing again.

Which was a profoundly stupid idea, considering what he wanted, what she wanted, considering the present—and their past.

"Do you hate me?" he asked. He remembered the way they had parted. She'd looked devastated, about to cry. Thank God she hadn't. But what she'd wanted—the hope of a lifetime of love—was his worst nightmare. It brought back memories that he'd turned his back on years ago. What had begun happening between them that weekend was something he wasn't ready for. Would never be ready for.

So there was no point in making her hope in vain. He regretted having hurt her when he'd left her. But he could never bring himself to regret that weekend. It was one of the best memories of his life.

"Of course I don't hate you," she said briskly now. "I don't care at all about you."

Her words were a slap in the face. But he supposed he had it coming. And it was just as well, wasn't it, that she didn't care? It meant he hadn't hurt her badly after all.

"Well, then," he suggested easily, "let's share a meal." He gave her his best engaging grin. "For old times' sake," he added when he could see the word *no* forming on her lips.

"We don't have old times."

"We have one old time," he reminded her softly.

Her cheeks grew brighter yet. "That was a long, long time ago. Years. Five or six at least."

"Five," he said. "And a half." He remembered clearly. It was right after that weekend that he'd made up his mind to stay in Europe, to buy a place in Paris.

It made sense businesswise, he'd told himself at the time. But it wasn't only business that had made him dig in across the pond. It was smarter to put an ocean between himself and the temptation that was Daisy.

She was still tempting. But a dinner he could handle. "It's just a meal, Daisy. I promise I won't sweep you off to bed." Not that he wouldn't like to.

"You couldn't," she said flatly.

He thought he could, but emotions would get involved. So he wouldn't go there, as tempting as it was. Still, he wasn't willing to walk away, either. "We have a lot to catch up on," he cajoled.

But Daisy shook her head. "I don't think so." Her smile was brittle. He saw none of the sunny sincerity he'd always associated with his memories of her. Interesting.

He studied her now, wondering what her life had been like over the past five years. He'd always imagined she'd found the true love she'd been seeking, had found a man who'd made her happy. And if the thought occasionally had made him grind his teeth, he told himself a guy couldn't have everything. He had what he wanted.

Now he wondered if Daisy had got what she wanted. Suddenly he wanted to know.

"Another time then," he suggested.

"Thank you, but no."

He knew he was going to get "no" if he asked a hundred times. And the knowledge annoyed him. "Once upon a time we had a lot to say to each other," he reminded her.

"Once upon a time is for fairy tales, Alex. Now, if you'll excuse me, I have to go."

"Let's," he said readily. "I'll walk with you."

"I don't mean go somewhere else," she said. "I mean I have to go back inside. I have work to do. In my office."

"Matchmaking?"

She shook her head. "Not tonight."

"Photography?" He remembered the camera, how it had been almost a natural extension of who she was.

She nodded, smiling a little. It was a real smile.

"You've got your own business then?" he pressed.

"Yes." She nodded. The smile stayed.

"Families? Kids? People of all shapes and sizes?" And at her further nod, he said, "Show me."

She almost moved toward the door, almost started to invite him in. But then she stayed where she was, gave her head a little shake. "I don't think so."

"You took photos of us." Sometimes he'd wished he had one. To take out and remember. But that was stupid. It was better to forget.

She shrugged and looked just a little uncomfortable. He wondered if she still had the photos.

"Why matchmaking?" he asked her suddenly.

She shrugged. "Long story." And no invitation to ask her to tell it.

He lifted a corner of his mouth. "I've got time."

"I don't."

"You're scared."

The color in her cheeks bloomed again. "I am not scared! What's there to be scared of?"

"I don't know. You tell me." He cocked his head. "Temptation maybe?"

She shook her head adamantly. "I'm not tempted. I'm busy. I have things to do. I haven't seen you in five years, Alex. I barely knew you then. We don't have a past to catch up on."

"We had a hell of a lot." He didn't know why he was persisting, but he couldn't seem to leave it alone.

"And we wanted to do different things with it. Goodbye, Alex." She turned away and started to go back inside.

But before she could, Alex caught her arm, and spun her slowly back, then did what he'd been wanting to do ever since he'd realized who she was.

He dipped his head and kissed her.

It was instinct, desire, a mad impetuous hunger that he couldn't seem to control. It was a roaring in his ears and a fire in his veins. It was the taste of Daisy—a taste he'd never forgotten. *Never.* And as soon as he tasted her, he wanted more.

And more.

For a second, maybe two, Daisy seemed to melt under the touch of his lips. She went soft and pliable, shaping her mouth to his. And then, in another instant, it was over.

She jerked away from him, stared at him for one horrified moment, cheeks scarlet, mouth still forming an astonished O. Then she pulled out of his grasp and bolted back inside the foyer.

"Daisy!"

The door slammed in his face.

Alex stared after her, still tasting her. Jolted, intrigued, stunned. Aroused.

Five years ago Daisy had been like a siren he'd followed eagerly, mindlessly, hungrily. He'd wanted her on every level imaginable. And having her that weekend over and over hadn't assuaged his hunger. He'd only wanted more.

Leaving, thank God, had removed the temptation.

And now—within minutes of having seen her again—it was back. In spades.

It was the last thing he wanted. The last thing he needed.

Alex turned and walked down the steps, pausing only to drop the paper with her name and address in the trash.

She had been right to say no. He would be smart and walk away.

Ten minutes later Daisy was still shaking.

She sat at her desk, staring at the photo she was editing, and didn't see it at all. Eyes closed or open, she only saw Alex—older, harder, stronger, handsomer—in every way *more*, even more compelling than the younger Alex had been.

She shuddered and scrubbed at her mouth with her fingers, trying to wipe away the taste of his kiss.

But all the scrubbing in the world wouldn't do that, and she knew it. She'd tried to forget it for years. It hadn't done a whit of good.

She hadn't even tried to forget him. That would have been impossible. But as time passed, at least she'd managed to put him on a shelf in the back of her memory's closet. He was still there, but he couldn't hurt her.

But now Alex was here.

She'd just seen him, talked to him. Been kissed by him. Had almost, heaven help her, kissed him back. It had felt so right, so perfect, so exactly the way it had felt the first time.

But she knew better now.

He had come. He had gone. The other shoe had finally dropped. He wouldn't come back.

"And it wouldn't matter if he did," Daisy said aloud.

Because if one thing was completely obvious, it was that however much more he had become, in fundamentals, Alex hadn't changed a bit.

He might want to get married now, but he obviously didn't want anything more than "friends—with benefits." He didn't want love. He didn't want a real marriage. He didn't want a family.

He didn't want her.

For a nanosecond her traitorous heart had dared to believe he'd finally come to his senses, had learned the value of love, of relationships, of lifetime commitment.

Thank goodness, a nanosecond was all the time it had taken her to realize that there was no point in getting her hopes up.

Of course he had proved he still wanted her on one level— the one he had always wanted her on. She wasn't such an innocent that she didn't know desire when she felt it. And she had felt it hard and firm against her when Alex had kissed her and pressed his body against hers.

But physical desire was just that—a basic instinctive response. It had nothing to do with things that really mattered— love, commitment, responsibility, sharing of hearts and souls, dreams and desires.

It was nothing more than an itch to be scratched.

And she wasn't about to be a matchmaker for a pairing like that. If he was interested in nothing more than a woman to share his bed—but not his heart—he wouldn't be interested in the sort of marriages she believed in. So he wouldn't be back.

And thank God for that—because if her heart still beat faster at the very sight of him and her body melted under his touch, at least her mind knew he was the last person she needed in her life.

Not just in her life, but in the life of the person she loved most in all the world—the one who, at this very moment, she could hear pounding his way up the stairs from the kitchen.

"Mom!" His voice was distant at first, then louder. "Mom!" And louder still as the door banged open. "Mom! Aren'tcha finished working yet? It's time to go."

Charlie.

Four and three-quarter years of sunshine and skinned knees and wet kisses and impatience all rolled up in the most wonderful person she knew.

He skidded to a stop in front of her and looked up at her, importuning. "Mom!"

"Charlie!" She smiled at him, echoing his tone, loving him with all her heart.

"Are you ready?" he demanded.

"Almost." She turned back to close the file she hadn't done a thing to since Alex had shown up on the doorstep. "Almost," she repeated, taking a deep breath to steady her nerves, then shutting the file.

She wished she could shut her memories of Alex down as easily. She couldn't. Particularly she couldn't right now— faced with the small boy staring up at her, all quivering impatience.

Impatience wasn't Charlie's middle name, but maybe it should have been. He'd been eager and energetic since the moment of his birth. Before his birth, in fact. He'd come almost two weeks early, right before Christmas. And he'd been taking the world by storm ever since.

He had a chipped tooth from a fall out of a tree back in May. He had a scab on his knee beneath his jeans even now. Daisy had told him last week she was going to buy stock in the Band-Aid company, and after he'd wrinkled his nose and said, "What's stock?" he'd listened to her brief explanation and said, "Good idea."

His stick-straight hair, the color of honey shot through with gold, was very close to the same shade as her own. But his light eyes were nothing like her stormy dark blue.

He didn't look like Alex—except for the shape of his eyes.

And after nearly five years, she was inured to it. She didn't see Alex in him every time she looked at him. She saw Charlie himself—not Alex's son.

Except today. Today the eyes were Alex's. The impatience was Alex's. The "let's get moving" was Alex down to the ground.

"In good time," she said now, determined to slow Charlie down—a little, at least. But she managed a smile as she shut the computer down. And she was sure she was the only one who noticed her hands were shaking.

"You said we'd go at six-thirty. It's almost six-thirty. The game's gonna start." He grabbed one of Daisy's hands and began to tug her back toward the stairs.

"Coming," Daisy said. But she straightened her desk, made a note to reorder the Cannavarro files, put her pencil in the drawer. All very methodical. Orderly. Step by step. Pay attention to detail. From the day that she'd learned she was pregnant, it was how she'd managed to cope.

Charlie bounced from one foot to the other until she finished and finally held out a hand to him again. "Okay. Let's go." She allowed herself to be towed down the stairs.

"We gotta hurry. We're gonna be late. Come on. Dad's pitching."

Dad. One more reason she prayed that Alexandros Antonides didn't darken her door again.

"Hey, Sport." Cal dropped down beside Charlie on the other side of the blanket that Daisy had spread out to sit on while they watched the softball game.

They had been late, as Charlie feared, arriving between innings. But at least Cal, Daisy's ex-husband, had already pitched in his half, so he could come sit with them until it was his turn to bat.

"We made a fire engine," Charlie told him. "Me 'n' Jess. Outta big red cardboard blocks—this big!" He stretched his hands out a couple of feet at least.

Cal looked suitably impressed. "At preschool?"

Charlie bobbed his head. "You an' me could make one."

"Okay. On Saturday," Cal agreed. "But we'll have to use a cardboard box and paint it red. Grandpa will be in town. I'll tell him to bring paint."

Charlie's eyes got big. "Super! Wait'll I tell Jess 'bout ours."

"You don't want to make him jealous," Cal warned. He grinned at Charlie, then over the boy's head at his mother.

Daisy smiled back and told herself that nothing had changed. Nothing. She and Charlie were doing what they often did—dropping by to watch Cal play ball in Central Park, which he and a few diehards continued to do well after the softball leagues ended in the summer. Now, in early October, there was a nip in the air, and the daylight was already going. But they continued to play.

And she and Charlie would continue to come and watch.

It was the joy of a civilized divorce, Daisy often reminded herself. She and Cal didn't hate each other—and they both loved Charlie.

"—you?"

She realized suddenly that Cal was no longer talking to Charlie. He was talking to her. "Sorry," she said, flustered. "I was just…thinking about something."

"Apparently," Cal said drily. Then he looked at her more closely. "What's wrong?"

"Nothing." She looked around. "Where's Charlie?"

Cal nodded in the direction of the trees where Charlie and the son of another one of the players were playing in the dirt. "He's fine. You're not. Something's wrong."

"No. Why should anything be wrong?" That was the trouble with Cal. He'd always been able to read her like a book.

"You're edgy. Distracted. Late," he said pointedly.

"I didn't realize you were timing me. I've got things on my mind, Cal. Work—"

But he cut her off. "And you're biting my head off, which isn't like you, Daze. And you must've come on the bus."

"The bus?" she said stupidly.

"You always walk, so Charlie can ride his bike." Cal looked around pointedly. There was no bike because, he was right, they hadn't had time to bring it. Charlie wanted to ride his bike everywhere. It was the smallest two-wheeler Daisy had ever seen, but Charlie loved it. Daisy was sure he would have slept with it every night if she hadn't put her foot down. Cal had given it to Charlie for his fourth birthday.

Daisy had protested, had said he was too young, that no four-year-old needed a bike.

"Not every four-year-old," Cal had agreed. "Just this one." He'd met her skeptical gaze with confident brown eyes and quiet certainty. "Because he wants it more than anything on earth."

Daisy couldn't argue with that. If Charlie's first word hadn't been *bike* it had been in the first ten. He'd pointed and crowed, "Bike!" well before his first birthday. And he'd been desperate for a bicycle last winter. She hadn't thought it would last. But Cal had insisted, and he'd been right.

Charlie's eyes had shone when he'd spotted the bike that morning. And over the past six months, his love for it had only grown. Since Cal had helped him learn to balance and he could now ride it unaided, Charlie wanted to ride it everywhere.

Usually she let him ride to the park while she walked alongside him. But they had been late today because...because of her visitor.

She was suddenly aware that Cal was watching her, not the game. "He doesn't have to ride his bike every time," she said testily. "And it's nearly dark."

"True." Cal stretched his legs out in front of him and leaned back, resting his weight on his elbows and forearms as his gaze slowly moved away from her to focus on the game, yelling at the batter to focus. Then, still keeping his gaze on the batter, he persisted quietly, "So why don't you just tell me."

He wasn't going to leave it alone. She'd never won an argument with Cal. She'd never been able to convince him of anything. If he was wrong, he couldn't be told. He always had to figure it out himself—like his "I can love anyone I will myself to" edict. He'd been as wrong about that as she had been about her "love at first sight" belief.

Clearly, when it came to love, the two of them didn't know what they were talking about.

Now he stared at her and she plucked at the grass beside the blanket, stared at it. *Nothing's changed. Nothing's changed.* She tried to make it into a mantra so she could convince herself. But she was no better at lying to herself than she was at lying to her ex-husband. Finally she raised her gaze to meet his as he turned away from the game to look at her. "I saw Alex."

There was the crack of bat hitting ball. Whoops and yells abounded.

Cal never turned his head to see what happened. His eyes never left Daisy's. He blinked once. That was all. The rest of his body went still, though. And his words, when they came, were quiet. "Saw him where?"

Daisy ran her tongue over dry lips. "He came to my office."

Cal waited, not pressing, allowing her to tell the story in her own way, in her own time.

And she couldn't quite suppress the ghost of a smile that touched her lips. "Looking for a matchmaker."

"What!" Cal's jaw dropped.

Hysterical laughter bubbled up just as it had threatened to do when Alex told her. This time Daisy gave in to it. "He's looking for a wife."

"You?" Cal demanded.

"No. He was as surprised as I was when he knocked on my door. He didn't know he was coming to see me."

"Then how—?"

"Lukas sent him."

Cal's eyes widened. His teeth came together. "Lukas needs to mind his own business."

"Of course. But Lukas never does. Besides, he didn't have any idea what he was doing. He never knew about Alex and me. No one did." No one ever had except Cal—and only because when she'd discovered she was pregnant, she'd had to talk to someone. "Don't blame Lukas. He thinks he's doing me a favor sending clients my way. And he is, I suppose. Most of the time. Not this time," she said quietly.

"No." Cal stared down at his fingers plucking at the grass for a moment. Then his gaze lifted and went toward Charlie who was still playing with his friend in the dirt. The question was there, but unspoken.

"I didn't say a word."

"But he—"

Daisy shook her head. "No. That hasn't changed. He wouldn't want to know."

"Still?" Cal persisted.

"No. He doesn't want relationships any more than he ever did," Daisy said firmly. "He doesn't want a real wife—he wants a woman to take to social events and go to bed with. It will save him the effort of having to go out and find one, charm one."

"He charmed you," Cal pointed out.

Cal, of course, knew that. He knew the whole sordid story.

She had met Cal Connolly when she'd taken the job with Finn after college. Cal had been the photographer she'd replaced, Finn's assistant before her.

Even after Cal hung out his own shingle, he had regularly come by Finn's to talk shop. Daisy had been included in the conversation. She learned a great deal from both of them.

Finn was brilliant, mercurial—and impatient. Cal was steadier, calmer, more methodical. He didn't yell quite as much. Finn had a wife and growing family. Cal was single, on his own. So it was Cal she began to spend time with. And while Finn had always remained her mentor, Cal had quickly become her best pal.

When she wasn't working for Finn, she had spent hours working with Cal, talking with him, arguing with him. They argued about everything from camera lenses to baseball teams to sushi rolls, from free will to evolution to love at first sight.

That had always been their biggest argument: did you love because—bang!—it hit you between the eyes? Or did you love because you decided who the right person was and made up your mind?

Because of her parents, Daisy had been a staunch believer in the "love at first sight" notion.

"I just haven't met the right person," she had maintained over and over. "When I do, I'll know. In an instant. And it will be perfect."

But Cal had scoffed at that. Ever the logical realist, he'd said, "Nonsense. I don't believe it for a minute. That makes you nothing but a victim of your hormones."

"It's not hormones. It's instinct."

But Cal had disagreed. "You can will whom you love," he'd told her firmly. "It's a rational decision."

So when he'd proposed to her, he'd been determined to demonstrate just that. "Obviously your way doesn't work," he'd pointed out. "So we'll try it my way now."

And Daisy, because she did love Cal—just not the way she thought she loved Alex—had faced the truth of her own folly. And she'd said yes.

It turned out they were both wrong. But they'd given it their best shot. And Daisy still did believe in love—now she had a codicil: it was apparently for other people.

Now Daisy let out a sigh and wrapped a blade of grass around her finger where Cal's wedding ring once had been.

"So, are you going to do it? Matchmake for him?" Cal asked.

"Of course not."

He grunted. "Good." He stared out across the field. "Was it...the same? Did you feel...this time...what you felt before?"

It was all Daisy could do not to touch her tongue to her lips. Instead she pulled her knees up and wrapped her arms around them, in full cocoon mode. "He's still charming," she admitted.

Cal had been watching the next batter swing and miss. But at her words he turned his head and shot her a sharp glance.

Daisy gave him a quick humorless smile. "Speaking objectively. Don't worry. I'm not a fool anymore."

"So I should hope."

The batter swung and missed. Cal hauled himself to his feet to go pitch another inning. "You all right? Anything I can do?"

"No. He won't be back."

Cal cocked his head. "No?" He didn't sound so sure.

"Why would he? I didn't invite him in. I didn't encourage

him at all." *I didn't kiss him back!* "And he doesn't want me. He wants some woman who won't care."

"And Charlie?"

"He doesn't know about Charlie. I'm doing him a favor, really," she said firmly. "He doesn't want kids. He never did."

"Because he doesn't think he has any," Cal pointed out. "What if he finds out he does?"

"He won't."

"But if—" Cal persisted. It was what she hated about him.

"Charlie is mine! And yours."

She had always told Charlie—not that he understood yet really—that he had two fathers—a birth father who had given him life, and Cal, the father he knew. Charlie didn't question it. Someday he would, no doubt. But by then it would be ingrained in his mind. There would never be a time when she had to "tell him" his father was not Cal.

Because in every way that counted, his father was Cal. Cal was the one who had been there for her. He'd been her husband when Charlie was born. Charlie bore his surname. He was the only father Charlie knew.

If someday he wanted to know about Alex, she'd tell him. If someday in the distant future, Alex learned he had a child, perhaps they would meet. But not now. Now Charlie was a child. He was vulnerable. He didn't need a father who didn't want him.

"You don't know what he'll do, Daze," Cal said heavily, "if he finds out."

"He won't find out." She would make sure of that.

Cal's smile was grim. "We hope."

CHAPTER THREE

A DAY went by. Two.

Daisy still kept looking over her shoulder—well, out the window, actually—feeling skittish. Apprehensive.

She checked the caller ID every time the phone rang. Her breath caught whenever she saw a shadow on the front steps.

She actually dropped the kettle she was filling this morning, even though it was just the FedEx man bringing an order to Mrs. Kaminski upstairs.

Now she was filling it again for her friend Nell, who had just brought Charlie home from preschool and was staying for a cup of tea and regarding her curiously all the while.

"Something wrong?"

"No. I just…dropped the kettle this morning. I'm trying to be more careful now." Daisy set it on the burner and turned the gas on.

"Cal giving you trouble?" It was always the first thing Nell thought of because her own ex-husband, Scott, was a continual source of irritation.

"Cal never gives me trouble," Daisy said. She glanced out the sliding door to the garden where Charlie and Nell's son Geoff were playing with trucks.

Nell grimaced. "Lucky you. Scott's driving me crazy."

Daisy wasn't glad to hear that Scott was creating difficulties in her friend's life, but talking about it did avert Nell's further interest in Daisy's edginess. She gave Daisy an earful about her ex while they drank their tea and ate biscotti. Daisy made soothing sounds, but Nell was still grumbling when she decided it was time to go. She called Geoff in and they headed out the front door.

Relieved that her life was nowhere near as complicated as her friend's, Daisy was feeling much more sanguine when the phone rang as the door shut behind Nell and her son.

"Daisy Connolly," she said brightly into the phone.

"Daisy." The voice was warm, slightly gruff and instantly recognizable. The intimate tone of it made the hairs on the back of Daisy's neck stand straight up. Why hadn't she checked the ID this time?

"Yes. This is Daisy," she said crisply. "Who is this?"

"You know who it is." There was a smile in his voice as he called her bluff.

"Alex," she said flatly because playing the fool any longer wasn't going to help matters a bit.

"See. I knew you'd figure it out." He was grinning now. She could hear that, too.

"What do you want?"

"Are you married?"

"What?"

"I remembered you weren't Daisy Connolly back then. Wasn't your last name Harris? Morris?"

"Harris."

There was a brief silence. "So you did marry." It wasn't a question.

"Yes," she said firmly.

"And now?"

"What do you mean, and now?" Why did he have to ask? What business was it of his?

"Are you still…married?"

What kind of question was that? Damn it. She wanted to lie. But she'd never been a good liar, and though her acquaintance with Alex hadn't been long, it had been intense. She was sure he would be able to tell if she did.

"I'm divorced." She bit the words out.

"Ah."

Which meant what? Never mind. She didn't want to know. "Alex," she said with all the patience she could muster. "I'm working."

"This is work."

"No. I told you, I'm not matchmaking for you."

"I got that. You don't want what I want." He parroted her sentiments back to her. "This is photography. Or are you going to turn me down for that, too?"

She opened her mouth, wanting desperately to do exactly that. But she wouldn't give him the satisfaction of knowing he'd rattled her. "What sort of photography?" she said. "I do family stuff."

"And weddings. And bar mitzvahs. And some professional head shots. Some editorial. Recreation. Ice skating," he added. "Frisbee in the park. Baseball games." He ticked off half a dozen scenarios that were all shoots she had actually done.

"How do you know that?"

"You have a website," he reminded her. "The internet is a wonderful thing."

Daisy, grinding her teeth, wasn't so sure. Her fingers tapped an irritated staccato on the countertop. Outside Charlie was making vrooming noises as he pushed his cars around the patio. Any minute he'd slide open the door and want a snack. To prevent it, she latched the sliding door and got some crackers out of the cupboard and cheese from the refrigerator, preempting his demand. "What did you have in mind?" she asked.

"I need photos. An architectural journal is doing a piece on me and some of the work I've done. They've got photos of my projects from all over the world. Now they want some of me on one of the sites." He paused. "They said they could send a photographer—"

"Then let them."

"But I'd rather have you."

She wanted to say, Why? But she didn't want to hear his answer. Besides, asking would open a whole new can of worms.

"Not my line," she said briskly as she slapped cheese between the crackers and made little sandwiches for Charlie.

"You do editorial. I've seen magazine articles."

"Yes. But I don't traipse all over the world. I work in the city."

"The building is in Brooklyn." He gave her a second to digest that, then added, "I seem to remember you cross the river."

They had crossed the river together coming back from the wedding on Long Island. Daisy felt the walls closing in.

"Yes, I cross the river. *If* I have time. I'm busy."

"Any time in the next two weeks," he said smoothly. "And don't tell me that every minute of your life is booked."

Daisy heard the challenge in his voice. It was just another way of saying, *I don't believe you're really over me at all. You still want me. And now that you're divorced you might not believe in that ridiculous "love at first sight" notion anymore. You might be glad for a roll in bed.*

And, if it weren't for Charlie, heaven help her, she might.

"Are you still there? Daisy?" he prompted when she didn't reply.

She drew a breath. "I might have something next week. Let me check." It was the only way she could think of to prove to him—and to herself—that she wasn't a weak-willed fool.

She put the cracker sandwiches on a paper plate, flipped up the latch and slid open the door. Charlie looked up and, at the sight of the plate, grinned and jumped to his feet.

Daisy put a finger to her lips to shush him before he could speak, grateful that she'd taught him almost since he could talk not to blurt things out where people on the phone could hear him. That way, she'd explained, he wouldn't have to have a babysitter as often if she could take calls as if she were in her office when, in fact, she was at home.

Charlie had learned quickly. Now he stuffed a cracker

sandwich into his mouth, then carried the plate back to his trucks. For a moment, Daisy just watched him and felt her heart squeeze with love. Then quietly she slid the door shut and went to look at her appointment book.

"Where in Brooklyn? What sort of photos?" she asked as she flipped through the pages of her day planner.

"Park Slope." Alex gave her the address. "It's a pre-war building."

"I thought you were an architect. Don't you design new buildings?"

"Not this one. I built this one from the inside out. The outside is pretty much intact, except for the windows. I fixed the windows. The place was in really awful shape and the guy who owned it wanted it removed. He wanted me to put up a new building there. But when I got into it, I couldn't see tearing it down. Structurally it was sound. And it had some really strong period architectural features. It fit the block, the surroundings. So I made him a deal. I bought it from him and he bought land a couple of miles away. Then I built him what he wanted there, and I kept this one for myself."

The eagerness and the satisfaction in his voice reminded her of when he'd talked about his hopes for his career. He'd already done some big projects for the company he'd worked for then. But those had been projects he'd been assigned, ones that had been the vision of someone else. Now it sounded like he had taken the reins and was making his own choices, his own decisions.

"Are you your own boss now?" she asked, unable not to.

"For the last five years." He hesitated, then went on so smoothly she might have imagined the brief pause. "There was never going to be the perfect time to leave, so I just… jumped in."

"You like it?"

"Couldn't be happier," he said. "What about you? You've obviously left the guy you were working for."

"Finn? Yes. And I like what I'm doing, too."

"You can tell me all about it—if you can see a way to work me into your schedule?"

He made it sound very straightforward. A job. No more. No less. Maybe this really was all business.

Daisy could almost—but not quite—forget the way he'd kissed her. Deliberately she shoved the thought away. "What sort of thing does the writer have in mind?" she asked. "What do they want to feature?"

"Me," Alex said ruefully. "Up-and-coming architect, blah, blah, blah. I designed a hospital wing—first one I've done—and it's up for some award."

"That's great." And not surprising, really. She imagined that Alex would be good at whatever he did. "Where? Nearby?"

"Upstate a ways. Same side of the river, though," he added drily. "They used staff photos for that. They want ones of me and of the place in Brooklyn because it's a new departure for me. So you'd be shooting it now—plenty of awful 'then' photos already available. And then they want some of me 'in my environment.'" His tone twisted the words wryly. "With a pencil protector in my pocket." She could hear his grin. "Playing with blueprints. I don't know. You will."

If she did it. And maybe she should. Maybe it was exactly what she needed to do—learn about the man, demythologize him, turn him into some digital files and eight-by-ten-inch glossies.

"I can spare a bit of time next Thursday afternoon. Say, around three?"

"Great. I'll pick you up."

"I'll meet you. Just give me the address again." It was business. Just business.

He gave her the address. She wrote it down.

Then he said, "See you Thursday. Bye."

And he was gone. Just like that.

She had second thoughts. And third. And thirty-third. By the time Saturday rolled around, it was all she could think about.

"So call him and tell him you can't," Cal said when he came by to pick up Charlie Saturday morning. Charlie had already given her a smacking kiss goodbye and bolted out the door eager to tell his grandfather about the fire engine they were going to make.

But Cal hadn't followed him. He was eying her curiously as Daisy told him about Alex's call and his offer of the photography job. She also admitted to her qualms.

"It's just…distracting!" She stuck her hands in her hair and tugged.

"Why do it then? Call him up and tell him no."

"He'll want to know why."

"You're not obliged to tell him."

"If I don't, he'll get suspicious."

"About what? Is he going to think you're hiding his son from him?"

"No, of course not. He'll think—" Daisy hesitated "—that I'm still in love with him. That I don't trust myself around him."

"Possible," Cal agreed. "Or maybe you don't trust him."

Maybe she didn't trust either of them. The attraction was still there on a physical level. She hadn't told Cal about Alex's kiss. Or her reaction to it. There were some things better left unsaid. Now she just shrugged. "It'll be all right," she murmured.

Cal gave her a long hard look. She tried to remain indifferent under his gaze, but Cal was a photographer, too. He saw things that other people couldn't see.

"Is it just hormones?" he said at last. "Or something more?"

Daisy flushed, giving him yet another telltale sign. "I'm curious about what he's done with the building. About the sort of work he's doing."

"Uh-huh." Cal wasn't having any of it.

"Really. I wouldn't jeopardize Charlie's future. You know that." She looked at him steadily.

"Keep it in mind," Cal warned.

"No fear. I'm not an airy-fairy fool anymore."

Cal looked as if he doubted that. But at last he shrugged. "If you say so."

"In fact," Daisy added, "I think this may be a good thing. I can learn more about his real life, so I'll be able to tell Charlie about it someday."

"Oh, there's a plus," Cal muttered.

"It'll be fine." She put a hand on his sleeve. "Really, Cal. Don't worry."

Cal let out a slow breath. "I'm trying not to." He started toward the door and then turned back. "Charlie hasn't seen him? He hasn't seen Charlie?"

"No!" She smiled her best reassuring smile.

"Someday…"

"Someday they'll meet. Someday when Charlie is older. Grown-up. Settled. And if he has questions in the meantime, I'll answer them. But I'm not setting him up to be hurt! You know that. We've discussed it." When a man felt about having kids the way Alex did, deliberately introducing him into Charlie's life wasn't a risk she wanted to take.

Besides, he had a perfectly fine father in Cal. And one father was enough—for the moment at least.

"C'mon, Dad!" Charlie poked his head out of the window of the car.

"Go on, Dad," Daisy urged him. "And don't you worry. I'm doing enough for both of us. And it's silly, really. I will be fine. I'll shoot his photos, admire his handsome face and come home. End of story. Trust me. I can take care of myself."

The building Alex had restored wasn't far from Prospect Park. Daisy found it easily. It sat on the corner of a residential street filled with brownstones and trees and a business cross street that was wider, had fewer trees to block the view, and gave her plenty of scope.

She'd arrived early to scope out the neighborhood, wanted to get herself in work-mode before she ever laid eyes on him.

The day was cool and crisp, the trees in their full autumn glory as she walked down the block, studying the building side on.

At a few minutes before three the sun was low enough that the shadows picked out some of the ornate carved relief on the facing of the top floor, sharpening the detail, showing the building to best advantage. Daisy took out her camera before she was halfway down the block, framed and shot. She took a dozen or more, then crossed the main thoroughfare to study the angles.

The building was tall and narrow, a four story redbrick like others in the neighborhood, but, unlike the rest of them, it seemed somehow to draw in the light.

She studied it more closely, trying to understand what she was seeing. The ground floor housed an electronics store which seemed an odd tenant for an old building. But somehow it fit the space easily and looked as if it belonged. Studying it, she began to realize why. The windows were taller than those in other buildings on the block and she remembered Alex saying he had changed the windows. But they still fit the period; they belonged. But he'd made the proportions just that little bit more generous.

Now they fit twenty-first century people. It made all the difference.

The second floor echoed the look with a series of gothic-arched windows and cream-colored facings that contrasted with the dark red brick. Stenciled just above waist height across the central largest window in black sans serif was Antonides Architectural Design. Simple, spare, elegant.

She could see possibilities forming as she moved quickly along the sidewalk. She would shoot Alex standing in that window, looking out, master of his kingdom. And another at his drafting table. She could envision him in her mind's eye bending over a drawing, black hair drifting across his forehead as he studied his work intently.

There would doubtless be plenty of other possibilities inside; an open staircase perhaps or a period elevator or maybe a skylight and, she grinned delightedly—enough light to make it happen.

Suddenly enthused and feeling like a real competent professional photographer for the first time since Alex had asked her to do it, Daisy turned—and came up hard against a solid male chest.

CHAPTER FOUR

"I saw you wandering back and forth across the street. I thought you might be lost." Alex had caught hold of her when she'd turned and crashed into him. He was still holding on now. Their bodies were touching.

Daisy's heart was going a mile a minute. Hastily she pulled away from his hard chest. "I wasn't lost," she said, hating her sudden breathlessness. "I was studying the building. Looking at all the angles."

She squinted up at him, trying not to be bowled over by the casual magnetism of the man. What was it about Alexandros Antonides that drew her like a moth to a flame?

Well, he was still gorgeous, there was that. Tall, whip-cord lean, broad-shouldered. Masculinity defined. Alex didn't have to flaunt the testosterone. It wasn't a veneer he put on. It was clearly bedrock in him.

"Well, if you're done assessing all the angles, let me show you around." He gave her one of those smiles, too, the one that had, from the beginning, undermined her common sense.

But she was older now, Daisy reminded herself. Made of sterner stuff. And she knew what he was made of, too.

"Fine," she said briskly. "Lead on."

He did just that, but not before he plucked her camera bag and one of the tripods out of her hands, leaving her with only her purse and the smaller tripod. "You could have left that in the building while you were looking around," he said over his shoulder as he crossed the street.

"I suppose."

"How'd you get here?"

"Subway."

He turned as he stepped up onto the sidewalk in front of his building. "With all this stuff? For God's sake, Daisy! They have cabs in Manhattan!"

"It's more efficient to take the subway."

"I'd have paid the cab fare."

"I don't need your cab fare. It's a business expense. When I want to take a taxi, I take one. I prefer the subway when I'm coming to Brooklyn. No bridge tie-ups. Now can we get going?"

She didn't want him fussing over her. He had no right. She didn't need him—of all people—thinking he knew best what was good for her.

Alex grunted, but still he shook his head as if despairing of her as he pushed open the door to the building. The electronics store she'd already spotted had its entrance off this interior vestibule on one side of the building. On the other was a stationer's shop—all fine paper and cards and pens.

"The old and the new," Daisy remarked, looking from the stationer's to the electronics store, nodding. She'd work that in, too.

Meanwhile he was leading her into the electronics store, pointing out the new windows and the old oak paneling, the new built-in oak cabinets and the old tin ceilings now restored. It was an artful blend of the best of both, and it showed off the latest electronic devices spectacularly well. After a quick tour there, he took her into the stationer's shop, and the same was true there, as well.

The exquisite paper products looked appealing against the same oak cabinetry. The displays of calligraphic pens and multicolored inks and artists' tools were equally appealing.

Against the tall narrow windows Alex had created window seats which the proprietor had set up as inviting nooks for one or two people to sit and try out the various products. They were all full—and many of the customers were as young and hip as those in the electronics store across the vestibule.

"I'll show you photos of how it was before when we go upstairs," he said. "In the meantime, shoot whatever you want. Den and Caroline—the owners of the stores—have given their permission."

"Great. Thanks. You don't have to hang around," she said when he made no move to go. "I'll shoot down here. Then I can come to your office."

"I've cleared my calendar." He set her bag down, then propped his shoulders against the wall and watched every move she made.

Daisy was used to going about her work single-mindedly forgetting everything and everyone else but the focus of her shots. She was, this time, aware every second of Alex's eyes on her. She tried to tell herself he was just being polite. But he didn't simply watch while she took photos in the stationer's shop and in the electronics store. He followed her outside so she could shoot a couple from down the block.

Daisy shot him a hard look. He smiled back blandly.

"Fine," she muttered, "if you're going to tag along…" Then she raised her voice loud enough for him to hear and motioned him to stand in front of one of the heavy oak and etched glass doors. "Stand there and look 'lord of the manor-ish.'"

He was Greek. What did he know about lords of the manor?

But apparently some things were universal, and he understood perfectly, leaning casually against one of the walls by the front door, a proprietorial air about him that said exactly what she wanted it to—that this was his domain. He owned the place.

"Got it," she said, clicking off half a dozen so she could have her pick.

"Come on upstairs, then." He led the way back inside.

The elevator was utilitarian, so she wasn't sure what to

expect when the doors opened—a hallway and doors to offices, she would have guessed. But that wasn't what she got.

The elevator opened into one big room facing north. There were expanses of gleaming oak flooring broken up by areas covered with dove-gray carpet. In one of the carpeted areas, a woman sat at a desk making some notes while she talked on the phone. Not far away, on another carpet there was soft furniture—sofas and armchairs that invited you to sit and peruse books from floor-to-ceiling bookcases.

Where the floor was wood, she saw several large tables with projects on display, detailed architectural models in place. Around the sides of the room, in their own spaces but accessible to everyone, there were drafting tables, a couple of which had people working at them. They had glanced up when the elevator doors opened, but seeing Alex, they'd nodded and gone back to work.

Daisy's gaze swiveled to take in the whole room. "Wow," she said, impressed. "Very nice."

"I like it. Let me show you around." He introduced her to Alison, his middle-aged office manager. Then he took her to meet the two at the drafting tables. A young dark-haired woman, Naomi, was deeply involved in whatever she'd been assigned and barely glanced up to smile. But the other, an intern named Steve, had some questions about his project, so Daisy was able to take some shots of Alex and Steve, leaning over one of the drafting tables, studying blue prints.

Then, while Alex answered Steve's questions, she wandered around, taking other shots of the room, of Alex on the job.

It was just the way she'd imagined him—in his element, his easy competence apparent. He drew her gaze as he bent over the table, his dark hair falling across his forehead as he pointed out something to Steve. She snapped off a couple of shots. But even when she lowered the camera, she couldn't seem to look away.

"Sorry," he said, coming back to her. "I didn't mean to spend so long with him."

"No problem. I got some good shots. Which is your table?" She nodded toward the vacant drafting tables.

"Upstairs. I'll show you."

He led her to a spiral staircase that ascended in one corner of the room. "We could use the elevator, but this is faster."

It was also a treat. It had caught her eye earlier, a bit of wrought-iron frivolity in stark utilitarian surroundings. And yet it belonged.

"Was it original to the building?" It was a little added lagniappe, and she had already taken a number of shots of it.

"No. But I wanted something to catch the eye," Alex said. "Something that was from the original period. I went to every salvage place in the boroughs, looking. I knew it when I saw it."

"It's perfect." She motioned him to precede her up the steps. "Turn around," she said when he was halfway up. She took several shots of him on the steps, and was seriously tempted to take one of his backside when, afterward, she followed him up. But she didn't need any more reminders of how tempting Alex Antonides was.

His office was out of the mainstream, but connected to it. "I don't let them up here," he said frankly. "I need my space."

"A perk of being the boss," Daisy acknowledged. But she had to admit she liked his private aerie, too. The room in which he had created his office wasn't large. Like the bigger room downstairs, it had tall, narrow, gothic arched windows and polished oak flooring. Floor-to-ceiling bookshelves held vast arrays of architectural titles, books about design, and a lot of history, art and photography books. Daisy studied the titles.

It was disconcerting to find many of the same titles she had on her own shelves. So, whatever it was, it wasn't just physical.

She wished it were. He would be so much easier to resist. Forcing herself to focus on the task at hand, she gave a little wave of her camera, asking permission to take photos. "May I?"

He nodded. "Of course."

"I've heard that there's a movement to minimize windows for energy conservation," she said as she pointed the camera in his direction. "You obviously don't believe that."

"There's a place for that. But light is good, too. And while you can conserve energy by building dark, I like light. So I try to make sure the windows are doing their job, too." He stopped. "Sorry. Boring."

Daisy lowered the camera. "It's not, actually. And I'm a photographer. I like light, too."

"Come on," he said suddenly. "I'll show you the best light of all."

Without looking to see if she followed, he started up to the next level on the same spiral staircase. Daisy followed, expecting more office space. But when he reached the landing and unlocked the door, she knew better.

This was where Alex lived.

If he hadn't said, "Welcome to my place," she would have known it anyway. The light walls, the earth tones, the casual modern but not stark furniture, the plush dark rust and blue and gold oriental rug centered on the polished oak floor created a visual backdrop for the man she had known. Even if he weren't standing there watching her take it all in, she would have known this was where he belonged.

There were, in the furnishings, in the books and papers on the coffee table, in the framed architectural drawings on the walls, signs of Alex everywhere. She was shaken by how instantly she felt at home, as if she, too, belonged here.

No. No, she didn't.

She took a breath, steeled herself and tossed his words back at him, "So show me the best light of all."

He smiled. "Right this way."

Wouldn't you just bloody know that it would be the skylight in his bedroom!

Daisy stopped dead at the door, realizing a split second before she crossed the threshold exactly where they were going. "I didn't mean—"

Alex turned, flashing her a grin. "You asked for it."

Daisy read the challenge in it—the very challenge she'd told Cal she could handle. And she could, damn it. So, deliberately, she stepped in and looked around. The skylight was above the bed. The bed looked to be the size of, perhaps, the Sahara Desert—but vastly more comfortable with its buff-colored duvet and a quartet of dark brown pillows.

"Very nice," she said, doing her best to keep her gaze fixed on the skylight until she turned back to the living room again. "Let me shoot some photos out here."

He smiled, but didn't challenge her further, just let her wander around and look her fill.

Daisy resisted looking her fill. She'd have been here for hours, curious about the man, wanting to know him better, at the same time she knew she shouldn't want to know him at all.

Alex's apartment was not some sterile showplace. There were dishes in the sink, a newspaper on the counter. Two pairs of athletic shoes, a gym bag and a racing bike sat by what she supposed was the main front door—the one that didn't lead down to his office. And one wall of the kitchen was painted as a mural of something that looked like the Greek islands—lots of blue sea and sky, white-washed buildings and blue domed churches. It drew her attention.

"Did Martha paint that?"

Martha was Lukas's twin sister. Daisy had met her several times over the years. She knew Martha now lived part of the year in Montana—of all places—and part of the year on Long Island and wherever her husband, Theo Savas, was sailing boats.

It seemed an amazing exotic existence to Daisy who had been born in Colorado, came to the big city for university, and never left—except to go back home occasionally.

"She did," Alex agreed. "Kind of bowls you over, doesn't it?"

"I like it," Daisy said.

"I didn't," Alex said, surprising her.

"What? Why not?"

He shook his head. "Memories."

That startled her until she remembered him telling her about his childhood, about his brother who had died young.

"You could paint over it," she suggested.

He shrugged. "I got used to it. I just wasn't expecting it. I was heading out of town and I told her to paint whatever she wanted. She thought it would make me happy. Can we get on with this?" he said abruptly, gesturing to her camera.

"Oh! Yes, of course!" Daisy grimaced, feeling a flush of confusion engulf her. That would teach her.

She pointed to the armchair near the window. "Go sit there and look at one of your books."

Alex picked up a book and sat down with it, opened it at random, studied it as if he cared what was in it while Daisy moved and shot, moved and shot.

He turned a page. "I hired a matchmaker."

Daisy's finger slipped on the shutter release. Then, taking a slow careful breath so as not to jar the camera, she clicked off several more shots and lowered it again.

"Did you?" she said, heart pounding. "Good for you. I'm sure you'll find exactly what you're looking for. Turn a little more this way."

He turned. "I found her on the internet."

A breath hissed through Daisy's teeth. "The internet? For heaven's sake, Alex! How do you know she's legitimate? She might be a charlatan—someone hanging out her shingle, looking to make money off poor unsuspecting fools."

He looked up from the book and raised a brow. "Poor unsuspecting fools...like me?"

Daisy's cheeks burned. "I didn't mean that! I never said—" She retreated behind her camera again. "I just meant that not everyone is reliable, honest. Did you get letters of recommendation? What do you know about her background?"

"She has a degree in human relations. She was born and raised in Virginia. She came to the 'big city' when she was just out of college. Reminded me a little of you."

"I'm not from Virginia," Daisy bit out. "And I don't have a degree in human relations."

"So maybe she's more qualified than you are," Alex mused, giving her a sly smile.

"Maybe she is. I've got enough here. Let's go back down to your office." Someplace less intimate. Someplace where she could focus on her work. She didn't want to hear anything more about his matchmaker.

Alex picked up her camera bag, then started down the stairs again. He glanced back. "I went out with one of her suggestions last night."

Daisy pasted on a bright smile. "How nice. Maybe you'll have a wife by Christmas."

He nodded. "Maybe I will. She's a stockbroker. Nice enough. Intense, though," he mused.

Daisy pointed him toward his drafting table. "Put out a drawing and focus," she directed. She did not intend to get sucked into analyzing his date.

"Too intense for me," he went on, even as he obediently pulled out a drawing, spread it on the table and stared down at it. "She'd talked nonstop about everything from chandeliers to parakeets to stock options to astronomy."

"Well, it's early days yet," Daisy said briskly. "Maybe the next one will be better."

If he'd been her client she'd have talked to him about that, tried to learn what he hadn't liked, what was "too intense." But she wasn't finding a wife for Alex Antonides. He was someone else's problem.

He kept his gaze on the drawing. "Maybe. I'm going out with another one tonight."

"Another one?" That fast? Where was the "matchmaking" in that? It sounded more like trial and error.

He glanced around. "Amalie—that's the matchmaker—has got a whole list."

A list. Daisy wasn't impressed. "Is she French? Or fake?" she added before she could help herself.

Alex raised a brow. "Her mother's French. Is that a problem?"

Daisy raised her camera again, refusing to admit she was taking refuge behind it. "Of course not. I just wondered. I suppose she's introducing you to French women then." It made sense. He spent a good part of every year in Paris.

"Career women," Alex corrected. "And I'm not looking for a French one. I live here now."

That was news. Daisy stayed behind the camera. She kept moving.

Alex picked up the drawing and rolled it up. Whether she was finished or not, it was clear that he was. "She has a list as long as my arm," he reported. "She said I need options."

Daisy grunted noncommittedly. She didn't think much of "options." But then, when she helped people find the right mate, she was trying to find their soul mate, not a sex partner who was willing to share a mortgage.

"So," Alex said, "I just have to find the right one."

Good luck with that, Daisy thought. But she kept her skepticism to herself. If she expressed it, he'd tell her she should do it herself.

"All done," she said, and began disassembling her camera and stowing it in her bag. "I'll get to work editing these early next week. I'm going to be out all day tomorrow, and I'm not working this weekend. If you'll give me your business card, I'll email you when I've finished. Then you can let me know whether to send you a disk or email you files or send them directly to the magazine."

Alex fished a card out of his wallet, started to hand it to her, then took it back and scribbled something on the back before pressing it into her palm again. "You can reach me at this number anytime."

Not likely. But Daisy just pocketed it and smiled as she zipped her bag shut, stood up and hoisted it onto her shoulder. Then, deliberately, she stuck out her hand to Alex for a businesslike shake. "Thank you."

He blinked, then stared—at her, at her hand. Something unreadable flickered across his face. Then in slow motion, he reached out and took her fingers in his. Flesh on flesh.

Daisy tried not to think about it. But his palm was warm and firm and there were light calluses on it, as if he didn't only sit in his office and draw. She remembered those calluses, those fingers—the way they had grazed her skin, had traced the line of her jaw, the curve of her hip, the hollow of her collarbone. Other lines. Other hollows.

She swallowed hard.

Still he held her hand. Then abruptly he dropped it. "Thank you, too," he said, his voice crisp. As businesslike as she hoped hers was.

"Goodbye." One more polite smile and she'd be gone.

Alex nodded, his gaze fixed on hers. The phone on his desk rang. He grimaced, then picked it up. "What is it, Alison?" There was barely concealed impatience in his tone. Then he grimaced again. "Right. Okay. Give me a sec." He turned back to Daisy. "I have to take this."

"Of course. I was just on my way."

She was down the steps and out the door without looking back. There. She'd done it—beard the lion in his den.

And survived.

Just like she'd told Cal she would.

Staring at the skylight in his ceiling in the dark didn't have much to recommend it. There were stars. There were a few small clouds scudding along, silvery in the moonlight.

There was Daisy.

Alex flipped over and dragged the pillow over his head. It didn't help. She was on the insides of his eyelids, it seemed.

The whole day had been a bloody disaster. Well, no, that

wasn't true. Before 3:00 p.m., things had been pretty normal. He'd been a little distracted, there had been a lot to do, but he'd got some work done.

And then Daisy had shown up. Exactly as he'd planned.

She was supposed to come, take her photos, and leave again. He was supposed to smile and look professional and competent and disinterested, and see her on her way. Asking her to take the photos was supposed to settle things between them, put them on a business footing.

It was supposed to pigeonhole her—and convince Alex that he wasn't really attracted, that he hadn't been thinking about her fifty times a day since he'd seen her again, that she didn't draw his gaze more than any other woman, that he was perfectly happy to watch her walk out of his office and out of his life.

The operative word was *supposed*. The truth was, well, something else altogether.

And the day hadn't been all that normal before three o'clock, either. He might have got some work done earlier in the day, but shortly before Daisy was due to arrive, he'd found himself walking over to look out the window every few minutes. It was a nice day, sunny, brisk. He was enjoying perfect fall weather. No more, no less.

So why had his heart kicked over at the sight of her down there on the sidewalk, pointing her camera up at his building? Why had he stopped Steve abruptly halfway through a question to go down and intercept her before she came in? Why had his fingers itched to reach out and touch her? And why had he had to fight to suppress the urge to kiss her when she'd turned and bumped straight into his chest?

She drove him crazy. She got under his skin. The minute he saw her, he couldn't seem to focus on anything or anyone else.

The feeling persisted the whole time she was there—this desire to touch her, to smooth a hand over her hair, to pull her against him, to touch his lips to hers. His heart had begun hammering the moment he'd seen her, and it was still banging away when he'd had to take that phone call and she'd left.

He'd wanted to stop her, to say, "Hang on. Wait," because it was too soon, there had been so little time, he had not had enough of her yet.

But at the same time, he knew it was stupid—*he* was stupid. Daisy Harris—Connolly!—was *not* what he wanted—or needed—in his life.

And it didn't matter that she was divorced now. She still apparently wanted things he didn't want. Wanted things he wasn't prepared to give. So the one bit of common sense he had, had kept his mouth shut.

He hadn't said, "Wait." Hadn't stopped her or called her to come back.

It was better she had left. And better still that he had had a date that night with one of Amalie's "options."

Whoever she was, she would erase Daisy from his mind.

Except she hadn't.

Her name was Laura or Maura or Dora. Hell, he couldn't remember. She had been pleasant enough in an airheaded sort of way. But he'd spent the evening making mental comparisons between her and Daisy.

Suffice to say, Dora/Maura/Laura had come up short on all counts.

She didn't have Daisy's charm. She didn't have Daisy's ability to listen. She didn't have Daisy's smile or Daisy's sparkling eyes or Daisy's eager enthusiasm.

She wasn't Daisy. He was bored.

He'd been polite enough. He'd listened and nodded and smiled until his jaw ached. He'd dutifully told her a bit about himself, but his comments were flat and uninteresting even to his own ears. It wasn't hard to tell she was bored, too.

"You win a few, you lose a few," she'd said, smiling and shaking his hand when they'd left the restaurant to go their separate ways.

It was nine-thirty. Shortly after ten he was home.

And that was when he began to realize his mistake. He'd not only lost, he'd lost big-time.

He hadn't vanquished Daisy from his mind by having her come take photos this afternoon. On the contrary he now had a whole host of new images of Daisy—on his turf.

Now when he stood at the window, he could look down at where he'd first spotted her, camera to her eye, taking pictures of his building, her hair loose in the wind. And when he grew tired of pacing his apartment and went back down to his office to do some work, the minute he sat down at his drafting table, he could almost feel her presence just over his right shoulder where she had been that afternoon.

He crumpled up half a dozen attempted drawings before he gave up, stomped back upstairs, stripped off his clothes and took a shower.

She hadn't been in his shower, at least.

Not this one, anyway. But he'd shared a shower with her five years ago, and the memories flashed across his mind with such insistence that he'd cranked the hot water down till only the cold beat down on his body. But his arousal persisted.

He wanted to go for a bike ride, burn off the energy, the edge. But not in Brooklyn. Not at midnight. There was stupid—and then there was stupid.

He was stupid, not suicidal.

He should have known better than to think he could see her again and forget her. He'd never been able to forget her. And he wouldn't be able to, damn it, until Amalie finally found him the right woman.

In the meantime he'd flung himself onto his bed, stared up at the skylight—and discovered the depth of his folly.

Daisy had been in his bedroom. He'd deliberately brought her in here—to show her the "best light"—wanting to get a rise out of her.

Well, she wasn't the one who was rising. Pun intended, he thought savagely. The joke was on him.

* * *

The trouble with doing an hour-long shoot with Alex was that the hour was just the beginning.

Oh, it was over for him. But Daisy had to work with the images, study them, analyze them, choose the best ones, correct them. Spend hours and hours and hours contemplating them.

It drove her insane.

She didn't want to see him in his element hour after hour. She didn't want to feast her eyes on that handsome face. She didn't want to focus on the lithe muscular body as he stretched across the drafting table to point something out to Steve. She didn't want to study the strong profile, the sharp angles, the hard jaw, and hawklike nose as he stared out the window.

He was everything she'd thought he would become.

And she couldn't bear to look at it.

She put the photos away and went to read books to Charlie. The next night she watched a movie instead. The following night she had a new shoot, some high school senior pictures to work on. She'd get to Alex's when the memory of being in his office, in his apartment—in his bedroom—wasn't quite so immediate.

She would do them.

Not now. Not yet.

She needed time. An eon or two.

She needed space. Would a galaxy be enough?

The trouble with the "options" Amalie was providing him with, Alex decided after his fifth disastrous date, was that not one of them—so far—had been worth the trouble.

He'd gone out with half a dozen since he'd contracted with her, and since the intense Gina whom he'd mentioned to Daisy and the airhead whose name he couldn't recall, there had been phlegmatic Deirdre and twitchy Shannon and a politician called Chloe.

But if they'd been bad, tonight's "flavor of the evening" was absolutely no improvement, though Amalie had sworn they would be perfect for each other.

"She's an architecture student. You'll have so much in common!" Amalie had vowed.

He met her at a restaurant near the Lincoln Center. She was at the bar when he got there, a red scarf looped around her neck. That's how he would recognize her, she'd told him on the phone.

He did a double take when he saw her. She looked so much like Daisy. Maybe a little blonder than Daisy, maybe a little taller. And her eyes were a sort of faded gray-green. She beamed at him when he arrived.

"I knew it was you!" She was like bubbly champagne. "You're even more handsome than your picture."

She might have meant it. He didn't know. Didn't care. Her eyes didn't sparkle like Daisy's.

They took their drinks to a table and he said, "Amalie says you're studying architecture."

Not quite. What Tracie knew about architecture she appeared to have memorized from Wikipedia. She started talking about the Acropolis before they ordered and had barely reached the Colosseum by the time their entrees arrived.

It was always interesting to learn which buildings inspired another architect, but Tracie wasn't an architect—or even a student of architecture, Alex was willing to bet. After two hours of her nonstop talking, he'd had enough. If she hadn't looked so much like Daisy, he doubted he'd have lasted that long.

But the truth was, the longer he spent with her, the less like Daisy she seemed. Tracie was nervous, edgy. She had a shrill laugh. Her voice grated on him.

Daisy's laugh made him feel like smiling. Her eyes always sparkled—either with joy or annoyance. It didn't matter which. They drew his gaze. When she was with him, he couldn't stop looking at her. Her voice was always like warm honey.

Not, of course, that he'd heard it since she'd walked out of his place a week and a half ago. She'd taken his picture and said she'd be in touch and he'd never heard from her again.

He set down his fork sharply.

"You're bored," Tracie accused, staring hard at him over his empty plate. He hadn't had to talk, so he'd eaten everything in front of him.

Now Alex shook his head. "No," he lied. "I'm distracted. I just realized I have to be somewhere. I have an appointment."

"Tonight?" Her eyes widened.

"I have to pick up some photos," he said. "I need to get them to an editor in the morning." It wasn't entirely true. But the editor did need them. She'd called him yesterday inquiring about where they were. He'd thought Daisy had sent them in so she wouldn't have to contact him again.

Tracie pursed her lips, then pouted. "But we've only reached the Duomo." Which meant they had about six hundred more years of architecture to cover.

"I'm sorry," Alex said firmly. "I really need to go."

He did finish his coffee, but then called for the bill, saw her into a taxi and watched it drive off. Not until it disappeared around the corner did he breathe a sigh of relief. He was free.

For what?

It was just past nine. Not really late—unless you'd just spent the past two hours being systematically bored to death. Then you wanted some excitement, something to get the adrenaline going.

But the adrenaline was already going—and so were his feet.

They knew exactly where they were headed, and before Alex even realized it, he was on the corner of the street where Daisy's office was.

Daisy—who was, let's face it, the reason he'd been willing to go on five dates in the past ten days—so he would bloody well stop thinking about her.

But he hadn't stopped.

Every night he lay in bed and stared at the damned skylight

and remembered her sparkling eyes, her smooth golden skin, her warm smile. And because he was in bed, he remembered other things, too.

He remembered touching her skin—all over. He remembered kissing her smiling mouth. He remembered stripping off her clothes and running his hands over her body, teasing, tasting—

Hell! He couldn't show up on her doorstep halfway to wanting to bed her. Not that she'd even be there. It was her office, for God's sake. Why would she be burning the midnight oil editing photos? Presumably she had a life.

She probably even went out on dates now that she was divorced. Maybe she had a boyfriend. His jaw tightened and he shoved his hands in the pockets of his jacket as he started walking down the street.

He didn't expect she would be there. So he was taken aback to discover lights on in the bay window of the apartment that was her office.

She didn't have a life, after all? He stopped across the street and stared.

Now what? Turn around and walk back to Columbus? Catch a cab home? And stare at the damn skylight again?

Abruptly Alex crossed the street, took the steps to the front door two at a time, opened the door to the vestibule and punched the doorbell.

He waited. And waited. He shifted from one foot to the other, and wondered if she left the lights on all the time. Maybe she wasn't even there.

He was ready to turn around and leave when all at once he heard the sound of the lock twisting and the door handle rattling. The door opened.

Daisy stared out at him, nonplused. *"Alex?"*

"I came for the photos."

"What?"

"The editor called me. She wants the photos. You said you'd have them ready."

"I said I'd call you when they were ready." She was gripping the door, glaring at him, and by God, yes, her eyes were sparking fire.

He almost smiled as he snaked past her into her office before she could object, then turned and let his gaze run over her again.

She was wearing a pair of jeans and a sweatshirt—about as inelegant as imaginable—and she looked as sexy as hell. Her blonde hair was hanging loose around her face. It was disheveled, as if she—or someone else?—had been running fingers through it.

"Am I interrupting something?" he snapped.

"What?" She frowned. Then she shrugged. "My work. If you want the photos, let me get back to them. They're not done yet. I'm sorry. I've been busy. I'll have them for you tomorrow. I—"

"Let me see them."

"No. Not while I'm still working."

"Why? Afraid of someone else's opinion?"

"Do I offer you opinions about the buildings you design?" she countered with saccharine sweetness. "Of course not. So go away."

But Alex didn't want to go away. He wanted to drop down in the chair and watch her work. He wanted to run his fingers through her hair and pull her close. He wanted to slide his hands down the curve of her spine, cup her buttocks—

He groaned.

"What's wrong?" She was looking at him intently, worriedly.

He ground his teeth, then turned away, knowing he should get the hell out of here, but somehow he couldn't go. It was as if she'd bewitched him, cast some spell that wouldn't let him find the woman he knew had to be out there, the woman who would actually be right for him.

"Alex?" she pressed in the face of his silence.

Finally he snapped. "I've had five dates, and they've all been disasters!"

Daisy's eyes widened. She stared at him, then let out a sound that might have been a laugh. Or a snort.

"What a shame," Daisy said in a tone that told him it had been both a laugh and a snort.

"It is, damn it! And it's a waste of time." Alex cracked his knuckles and spun away to pace irritably around her office. But every step brought him closer to her. And he wanted her. Badly.

She stepped past him and moved toward her desk, and he wheeled to follow her when he found himself face-to-face with the photos on her walls.

None of them, of course, was Daisy.

But they all spoke of Daisy. Of what she wanted and he didn't.

Families. Children. Pets.

He looked at her. Her cheeks were flushed. She ran her tongue over her lips. She watched him warily, worriedly.

"Never mind," he said abruptly. "I have to go."

Ignoring his desire, forcing himself to turn away from the most beautiful woman he'd ever made love to, he stalked out the door. He was halfway down the steps when he turned his head, his heart still hammering. "Send me those photos, damn it."

CHAPTER FIVE

THE next day Alex got an email with a link to a site where he could download the photos Daisy had taken.

Here you are, the email said. Sorry it took so long. Hope they meet with your editor's satisfaction. Thank you for the opportunity to work with you.

Kind regards, Daisy Connolly.

Kind regards? Daisy *Connolly?*

As if he would need her last name to distinguish her from all the other Daisys in his life.

Blast her, anyway! Alex smacked a hand on the desk next to his computer screen. So all it had needed was for him to turn up on her doorstep and make an idiot of himself and Daisy was suddenly inspired to finish editing the photos, send them along and get him out of her life.

Swell.

He'd lain awake half the night—staring at the damned skylight and cursing his own misplaced desire—and wishing Amalie would come up with a viable "option."

In the morning he called her and demanded a better selection. "The last one was a charlatan," he said. "If she was an architecture student, I play center field for the New York Yankees."

"I'm talking to another young woman today," she promised. "You're very discerning. It takes time."

It didn't take time, damn it. That was the trouble. If Daisy wanted what he wanted there wouldn't be any problem at all.

But she didn't. That was perfectly clear. She probably hadn't been stalling. She'd probably actually been busy, too busy to get right to his photos. But once he'd turned up on her doorstep, making demands, she'd outdone herself getting the photos finished so she didn't need to have anything more to do with him.

They were amazing photos, though.

He stood in his office, staring at them now. He'd spread them out on his drafting table, studying them, seeing himself through her eyes.

They were every bit as sharp and insightful as the ones he'd seen on her wall last night. She'd taken most of the shots in black and white which, on first glance, surprised him.

But the more he studied them, the more he saw what she was doing: she had used the monochrome scheme to pare him down to his essence, exactly the way an architectural drawing or a blueprint did.

She caught him clearly—a man who had little patience with subtlety, who knew what he wanted.

He wanted her.

She had to know that. Didn't she know that?

He sighed and scraped the photos into a pile and put them back into the envelope. Of course she knew it.

She didn't want him—not on his terms.

So he'd seen the last of her.

End of story.

Daisy was still taking deep breaths and letting them out slowly a week later. But it was her own fault. She knew she should have got the photos edited and sent off right away. She hadn't.

And so Alex had turned up on her doorstep. An intense, edgy, irritated Alex. An Alex who had looked at her with fire in his normally cool green gaze. An Alex who had shot into her office so quickly, she hadn't even thought about how to stop him. And once he was there, it had felt like being trapped in a cage with a full-grown, very hungry panther.

A panther who had complained about the meals he was being offered at the same time he was looking at her like he intended to make her the next one.

She'd skittered away, crossed the room, needing to put space between them, because the mere sight of him had set her heart to pounding. All her senses went on alert with Alex. Her body wanted him no matter what her brain—and her mother's-heart—told her was wise.

She had been determined to resist—not just Alex, but her own desire.

Then abruptly he had turned and walked out!

And Daisy had been left staring after him as he strode off into the cold dark windy night. Then she'd shut the door and leaned against it, her heart still slamming against the wall of her chest, her pulse racing.

The adrenaline had kept her working half the night.

It took a week to wear off, more for her to be able to say with confidence to Cal that life was back to normal, and still more until she believed it herself.

So it was a blow on the first Saturday evening in November to hear a knock on the door, expect to get the Thai takeaway she'd ordered, and find Alex standing on her doorstep again.

She stared at him, dumbstruck.

"Good evening to you, too," he said cheerfully. His tone was mild, friendly, completely at odds with the Alex who had shown up last time.

"Good evening," she replied cautiously, trying not to look at his smooth-shaven face, his quirking smile, that groove in his cheek she always itched to touch. Deliberately she curled her fingers into the palm of her hand.

He hesitated a split second, then said, "I just wanted to say that I may have found the one."

Daisy blinked. "The one? The one what?"

His smile widened. "Woman." There was a pause. Then, "Wife," he clarified.

Daisy's stomach did an odd sort of somersault. She swallowed, then mustered her best polite smile. "Really. How nice."

She shut her eyes for an instant, and opened them to discover that he'd done it again—slipped past her and was suddenly standing in her office. How did he do that?

"She's a vice president in marketing for an international cosmetics firm," he reported, his handsome face looking very pleased. "She runs campaigns in half a dozen places all over the world. Always on the move. She has two phones. A red one for emergencies." He grinned, as if this were a good thing.

"Does she?" Daisy said drily. "Sounds perfect for you."

"You think so, too?" He was still grinning, so she didn't know if he heard her sarcasm as it had been intended or not. "That's what I thought. I read Amalie the riot act after the first bunch, said if that was as good as she could do, I was finished. And then she came up with Caroline."

Caroline. Even her name was right. Sophisticated, but approachable. She did sound perfect.

"And," Alex went on with considerable enthusiasm, "there are other things, too—she's beautiful, bright, funny, articulate, well-read."

Daisy shut the door but stayed by it, keeping an eye out for the Thai deliveryman and thanking God that Charlie was at Cal's this weekend. "So have you asked her to marry you yet?" she asked Alex flippantly.

"Considering it."

Her jaw dropped. "On the basis of a couple of dates?"

"Three," Alex corrected. He was moving around her office in panther mode, but looking better fed. He picked up an alabaster cat on the bookcase, and examined it while he talked. "Well, two and a half." His mouth twisted wryly. "The red phone rang tonight. She had to leave in the middle of dinner. She's on her way to San Francisco right now."

"You're joking." He had to be joking. *Didn't he?*

But when he didn't immediately agree that he was, Daisy shook her head, torn between despair and the prickling of awareness and wholly useless desire she always felt faced with Alexandros Antonides. Still. Damn it. "You're insane."

He put the cat down again and looked at her quizzically. "Insane? Why?"

"You can't make a decision like that in a few weeks' time!"

"Why not? She's what I want."

"But are *you* what *she* wants?" Daisy didn't know why she was asking that. Didn't know why she was arguing with him.

"That's her problem."

"Yours, too." She couldn't seem to help herself. "If you get married without knowing each other well, without thinking things through—"

"I could end up like you did?"

Daisy rocked with the punch of his words. *"What?"*

"That isn't why your marriage didn't work?"

"No, of course it isn't!" Daisy felt the heat of his accusation. But she denied it, and it wasn't a lie, either. "And we're not discussing my marriage." She wrapped her arms across her chest, as if they would defend her. Fat chance.

"Why didn't it, then?" he persisted.

"This is not about me!"

He raised his brows. "Maybe I'm trying to learn from your mistake."

"You and I are not likely to make the same mistakes."

Alex shrugged. "How will I know if you don't tell me?"

"I'm not going to tell you, Alex! My marriage is none of your business." She shoved away from the door and jerked it open. "I think you should go."

But Alex didn't go anywhere. On the contrary, he turned and flopped down into one of the armchairs, settling in, folding his arms behind his head. "Not yet. I want to hear why I shouldn't pop the question."

Daisy wanted to strangle him. But the quickest way to get him out of her life was to answer his questions. So she did.

"Because," she said slowly and with the articulation of an elocution teacher, "you don't want to get a divorce. Do you?" she challenged him. "Maybe you don't care whether you do or not because you won't care about her."

"I don't want a divorce," he said evenly. The green eyes glinted.

Daisy shrugged. "Fine. Then take your time. Make sure you're on the same page. That you want the same things. That… Oh, hell, why am I telling you this? You don't understand!"

He cocked his head. "Weren't you on the same page, Daisy?" He sounded almost sympathetic now.

She pressed her lips together and didn't answer.

He gave her a little half smile. "Are you going to marry again?"

"I doubt it." She turned away, then turned back and shrugged. "Maybe someday. It depends."

"On?"

"On whether or not I'm in love with him."

Alex's jaw clenched.

Daisy smiled. It was a painful smile, hard-earned. "Yes, love. Still. I want the whole package, Alex. Now more than ever."

Alex didn't move. A muscle ticking in his temple was the only betrayal of anything beyond casual interest in what she had to say. Then, with studied nonchalance, he rose slowly. "I wish you the joy of it then."

"And I you," Daisy said automatically.

He gave her a sardonic look.

"No, truly." She almost put a hand on his arm as he passed. But then she laced her fingers together instead. Still, she looked up at him earnestly. "I mean it, Alex. You deserve a wonderful life. I hope…Caroline is the right woman for you. I hope she gives you what you want."

He had stopped and was standing now, quite close. She kept her gaze on the rise and fall of his chest, knew that she could reach out and touch him. Knew she should back away.

But she didn't. She stayed quite still and met his gaze. "Regardless of what you think, marriage is more than you expect. You should…take your time, get to know this…woman you're considering marrying. Make sure it's right for both of you."

Alex stood staring at her as if he couldn't believe the words coming out of her mouth.

Daisy couldn't believe them, either. It wasn't any of her business. But she couldn't seem to stop herself. And maybe she did owe him the benefit of her experience with Cal. Certainly it had taught her something.

"No matter what you think you want out of marriage," she finished, "it can surprise you. You shouldn't take it lightly."

Alex's eyes narrowed further, and she expected he would tell her to mind her own business. But his jaw just tightened again, then he nodded. "I'll keep it in mind."

Their gazes locked—all the electricity flowing through New York City at that moment had nothing on what arced between them.

Then, carefully, consciously, Daisy swallowed. "Have a good life, Alex."

For a long moment he didn't reply, and she couldn't read his gaze. Then he said flatly, "I will. Shall I invite you to the wedding?"

No! It was her gut-level response. But she squelched it. "When you're sure she's the right one," she said slowly, "I would be delighted to come."

Alex's lips pressed together in a thin line. He nodded, then walked past her wordlessly out the door.

She closed it after him, leaned back against it, knees wobbling. Only after the sound of his footsteps had long faded away, did Daisy breathe again.

Moving on.

That's what her father always used to say when Daisy or her sister got all wrought up about something they could do nothing about. He'd listen to them anguishing for, oh, maybe thirty minutes, and then he'd say, "Can you do anything about it?"

They'd say, "No."

And he'd flash them his sunny grin and say, "So...moving on..."

He didn't mean, *get over it.* He meant, *stop dwelling on it. Get past it.*

You might still ache with disappointment. You might remember it forever. But you'd done all you could do. Now it was time to pull up your socks and move on.

Daisy moved on.

She still thought about Alex. How could she not? She had loved him once. He was the father of her child, even if he didn't know it. She owed him for that—for Charlie. And she wished things could have been different.

But they weren't.

Life moved on, and determinedly Daisy moved on with it. She did her work. She introduced a great couple, Debbie whom she'd met at a yoga class and Mark, who played baseball with Cal, and was delighted when they seemed to hit it off. She wasn't losing her touch with other people at least. Cal bought Charlie a point-and-shoot camera, and she went with the two of them for walks in the park and on the streets and took loads of pictures. It was fun to discover Charlie's interest, and restful to be with him and Cal.

Every time her thoughts drifted to Alex and she wondered if he'd proposed yet, she deliberately focused them elsewhere. So she wasn't even thinking about him the Sunday evening before Thanksgiving when Cal came into the kitchen and asked, "Whatever happened with Alex?"

Her ex had stopped by that afternoon to take Charlie for a bike ride in the park. When they'd come back, Daisy had invited him to stay for leftovers. After, he'd helped Charlie build a fire station with his Legos. Now Charlie had gone upstairs to get ready for his bath while Daisy put dishes in the dishwasher.

She felt a moment's jolt at the sound of his name. But then

she just shrugged. "No idea. Haven't seen him for a while. I believe he's got a woman in his life. He seems to think she's 'the one.'" Daisy couldn't help adding that.

Cal looked at her closely. "I'm sorry."

"I'm not," Daisy said, dropping forks in the silverware slots. "He was never the man I thought he was. He still isn't."

"Life sucks," Cal said with a faint grin.

"It has some good bits," Daisy countered, nodding toward the stairs where they could both hear Charlie banging around in the upstairs hall.

Cal's grin widened. "You're right. It does." He shoved away from the doorjamb and flexed his shoulders. "I'll be going then. Thanks for letting me take him to the park."

"Anytime." She walked to the front door with him and kissed him on the cheek and he gave her a hug. Then he shrugged on his jacket. "I'll pick Charlie up Thursday morning. I told my folks we'd be up there by noon."

Daisy nodded and forced a smile even as she felt her throat tighten. "He'll have so much fun."

Cal was taking Charlie to his parents' upstate for Thanksgiving. They wouldn't be back until Sunday morning. The thought of rattling around by herself for four days was horrible. But it was good for Charlie and for Cal and his family. It was a part of the life they'd made.

"My folks are really looking forward to it," Cal said. He looked at her closely. "You can come if you want." He must have seen some of the hollowness she felt.

Daisy shook her head. "Thanks, but I can't. You know that."

If she did Cal's parents might think there was hope of them getting back together. They had been upset when she and Cal divorced. Now they seemed to be coming to terms with the way things were. It wouldn't do to get their hopes up again.

"You're probably right. No, you are right. It's just—I'm sorry. Especially this year."

Daisy shrugged. "Don't worry. I'll be fine. I'm going to

Finn and Izzy's. It will be chaos. I'll never miss you. What do you have planned?"

"Going fishing if the weather stays warm enough. Chopping wood otherwise. Getting ready for winter." He grimaced.

"You'll have fun."

"Charlie will make it fun. He and Dad are something else when you get them together." Cal shook his head, grinning. "Like two kids."

"I'd guess there were three." Daisy cocked her head and smiled at him.

Cal rubbed a hand against the back of his neck. "Well, yeah."

Their eyes met, both of them rueful.

"Moving on," Daisy said with all the briskness she could muster.

And Cal nodded resolutely. "Moving on."

He went out, and Daisy locked the door after him. Then she went back into the living room, rubbing her hands up and down her arms. Was Alex having Thanksgiving with the woman in his life? Or was he working on one continent while she was on another?

What did she care? Daisy asked herself irritably.

She didn't, damn it. But sometimes moving on felt curiously like walking through molasses with her shoelaces tied together. Hard and lonely.

She felt suddenly very, very cold.

CHAPTER SIX

FINN and Izzy's at Thanksgiving *was* chaos. Finn's nieces, Tansy and Pansy, were both there, along with Rip and Crash, Finn and Izzy's sons, and a dozen or so other friends, several slightly giddy from having spent the night before over by the Museum of Natural History where all the gigantic balloon floats for the annual parade were being inflated.

Daisy had gone to the MacCauleys' early and she'd stayed late. Friday she'd spent the entire day catching up on photo editing. More often than she'd liked, she'd been tempted to open the folder where Alex's photos were.

Every time, she'd steeled herself against it and had resisted.

Saturday was harder. Her backlog of work was gone. The house was reasonably clean. The laundry was done, folded, put away. The rugs vacuumed, the furniture dusted. She supposed she could clean the oven, but that seemed like taking things too far.

Instead she took the dog Murphy for a long walk in the park, then decided to do some Christmas shopping. Closer to Christmas, stores would be jammed. Of course, they were on Saturday, too. But it wasn't as lonely as being home by herself, wondering if Charlie and Cal were having a good time.

Wondering what Alex was doing.

It was a relief when Cal and Charlie got back late Sunday afternoon. Charlie was full of stories about hiking in the woods and stacking firewood.

"No, I didn't let him chop it," Cal said before she could ask.

"An' we caught fish," Charlie told her, hopping from one foot to the other. "We got pictures. Look."

Daisy admired the pictures Cal had taken of Charlie and the fish. One of them, though, startled her as his expression in it was so much like Alex's. She never thought he looked like Alex. She really didn't know who he looked like, except that he had her color hair. But in that photo of him grinning up at his grandfather she could see that he had Alex's profile. It made her catch her breath.

"What's wrong?" Cal asked.

"Nothing," she said, papering over her surprise. "I was just amazed at the size of the fish."

"It was huuuuuge," Charlie told her proudly. He spread his arms to their fullest extent.

"Well, maybe not quite that big," Cal said.

But to Charlie it was the biggest fish in the world, and he'd had the best time in the world. And he proceeded to tell Daisy all about it after Cal went home and all through dinner and during his bath.

And Daisy nodded and smiled as she listened to her son's nonstop commentary. He'd had a wonderful time. She was glad he had gone. Glad Cal and his parents had had the joy of him.

Mostly, though, she was glad he was home again.

And when she went to bed that night, she thought, *I can do this. I'm going to be fine.*

She and Cal could cope with trading Charlie back and forth. Charlie wasn't a basket case. He was a normal happy little boy. Life was good.

She didn't think about Alex—or his perfect woman.

At least she tried not to.

"How much longer till Christmas?" Charlie asked. He'd been asking for the past four days, ever since he'd got back from Cal's parents'.

"Oh, a long time," Daisy said, tucking him into bed. She'd been saying the same thing every day since, too, because a person who was Almost Five had no concept of time, and she'd quickly discovered that if she said "soon," Charlie expected it to be "right after lunch."

"And my birthday?"

"Not quite as long."

Charlie made a face. "They should hurry up."

"All in good time." Even though she had caught up on things over Thanksgiving already, four days later, she felt her to-do lists getting longer by the minute. Lots of people suddenly remembered they wanted family photos for Christmas, and Daisy, understanding the desire, tried not to disappoint any of them.

She had other jobs, too. Most were from repeat customers who wanted her to do some editorial work, and a promo for a boutique in Soho. But one phone call the day after Thanksgiving had surprised her.

"This is Lauren Nicols," the woman had said when Daisy answered. "You did the photos for my piece on Alexandros Antonides."

"Oh! Yes, of course. I hope they were suitable," Daisy said, her heart quickening.

"More than," Lauren Nicols said warmly. "I was delighted. Alex told me you'd be good, but they were better than I'd hoped. The black and white surprised me, but it was perfect. You caught the man."

"I hope so," Daisy said honestly. "I tried."

"Oh, you did," the other woman assured her. "I wondered if you'd be willing to do some more for me."

"Of Alex?" Daisy asked, startled.

"No, Alex's article is in production. But I do other personality pieces for trade periodicals, usually three or four a month. Would you be interested in working with me on a couple of them at least?"

"I—" Daisy stopped herself before she could refuse, because really, why should she? She had enjoyed doing the photo shoot of Alex, and what better way to make sure her brain kept him in the "business" folder of her mind than to start filling it with other assignments, as well? "Yes," she had said. "I'd like that."

And so she had two shoots for Lauren to do before the holidays, as well.

"Go to sleep," she told Charlie now. "It will get here sooner."

"How much sooner?"

Daisy bent and kissed him good night. "You'll just have to wait and see."

Charlie made a face. But eventually he screwed his eyes shut, and Daisy, knowing that was going to be his best attempt, smiled and turned out the light. "Night, Chaz," she said softly. Then she pulled the door and went down the hall to her office where she'd be working until midnight at least.

First on the docket were the wedding photos she'd taken last night. Wednesday night weddings weren't common, but this had been a small intimate affair to which Daisy had been thrilled to be invited—and eager to take the photos.

They were her wedding present to the couple because both the bride and the groom were "hers."

Seeing Rafaela Cruz, a tech at Murphy's veterinarian's office, and Gino Martinelli, a cop who lived in Finn MacCauley's building, standing at the altar together made Daisy's heart sing for she had helped them find each other.

When she'd learned that besides being a photographer, Daisy was a matchmaker, Rafaela had said, "Huh. Not sure I believe in that."

"Some people don't," Daisy had replied. She wasn't in the market to twist anyone's arm. But Rafaela had wanted to know more because, as she said, "I don't believe there's any good men left." So Daisy had spent time talking to her, trying to discover who, beneath her bluster, Rafaela really was.

Even when she finally said she wanted to try it, Rafaela had had her doubts.

And she and Gino had definitely not been "love at first sight."

Gino, who was Rip MacCauley's soccer coach, had been badly burned in an earlier relationship. But somehow he was the one Daisy had thought of when Rafaela had challenged her to "prove there's one good man."

"Come watch him coach," Daisy had suggested.

Rafaela had dismissed the idea. "I don't want a coach. I want a husband."

"You want a patient man," Daisy said. "A man who works hard and values kids and will be there for you and your family no matter what."

"Yes, but—" Rafaela had protested.

"Maybe Gino could be that man. Unless you're afraid to try?" Daisy had challenged her right back. Then she'd turned around and challenged a reluctant Gino, too.

"She's too pretty," Gino had said. "She'll want some hotshot stud."

Daisy had just looked him up and down. "And you're not a stud?"

Gino had laughed at that. "All right. Bring her on."

They'd been cautious to the point that Daisy sometimes wanted to bang their heads together. But gradually Rafaela and Gino had faced their doubts, had given each other a shot. Had discovered in each other what Daisy had seen from early days. Over the summer they had fallen in love.

And now they were married.

Daisy's gift to them was going to be a book of photos she'd taken throughout their courtship and at their wedding. She just needed to get it finished. The pages from the courtship were done. Now she picked up the wedding invitation and set it on the flatbed scanner. It was high rag content paper, heavy and elegant.

Daisy remembered when she'd plucked it out of the mailbox right before Thanksgiving. She had stared at it, feeling an odd sinking sensation in the pit of her stomach because she hadn't thought it was Rafaela and Gino's invitation at all.

She'd thought it was Alex's.

She'd been shocked at the relief she'd felt upon opening it to discover Rafaela's and Gino's names inside.

Of course, she'd told herself logically, even if Alex had run right out and asked his perfect woman to marry him the minute he'd left her that night, they wouldn't have been sending out invitations right away.

But logic had never had much to do with anything where her relationship with Alex was concerned.

Now, taking an expansive breath, Daisy smoothed the invitation flat and lowered the lid, then pushed the scanning button.

The phone rang as it was appearing on her screen. She picked it up absently. "Daisy Connolly."

"Daisy." The voice was gruff and instantly recognizable. "I have a favor to ask."

"Alex," she said as soon as she could breathe again. "What do you want?"

"A date."

Once more Daisy's breath caught in her throat. Then she realized what he was really asking for. "I am not matchmaking for you."

"I don't want you to fix me up with a date. I want you."

I want you. She knew he didn't mean it the way it sounded. She didn't *want* him to mean it the way it sounded. But she didn't know what he did mean, either. *"What are you talking about?"*

"I need a date for Saturday night."

"Need a date?" That had to be a first.

"There's a big charity fundraising dinner and dance at the Plaza. Remember I told you I designed a new wing for a hospital? Well, I'm on the guest list—and they're giving me some plaque or something—so I have to show up. With a date."

Daisy waited a beat. "What happened to Caroline?"

"Caroline had to fly out to Hong Kong this afternoon. Unexpected breakdown of some project she'd been overseeing. She won't be back for a week. I can't show up alone. I've already committed for two. They expect me to bring someone. Head table and all that."

"Head table?"

He grunted. "So I need a replacement." And apparently in his mind it was perfectly logical that she would drop everything and accompany him to some society event in another woman's place.

Daisy focused on the wedding invitation on her screen. "Get your matchmaker to find you one."

"Can't."

"Of course you can."

"No," Alex said tersely. "I can't. Thanks to you."

That startled her. "Me? Why me?"

"Because, damn it, you're the one who told me to take it slow. 'Don't ask her to marry you yet. Get to know her,' you said. Make sure she's 'the one.'"

He'd listened?

"So I have been. It isn't easy because half the time I'm out of town or she is. But we've gone out more."

"As well you should," Daisy said firmly, still surprised that he'd done it.

"So I can't ask Amalie to find me a date, can I?" Alex said. "If I went out with someone else now—someone new—what would that say to Caroline? Not to mention that I'd be creating false expectations in whoever Amalie found."

Daisy was somewhere between dazed and amazed. "You thought of that all by yourself?" Since when had Alex put thought into the repercussions of relationships?

"Can I help it if you put ideas in my head?"

"Good for me." She grinned in spite of herself.

"So you see the problem. It has to be you."

Daisy pressed back against the desk chair she sat in and asked, "Why won't I upset Caroline?"

"She knows I need a date. I told her I was going to ask you. She'll be glad I've found an old friend to go with."

"Old friend?" Daisy echoed.

"You know what I mean. So," he went on briskly, "Saturday night. Black tie. The equivalent for you. I'll pick you up a little before eight. Where do you live?"

"What? No! Wait. I didn't agree."

"So you don't stand behind your own advice?"

Daisy opened her mouth to object, and couldn't find words to convince herself, let alone ones that would convince as stubborn a man as Alex.

"I can't," she said feebly.

"Why not?"

Because I don't have a babysitter. She didn't say that, even though it was certainly true. "I— My wardrobe doesn't run to that sort of thing."

"Get something suitable," he directed. "I'll pay for it."

"You will not. I can't—"

"Did you or did you not tell me to take my time, get to know Caroline?"

"Yes, but—" She stopped, waiting for him to cut her off, but he didn't. He waited in silence for her next reason she couldn't go. And she didn't have one—other than self-protection.

Maybe she was protesting too much. Maybe going with him would be the best self-protection there could be.

Maybe spending an evening with Alexandros Antonides, going on a date with him, would actually force her to "move on" once and for all.

Last time she'd felt like Cinderella going to the ball—and she'd believed she'd found Prince Charming. If she went now, she would go with no illusions at all.

She could even dance with him—but know it ended there— know that her happy ending was waiting at home in her life with her son.

She would be in no danger of succumbing to airy-fairy fantasies. She would enjoy the evening and come home at midnight—unlike Cinderella—with both shoes on and her heart intact.

Daisy took a breath. "Yes, all right. I'll do it."

"Great." He sounded pleased. "What's your address?"

"I'll meet you there."

Alex argued. Daisy was adamant. He said she was being silly. She said she didn't care.

"I'm not your real date. I don't need to act like one. I will see myself to the Plaza and I'll see myself home afterward."

"Daisy, that's ridic—"

"Take it or leave it."

There was a long silence, then an exasperated sigh. "Fine. Quarter to eight. Front steps of the Plaza. This Saturday. Don't be late."

She was out of her mind.

Absolutely insane.

She couldn't go out with Alex! She didn't have a babysitter. And even if she could find one, she didn't have a dress. Nor did she have a fairy godmother and some talented singing mice who could whip one up in an afternoon.

She was in a complete dither the next afternoon when Izzy and the boys stopped by for a visit after Rip's orthodontist appointment.

Izzy took one look at Daisy pacing around the kitchen and demanded, "What's the matter with you?" Her boys went running out back to play with Charlie, but Izzy stood right where she was and studied Daisy with concern.

"Nothing's wrong with me."

"Really?" Izzy's tone dripped disbelief. "You're pacing the floor. You're tearing your hair."

True, but Daisy stopped long enough to put the kettle on. "I have to go out tomorrow night. To the Plaza."

Izzy's eyes widened. "A date? At last!" She beamed and rubbed her hands together.

"Not a date! Nothing like that," Daisy said quickly. "It's business. Well, sort of business." She couldn't quite explain.

"Who with?" Izzy demanded.

"A cousin of Lukas's. An old...friend." Which was the truth, wasn't it? Alex had even called her "an old friend." "I knew him years ago. He's interested in getting married. Wanted me to matchmake for him. I said no. Now he's got a serious girlfriend, but she's out of town. So he asked me to go in her place."

It sounded quite believable to Daisy.

Izzy immediately caught the snag. "Why wouldn't you matchmake for him? I thought you loved matching people with their soul mates."

"Yes, but—" She wasn't going into what Alex thought about soul mates. "I didn't feel I knew him well enough." Daisy turned away and started rearranging the forks in her silverware drawer. A Tarzan-like yodel from the backyard turned her around in time to see Izzy's oldest son, Rip, hurtle out of the tree at the end of the garden. He and his younger brother, Crash, were Charlie's heroes.

"Mountain goats," Izzy muttered. "I can make them stop if you want."

Daisy shook her head, grateful the conversation had veered away from Alex. "It's all right. Charlie loves trying to keep up with them. And it's good for him to have them. He needs older brothers."

"Not these two." Izzy winced as Crash followed his brother's leap with one of his own. "What's he like? This cousin of Lukas's," Izzy elaborated at Daisy's blank stare. "Your 'old friend'? One of the dark handsome Antonides men, is he?"

Daisy did her best at a negligent shrug. "I guess."

"Not a wild man like Lukas, I hope."

"No. He's not like Lukas," she said. "He's very...driven."

"Is that why you're chewing your nails?"

"I'm chewing my nails because I can't find a babysitter. I already called your girls."

"Tansy and Pansy are hopeless now they're in college," Izzy agreed cheerfully. "They have lives." She sighed. "But no worries. I'll keep him."

Daisy blinked. "You will? Are you sure?"

"Absolutely. If you don't mind me having him at our place." Izzy picked up the kettle and began pouring boiling water because Daisy wasn't doing it. "He can even spend the night. In case you don't want to turn into a pumpkin right after the Plaza." She grinned.

Daisy flushed and shook her head. "Not a chance. I am a pumpkin. Home before midnight. This is not a date. But Charlie would love to go to your place, if you're sure."

Izzy waved a hand airily. "I'll never notice he's there." She zeroed back in. "What are you wearing?"

"That's my other problem," Daisy admitted. Nothing in her wardrobe lent itself to upscale fundraisers at the Plaza. And despite his brusque "Get something. I'll pay for it," she had no intention of allowing herself to feel beholden to Alex.

Izzy was thoughtfully silent for a long moment. Then, "I might have something," she said, looking Daisy up and down assessingly. "Ichiro Sorrento," she said.

"What?"

"That new designer whose collection Finn shot last year. Japanese-Italian. You remember him?"

Daisy did. But she shook her head. "No way I can afford anything with his label."

"You don't have to. You can wear mine. Remember that gorgeous dress and jacket I wore to Finn's opening last spring?"

Daisy's eyes widened. "*That* dress?" The dress had been a deep-sapphire-blue silk, spare and elegant, with an exquisitely embroidered jacket in the same deep blues, emerald-green and hints of violet. "You don't want me wearing your gorgeous dress. I'd spill something on it."

"I already have. It doesn't show," Izzy said cheerfully.

"I'm taller than you are."

"Everyone is taller than I am," Izzy countered. "So what? You'll just show more leg. I doubt anyone will mind. Especially—" she grinned "—not a male Antonides."

"Not. A. Date," Daisy reiterated firmly. "I'm not trying to show off my legs."

"Of course not. But you're not a nun, either. You need to knock Mr. Driven Antonides's socks off. Make him forget all about his serious girlfriend and run off to Vegas with you!"

It was as if a little devil called Izzy was sitting on her shoulder tempting her. "Dream on," Daisy scoffed.

"A little dreaming never hurt anyone," Izzy retorted.

Daisy let her have the last word.

But in her heart she begged to differ.

Where the hell was she?

Dozens of hired cars and limos and taxis slid up to the Plaza's entrance Saturday evening while Alex stood on the steps, shifting from one foot to the other, watching and waiting. There were snowflakes in the air. Alex could see his breath, and his shoulders were getting damp as the snow melted, but he couldn't bring himself to go inside and wait and pace.

There were scores of black-tie-clad men and elegantly dressed women getting out of taxis and limos—and not one of them was Daisy.

He'd told her quarter to eight. It was almost ten after. He'd got here early, to be sure he was here when she arrived, and she was nowhere to be seen.

He should never have given in to her demand that she come on her own, that he neither pick her up nor take her home after. He'd agreed only because she would have refused to come otherwise. The sweet and malleable Daisy he had known five years ago might still be somewhere inside this Daisy Connolly, but he hadn't caught a glimpse of her in a long, long time.

Was this her revenge? Was standing him up payback for

his having said he wasn't interested in marriage all those years ago?

He shouldn't have asked her to come. It was a damn fool idea. When Caroline had said she couldn't make it, but suggested he invite his friend Daisy, he'd been surprised.

"My friend Daisy?" he'd echoed, puzzled.

Caroline had shrugged. "I assume she's your friend. You talk about her all the time."

Did he? Surely not. But he could hardly deny their friendship if it came across that way to Caroline because how could he justify talking about her if she wasn't a friend? What would Caroline think if he said she wasn't a friend at all, she was...a thorn in his side, an itch he never quite managed to get rid of. Like poison ivy, perhaps.

So he'd shrugged and told Caroline he'd ask. And, hell, why not? He could prove to Daisy that he'd listened, that he hadn't gone straight home and asked Caroline to marry him. He'd done what Daisy suggested and got to know her.

He hadn't fallen in love with her. That wasn't going to happen. He knew it. Caroline knew it.

They had seen each other as often as their schedules allowed. They always had a good time. Relationship-wise they were on the same page—and perfectly happy to be there. And if they still hadn't managed to make it to bed together, well, the time had never been right.

She'd had an early meeting or he was flying off to Paris. She was in Rio or he was in Vancouver. It had nothing to do with memories of Daisy in his bed. She hadn't been in this bed.

Only in his bedroom. And the fact that he couldn't forget that was still driving him nuts.

"Alex!" A hearty booming voice from the doorway startled him back to the present—back to the lack of Daisy anywhere in sight. He turned to see Tom Holcomb, the hospital's vice president in charge of building development.

Tom was grinning broadly, holding out a hand to shake.

"Good to see you. Big night for you." He pumped Alex's hand, then looked around. "Where's your date?"

Alex opened his mouth, hoping that a suitable polite reply would come out when, all of a sudden, from behind a hand caught his.

"Sorry," Daisy said, catching her breath.

Alex turned his head, saw her smiling up at him, and felt his heart do some sort of triple axel in his chest. There was a glow to her cheeks, as if she'd been running, but she was smiling.

And so was he. His heart which, after the triple axel, had seemed to stop all together as he looked at her, began beating again. "About time," he said gruffly, swallowing his relief. She was gorgeous. She wore a long black wool dress coat and he could barely get a glimpse of the dress beneath it, but what he could see seemed to sparkle—just as Daisy did. Her eyes were alight, electric almost, taking in everything. She'd pinned her hair up in some sort of intricate knot which reminded him of the way she'd worn it at the wedding when he'd met her. He remembered taking it down, running his fingers through it. Felt a quickening in his body at the temptation to do it again now. It was, after all, already slightly askew, as if she had been running.

"My cab got stuck in traffic. Think I stood you up?" She laughed.

"No." He wiped damp palms down the sides of his trousers. He wasn't admitting anything.

"Your date, I presume?"

Alex was suddenly conscious of Tom Holcomb still standing beside him, looking with interest at Daisy.

Alex nodded and drew her forward. "This is Daisy Connolly. Daisy, Tom Holcomb. He is the VP in charge of building development, the man I worked with on the hospital design."

"The man who rubber-stamped his terrific ideas," Tom

corrected, shaking the hand Daisy offered. "I'm delighted to meet you. Are you an architect, too?"

"No. A photographer," Daisy said, shaking the hand he held out. "I recently did a photo shoot of Alex at a building he restored in Brooklyn."

"A man of many talents," Tom agreed. He drew Daisy with him into the hotel, asking questions about her own work which she answered, still smiling. And Daisy, with a glance back at Alex, went with him.

Alex stood watching, bemused, and somehow a little dazed.

Dazed by Daisy. Dazzling Daisy, he thought, smiling wryly at his own foolishness. But it was true. And he didn't mind following, it gave him a chance to admire her from another angle.

From any angle tonight she was elegant, sophisticated, tailored, stylish. She would never be the stunning classical beauty that Caroline was. Daisy's nose still had a spattering of freckles, her cheekbones were not quite as sharply pronounced. Her mouth was less sculpted than impish. And you could never say that Daisy had every hair in place.

But everything about her was alive—from her unruly hair to her lively sparkling eyes to her kissable lips.

Alex tried not to think about her kissable lips. It wasn't as if he was going to be tasting them again this evening. Furthermore, he reminded himself, he shouldn't even want to. He was this close to buying Caroline an engagement ring.

But Caroline's kisses had never intoxicated him. They'd never made him hot and hard and hungry in a matter of an instant. He'd lost every bit of his common sense that weekend with Daisy—and she hadn't had any at all.

There had never been anything cool, calm and collected about her. She was a lead-with-her-heart, damn-the-torpedoes, full-speed-ahead sort of woman.

Basically the anti-Caroline. And Caroline was what he wanted.

Wasn't she?

"Are you coming?"

Alex jerked his brain back into gear to see that Tom had disappeared into the hotel, but that Daisy was still standing at the top of the stairs by the revolving door, waiting.

"Got distracted. Sorry." He bounded up the steps, feeling awkward, caught out. And feeling that way, he challenged her. "Been running?" he asked her gruffly.

"I told you," she said with some asperity. "The cab was caught in traffic. I left it in the middle of Columbus Circle."

"You *walked* from Columbus Circle?" Wide-eyed he stared at her high pointy-toed heels.

"No," she said flatly. "I ran."

Definitely the anti-Caroline. Alex shook his head, dazed and amazed, and unable to keep from grinning. "Of course you did."

Daisy glared, her eyes flashing. "You said not to be late!"

"So I did." His grin widened briefly, then he met her gaze. "Thank you."

Their eyes locked. And Alex felt the electricity arc between them exactly the way it always did. It didn't seem to matter that she was all wrong for him. He jerked his gaze away from hers, but it only went as far as her lips. Nervously she licked them.

Alex's body went on full alert.

Daisy tore her gaze away. "It sounded like the sort of occasion where it wouldn't do to waltz in late," she said, a little ragged edge to her voice. "Not if you're at the head table."

She was right, of course. He was being a fool—again.

Impatient with his own weakness, Alex gestured her brusquely into the revolving door. "Well, let's not waste your sacrifice, then. We'll go in."

Daisy was in complete control.

She might as well have had a squadron of singing mice and a fairy godmother the way everything had fallen into place. Izzy was keeping Charlie, the glitzy shimmery dress fit perfectly, the sophisticated black dress coat her mother had given her for her birthday was beautifully appropriate. Other than the stupid traffic jam and having to run quarter of a mile and that she could feel her hair slipping from its knot, she didn't have a care in the world.

Granted her first glimpse of Alex in formal attire, complete with black tie, pristine white shirt, checking his watch impatiently as he waited for her, had made her mouth dry and her heart gallop. But, Daisy assured herself, that was because she'd just been running, not because of the man himself.

Still, once in the hotel, on the arm of the handsomest man in the room, it was hard not to believe she was channeling Cinderella.

Daisy had been to the Plaza before. But she'd never been to An Event.

This was An Event—in a cavernous room that despite its immensity, managed somehow to seem warm and appealing and elegant with matte gold walls, burgundy drapes, glimmering sconces and crystal chandeliers. The dozens of tables wore pristine white damask linens, sported napkins folded by origami experts, and had settings of gleaming china and rows of delicate stemware.

Not a bowl of mac and cheese in sight.

When she worked for Finn, Daisy had gone to plenty of glitz-and-glamour events. In the fashion industry they'd been brasher and flashier, not to mention, thousands of decibels louder than this one. A girl from small town Colorado had been very much out of her league. But after the first half dozen or so, she had become blasé and soon she began waltzing through them without batting an eyelash.

Of course those rarely required her to look suave and elegant and remember which fork to use. Tonight there looked to be a surfeit of forks. But it wasn't the number of forks that was making her blood race. It was Alex.

"Can I get you something to drink? Wine? A cocktail?"

"I'll have a glass of wine," Daisy decided. "Red."

They'd drunk a smooth dark burgundy when they'd first

met. If she was going to rewrite the ending of their encounter, she would begin tonight the way they'd begun before. But this time she wouldn't let herself embroider the circumstances with airy-fairy fantasies of happily ever afters.

"Burgundy," Alex said, surprising her. Did he remember? But she couldn't—wouldn't—ask.

"I'll be right back." He headed toward the bar.

When he returned, drinks in hand, Daisy was standing near the wall right where Alex had left her. She drew his eye clear across the room. The dress he'd glimpsed before she'd shed her coat definitely lived up to its promise. Its blue-green iridescence sparkled like northern lights as it molded her every curve. The short embroidered jacket covered more than he wished, hinting at bare shoulders beneath, smooth shoulders he remembered kissing all too well.

But it was more than the dress that drew his gaze, more than the dress that made the woman. There was a warmth and a vibrant energy in Daisy—as if she were the only person there in three dimensions. Everyone else seemed flat by comparison.

She had been alone when he'd left her, but now she was chatting with hospital CEO Douglas Standish and his wife. Daisy's expression was animated, interested. He remembered her that way from the moment he'd first seen her. She engaged with people, drew them out. She had drawn him.

Never particularly social, Alex had attended the wedding with the intent of leaving as soon as it was reasonable to do so. He'd drifted around the periphery of the room, keeping his eye on the exit—until he'd seen Daisy.

Then he'd only had eyes for her. It was still that way.

Now he wound his way through the crowds of people, heading toward her as determinedly as he had that long-ago day.

"Here you go." He handed the drink to Daisy, then turned to Standish's wife. "May I get you a drink?"

"No, thank you, dear. Douglas will do that. I just wanted to meet your lovely lady—and tell her how lovely you are—"

her eyes twinkled merrily when Alex opened his mouth to protest "—and what an amazing gift you've given us with the design for the hospital wing."

"Thank you for saying so."

She patted him on the sleeve. "Have a wonderful evening. You deserve it. So nice to meet you, dear," she said to Daisy, before taking her husband's arm and guiding them into the crowd.

"So," Daisy said, looking him in the eye when the other woman had left, "you're the guest of honor. And you couldn't be bothered to tell me?"

Alex shrugged. "It's no big deal."

Daisy's eyes glittered. "It's a huge deal," she contradicted him. "Huge. Apparently your hospital wing has broken new ground in patient services. It's celebrated worldwide." She had gone beyond glitter to glare now. "They're giving you an award."

"I told you that when you did the photos for the article."

"An award, you said. You didn't tell me anything about it. It might have been for perfect attendance at meetings for all I knew! This is wonderful!" And now her wonderful eyes sparkled with warmth and delight, and in spite of himself, Alex felt a rush of pleasure. "Did you tell Caroline?"

"No," he said, surprised.

"Why not?"

He shrugged. "It's nothing to do with her."

"Of course it is!"

Baffled, he shook his head. "Why?" She hadn't done anything. He hadn't even known her when he'd done it himself.

"Because *you* did it! Because you're her man."

But he *wasn't* Caroline's man. He wasn't anyone's man. But he wasn't going to have that argument with Daisy now. Fortunately people were beginning to head to their seats. So he just said, "Come on. We need to go sit down." He took her arm, more aware of touching her than he was whenever he touched Caroline. He led her to the table where they would be sitting, then pulled out her chair.

Daisy flounced down into it, but she still wasn't done. She looked up at him, her expression annoyed. "She'd be thrilled," she told him. "And proud. I am—proud," she said, "and it's nothing at all to do with me."

Alex felt a warm flush of pleasure at her admitting that. What he didn't do was tell her that it wasn't entirely true.

He would never have taken the commission at all if something she'd said to him hadn't stuck with him for the past five years. Initially he'd said no. He had no interest in hospital design. He didn't like hospitals. Hated them, in fact.

After his brother had got leukemia, Alex had spent far too much time in hospitals watching his brother suffer and become more and more remote. It had devastated him. Even now Alex associated hospitals with the most painful period of his life.

After Vass's death, Alex had never set foot in one again. Even when he broke his arm playing lacrosse in college, he'd insisted on having it set at a doctor's office. "No hospital," he'd said firmly. It was the last place he wanted to be.

He didn't talk about hospitals, either. Didn't talk about Vass. Never had to anyone. Except that weekend when Daisy had got under his skin.

He supposed it was because she was just getting her equilibrium back after losing her father. Barely fifty, he'd been born with a heart defect that had grown worse over time. He'd been in and out of the hospital often, she'd said. And the sad wistful look on her face had prompted Alex to confide that he, too, hated hospitals.

"They take away your life," he'd said harshly, remembering how remote and sterile they had seemed, how they'd isolated his brother, how Vass had wanted to come home so badly, to be out, to be anywhere but there. "They don't save it."

He'd expected her to agree.

Instead she'd shaken her head. "It wasn't the hospital's fault. Without the care my dad got there, we'd have lost him sooner.

But it was hard for him to feel connected. He felt so isolated, like he wasn't really a part of things anymore."

Vass had said the same thing.

"There was only one window," she'd gone on. "But he couldn't see outside from his bed. So we used to pretend. We'd close our eyes and pretend he was home or we were going fishing in the San Juan or even doing chores, chopping wood for the fireplace. He loved that fireplace..." Daisy had swallowed then, and her eyes had glistened with unshed tears. She'd blinked them back rapidly. "It wasn't the hospital's fault," she repeated. "But it could have been better. It could have been more."

Her words had made Alex think.

What if Vass had had a chance to spend time in a hospital that had allowed him to feel connected. What if he'd been able to do, at least virtually, the things he wanted to do—like go back to the beach near their island home, or drive a race car, or sail over the Alps in a hot-air balloon?

Once Alex opened the floodgates, the ideas wouldn't stop coming. And what hadn't been possible twenty-five to thirty years ago was within reach now.

Alex's hospital wing was full of windows—floor-to-ceiling in many rooms. Even treatment rooms, wherever possible, brought the outside in. If a patient wanted to see the world beyond the walls, he could. The semirural setting just across the river north of the city provided views of the countryside as well as the city skyline. And it wasn't just about the visuals. Alex worked in sound systems and even olfactory ones, connecting senses to the world beyond the hospital's confines.

He had provided virtual worlds, as well. Patients in the wing he'd designed could close their eyes as Daisy's father had, but they could also use modern electronics to create the sights, sounds and smells of the seashore, the woods, the inside of a race car or the ballroom of a fairy-tale palace.

He told her about it now, aware of the way she looked at him, as if he could hang the moon. The salads that had been in front of them when they'd sat down remained virtually untouched.

"It sounds like an amazing place." Daisy smiled, a smile that went all the way to her eyes, that touched—as it always did—a place hidden somewhere deep inside him that no one ever reached but her.

He cleared his throat. "If you have to be in a hospital," he agreed gruffly, "if you can't have what the rest of the world takes for granted, I guess it will do."

Their eyes met. And Alex knew that whether or not he mentioned his brother or her father, Daisy remembered. Daisy knew.

What surprised him, though, was her withdrawal. One minute she'd been gazing at him with warmth and admiration. The next some shadow seemed to settle over her, her expression shuttered.

"I'm sure that all the children will appreciate it." Her tone was polite, but she seemed suddenly more remote. She turned to her salad and began to eat.

Alex was more nettled by her withdrawal than he would have liked. But really, what difference did it make? He hadn't done it for her. He'd done it for people like her father, his brother. He dug into his own salad.

Neither of them spoke until the salads were taken away and the entree was set before them. Then Daisy turned toward him again. "What sort of building are you working on now?"

So they were going to be polite and proper and distant. Fine by him. Alex was glad to talk about the present so he told her about the office building he was designing on the edge of Paris.

Daisy had never been to Paris. And as he talked, he saw her eyes begin to sparkle again. Her remoteness vanished. Her questions came more quickly, and her enthusiasm was contagious. He wanted to make her smile, wanted to have her cock her head and listen eagerly. Alex found himself telling her not just about his work in Paris, but about the city itself, about places he liked, things he'd seen, galleries he visited, buildings he admired.

"You used to live there, didn't you?" It was the first time she'd alluded to the past.

"Yes. And then I was here for a while. But I went back four or five years ago," he said. He knew precisely when he'd gone—and why. After the disastrous end to his weekend with Daisy, New York had more memories than he wanted. Paris seemed like a far safer place to be.

It was only in the past six months or so—when he'd made up his mind to marry, in fact—that he'd returned to live more or less permanently in New York. Even now, though, he kept his small flat in the fifth arrondissement.

Their talk moved from Paris to the Riviera, to other places he'd been. Daisy asked about all of them. The women Amalie had set him up with had asked questions, too, but not like Daisy. Not as if they cared about the answers.

Daisy did. And her interest and enthusiasm drew him out. He would have liked to show her Paris, to walk the wide boulevards and narrow lanes with her, to sit at a tiny table in an outdoor café and drink strong dark coffee with her, to wander through the museums and the galleries hand in hand with her, to walk along the Seine with her and kiss her there, to run through a rainstorm with her.

To take her back to his little garret flat and make love with her. He could imagine Daisy there, letting him strip off her little embroidered jacket, then letting him find the zip at the back of her dress and lower it slowly. He'd kiss his way down—inch by luscious inch and—

"And what?" Daisy was looking at him, curious and impatient.

Hot. God, he was hot. And hard. And suddenly aware that he was in the middle of a crowded room with the object of his fantasy studying him worriedly. Her eyes were still bright and eager, but she was looking at him with puzzlement.

"What happened? You stopped talking," Daisy said. "Did you just get distracted?"

Alex's heart was still hammering, his body still feeling the effects of what he'd been thinking about—her. He shifted in his chair and cleared his throat. "I did, yes." He gave a quick shake of his head. "Sorry about that."

He didn't let it happen again, even though he was still intensely aware of her. It was almost a relief when dinner ended. Except then the speeches began, and Alex knew he would have to say something when the award was presented.

Public speaking wasn't his forte. He preferred to speak with his work, with his design, with his buildings, not his words.

But when the time came, Daisy clapped madly and beamed at him encouragingly when Douglas Standish beckoned him to the podium to accept his award.

Alex made it brief. He gripped the podium and stared into the bright lights as he thanked the hospital board who had given him the opportunity to design the wing and the committee who had given him the award. It was what he had prepared, and it was all he had intended to say.

But before he could walk away, his gaze slid across the hundreds of people in the room and, looking down, he didn't see the lights. He saw Daisy.

His mouth went dry at the sight of her upturned face, at her avid expression, her tantalizing smile. And he didn't walk away. He looked at her, spoke to her.

His voice was less stilted and more ragged as he said, "I hope this wing makes a difference to the patients. I hope it gives them the safe haven they need to get well and—" he paused, his eyes still locked with hers "—the connections to the world outside to keep them strong."

Like your father never had. Like my brother never had. And you're the only one who knows why I did it.

He could see that in her eyes, the realization dawning, her lips parting in a silent O.

Alex jerked his gaze away and abruptly shut his mouth.

Then, clutching the award in a sweaty hand, he said hoarsely, "Thank you all," and strode back to his chair and sat down.

His heart was crashing in his chest. He didn't look at Daisy. He didn't have to. He could sense her eyes on him. The awareness, the emotion vibrated between them. So damn much emotion it felt like being swept off by a tidal wave. He kept his gaze resolutely on the platform where Douglas was coming back to speak.

With a few brief words he thanked Alex again, then thanked all the hospital's staff and benefactors for their support. Then the doors opened to the adjoining ballroom and the small live orchestra just beyond those doors began to play.

People stood up, couples headed toward the dance floor. Alex breathed again.

Abruptly he stood and held out a hand. "Let's dance."

CHAPTER SEVEN

PUTTING her hand in his was like touching a live wire.

A current of electricity seemed to flow between them, one even stronger than the flickering awareness she'd felt all night.

Daisy was aware of the pressure of Alex's strong fingers wrapping around hers as he led her through the doors and onto the dance floor. But it was nothing compared to her awareness when he took her in his arms.

She almost stumbled against him as she tried to do the opposite and keep a respectable distance between them. It was a battle because every instinct in her went to him like a moth to the proverbial flame.

Every touch was memorable. His fingers encased hers warmly. She was exquisitely aware of his hand pressing lightly at the small of her back. She was close enough that she could catch a faint hint of soap and aftershave. And a quick glance showed her how smooth-shaven his jaw was. She remembered it rougher, had loved to stroke her hand over it, stubbled one way, smooth the other.

Abruptly she turned her head, trying to follow his lead at the same time and nearly tripped over his foot. He caught her, pulled her closer. And Daisy knew the sensation of her body melting into his, as if she belonged there, wrapped in his arms.

She had danced with lots of other men. She had felt other men's hands on her body. None—not even Cal's—evoked such strong reactions.

Even now, knowing he was not for her, knowing for a fact that she and Alex had no future, Daisy could not deny that Alex's touch, Alex's smile, Alex's gaze brought to life something inside her that no other man's ever had.

Dancing with Alex was, just as it had been five years ago, the Cinderella experience that Daisy had remembered.

She understood now how she had been swept away by it. There was a feeling of rightness, of perfect understanding, that she'd never had with anyone else. And it scared her to feel it again and know how wrong it had been.

She forced herself to remain clearheaded and sane. She looked away from his hard jaw to study the room, determined to commit it to memory. She focused on the music, tried to think of the title, the composer, to isolate the instruments. And all the while she was aware of the man who held her in his arms.

His breath teased the tendrils of her hair. His trouser-clad legs brushed the silk of her dress. And every touch, every brush set off a hum of something electric. And the study of the room and the music and everything else faded away.

It was all right, she told herself. Nothing was going to happen on a dance floor. He couldn't sweep her off her feet. She couldn't slide a hand between the buttons of his shirt.

So where was the harm in appreciating the feel of hard muscles under her fingertips? Why not give in, just for the moment, to the instinctive rhythm they seemed to engage in when they moved to the music? As long as she didn't allow herself to remember the instinctive rhythm they'd brought to their lovemaking…

There was a point beyond which lay foolishness. Daisy had been there once. Never again.

Careful, she warned herself. Be careful.

But her head turned and so did his. Her lips brushed his jaw. His touched her ear. A shiver ran from the hairs on her neck to the tips of her toes. Her body trembled. Her knees wobbled. And deep in the center of her, something ached with the desire she refused to admit.

She took a breath. "So," she said, "tell me about Caroline."

She was gratified when Alex seemed briefly to stumble. But then he caught himself and without even looking directly at him, she saw his jaw ease as if he were smiling.

"Caroline is amazing," he said. "She's quick. Witty. Beautiful."

His voice was warm, animated. Of course it was. Caroline was his woman. *Remember that,* Daisy told herself sharply and kept asking him Caroline-related questions.

Maybe it was masochistic. Maybe it was just the only way to keep her common sense. Whatever it was, it helped. Daisy made herself listen as he told her all about the ad campaign Caroline was developing that had taken her to Hong Kong. Alex told her about how Caroline had been headhunted by five different companies in the past two years.

"She's amazingly successful. Definitely making her mark. She's even thinking she might go out on her own in the next couple of years." He clearly approved of her ambition and her talent. Daisy forced herself to think about that and not about the way his legs brushed against hers.

"So what are you waiting for if she's so wonderful?" She ventured a glance at his face, wanting to see his expression.

A tiny crease appeared between his brows. The muscles in his shoulder tensed beneath her hand, and hard green eyes looked down into hers. "I thought you weren't in favor of quick decisions these days," he said sharply.

"Yes, well, I'm not you."

Alex grunted. He didn't say anything else. Didn't answer. Didn't talk about Caroline anymore, either.

Daisy tried to stifle her irritation. She told herself it didn't matter, but for some reason it did. It would be easier if he were engaged. Easier to stop thinking about how damned appealing he still was.

Well, fine, if he wouldn't help her out by talking about

Caroline, she'd talk about the pulmonologist whose photos she'd taken for Lauren Nicols.

"I have to thank you for sending Lauren my way," she said. She didn't really want to be beholden to him. But it was her own work that had caused Lauren to call, nothing he'd done. So she talked about that. And Alex seemed grateful enough to take up that topic of conversation. Then the dance was over, and Douglas Standish asked to partner her for the next one.

She danced with half a dozen men, and only reaffirmed that no one's touch affected her the way Alex's did. She seemed to be aware of him—where he was, who he was dancing with— even when he was nowhere near. Actually though, he always seemed to be somewhere fairly near. Wherever her partners danced her, Alex was never far away.

She tried not to look at him, tried not to envy the women he held in his arms, tried not to gauge if he had held them as closely as he'd held her. But she couldn't help noticing that while he danced and chatted with them, his gaze often sought her.

It didn't mean anything. It couldn't.

But she couldn't quite stifle the gratification she felt every time she felt his eyes on her. She didn't dare catch his eye, though. It would be playing with fire. And Daisy had no intention of playing with fire, though there seemed to be one kindling somewhere just south of her midsection, and every time she looked his way, the fire grew.

The evening passed quickly. It was nine-thirty. Ten. Then nearly eleven. They danced. They visited with people Alex had worked with. They danced again. And this time the flames burned even hotter than before.

His eyes seemed to bore into hers whenever she looked at him. Their legs brushed. Their bodies touched. Against her breasts, she could feel the beat of his heart. With everyone else they spoke easily, casually. But when they danced, they had little to say to each other, and the conflagration continued to build.

It wasn't yet midnight, not even eleven-thirty. But Daisy knew she needed to be sensible. While she wouldn't turn into a pumpkin at midnight, and Izzy was keeping Charlie until the morning, a woman could stand just so much temptation.

But one more dance wouldn't hurt, she thought as the music began again and, wordlessly, Alex drew her once more into his arms. They hadn't danced with each other two dances in a row. But it seemed natural now. Right.

Inevitable.

Just as, inevitably, in a few minutes she would say thank-you for a nice evening and take her leave.

But now—just for a few moments more, Daisy allowed herself the luxury of lingering close to him, to luxuriate in the warmth and the nearness of his body, to relish the shiver she felt at his warm breath against her hair.

It's all right, she assured herself. It's just now. Just this moment. Not forever. She had no expectations this time. She was only making memories that would last her through the years.

Her body trembled. Vibrated. Particularly her hip.

Her hip? For a moment she didn't know what was happening. The vibration stopped, thank God. But almost instantly, it started again.

Daisy stumbled, realizing that this vibration had nothing to do with the nearness of Alex and everything to do with the tiny mobile phone she'd tucked into the on-seam pocket of the dress.

"You won't need it," Izzy had said.

But Daisy had insisted. Most glitzy high-fashion dresses clung so tightly that anything more than underwear—and sometimes even that—was too much. But Izzy's gorgeous kicky swirly dress flared at the hips, and Daisy had put her phone into one of its tiny pockets.

"Just in case," she'd said, patting it.

"Suit yourself. I won't be calling you," Izzy had vowed.

But someone was calling her now.

Alex caught her when she stumbled. "What's wrong?"

"It's my phone."

His brows drew together. "Your *phone*? Who the hell do you need to talk to tonight?"

Daisy didn't answer that. "Sorry." She shrugged, half apologetic, half worried as she slipped out of his arms and moved to the edge of the dance floor. "I have to get this."

Alex followed her. "One of your clients out on a hot date and need advice?" he growled.

Daisy glanced at the caller ID. It was Izzy. She answered at once. "Is it Charlie? What happened? What's wrong?"

"He's fine," Izzy said quickly. She sounded as out of breath as Daisy felt. "Well, not entirely fine. But nothing life-threatening. Really. Don't panic."

"What *happened*?" Daisy pressed the phone hard against her ear, trying to hear above the music.

"He was following Rip," Izzy reported ruefully. "Doing what the big boys do. They were climbing on the bunk beds. Rip has this notion that he can move all around their bedroom without touching the floor—"

"Oh, God."

"Well, he can," Izzy admitted. "Of course he's bigger than Charlie. He has longer arms and legs. More wingspan."

Daisy didn't need to have it spelled out. "Oh, God," she said again, knees wobbling.

"Charlie's a pretty impressive climber," Izzy said with the calm that came from having got sons through the first decade of their adventurous lives. "And jumper—but he didn't quite make it to the top of the chair from Rip's bunk. He's broken his arm. I'm so sorry, Daisy. I feel terrible. I—"

"Where is he? St. Luke's?"

"Yes. Finn's taking him. We're on a first-name basis with the emergency room staff."

"I'll meet him there." Daisy was already headed for the nearest exit so she could grab her coat and then a cab.

"I'm so sorry," Izzy repeated. "And Rip is devastated."

"Tell him not to worry. I'm sure it will be fine." She just needed to get there. Now.

"I feel so responsible. Or, as Finn says, irresponsible."

"Don't. It's not your fault."

"It is. I forget how much younger Charlie is. Call me as soon as you've seen him. Promise?"

"I promise." Daisy stuffed the phone back into her pocket and headed for the cloak room.

"What is it? What happened?"

Dear God, she'd forgotten about Alex!

Daisy shot him a quick glance and apologetic smile over her shoulder. "I— It's…an emergency. A friend…" She gave a vague wave of her hand as she skirted around groups of people in the foyer. "I'm sorry. I have to go."

"I figured that out," Alex said gruffly. "Not a client."

"No."

"Your ex?" he bit out.

Daisy blinked at him. "What?"

"Guess not. A new boyfriend?" His gaze narrowed. When she didn't answer, it narrowed further. "Did you tell him you were coming out with me?"

There were no answers to anything he was likely to ask now. "I need to go, Alex," she repeated, then forced herself to stop and face him squarely, even managing to paste a smile on her face. "Thank you for this evening. I enjoyed it."

"I did, too," he said, a grim set to his mouth. Then he stepped around her to present the claim check for her coat to the lady behind the desk.

"Thank you. You don't have to wait. I'll just catch a cab."

He didn't reply. But he didn't leave, either. And moments later, when the lady brought her coat and she reached for it, Alex was there first, shaking it out and holding it so she could slip it on.

"Thank you." As the coat settled on her shoulders, Daisy flicked a grateful smile in his general direction. "I'm sorry to run off. I did have a lovely evening." She paused, hoping he'd say, *Of course, I understand. Thank you for coming.* Then, niceties observed, she could dart away.

He said, "I'll come with you."

"No! I mean, no, thank you. It's not necessary. Really, Alex. I mean it," she said when she saw his jaw tighten. "Thank you for everything, but I'll say good-night here." There was a moment's silence. Then, not knowing what else to do, she thrust out a hand for him to shake.

He looked at it as if she'd offered him a poisonous snake.

Hastily Daisy withdrew it. "Good night, Alex." And without giving him time to reply she turned and darted out of the hotel to catch a cab.

He should just let her walk away and get on with his life.

It was clearly what she wanted. Whatever the hell she was doing, dropping everything and running off at the drop of a hat, it wasn't any of his business.

Alex knew that.

She didn't want him there. He knew that, too.

But he couldn't let her go and face whatever the hell she was about to face when the mere thought of it turned her white-faced and stricken.

So what if it was a boyfriend? Once he saw that she was all right, he'd leave her to it. To him—the boyfriend. Though he couldn't help grinding his teeth at the thought.

The cab he'd grabbed outside the Plaza took a right on Fifty-seventh and headed west. It was Saturday night in midtown, and the traffic was bumper-to-bumper traffic. The theaters had just disgorged people by the hundreds onto the streets. Progress was excruciatingly slow.

He should have just followed her straight out the door. But she'd got a head start on him, and then Standish had called his name. There was no way to pretend he hadn't heard, and impossible to be impolite and brush the older man off—not without being able to offer a convincing excuse.

And what was he going to say? "My date had to rush to

the hospital because she thinks her ex-husband…or maybe her boyfriend…or some guy she knows called Charlie needs her?"

Damn it. Didn't she have any pride?

He glared out at the traffic, willing it to move. At least Standish had told him where St. Luke's was. It wasn't that close to Daisy's office, though perhaps it was near where she actually lived.

He didn't even *know* where she lived. Something else she hadn't shared with him. And something else to fume about until the driver dropped him off outside the emergency services department and sped away.

Facing it, Alex's feet suddenly felt rooted to the pavement.

He didn't do hospitals. Of course he'd been in and out of the hospital he'd designed the wing for. But he'd never been in it other than for work. He'd never been in a hospital for anything resembling a medical reason—for anyone—since the day Vass died. Everything in him wanted to walk away.

Only the memory of Daisy's stricken face made him take a breath, then another deep one, and stride straight in.

It was a zoo. There were people everywhere, sitting, standing, crying, bleeding, filling out forms.

Not one of them was Daisy.

Alex stood by the door, cracking his knuckles. He didn't even know who to ask for. Charlie Somebody.

Hell, he didn't even know the guy's last name. He got in line anyway. Maybe he'd spot her before he had to come up with a name.

He was two cases from the desk when he heard the sound of her voice. His head jerked around, his heart lurched at the sight of her drawn pale face.

She stood in the doorway of one of the examining rooms, her expression intent as she listened to a white-coated doctor. Whatever he said, she nodded, still looking fragile. The doctor patted her arm, then went into the room. Daisy started to go after him.

Alex went after her. "Daisy!"

She jerked as if she'd been shot. Then she spun around, white as a sheet.

He started to go to her, but instead she hurried toward him. "What are you doing here?" Her voice was thready, strained.

He just looked at her. "You're here."

She swallowed. Something shuttered in her gaze. "You don't need to be here."

"You look like hell."

"Thank you so much."

He moved closer. She moved back until he'd cornered her between a chair and the wall. Then he put a hand on her arm so she couldn't pull away. "I came to see if I could help, Daisy."

She shook her head almost fiercely. "I don't need your help. I told you that. It'll be all right."

"Charlie will," he clarified, needing to see her reaction to his name. He tried to keep his voice even, nonjudgmental, but he didn't like it when she flinched.

Her jaw tightened. Her fingers knotted.

"Is it bad?" he asked. He didn't want the guy to die, for heaven's sake. He just didn't want Daisy dropping everything to race across the city for him.

"He has a broken arm."

"A broken arm?" Alex almost laughed with relief at the same time he felt a surge of annoyance. "All this hysteria for a broken arm?"

"I'm not hysterical!" Daisy said indignantly. There was color in her cheeks again.

He couldn't help grinning. "No? Taking a phone call in the middle of a dance? Rushing out of the hotel? For a broken arm?"

"I apologized," Daisy said tightly. She hugged her arms across her chest. "You didn't have to come. I certainly didn't invite you!"

"I thought he might be dying. You looked devastated. I didn't want you to have to face it alone."

Something flickered across her features. She hesitated for

a moment, as if she was giving him the benefit of the doubt. Then she nodded. "That was kind of you. Thank you. But it really wasn't necessary." She straightened, pulled her arm out of his grasp, and gave him what he supposed was a dismissive smile. "It will be fine. *He* will be. I just… Maybe I overreacted. Don't worry. No one's going to die. Now, please excuse me." She tried to slip around him.

But Alex was in no mood to be dismissed and he blocked her way. "Who is he, Daisy?"

She didn't answer. He didn't think she was going to. But then a nurse poked her head out of the examination room. "Mrs. Connolly, Charlie's asking for you. Doctor is going to put the cast on now."

Once more Daisy started to move away, but Alex caught her arm. "He's *asking* for you?" he said mockingly. "To what? Hold his hand?"

Her teeth came together. Her eyes flashed. "Maybe. He's a little boy," she snapped, her eyes flashing anger. "He's my son."

Her *son*? Daisy had a *son*?

But before he could do more than reel at her words, Daisy had jerked her arm away, cut around him and stalked back into the examination room. The door shut behind her with a resounding bang.

A dozen people stopped talking and looked around in surprise.

Alex felt as if he'd been punched. *Where the hell did she get a son?*

Well, of course, he supposed she'd got the boy the time-honored way—she and her ex. But why hadn't she mentioned him?

Not that it was his business. But still…

Alex glared at all the people who were still murmuring and staring at him as if it were his fault she'd stormed away and slammed the door. He wouldn't have minded slamming one or two himself. Instead he stalked over to an empty chair by the windows and flung himself down.

He didn't know how long he waited. Long enough to have plenty of second thoughts. Daisy wasn't going to be happy to come out and find that he had waited. She'd made that perfectly clear.

And did he really want to meet Daisy's child?

It was annoying enough to think that she had professed to love him, then turned around and married someone else. To be honest, Alex had felt a certain satisfaction knowing her rebound marriage hadn't lasted.

That it had resulted in a child was somehow disconcerting.

A child. Charlie.

Alex tried to imagine a little boy who looked like Daisy. Would he have her mischievous grin, a dimple in one cheek, freckles across his nose and a mop of honey-colored hair?

Or would the boy look like her ex-husband? Was the ex holding Charlie's other hand in the exam room with them now? Alex straightened in the chair, scowling at the thought.

Maybe he was going to be sitting here when all three of them came out of the room together. And wouldn't that be awkward as hell?

The noise of a crying baby, a croupy cough, a parent and teenager arguing washed right over him. Alex paid no attention. So it would be awkward. So what? He'd walked out on her and their child, hadn't he?

Alex almost hoped the S.O.B. was here. He'd like to see what was so wonderful that Daisy had ever married him. Scowling, he shifted irritably in the chair, then looked up to see Daisy coming out of the examining room.

On her hip was a little boy with a mop of brownish-blonde hair and one arm in a bright blue cast. He'd expected a two- or three-year-old. But this boy looked bigger. Alex leaned forward, studying him intently. But he couldn't see much. There were people in the way.

Daisy was listening to the nurse. They were standing just

outside the exam room door. The boy was listening, too. Then he turned his head to look out at the waiting room.

Alex's breath caught. His heart seemed to stutter even as he stared.

Charlie's jaw was squarer than Daisy's, his lower lip fuller, his nose a little sharper, his cheekbones higher. His eyes weren't blue, they were green.

He didn't really resemble Daisy at all. Even his hair was actually a deeper gold than Daisy's. But Alex knew exactly who he was. He had known another boy with those eyes, that jaw, whose hair had been exactly that color.

His brother. Vassilios.

CHAPTER EIGHT

For a moment Alex couldn't move. Couldn't think. Could only stare.

And understand the implication. It hit him like a fist to the gut.

He moved on automatic pilot, putting himself between Daisy and the door. And all the while, he couldn't take his eyes off the child.

The boy was Vass all over again. Alex's heart squeezed in his chest. His throat tightened. He couldn't swallow. He barely had a toehold on his composure when Daisy finished talking to the nurse and turned—and saw him.

She stopped, rooted right where she was.

Their eyes locked and he watched her color fade. Her lips parted and trembled. Her arms tightened around the boy in her arms and she glanced around as if looking for another way out.

Bad luck, Daze, Alex thought grimly. Nowhere to go but through me.

She understood that, for a second later she straightened her shoulders, lifted her chin and walked straight toward him.

"I told you that you didn't need to wait."

Alex felt a muscle in his temple tick. He swallowed, seeking words. There were none. Only a well of pain.

How could you? His eyes asked her. The boy—his son!—was close enough to reach out and touch.

He balled his fingers into fists, every fiber of his being

wanted to reach out to the little boy, to take him in his arms
and never let him go. But the boy didn't know, wouldn't understand. Even Daisy seemed to think he was behaving oddly.

"Are you all right?" she asked when he didn't reply.

She had no idea. Didn't realize what he knew. Of course,
she wouldn't. She had no idea Charlie could've been Vass's
clone. Alex managed a curt nod. "Fine." Poleaxed, in truth.

"Good." She smiled briefly. "It was kind of you to bother,"
she said. "But not necessary."

It was necessary. Alex knew that down to his toes. He just
looked at her. For a moment neither of them spoke, neither
moved.

"Mommy."

Daisy shifted at the sound of the small plaintive voice.
She hugged the little boy close. "This is Charlie," she said.
"Charlie, this is Mr. Antonides."

Your father.

God, how he wanted to say the words. He didn't. He just
studied the boy up close. His cheeks were fuller than Vass's
had been. But at that age, maybe his brother had had round
cheeks, too. Alex would have been too young to recall. But
Charlie had the same freckles across his nose that Vass had
had, the same long lashes.

"I got a brok'n arm," the boy told him in a froggy little
voice.

Alex nodded and met his chocolate gaze. "Yeah, I see that
you do."

Daisy shifted under the boy's weight. "I need to get him
home. Thank you. I'm sorry that the evening ended this way."

I'm not. Alex didn't say that, either. He dragged his gaze
away from the boy long enough to meet hers. It all made
sense now—her distance, her coolness, her determination to
shut him out.

But he wasn't out any longer—and he had no intention of
ever being out of this child's life again.

"Come on," he said. "Let's get you into a cab." He stepped

back to let Daisy go through the door. It was late, well after midnight, and the snow was still falling. Charlie couldn't put his arm in his jacket, and Daisy was trying to pull it more closely around his shoulders.

"Let me." Alex took the boy's puffy red down jacket and settled it around small bony shoulders. His hands trembled as he brushed them over him, then tucked the jacket close between Charlie's body and his mother's. "There you go." Even to his own ears, his voice sounded hoarse.

"Thank you." Daisy flicked him a quick smile.

There were no taxis right outside. So he strode off to the corner to flag one down. He half expected Daisy to have vanished by the time he got back with it. But sanity must have prevailed. Either that or she was too shattered by the events of the evening to pull a disappearing act.

Alex opened the door to the taxi. "After you. I'll take him." He held out his arms.

"I can manage." She tried to get in with the boy in her arms, but she nearly lost her balance, and Alex scooped him away.

And the moment the boy's solid body settled in his arms, Alex felt something in him change. Something strong and protective took root, dug in. Instinctively he moved his face closer to the boy's soft hair, drawing in the scent of antiseptic, bubble-gum shampoo, laundry soap and earthy little boy.

His breath caught, his grip tightened.

"I can take him now." Daisy's hollow-eyed gaze locked with Alex's as she held out her arms to the little boy.

Slowly, carefully—reluctantly—Alex settled him on the seat next to her. Then, not giving her a chance to tell him he didn't need to come along, he slid into the backseat as well and shut the door.

There was silence except for the taxi's public service babbling. The car didn't move.

"You'll have to tell him where we're going," Alex said at last. "I don't know."

Daisy hesitated for a split second, then in a low voice gave the cab driver the address. It was the same address as her office.

As the cab lurched forward, he narrowed his gaze at her. Daisy kept hers focused straight ahead. Charlie huddled between them. Alex could feel the little boy's bony shoulder pressed against his arm. He angled his gaze down to see the top of the boy's head, the burnished gold of his hair, the sharp little nose and what looked like a stubborn chin. Looking at him, Alex felt his throat tighten with so many emotions he couldn't name them all.

Charlie.

His son.

Alex turned the notion over in his mind. Tested it. Tasted it. Wrapped his entire being around it. Then he lifted his gaze and looked over the top of Charlie's head at the woman who hadn't even bothered to tell him and felt his whole body stiffen with anger.

As if he were aware of something wrong, Charlie stiffened, too. He edged closer under his mother's arm.

Was he scared? Certainly he sensed something was amiss. Kids could do that, Alex remembered. He certainly had.

He'd read his parents' body language for years. He had sensed their worry about Vass, even when they'd tried to say everything would be fine. He'd felt their pain, their hurt at his brother's illness. He'd felt, without needing words, their emotional withdrawal.

He didn't blame them. His brother had been his idol. His hero. He knew as well as they had that Vass was the best person in the world. And he instinctively felt what they felt: that if they had to lose one of their sons, it should not have been Vass.

Moody, temperamental, fidgety, less-than-perfect Alex was the one who should have died.

Of course no one said so. No one had to. Kids could read body language. They could hear the feelings in the silences—as Charlie could no doubt hear his now.

Consciously Alex relaxed his body and stopped glaring at

Daisy. Instead he shifted slightly away so that he could look down at Charlie more easily.

"I'm not Mr. Antonides. I'm Alex," he said.

The boy flicked a quick glance up at him and dipped his head in acknowledgment.

"Want to shake left hands?" Alex asked.

Charlie's gaze lifted again to meet his. Alex could feel Daisy's eyes on him, as well. Wary, suspicious. Charlie hesitated a moment, then nodded and stuck out his left hand. Small fingers gripped his.

And Alex knew that this first mutual touch was momentous, and that the feel of that small warm hand in his was a memory he would carry with him to his grave.

"I broke my arm once, too," he told the boy, "when I was ten."

"Did you jump off a bunk bed?"

So that was what Charlie had done. Alex smiled and shook his head. "I was climbing some cliffs. One crumbled and I fell."

If he had been on the cliffs near their Santorini home, he didn't think it would have happened. He knew those cliffs like he knew the inside of his bedroom. He and Vass had climbed them their whole lives.

But they hadn't been in Santorini. They had been at a place they were renting in Athens while Vass was in the hospital for treatments. Alex had hated it there, hated the hospital, hated the house, hated having to play by himself all the time because Vass was too ill to do anything.

And he'd only made things worse when he fell.

"You don't think!" his mother had raged. "You never think!"

"You should be glad it hurts," his father had said sternly. "Maybe you will not be so inconsiderate again."

"I wish I'd been with you," Vass had whispered when Alex finally got to see him. His brother's eyes had had dark circles under them. But they had still glittered with urgency and desire.

And Alex had said fervently, "Me, too."

Now, trying to push aside the painful memory, he smiled at the little boy who was looking up at him with Vass's eyes. "Did you break yours jumping from a bunk?"

"I was tryin' to get to the dresser like Rip does."

"Who's Rip?" Whoever he was, Alex liked his name.

"One of Finn and Izzy MacCauley's boys," Daisy said. "Rip is Charlie's hero. He tries to do whatever Rip does, in this case, apparently, to get around the house without touching the floor," she said despairingly.

Alex grinned. "I used to do that, too."

Charlie's eyes widened. "You did?"

"It's something all boys do?" Daisy looked dismayed.

"It's a challenge," Alex told her. "Boys like challenges. How old is Rip?"

"Almost twelve," Daisy said. They were speeding down Central Park West. There was little traffic now and they were hitting the lights. It would be a matter of minutes until they were at Daisy's office.

"That explains it," Alex told the little boy. "You've just got to get bigger."

"Mom says I can't do it again."

Daisy looked mulish. "I don't want him killing himself."

"He won't," Alex said. He smiled at Charlie. "You look like a pretty tough guy."

The boy's head bobbed. "I am. My dad says so."

"Your dad?" Alex lifted his gaze to look from Charlie to Daisy. "His dad?" he said to her.

"His dad." Daisy's look was even more mulish and her tone even firmer than before. "My ex-husband. Cal."

Alex's jaw tightened at the lie. He stared at her.

And just as if she were telling God's own truth, Daisy stared defiantly back. Their gazes were still locked when the cab turned the corner on Daisy's street and pulled up midblock in front of her place. He understood it was more than her office now. She damned well lived here, too.

"Here's where we get out," Daisy said briskly. She reached into the pocket of her coat and pulled out money for the cab.

"I'm paying," Alex said flatly.

Daisy opened her mouth as if to protest, but then shrugged. "Thank you."

He paid the driver, then opened the door and got out, reaching back in and lifting Charlie carefully up into his arms, settling him against his hip. Charlie looped an arm over his shoulder.

Daisy scrambled out and looked disconcerted to see the boy in Alex's arms and not standing on the sidewalk where she had apparently expected to see him.

Alex nodded toward the building. "After you."

He wasn't surprised when Daisy fished a key out of her pocket and, instead of going up the stoop, led the way through a wrought-iron gate and down the steps to the door below. Her movements were jerky as she fumbled the key, but finally unlocked the outer door and pushed it open, then did the same with the lock on the front door, and turned to hold out her arms for her son.

Still carrying Charlie, Alex pushed straight past her into a tiny foyer filled with jackets and boots and roller skates and the smallest bicycle he'd ever seen.

"Yours?" he asked Charlie.

The boy's head nodded against Alex's shoulder.

"Can you ride it?"

Another nod, this one firmer than the last.

"Good for you. I had a bike when I was your age." Alex smiled. Bikes had been his thing—never Vass's. And already Charlie rode one. So there was that bit of himself in his son. "We'll have to go riding."

"He has a broken arm," Daisy said sharply.

"Not now." Alex turned and faced her. "There will be time."

He watched that register in her brain before he said to Charlie, "Plenty of time."

"Alex," Daisy protested faintly.

He turned his stare back on her until her gaze slid away.

"You got a bike?" Charlie asked, interested.

"Yep. I race bikes."

Charlie looked fascinated. Daisy looked dismayed. She shook her head, as if resisting everything. Then quickly and deliberately she stripped off her coat and hung it on one of the hooks in the foyer and crossed the room, holding out her arms.

"Give him to me. He needs to get ready for bed. Now."

Alex wanted to argue. Wanted to defy her, hang on to his son. But for all that he was furious with Daisy, none of it was Charlie's fault. But his jaw was tight, his whole body felt rigid as he loosed his grip and eased the boy into his mother's arms. He took special care not to jar Charlie's arm. And once he'd let go, he smoothed a hand over Charlie's hair, letting it linger.

"You're a brave guy," he said, keeping his gaze on Charlie.

The boy nodded solemnly.

"We'll ride bikes together sometime soon," Alex promised, his smile crooked. "Okay?"

Another nod and a tentative smile.

He could hear Daisy's indrawn breath. "Good night, Alex." She paused, then added evenly, "Thank you for…everything."

For everything? His eyes asked her.

For giving you a son?

"Who's he?" Charlie asked as Daisy carried him up the stairs.

"A man I used to know. A…friend." But she was distracted as she spoke, remembering Alex's narrowed gaze as he'd watched her carrying Charlie across the emergency room.

He didn't know, she assured herself. He couldn't.

It was Charlie's mere existence that had surprised him—that *she* had a son. And his terseness simply meant that he was annoyed she hadn't told him.

In Charlie's room, she flicked on the light and deposited

him gently on the bed. She rarely carried him anywhere these days, and having done so now, she was almost out of breath, surprised at how big he'd gotten since she used to carry him all the time.

"My arm hurts."

"I know. I'm sorry." She bent to kiss his soft hair, then smoothed her hand over it, pulling back as she remembered that Alex had just done the same thing. "I guess maybe you won't leap from bunk beds anymore?"

Charlie pursed his lips, considering. "Not till I'm bigger," he decided. "Crash can do it."

"Maybe you should wait till you're nine or ten then." She got his pajamas off the hook behind the door.

"Maybe." Charlie took the pajamas, then tried to wriggle out of the jacket he still had over his shoulders and one arm.

"I'll help you tonight," Daisy said. "But you're going to have to figure out how to do it yourself, too." She eased off the jacket, then lifted the hem of his shirt and began to slide it up and over his good arm and his head.

"Maybe Alex could teach me."

"What?" She jerked back, then stared at the pair of bright eyes that popped into view as the shirt came off. "Why would he?"

"'Cause he broke his arm," Charlie said simply. "He'd know how."

"Oh. Well…" Daisy made a noncommittal sound. "I'm pretty sure you can figure it out without Alex's help." She finished getting his clothes off and his pajamas on. "Go wash your face and brush your teeth."

Charlie flopped back on the bed. "But I'm tired. Do I hafta?"

"Yes. Even boys who fall off bunk beds have to maintain a minimum of civil decorum."

"I didn't fall," Charlie protested. But he allowed her to pull him up. "I jumped. An' what's 'civil deck-somethin'?" Charlie loved big words.

"Civil decorum," Daisy repeated. It was what she had tried to maintain for the past hour and a half. She said, "Behaving like a well-brought-up *clean* child."

"Ugh." But Charlie slid off the bed and padded toward the bathroom while Daisy gathered up his clothes. "Oh!" she heard him say brightly. "Hi."

"Hi." The unexpected sound of Alex's voice right outside the door sent Daisy hurrying out. She skidded to a halt a second before she collided with his chest.

"You didn't leave."

"No." He had propped a shoulder against the wall outside Charlie's bedroom door and stood there meeting her gaze, then his eyes dropped to Charlie, and Daisy felt more than a flicker of unease.

He didn't say anything. But even quiet and unmoving, his presence seemed to overpower everything else. He was too big. Too close. The space was too intimate. And the situation didn't bear thinking about. She didn't want him here.

But she didn't know how to get rid of him without causing Charlie to wonder what was going on. He already had to wonder. No man but Cal had ever been upstairs.

But Alex was, right here in the hallway, his dark hair disheveled, as if he had run his fingers through it. He looked incongruous here in his formal evening wear, but even as she thought it, she realized the formal evening wear wasn't so formal anymore. He'd removed his tie—it dangled from his pocket—and he'd undone the top two buttons of his shirt.

It had the effect of making him look more masculine and primal than ever—with the added misfortune of reminding her of how he'd looked five years ago when she'd brought him into her tiny apartment after the wedding. He was all the things he'd been then and all the things she'd been at pains to resist earlier this evening—too broad-shouldered, too imposing and too damned predatorily male.

"I came to say good night to Charlie." His tone was mea-

sured, his words easy, understandable and, to Charlie, un-
threatening.

But Daisy knew a threat when she heard one. She took a
quick breath. "Say good night, Charlie."

Charlie tipped his head back to look up at Alex, but instead
of saying good night, he said, "Can you teach me to get my
shirt on an' off over my cast?"

Alex nodded. "I can."

"No, he can't. It's after one in the morning. You need to go
to bed," Daisy said firmly.

"I'll show you," Alex promised smoothly. "Tomorrow."

"But—" Charlie began.

"Your mother's right," Alex said firmly. "You need to
sleep."

"I can't sleep. My arm hurts," Charlie argued.

"But you're tough," Alex reminded him. The two of them
looked at each other. Two men understanding each other—
even though one of them was only four.

"Teeth, Charlie," Daisy said firmly. "And wash your face.
Now." She took hold of his shoulders and steered him past
Alex, doing her best not to brush against him in the narrow
hallway. If she'd hoped he'd take the hint and go, she was out
of luck.

He didn't budge, just waited until Charlie had brushed his
teeth—awkwardly because he had to do it left-handed—and
scrubbed at his face with a washcloth. He didn't use soap, but
Daisy didn't make him do it again. She just wanted him in bed.

"Right," she said briskly. "Off to bed."

Obediently Charlie headed back down the hall, but stopped
directly in front of Alex. He looked up again. "G'night."

And Daisy remembered when she'd seen the photo of
Charlie looking up at Cal's father and had realized how similar her son's profile was to Alex's. They were indeed remarkably alike.

Was that how Alex had known? Or was it some scary primal innate recognition between father and son? She didn't

know. She only knew that the still-deep emotion that she could sense simmering in Alex was more elemental than just a response to discovering she had a child she hadn't told him about.

The question was no longer: *Did he know?*

The question was: *What was he going to do now?*

He reached out a hand and brushed the top of Charlie's head once more. "Good night," he said gravely. "It was nice meeting you, Charlie." His fingers lingered for a moment, then he withdrew them and tucked them into the pocket of his trousers and brought his gaze up to meet Daisy's. "At last."

She suppressed a shiver, then swallowed. With her eyes she beseeched him to be silent, and was relieved when he didn't say anything else. Giving him a fleeting grateful smile, she slipped past him to follow Charlie into his bedroom where she shut the door with a solid click.

Whatever Alex might have to say to her—and she had no doubt he had plenty to say—he could say it tomorrow. Or next month. Not now.

Her priority was Charlie. It was the middle of the night and he'd been hurt, and it didn't matter that her brain was whirling a million miles a minute. If she pushed him, he would balk and take even longer.

So she did everything in his bedtime routine. She tucked him in, then read him a bedtime story. She listened as he told her about his day, including a long involved account of everything he'd done at Rip and Crash's house, what he didn't like about the emergency room, and ultimately, as she'd feared, questions about Alex.

"Do you think he'll ride bikes with me?"

"I don't know," she said. "He's a busy man."

"He said he would."

"Yes. And maybe he will."

"Remind him."

Daisy made a noncommittal sound. "Prayers," she reminded him, and when he'd finished, she added a desperate silent one of her own. Then she kissed her son good-night.

Charlie clutched her hand when she got up to leave. "Stay."

"Charlie."

"My arm hurts. Sing to me," he pleaded.

That wasn't part of the regular nightly routine, but sometimes when he was sick and irritable, she could calm him with some silly songs. "You're tired."

His big eyes drooped even as he nodded. "I'll sleep. Sing."

So Daisy turned out the light, determinedly shut out the turmoil roiling around in her mind, and sat back down on the bed beside him.

Maybe it would soothe them both, she thought as she began to sing. There was a boat song, and a campfire song, and a bus, train and truck song. She had made them up about Charlie's life when he was a toddler. He knew them by heart. Now he settled against her, his eyes shut, the blue cast dark against the pale blanket that covered him. His breathing slowed.

Her voice slowed, too, and finally stopped. Waited. Watched him. And finally when she was sure he was asleep, she dipped her head and kissed him.

"I love you," she whispered, brushing a hand over his hair. Then she put out the bedside light and slipped quietly out of his room, shutting the door after her.

The clock in her bedroom said five minutes of two. Daisy felt as if she'd been up for two days. Or weeks.

Wearily, she stripped off Izzy's dress. It still sparkled in the soft bedside light. It had made her sparkle in the beginning. She didn't sparkle now. She felt as if she'd been run over by a truck. She flexed her bare shoulders and shivered as she stared into the mirror over her dresser. A pale, hollow-eyed, haunted version of herself stared back.

She felt ill. Exhausted. And scared.

Alex knew. And soon he would confront her about Charlie. He would say whatever he had to say about the son he hadn't known he had. The son he never wanted. She felt a tremor run through her.

Whatever he said, he could say it to her. He wasn't going to say it to Charlie. Charlie wasn't ever going to hear that he wasn't wanted. Ever!

Maybe, with luck, Alex would pretend he didn't know. Maybe he would simply walk away. She could hope.

Quickly pulling on her nightgown, she wrapped up in her fuzzy chenille robe and tiptoed down the hall to brush her teeth and wash her face. Then she went downstairs to let Murphy out. She would have done it when she first got home, but Charlie had taken precedence.

Murphy wagged his tail, delighted to see her. She rubbed his ears and kissed the top of his head. Then she slid open the door to the back garden, Murphy went out, and she slid it closed against the snowy December night. Then, while he was out there, she went to put the dead bolt on the front door. Alex couldn't have done it when he left.

If he had left.

He hadn't. He was sprawled, eyes closed, on the sofa.

CHAPTER NINE

FOR a moment Daisy didn't even breathe, just pressed a hand protectively against her breasts and felt her heart pound wildly beneath it.

She dared hope he was asleep—because hoping he was a figment of her imagination was not a possibility. But even as she did so, Alex's eyes fluttered open and he rolled to a sitting position.

"What are you doing here?" she asked.

Alex rolled his shoulders, working the stiffness out. He had taken off his coat and the stark white of his shirt made his shoulders seem broader than ever. He looked at her levelly. "Waiting for you."

"It's late!"

His eyes bored into her. "Five years late."

"I don't know what you mean," she said. Her fingers knotted together.

"You know." His gaze was steady, his eyes chips of green ice.

"Alex," she protested.

"We're done playing games, Daisy."

"I'm not—"

"We're going to talk." There was a thread of steel in his voice now, and as he spoke, he stood up. Slightly more than six feet of whipcord muscle and testosterone somehow filled the room.

Daisy stepped back. "I have to let the dog in."

He shrugged. "Go ahead. I'm not going anywhere."

Exactly what she was afraid of. She hurried through the kitchen and fumbled with shaking fingers to open the sliding-glass door for Murphy. It wasn't just her fingers shaking, her whole body was trembling, and it had nothing to do with the cold December night. The cold in Alex's stare was a different story.

Murphy trotted in, wagging his tail cheerfully. Daisy shut the door and slid the bolt home, then cast a longing look at the stairs that led up to her room. But retreat wasn't an option. So, wiping damp palms down the sides of her robe, she went back to the living room.

Alex was standing by the mantel, holding the photo of her and Charlie and Cal taken last Christmas. At her footsteps, he took one last look and he set it back on the mantel, then looked over at her. "Is this your ex?"

She nodded. "That's Cal."

"Very cozy."

"It was Christmas. Christmas is cozy."

"You look happy."

"We were happy." She hugged her arms across her chest.

"You were still married to him then?"

"No."

One dark brow arched in surprise. "But you had a picture taken together?"

"Yes." She wasn't giving him any explanations. She didn't owe him any.

"He's not Charlie's father."

"Yes, he is." She had been married to Cal when Charlie was born. He was the father on Charlie's birth certificate. He was the father that Charlie called Dad. He was a father to Charlie in every way that mattered.

"Not by blood, he's not."

Daisy swallowed, then lifted her chin. "And you know this how?"

He reached into his back pocket and pulled out a thin black leather billfold. Opening the wallet, he took out a photo, crossed the room and handed it to her. It was a small color snapshot of two young boys, grinning at the camera.

Daisy saw only one. He could have been Charlie.

He was older than Charlie, maybe nine or ten. But his eyes were Charlie's—the same shape, the same light color. He had the same sharp nose, spattered with freckles, the same wide grin. He even had the same straight honey-blonde hair that she'd always assured herself had come from her side of the family.

She clutched the photo so tightly, her fingers trembled. Her throat tightened and she shut her eyes. She couldn't breathe.

Alex didn't seem to be breathing, either. He was stone silent and unmoving. Waiting for her to speak?

But what could she say?

Slowly she opened her eyes again and began to study the picture more carefully. The two boys were standing on a beach, bare-chested and wearing shorts, the sea lapping bright blue behind them. They had their arms slung around each other's shoulders and they were laughing into the camera. The older boy was the one who looked like Charlie. The other was younger, maybe six or seven, with a front tooth missing. He had dark shaggy hair and light eyes. Daisy knew those eyes.

Slowly, cautiously, she looked up at them now. "It's you..." she said so softly she doubted he could hear her. Her thumb stroked over the dark-haired boy's face. "And your brother."

A muscle ticked in his jaw. He nodded. "Vassilios."

Of course it was. His beloved brother, his hero, the beautiful loving boy whose death had destroyed his family looked almost exactly like Charlie.

Dear God, what a shock seeing his son must have been.

Outside a siren wailed as a fire truck went up Central Park West. Inside, the room was so silent she could hear the old oak mantel clock tick. She could hear Murphy two rooms away in the kitchen lapping up water. It was the calm before the storm.

"Why the hell didn't you tell me?" His voice accused her, anguished, ragged, furious. He plucked the photo back out of her hand, his fingers fumbling as he slid it back in his wallet and shoved it into his pocket.

She heard the pain, the anguish, the accusation. On one level she understood them. But she remembered pain and anguish of her own.

"Why the hell should I?" she countered, stung by his fury. "You didn't want a child. You said so! I babbled about marriage and family and you were quite clear. No marriage. No family! Why should I have told you?"

"That was before I knew I had one! How could I say I didn't want my son when I didn't even know he existed?"

"You didn't want him to exist!"

His nostrils flared and his jaw clamped shut. He balled his fingers into fists, as if he were trying to control what he did with them. Like strangle her. "You kept my son from me!"

"I took you at your word!"

"Damn it!" Alex let out a harsh breath. He glared at her, then raked his fingers through his hair and paced the room. At the far end, he whirled around. "You knew how I felt about my brother!"

Yes, she had known. She knew that Vassilios had been the favorite son, the star, the heir. She knew that everyone had loved him. Even Alex. Especially Alex. Vassilios had been bright, funny, caring, social. Everything, Alex had told Daisy five years ago, that he himself was not.

But Vass had been so wonderful that Alex hadn't envied him. He'd only wanted to be like him. He had loved his brother deeply. Vassilios's death had irrevocably changed his life.

She had known that losing his brother was the main reason Alex never wanted children. It was the reason Alex had originally never wanted to marry. He didn't want to love, he'd told her. Love hurt.

Dear God, she could agree with that. She'd hurt more in the aftermath of his leaving and her discovering she was having his child than she could ever have imagined. She'd loved him—and lost him—and for nearly five years now had Charlie to remind her of that loss.

But she couldn't regret it. She couldn't even regret marrying Cal. At least they'd had some sort of love. They'd tried.

Alex had refused to even try. Not then. Not now. He still wanted a marriage on his terms, a marriage without love. And children had still been a deal breaker. He'd made that clear.

So now she met his accusation squarely and told him the honest truth. "Yes, I knew," she agreed. "But mostly I knew you didn't want children. I did what I had to do. I did the best that I could for my son."

"Really? And you and dear Cal have such a spectacular marriage." His tone mocked her, infuriated her.

Daisy had to fight her own inclination to look away. Even so she felt her face heat. "Cal is a great father."

"And I wouldn't have been?" His challenge was loud and clear. Mostly loud.

"Not if you didn't love him! And be quiet. You'll wake him up."

Alex's teeth came together with a snap. She could hear his harsh breathing, but he didn't claim he would love Charlie. How could he? He'd already hardened his heart.

"Why would I think you'd be a good father to a child you didn't want?" she said. "Cal was. Cal was there when he was born—"

"Because you damned well didn't tell me!"

"Cal loves him," she finished quietly.

"And I've never had a chance to!"

"You didn't want one. You'd already made your choice. And when I found out I was pregnant, I had to make choices, too. I chose to do what I thought was best for Charlie. He needed love. He needed parents. A family. You didn't want that. You said, 'No entanglements, no hostages of fortune.'"

He had actually used those terms, and when she repeated

them now, she saw him wince. "You said love hurt too much. You wanted nothing to do with it."

They glared at each other. Daisy wrapped her arms across her chest and stared unblinkingly at him. She knew what he had said, and Alex would be lying if he denied it now.

He didn't deny it. He didn't say anything at all. His jaw worked. His eyes reflected his inner turmoil. Seconds passed. Daisy could hear Murphy's toenails clicking down the hallway as he came out from the kitchen to look at them inquiringly.

Alex didn't notice. He was cracking his knuckles, then kneading the muscles at the back of his neck. He paced the room like an agitated animal trapped in a cage. Finally he flung himself down on the sofa and rubbed his hair until it stuck up all over his head. He dragged his palms down his face and stared at her bleakly over the top of them. "Hell."

In a word, yes.

It was a hell she was already familiar with. The confusion, the anguish, the damned-if-you-do, damned-if-you-don't choices she had faced when she'd discovered she was pregnant. She remembered the hollowness she'd felt at Alex's flat-out rejection of any sort of relationship. In the face of her hopes and dreams and—let's face it—fantasies, he had been crystal clear.

She hadn't even wanted to imagine what he would have said if she'd turned up on his doorstep and announced she was expecting his child. The very thought had made her blood run cold. Even now she shivered inside the thick robe she was wearing. Tucking her hands inside the opposite sleeves, she chaffed her arms briskly, trying to warm them.

Alex just sat there. He didn't speak. He didn't move, except for the rise and fall of his chest. His expression was grim as he stared across the room. He wasn't looking at her now.

She wondered what he was seeing in his mind's eye. His dying brother? His unknown son? The parents who had rejected him and each other? His life, as carefully designed as any building he'd ever planned, going down the drain?

She couldn't imagine. Didn't want to.

Murphy stood between them, looking from one to the other as if wondering what they were doing in his living room in the middle of the night. Finally, accepting it as dogs always did, he curled up on his bed in front of the fireplace and put his head between his paws.

Alex looked up and met her gaze. "I want my son."

"Want your...?" Daisy stared at him, breathless, as if he had punched her in the gut. "What does that mean? You can't take him!" she blurted, anguished. "You don't have any right!"

"I didn't say I was going to take him." Icy green eyes collided with hers. "But I'm not walking away, either."

Daisy swallowed, tried to think, to fathom what Alex's "not walking away" meant. For Charlie. For her. She didn't have a clue.

She only knew what she must not let happen. "You're not hurting him," she said fiercely. "I won't let you."

Alex rubbed a hand over his hair. His brows drew down. "Why the hell would I want to hurt him?"

Daisy had started to pace, but she stopped and turned to face him. "I didn't say you would intend to. But it could happen. He's only four, Alex. He won't understand. Besides, he has a father."

Alex's jaw tightened. "Cal." He spat her ex-husband's name. "Did you marry him because of Charlie?"

Daisy ran her tongue over her lips as she tried to decide how to answer it, how to be honest and fair to both Alex and to Cal.

"Did you?" Alex persisted when she didn't reply.

She sat down in the armchair across from the sofa where he was leaning toward her, his elbows on his knees, his fingers laced. "Yes," she admitted. "But it wasn't as simple as that. I didn't go find the nearest eligible man and ask him to marry me."

"No?" He mocked her.

Daisy tried not to bristle. "No," she said firmly. "Cal asked me."

"And you jumped at it."

In fact she'd been shocked. It had never occurred to her. They'd been friends. Nothing more. "I thought about it. He insisted we could make it work."

"Sounds passionate," Alex drawled.

"Cal and I had been friends for a long time. He said love wasn't just a matter of passion. It was a matter of choice. I thought he was right. He wasn't. But—" she met his mockery defiantly "—I love Cal."

"You thought you loved me."

"I did," Daisy agreed. "But that was before I found out you didn't give a damn."

Alex stiffened as if she'd slapped him, then surged to his feet and loomed over her. "So you fell out of love with me and in love with What's His Face in, what? Six weeks? Less?"

"It wasn't like that."

"No? So, what was it like?"

She knew he didn't really want to hear the answer. He was angry and he just wanted to put her on the defensive, pick a fight.

But Daisy wasn't buying into that. "Sit down," she said, and pointed at the sofa when he didn't move. "Sit down and I'll tell you what it was like," she repeated sharply.

His gaze narrowed on her, but when she kept pointing, he dropped onto the sofa, still staring at her unblinkingly.

When he had settled again, Daisy tucked her feet under her and tried to find words that would make him understand.

"I was hurt when you didn't feel what I did that weekend," she began.

Alex started to interrupt, but she held up a hand to stop him. "I know you think I shouldn't have been. You think I presumed too much, And—" she took a steadying breath "—you were right. I presumed far too much. But I was young and foolish, and nothing like that had ever happened to me before."

Alex's mouth was a thin line, but he was listening at least.

Daisy twisted the tie of her bathrobe between her fingers,

staring at it before lifting her gaze again. She shrugged and told him helplessly, "I fell in love with you. It was a mistake, I admit that." She laced her fingers in her lap and dropped her gaze to stare at them. If she looked at him, she'd realize that she was actually saying these things—and she didn't want to be saying any of them.

She wanted her life back—the way it had been before she had gone to the dinner with him tonight, the way it had been before everything she'd worked so hard to build and hold together for the past five years had all come apart at the seams.

"When you walked out, I was humiliated," she said. "I felt like an idiot. Sick."

Alex's jaw bunched. She knew he wanted to argue. He shifted uncomfortably. Daisy didn't care. She was uncomfortable, too. They could suffer through this together.

"Weeks went by," she continued. "Two, three, four—and instead of being able to put it behind me, I just felt sicker. And sicker. I started throwing up every morning. And that," she said, lifting her eyes to look at him squarely now, "was when I realized that it wasn't the memory of my idiocy that was making me sick. It was being pregnant."

He flinched, then let out a slow breath.

"I didn't even think about trying to find you," she said levelly. "You'd made it quite clear you weren't interested in any sort of involvement at all."

"You could've —"

"No," she said flatly. "I couldn't." She hesitated, then just told him the truth. "I was afraid you might want me to get an abortion."

He stared at her, shocked. "How could you think—?"

"Why wouldn't I?" she demanded. "You didn't want to care! I was afraid you'd say, 'Get rid of it before *anyone* cares.' Well, *I* cared. Even then I cared!" She could feel tears stinging the back of her eyes.

"Jesus," he muttered.

"Exactly," Daisy said, understanding the desperation that

made him say it. "I did a lot of praying. You can believe that. I was scared. I didn't know how I was going to cope. I could keep working for Finn while I was pregnant, but after the baby came, I thought I might have to go back to Colorado and stay with my mother till I could work something out. And then—" she breathed deeply "—Cal proposed."

"Your savior. He was just standing around, waiting in the wings, for exactly that moment?" Alex demanded bitterly. "Ready to take some other man's woman?" Alex ground out. "His *pregnant* woman?"

"I was *not* your woman! And he was my friend. He *is* my friend."

"And yet you couldn't stay married to him," Alex said derisively.

Her jaw tightened. "It didn't work out." She folded her hands in her lap.

"Why not?"

"That's not your business."

Alex scowled blackly. "He married you, then dumped you? It doesn't make sense. None of it makes sense."

"He didn't dump me! And it made sense," Daisy insisted. "We hoped it would work. We wanted it to work. Cal's a good man," she said, looking over at the photo on the mantel. She stared at it for a long moment, then turned her gaze and met Alex's, smiling a little sadly. "He's been a good father."

"But not Charlie's only father!" Alex insisted.

"He knows he has a biological father. Well, as much as any four-year-old understands that. He knows he has two fathers. I figured I could explain you more to him as he got older."

"I'll explain myself to him now."

"No," Daisy said. "Not until I know how you feel."

"You know damn well how I feel. I want my son!"

Their gazes locked, dueled. And in the silence of battle, the stairs creaked.

"Mommy?"

Daisy's head jerked up to see Charlie peering over the bannister halfway down them. Alex stared up at him, too. Dear God, had he heard?

Daisy hurried up the stairs and scooped him up into her arms. "What is it, sweetie?"

"My arm hurts," he whimpered, and tucked his head between her jaw and her shoulder. He clung to her, but his gaze was fixed on Alex who was slowly coming to his feet.

Daisy shifted so that her body blocked his view. "I know." She kissed his hair and cuddled him close. "I wish it didn't. I'll take you back upstairs and sing to you. Okay?"

Charlie nodded. "Can Alex come, too?"

"Alex was just leaving." But she turned and carried Charlie down the stairs. "We'll just say good-night and see him out the front door." She smiled into Alex's suddenly narrowed gaze. "That will be nice, won't it?" she said to her son.

Solemnly Charlie nodded. He looked at Alex.

Alex looked back with an intensity that made Daisy quiver. Then Charlie lifted his head off her shoulder. "Night, Alex."

Daisy held her breath as, slowly, Alex shrugged into his suit jacket and crossed the room, stopping mere inches from them. He didn't look at her. He had eyes only for Charlie. To Daisy he looked dark, forbidding and positively scary.

But then he lifted a hand to touch Charlie's cheek and his expression softened, a smile touched the corner of his mouth. "Good night, son."

CHAPTER TEN

IT was like waiting for the other shoe to drop.

Daisy half expected to find Alex standing on the stoop when she got up. But a peek out the curtains as soon as she got up proved that no one was there.

He didn't call, either, though she jumped every time the phone rang.

Charlie, pushing his scrambled eggs around his plate, wanted to know what the matter was with her. "You're all jumpy," he remarked when a sound on the sidewalk made her flinch.

"Nothing's the matter." Daisy turned away, busying herself putting the dishes in the dishwasher. "Izzy said she and the boys were coming by."

Izzy's had been the first phone call she'd got this morning.

"How is he?" her friend had demanded even before Daisy had dragged herself out of bed.

"Still asleep," Daisy reported. In fact he was asleep on the other side of her bed. She'd got him back to sleep after Alex had finally left, but he'd awakened and come into her room again at five-thirty. Barely able to pry her eyes open, Daisy had taken the easy way out and let him clamber into bed with her. Fortunately he'd gone straight back to sleep, and when Izzy had rung at eight, he was still dead to the world.

"Sorry. We've been up for hours thinking about him."

"He's going to be fine," Daisy assured her. At least his

arm was. How his life was going to change now that Alex was going to be part of it, she didn't know. But at least Alex had been kind last night. He'd actually behaved—toward Charlie—very well. Maybe, given that, he would be fine. And kids were resilient.

It was her own resilience Daisy was worried about.

How was she going to deal with Alexandros Antonides in her life?

She didn't want to think about it. So when Izzy asked if they could come and see Charlie in the afternoon, Daisy said yes without hesitation. The distraction would do them both good.

By midafternoon with no Rip and no Crash, Charlie was getting restless. Daisy had watched a Disney DVD with him, then read him a couple of dozen picture books. She tried unsuccessfully to talk him into a nap.

"I'm too big for naps," he told her. "An' I'm not tired."

No, just cranky. She had a photo shoot to finish editing before tomorrow afternoon. So she brought her laptop down to the living room and worked on it there while Charlie played with his cars and his Legos on the floor.

"Maybe that Alex will come back," he said hopefully, looking up from his cars.

"Mmm." Daisy didn't encourage that line of thinking. A man who had been as adamant as Alex had been about not wanting children might have had a brief change of heart when faced with a little boy who looked very much like his beloved deceased brother.

But having a son was a huge responsibility. And it wasn't one that you could just pick up and put down as the whim struck you. Alex wasn't a fool. He had to realize that. It was possible that Alex had gone home in the early hours of the morning, thought about the implications of having a son, and come to the conclusion that he'd made the right decision five years ago. Whatever he decided, Daisy was determined that she wouldn't let him upset Charlie's life to suit himself.

She didn't have time to think about it more because finally the doorbell rang.

"They're here!" Charlie scrambled up from the floor and raced to open the door.

Daisy unlocked the door, and Charlie tugged it open.

Rip MacCauley took one look at Charlie's cast and said, "Oh, wow. Your cast is blue? That's cool."

The first smile of the day flickered across Charlie's face. "You think?"

"Oh, yeah," Rip said, coming in and taking off his jacket. "I only ever had a white one."

"Mine was purple when I broke my ankle," Crash announced. "Here. This is for you." He thrust a package wrapped in newspaper comics into Charlie's hand.

"A little something to keep him busy," Izzy told Daisy as the boys headed instinctively for the cars and the Legos on the floor and she followed Daisy into the kitchen. "Rip and Crash have been really worried. They seem to think they're indestructible, but when Charlie got hurt, they were, like, 'Oh, no! What if he dies?' They felt very responsible. As well they should, Finn says."

"Finn being such a pattern card of model behavior." Daisy grinned.

Izzy laughed. "That's what I said." She perched on a bar stool while Daisy made them coffee. "I was amazed when Finn got home so quickly last night. Why didn't you let him stay for a bit and help you with Charlie?"

"No point. We were fine." And she was very glad he hadn't been there to witness the meeting of Alex and his son.

"I'm sorry we interrupted your evening. How was the Plaza? Tell all." Izzy leaned forward eagerly.

It took Daisy a moment to even begin to remember the details, so much had happened in the meantime. "It was…fine," she said vaguely. "The Plaza is elegant, of course. The dinner was wonderful," she added dutifully, because "fine" wasn't going to satisfy Izzy.

"And the dress?"

"It was fantastic."

"Knocked his socks off?" Izzy's eyes were bright.

"It wasn't supposed to knock his socks off," Daisy reminded her. "He's got a girlfriend."

Izzy looked disappointed. But then she shrugged philosophically. "So you had a good time."

Daisy did her best to sound bright and enthusiastic about the evening. She didn't tell Izzy that Alex had turned up at the hospital. She didn't mention anything that happened after that. Until she had some idea of what Alex intended, she wasn't borrowing trouble—or discussing him with anyone.

She was glad Izzy and the boys came because it took the edge off Charlie's boredom and irritability. The matchbox cars that Rip and Crash brought him were a big hit. But Daisy was, honestly, glad when they left again because it was hard to give the impression of cheerful equanimity when she felt edgy and stressed and as if her world was splintering into a million pieces. She left Charlie playing with his cars on the floor in the living room and retreated to the kitchen to wash up the cups and plates from the MacCauleys' visit.

And then the doorbell rang.

"It's Alex!" Charlie yelled, jumping up and running to the door.

Wiping nervous hands on the sides of her jeans, Daisy followed him to answer it. She dragged the door open a few inches and, as always, felt her heart do a somersault in her chest at the mere sight of him.

Gone, of course, was the formal wear of last evening. This afternoon Alex was in jeans and a hunter-green down jacket, his dark hair windblown and dusted with snowflakes, his jaw stubbled. His eyes were bloodshot, but they met hers squarely.

"Daisy." His voice was soft but firm, and gravelly as if he hadn't slept.

"Alex," she replied, holding herself rigid, trying to relax, but unable to. Still she swallowed and tried to sound cordial and polite.

"Hi, Alex." Charlie poked his head around to beam up at the man on the doorstep. "Come 'n' see my new cars."

"Cars?" Alex grinned and stepped across the threshold.

Daisy backed up hastily. "Charlie's much better," she said as he brushed past. "You didn't have to come."

He gave her a look so intense it could have leveled buildings. "I wanted to come." Then he turned his attention to Charlie. "You're better, are you?" he said, his tone far lighter. "Good. I thought maybe we could go to the park."

"The park?" Daisy echoed doubtfully.

But Charlie cheered. Obviously no one had told him he was an invalid.

"But let's see your new cars first." Alex was already shedding his jacket, dropping down onto the floor next to Charlie, making himself at home.

Charlie was clearly delighted to have the attention. He showed Alex the new set of Matchbox cars that Rip and Crash had given him. "Sports cars," he told Alex eagerly. "They go really fast. See?" He raced them around on the floor, making car noises.

Alex stretched out his long legs and leaned back on an elbow, watching, not just indulgently, but with real interest. He picked up the cars by turn, examining them, commenting knowledgeably because, of course, he knew all about cars. It must come standard issue with the Y chromosome.

Daisy stood there, watching, unable to pull herself away. Seeing the two of them together—father and son—was something she'd barely ever dreamed of. Hearing Charlie's eager chatter and Alex's low baritone in reply set something deep inside her quivering, aching.

Wanting. Far too much.

Abruptly she wheeled away. "I'll be upstairs," she said. "I have work to do."

He had come to see Charlie, not her. And while it was

hardly an honest introduction to the demands of fatherhood, if he came looking for reinforcements in fifteen minutes, she'd know it wasn't going to last.

Charlie came in half an hour later. "Alex an' me want to go to the park. He says to ask if you want to go along."

Annoyed that he would presume to decide what he and Charlie were going to do without consulting her, Daisy hurried downstairs.

The Legos and Matchbox cars had been neatly put away and Alex was zipping up his jacket. "Good," he said. "You're coming, too."

"You don't presume. You should have asked!"

"Charlie did ask."

Charlie bobbed his head. "I said we wanted to go, and did you want to come."

Daisy opened her mouth, then closed it again. "Fine," she said shortly. "I'll come."

It was torture, seeing him with Charlie, being with him herself, acting as though they were some lovely happy family, all the while knowing it was a sham.

"Take it easy," Alex said in an undertone as she jerkily shoved her arms into her jacket. "I'm not going to steal my son."

My son, she wanted to correct him. *And no, you're damned well not!*

But Alex had turned and was helping Charlie with his jacket. Daisy wanted to push him away and do it herself. But one look told her that Charlie was more patient with Alex helping than he would have been with her. And Alex did take the time to show him how to do it himself—except for the zipping up part.

"Guess we'll have to help with that," he said easily, then zipped the jacket up to Charlie's chin. Then rising again, he reached down to ruffle the little boy's hair.

It was a casual movement, but it already spoke of a connection that made Daisy's insides clench, especially when Charlie flashed him a happy grin.

Turning abruptly, she called Murphy and snapped on his leash. Then the four of them went out the door and headed to the park—just like a family.

She shouldn't have come. She should have stayed back in her office and got more work done. But the temptation of watching Alex with Charlie was too great. It was terrifying, too. But Charlie was having such a good time.

There was still lots of snow on the ground. Once they got to the park, they built a snowman. And they had a snowball fight. Then Charlie made snow angels.

"A snow devil more like," Daisy said, laughing as she watched him, then taking photos with the small pocket-size camera she always carried. She got quite a few of Charlie and Alex rolling balls to make the snowman, then more of Alex lifting Charlie onto his shoulders so he could put an old hat on the snowman's head.

They were laughing as they did it, Alex lurching around in the snow while Charlie gripped Alex's hair with his free hand and laughed madly. Then Alex tipped his head back to grin up at his son, and the look they shared made Daisy feel as if she'd caught a snowball square in the heart.

Later she nearly did as she helped Charlie pelt Alex with snowballs. She got several shots of Charlie and Alex throwing them at each other. Then Alex took the camera out of her hand.

"What are you doing?" She tried to grab it back.

But Alex held it out of her reach, his green eyes mischievous. "Go play with your son."

Self-consciously at first, Daisy did. But then she got caught up in Charlie's enthusiasm. And while she pushed Charlie on a swing and helped him build a little snow dog to go with the snowman, Alex took pictures. Finally, when Daisy said it was time to leave, he set the camera's timer and hauled them all into a picture together, scooping Charlie up into one arm while he flung the other around Daisy.

And once more when his arm pulled her close, Daisy felt the hum of electricity between them. She felt desire all over again, and knew it for the hopeless feeling it was. It was a relief when the timer went off, the shutter clicked, and he let her go, slung Charlie onto his shoulders and they all walked home.

On the doorstep, when Alex set him down, Daisy smiled politely. "Thank you. He enjoyed that."

"Did you?" Alex asked.

She heard the pointedness of his tone and chose to ignore it. "Of course." She fumbled to get the key in the lock. He was wearing sunglasses and before she'd turned away she couldn't read his expression, but she could still feel the intensity of his gaze.

"Good." He took the key out of her hand and opened the door himself. Then he pushed it open, let them go in, then followed and shut it behind him.

"I need to get dinner started. Don't let us keep you. I'm sure you have things to do." Daisy said briskly and, slipping off her jacket, started toward the kitchen.

"We can get takeout. What do you like?"

"I'm making stew. Charlie likes it."

"So do I." Alex smiled guilelessly.

"Alex can stay, can't he?" Charlie asked.

What was a mother to do? Of course she had to be polite. She was teaching Charlie to be polite.

The evening was interminable. Dinner. Then Charlie's bath. Then bedtime stories. And awareness of Alex at every single moment. Watching him with Charlie, catching him looking at her when he thought she wasn't noticing. Charlie's stories took forever, even though Alex read several of them. Prayers were longer, too, because Alex, of course, was added to them.

"No singing tonight," Daisy decreed before Charlie could even suggest it. "You need to go to sleep. Remember, your class is going to the zoo tomorrow." The preschool trip to the Bronx Zoo—and a program about animals in winter—had been much anticipated.

Now Charlie looked up from his pillow and asked, "Can Alex come?"

"No," Daisy said without giving Alex a chance to reply.

"But—"

"I have to work," Alex said, sounding regretful. "But we had fun today. We'll do this again."

Charlie popped up. "When?"

"That depends on how well and how fast you go to sleep now," Daisy said, no stranger to manipulative children. She gave him a speaking look.

Charlie sighed, sank back against the pillow and shut his eyes. "I'm sleepin'."

"So I see," Daisy said drily, bending to kiss him. "Good night, Mr. Sleepyhead."

"Night," Charlie murmured, not opening his eyes.

She stepped back, and found that Alex had taken her place at Charlie's bedside. He brushed a hand over Charlie's head, then dropped to one knee and pressed a light kiss on Charlie's forehead.

The boy's eyes popped open and small hard arms and one very hard blue cast wrapped themselves around Alex's neck.

Alex stiffened. And Daisy held her breath.

Then slowly his posture eased, and his arms went around Charlie, too. He scooped the boy up for a fierce hug, burying his face in the crook of Charlie's neck. Then slowly he drew back and lowered the boy to the pillows again. "G'night, sport." His voice was rough. He straightened and stood looking down at the little boy for a long moment.

Then his gaze turned to Daisy. Their eyes met. She shut off the light and headed down to the kitchen.

If he wanted to talk, he could do it while she washed the dinner dishes. But frankly, she didn't know what else there was to say. She began to run water in the sink, all the while aware of exactly where he was, hip propped against the counter beside the refrigerator, watching her.

"Sorry I didn't get here earlier," he said over the running water.

"You didn't need to come at all." Daisy set the plates in the soapy water.

"Of course I needed to come. But I had to get hold of Caroline. I needed to tell her first."

Daisy did turn then. "That you had a son? How did she take that after your 'no children ever' edict?"

Alex's mouth twisted wryly. "She was…surprised."

"I'll bet." Daisy turned away again, picking up a mug and scrubbing it so furiously that the tiny sprays of yellow primroses on it threatened to disappear.

"But she understands."

Daisy's teeth came together as she swallowed half a dozen remarks that were far snarkier than the previous one. "I don't want her *understanding*. If she's like you, she doesn't want kids around!"

"She won't have them. We've broken it off."

Daisy stared at him. "What?"

Alex lifted his shoulders. "Circumstances changed. I called Amalie, too. Told her I was cancelling the rest of our agreement. My matchmaker," Alex said when Daisy stared at him blankly.

She was still processing Caroline's departure. "Why?"

"Because I don't need one now. Obviously. She gets her money anyway, so she doesn't care. She wished me all the best." He paused, then exhaled slowly and said, "So, the decks are clear."

There was a moment's stark silence as the implication of his words set in. Daisy felt a sudden chill but it started inside her, not out.

"Clear," she echoed. "Clear for what?"

But as soon as she asked, she knew she couldn't let him answer. She already knew—and she didn't want to hear it. "For you to be noble? For you to do something stupid like ask me to marry you?"

Alex stared at her, taken aback. "Damned right I want to marry you. Why the hell not? It makes perfect sense."

Exactly what she wanted to hear. Daisy wasn't cold any longer, she was burning up. She wouldn't have been surprised if steam was coming out of her ears.

"You're just like Cal! What is it with men, anyway? Why do you always think you can make the world act the way you want it to?"

"Daisy—"

"It's all control with you, isn't it?"

"Daisy, stop it! Stop being stupid. And this has nothing to do with your ex or anyone else." He shoved away from where he was leaning against the countertop and came toward her. "Be sensible, Daisy. I want to—"

"No. Don't do it, Alex," she said fiercely. "Don't say it. I don't want to hear it." She flung the sponge away and put her hands over her ears. "I won't!"

Of all the bloody-minded females!

Alex couldn't believe it! But Daisy was glaring at him, her cheeks flushed, her eyes flashing. She'd flung the sponge into the sink and put her hands over her ears, defying him to…what?

Propose?

Of course he was damned well going to propose. It was the right thing to do. If he had fathered a child—and he quite obviously had—it was his duty to marry his child's mother, be her husband, a father to their child and…and then what?

Live happily ever after?

He wouldn't let himself think about that.

Because in his experience, people didn't get to. Well, maybe some did. But how did you know? How could you ever be sure?

You couldn't. But the decision was no longer his. He'd made it five years ago when he'd made love to Daisy. He'd spent all night coming to terms with what that meant, and he was ready to do it. Determined to do it.

And now...

Now he didn't have to.

Just like that, Daisy had popped his balloon of self-righteous nobility before he'd even had a chance to let it fly.

He should be relieved, Alex told himself. Somewhere deep down, he supposed he *was* relieved. But at the same time, he was madder than hell. He didn't like being dismissed, being told his presence wasn't needed, wasn't valued.

And if she expected he would just turn around and walk away, she was bloody well out of her mind. At least she'd taken her hands off her ears now and had turned back to the pots and pans with which she was making an almighty racket.

Alex scowled at her back. "I seem to recall," he pointed out, "that you wanted marriage."

The pots continued to clatter. She shot him a quick furious glance over her shoulder. "Five years ago, yes. When I was besotted, yes. When I thought you loved me, too. Not now! I don't want you now!"

It surprised him that her words actually hurt. They made him stiffen as if he could defend himself against them, against her. His jaw felt as tight as a steel trap. "Fine," he said tersely. "You don't have to 'have' me."

Daisy turned, a look of consternation flicked across her features, followed by a faint sheepish smile of relief. "Well, um, good. Thank you," she said gruffly.

"But that doesn't mean you're getting rid of me."

She blinked. "But—"

"For God's sake, Daisy. You have my son! You might not have seen fit to tell me, but I know it now. And I'm not going to walk out of his life. I want to be part of it. I want him to be part of mine."

"For how long? Are you going to be buddies like you were today? For as long as it suits you? Are you going to be here when he needs you or are you going to walk when the going

gets tough? Do you imagine you can be here and not *care,*
Alex? You said—you told me plainly—brutally—that you
didn't want to care—about anyone!" Her eyes flashed with
accusation.

"You never let me care," he pointed out, trying to sound
calmer than he felt. "You didn't even tell me he existed!"

"To protect him! To protect him from the knowledge that
for you love is a one-way street!"

Stung, for a moment Alex didn't reply. Deliberately he
swallowed his discomfort at the truth of her words. But at
the same time, he lashed back. "Is that what it is?" he challenged her. "Or maybe—" he flung at her because, damn it,
he wasn't the only one in the wrong "—it's all about protecting yourself!"

"I don't need to protect myself from you anymore. I know
the score now. But Charlie doesn't. He'll give his love, wholly
and completely, to you! To a man who can't let himself care—
to a man who thinks love is worth nothing! And how do you
think that's going to make him feel? I know what that's like,
remember? And I wasn't four! I know what's right for my
son!"

"And you're the arbiter of all things 'right' in Charlie's
life?"

"I know him better than anyone. I love him more than anyone. I want the best for him."

"The best thing would be if he had a family," Alex told her
flatly. "And you know it."

Daisy didn't reply. She just stared at him stonily. Then she
reached for a towel, dried her hands on it, and marched past
him, heading straight into the living room where she twisted
the locks and yanked open the door. "I think it's time you
left now."

Alex followed her into the living room, but he stopped
there, staring at her, trying to fathom what was going on in
her head. She wasn't being sensible, wasn't being rational.

"You know I'm right, Daisy."

She just looked at him, then at the door. When he still didn't move, she yanked his jacket off the hook where he'd hung it and thrust it at him. "Goodbye, Alex."

Wordlessly he reached out and took it, shrugged it on and zipped it up. "Fine. I'll go. But this isn't over. I'll be back. And while I'm gone, don't just think about Charlie. Think about what you want, too."

And he pulled her into his arms and took her mouth with his.

He'd been wanting to do this all day, all yesterday, every minute, it seemed, since he'd kissed her last. The hunger was so fierce he ached with it.

Now he felt her whole body stiffen. She raised her arms between them, her forearms pressing against his chest as if to hold him off. It didn't matter. While he would have liked to feel her body melt against him, to have her arms wrap around him, to know her eagerness matched his, he didn't need it to prove his point.

He had his lips to convince her, to taste her, to tease her. He had his tongue to touch her lips, to part them, to slip between and find her sweetness. God, she made him crazy, made his whole being quiver with need, made the blood sing in his veins.

He wasn't going to let her pretend that it meant nothing. Kissing Daisy *never* meant nothing. Kissing Daisy was amazing, wild, always potent, always drugging. Kissing Daisy always made his heart slam against the wall of his chest, made his loins tighten and his body hum with desire.

And damn it, he knew—absolutely knew—it was the same for her.

She fought it. He could feel her resisting. But she was fighting herself, not him. Her lips trembled, pressed together, denied him. But she denied herself, as well.

So he touched them anyway. He drew a line with his tongue, coaxed, teased. And they gave, opened just a fraction. He took advantage, darted within. He heard her whimper, and her fingers opened to clutch his jacket, hanging on. Her lips softened, parted farther. And he felt a jolt as her tongue tangled with his.

Yes, like that. It was always like that between them. Always had been. Alex wanted to cheer, to exult, to press his advantage and take them where they both wanted to go. He wanted to slide his fingers beneath her sweater and stroke her curves, her breasts, her very bones. He wanted to tease beneath the waistband of her jeans, slide his fingers south, touch her— there. Damn she was killing him. His breath came hard and fast. He wanted to taste, to tease, to sample and suckle. He wanted to devour. He wrapped her in his arms, thrust his fingers in her hair, kissed her hard one more time.

Then he pulled back, dragging in lungfuls of air as he looked down into her stunned feverish gaze. "While you're thinking," he said roughly, "think about that."

Her palm connected with his cheek so fast he didn't even see it coming.

"What the hell was that for?" he demanded. His fingers curled. He jammed his hands in his pockets.

"What was the kiss for?" she countered furiously.

His gaze narrowed. "*That's* why you slapped me? For reminding you that we had something good?"

"I don't need any reminders, thank you very much. And it turns out we didn't have anything at all."

"You don't believe that."

"I do. And I don't need you trying to bribe me with sex."

He gaped at her. "Bribe you?"

Her eyes flashed. "Bribe me, get around me, coerce me, make me do what you want because I'm somehow susceptible to you! Call it what you like. It's not going to work."

"For God's sake, Daisy." He raked fingers through his hair. "I was trying to show you it isn't all about Charlie."

"No, it isn't. It's all about you—what you want, when you want it, and not when you don't. You don't love Charlie. You don't love anyone. You don't want to. You push people away. At least Cal wanted to," she spat at him furiously.

"Cal?" he retorted. "This is all about Cal? All about your 'failed' marriage? Has it really made you that bitter?"

"I'm not bitter at all. Not at Cal. Not at our marriage." She lifted her chin as if defying him to argue. "We went into it with our eyes open."

He watched her, saw a host of conflicting expressions cross her face. Then she lifted a shoulder as if shrugging off a burden and said, "Cal is gay."

Alex stared at her.

"He's my friend. And he didn't have a lover. So when he saw what I was going through, he tried to make it easier for me." She ran her tongue over her lips. "He was convinced that he could will himself to love whoever he wanted to love." She shrugged. "He believes in the same things I do—commitment, long-term relationships, responsibility. Love."

Alex's gaze narrowed.

"He never lied to me. And I didn't lie to him. He knew I loved you. He knew you didn't love me. He offered his name, his support, everything he could. And I did the same for him. But—" she lifted her shoulders "—it wasn't enough. We tried to make it work. It didn't. In the end we knew that. We'll always be friends. But there's more to real love, real marriage than that. And we both wanted…more."

"I'm offering you more," Alex pointed out indignantly.

Daisy just looked at him. She took a slow breath, then swallowed and shook her head. "No, Alex. You're not. You're offering far, far less."

She pushed him out the door and closed it after him.

CHAPTER ELEVEN

DAISY leaned against the door, tears blurring her eyes. She dashed them away with a shaking hand. Of course he thought she was mad. The way he'd looked at her, patent disbelief in his eyes.

He was offering her marriage, wasn't he? Hadn't that been her heart's desire five years ago?

Yes, then. Not now.

Because this was exactly the sort of "marriage" he would have been offering Caroline. A wedding, a legal, convenient version of friends with benefits. Now as she stood with her back to the front door, still hearing Alex's footfalls moving quickly away, Daisy wiped a hand over her face, touched the tears, wanted to deny them. Knew she couldn't.

They were as real as the truth she'd just told Alex: marriages of convenience didn't work. Not for her. She and Cal had done their best. But friendship and responsibility only went so far.

They were only a part of the deep abiding fullness of heart, soul, mind and body that real love was.

She knew it wasn't easy. She knew, just as Alex knew, that real love hurt.

She didn't care. If she could have the love, she could endure the pain. She'd been raised in the real love of her parents' marriage. She remembered their joys and their sorrows. She remembered all too well her mother's pain at her father's death.

But she remembered, too, the sight of her mother smiling through her tears as she'd said, "I don't regret it for an instant. Loving Jack was worth all of this."

This was sometimes heartache, sometimes pain, sometimes joy, sometimes the simple act of heart-deep sharing.

Daisy wanted that.

She had the pain part down pat, she thought, tears streaming down her face.

But she knew she'd done the right thing—even if Alex had been right, that she'd been protecting herself. If marrying Cal had been a mistake, marrying Alex would be a disaster—because she could not stop loving him, and he didn't know what real love was.

He couldn't draw a straight line.

He broke the lead in all his mechanical pencils. He snapped the nib off his best drawing pen. His hands shook so badly as he sat at his desk and tried to find the calm he always felt designing, that he crumpled up page after page of the paper in his sketchbook.

Finally Alex threw the whole damn thing out and went to stand and stare out the window, dragging in deep breaths. But for once even the sight of the spectacular Manhattan skyline didn't soothe his furious soul.

He pressed his forehead against the cold glass of the window, then lifted a hand and rubbed it against his stubbled cheek.

The physical sting of Daisy's palm was long gone. But the emotional sting was imprinted on his soul. So were the words she'd flung at him: *It's all about you. You don't love Charlie. You don't love anyone. You don't want to.*

His throat tightened. His eyes blurred. He sucked in another breath and shook his head, wanting to deny it.

But he couldn't. Not entirely. At least a part of what she said was true: He *hadn't* wanted to.

For years—ever since Vass's death and his parents' divorce—Alex had done his best to make sure that anything as messy and painful as love would not be a part of his world. He'd deliberately built himself a life without it. He had his business, his design projects, his friends, and recently he'd figured that he could do marriage as long as it was on his terms, where his wife didn't want anything deeper or more demanding than he did.

He'd wanted a world he could control.

Which was why he had turned his back on Daisy five years ago.

She had threatened his control. She had bowled him over that weekend, had loved and given and enchanted in equal measures. He'd never met anyone so unguarded, so genuine, so warm and real.

Letting Daisy into his life would have been opening himself up to a tidal wave of emotions he couldn't control, a future he couldn't predict, the possibility for pain he didn't ever want to experience again.

God knew what would happened if he let down his guard.

So he hadn't. He'd turned away from her warmth, rejected her love, shut her out of his life. And having done so, he'd thought he was safe.

He was wrong.

But she was wrong, too.

Daisy had thought he *couldn't* love, and Alex had believed he *wouldn't*.

But God help him, he did. He loved Charlie. He'd only had to see the boy, watch the joy of life in his eyes, listen to him, hold his hand, touch his hair—and he loved. But more than that, before he recognized that he loved Charlie, he knew he loved her.

Daisy.

In spite of himself and his determined intentions, the day Daisy had come into his life, she had created a tiny rent in his armor. She had pierced his defenses, had touched his heart and planted a seed deep in his soul. For two days she had given him a glimpse of what life could be like if he had dared to let it grow.

He hadn't. He'd turned his back. But while he thought he'd walked away heart-whole, it wasn't true.

The minute he'd seen her again this autumn, everything he had felt when he'd been with her the first time—the need, the emotion, the connection—the sense that the world was a brighter, warmer, fuller, more welcoming place—had broken through.

He hadn't given in, of course. Though he had felt the attraction all over again, he'd still tried to do it his way—to control it. To control her.

He couldn't.

She wouldn't let him.

He knew what she wanted. Demanded. A real future, a no-holds-barred willingness to love and, admitting that love, to face the possibility of pain, of loss of control, of helplessness—all the things he'd said no to.

He didn't know if he could do it now.

But he loved. He had no choice. It was simply there—in him. For better or worse. But he knew he couldn't face the future until he was able to face the past.

Rubbing a hand over his face, Alex turned away from the window, from the cool remote perfection of the distant skyline, to the emotional minefield that he carried inside him. He padded into his bedroom.

The room was spare, unadorned. It held a wide bed, a tall oak chest of drawers, a closet. Nothing more. He went to the chest of drawers, then crouched down and pulled open the bottom drawer.

It was empty except for one thing—a single sturdy, flat, dark green cardboard box, perhaps a foot-square, two inches deep.

For a long minute, he just looked at it. Didn't immediately reach for it. Didn't really want to touch it even yet.

He hadn't touched it except when he'd moved it, since he'd

left for university at the age of eighteen. He hadn't opened it since he'd put the lid on it when his parents separated, when they sold the house, when his mother moved to Athens and his father to Corfu.

"Don't look back," his father had said as he'd sold off everything and buried himself in his scholarly books.

But Alex had put the things that mattered in that box, the things he couldn't let go of, even if he couldn't bring himself to look at them.

He'd carried the box with him ever since. He'd taken it to university in London, to his first job in Brussels, to the dozen or so places he'd lived in his adult life. He had brought it with him here.

Wherever he was, he always put it carefully in its own drawer where he wouldn't accidentally stumble across it when he was looking for something else. He didn't want to be blindsided when he wasn't prepared.

Someday, he always promised himself, he would open it. When the time was right he would once again let himself remember. But as time had passed, he'd learned to cope, he'd shut off the past, had refused to give it the power to hurt him. It was easier to forget. The time had never been right.

Until now.

Now he hurt anyway. Now Daisy's words had cut right through his protective shield, had looked inside him and found him wanting.

His hands shook as he drew the box out of the drawer and carried it over to sit on the bed with it. He was surprised how light it was. In his imagination it was the heaviest thing he owned.

He ran his fingers over the top, then carefully eased the lid off and set it aside. There were only a handful of things within—and just as he had feared, the sight of them brought a thousand memories flooding back.

There was the postcard of the Matterhorn that Vass had sent him when he was six and Vass was nine. Vass had been with their father in Switzerland. "It's s'cool," he had written. "You and me will climb it someday."

They hadn't, of course. But when Vass came home, they'd begun climbing the cliffs by their island home with eager purpose. Just as they'd earnestly practiced tying ship's knots in the two feet of line that lay in the box, as well.

"Learn to tie the knots and I'll teach you to sail," their father had said.

Now Alex drew the piece of line out of the box and his fingers moved automatically to make a Spanish bowline, a clove hitch, a figure eight while in his mind's eye he saw the summer days they'd spent on the water, the three of them. He remembered the heat and the sun and the wind—and the stories and the laughter that came with them.

He picked a small reddish-brown pottery shard out next, rubbing his thumb over its worn contours and remembering Vass finding it and saying he was going to grow up and be an archaeologist like Indiana Jones. And there were two very well-used Star Wars figures—Luke and Han, of course—they'd played with for years. There was a painstaking drawing of the Battlestar Galactica that Vass had drawn while he was in the hospital, and a far more precise elegant one that Alex had drawn at the same time because, after all, he was the one who was going to be the architect, not Vass.

And then there was a single silver Porsche Matchbox car.

Alex had faced all the other bits of memorabilia with a tight jaw, a strained smile, blinking eyes.

But the silver Porsche felt like a dagger to his heart.

They had fought over the silver Porsche, he and Vass. It had been his brother's, but Vass had been indifferent until Alex wanted it. And they had fought—actually came to blows— and Vass had punched him in the stomach and he had given Vass a bloody nose.

He stared at the small car now, picked it up and ran his hands over the lines of its frame. Then he closed his fingers around it until he felt the cold metal bite into his hand. He wanted to feel it. Needed the pain.

It hadn't been Vass's first bloody nose. He'd had several that summer. But this one they hadn't been able to stop. Not until they'd taken him to the doctor. And then there had been murmurs of concern. His mother's worry. His father's pacing. More doctor visits. A flight to Athens to see a specialist. A hospital. Tests.

A diagnosis. Leukemia.

Because of a bloody nose. A bloody nose that was Alex's fault.

It wasn't, of course. He knew that now. But at the time, he was not yet nine years old. He hadn't known—and no one had bothered to reassure him. They'd all been far too worried about Vass. He had been worried, too.

But he'd swallowed his worry and his guilt because there hadn't been time for it, there hadn't been room for it. His parents hadn't even seen it.

When Vass had come home from the hospital the first time, Alex had been scared to go into his room, afraid he might do more damage.

But Vass had said scornfully, "You can't give somebody leukemia. You're not that powerful, brat." Then he'd grinned, Vass's old wonderful "I can do anything" grin, and Alex had had his brother back.

Then he'd believed Vass would recover. Then he'd hoped for the best. Two and a half years later, there was no best.

The last time he'd been in Vass's hospital room, Vass had said, "Keep the Porsche. It's yours."

"I don't want it," Alex had protested, tears streaming down his face.

Now slowly, painfully, he unbent his fingers, and stared at the little car. He rubbed his fingers over it, remembering Vass doing the same thing. He squeezed his eyes shut and saw Vass's frail body and thin pale face, and he let the pain wash over him.

But other memories came, too. Along with the pain, he remembered the good times, the joy, the sharing and laughter. And he knew you couldn't have one without the other.

For years he'd put the Porsche and the memories in a box and tucked them away, unable to face them.

You don't love anyone. You don't want to. Daisy's words echoed in his mind. He heard them again, along with her parting shot: *You're offering far, far less.*

Alex knew what he had to do.

He just hoped to God he could do it.

"'S Christmas!" Charlie jiggled Daisy's shoulder, waking her, peering wide-eyed into her sleep-gritted ones. "An' Santa came!"

The pure joy of youth and belief beamed at her. She rolled over and shoved herself to a sitting position, then reached out to pull him into a fierce hug. "Of course he did. Were you worried?"

Charlie gave her a quick, hard, fierce hug in return, then wriggled out of her grasp, his head shaking to and fro. "Nah. I knew he'd come." He held out a hand to her and Daisy let him pull her to her feet.

"I did, too," she confided, snagging her bathrobe as he dragged her toward the living room, toward the Christmas tree which was already lit with small bright multicolored lights, because obviously Charlie had been there first, poking around.

But he hadn't opened any gifts. He had waited for her. Now he looked at her expectantly.

And deliberately, mustering all the joy she could manage, Daisy put her game face on. "Let me put the coffee on. Then we'll see what Santa brought."

There was no time to brood on Christmas morning. There were gifts to unwrap and ooh-and-aah over. Santa made a just-turned-five-year-old boy very happy. There was a set of Legos and some action figures, three new books, a soccer ball, and a floor mat with the outline of streets and buildings—a city to drive his cars around in. Daisy's mother had sent him a build-it-yourself racetrack for his little cars and a stash of art supplies for rainy days.

Charlie was thrilled. He wanted to play with all of it now. Daisy wanted to let him. But Cal was coming to get Charlie at noon. His parents were already here from Cooperstown and were looking forward to spending the day with Cal and their grandson. All of Cal's siblings and their families were coming, too.

"They'd be happy to see you, too," Cal had assured Daisy last week when they'd discussed plans. "You don't have to be alone."

But Daisy had shaken her head. "I'll be all right. I've booked a photo shoot." She had done it deliberately, agreeing to a plea from one of her old college classmates that she do a four-generation family shoot on Christmas afternoon.

"They're all only here for the day," Josie had apologized when she'd asked. "I know it's probably impossible being Christmas and all…but just in case…"

"Sounds great," Daisy had said firmly. It would keep her from sitting at home alone and miserable. "It'll be fun." She'd pasted a bright determined smile on her face. "If it's nice and there's snow on the ground, we can shoot it in the park."

It was nice. There was even, amazingly enough, a few inches of new snow on the ground. And more was drifting down by the time Cal appeared at the door.

He was smiling and looked happier than she could remember. She knew he'd met someone. It was early days yet, he'd told her last week. But there was a light in his eyes she hadn't ever seen before.

He took one look at her pale face and the dark circles under her own eyes and said, "You look awful."

Daisy laughed wryly. "Thank you very much."

But Cal frowned. "I shouldn't be taking him away from you today. Come with us."

Adamantly Daisy shook her head. "I'm meeting Josie's

family at their place at one to do some indoor shots, then we're going to shoot at the Bow Bridge in the park if it's still snowing."

"Come after you finish."

"I'll be fine," she insisted. "Go on. Have a good time." She gave Charlie a hug and a kiss. "Behave."

"I always behave," he said stoutly. "I'm bringin' my new guys to show Grandpa."

"He'll like that." Daisy gave him one more squeeze, then stood up. Her smile was strained. Of course Charlie didn't notice. She hoped Cal didn't, either. "See you tomorrow," she said with all the cheer she could manage. Then she shut the door behind them, leaned back against it, and pressed her hands to her eyes.

It was letting Charlie go, she told herself. This was, after all, the first Christmas that she hadn't had him with her all the time. Always before, after their divorce, Cal had come here and they'd celebrated together. But they both knew that couldn't last. He had a life now—and she had to get one.

Now she scrubbed at her eyes and took a deep, hopefully steadying breath, then she went upstairs to get ready to go, picking out the lenses and filters she wanted to take, determined to keep her mind busy so she wouldn't think about where Charlie was and what he was doing and…

…about Alex.

She *had* to stop thinking about Alex.

It had been two weeks since they'd had their confrontation. Two weeks since she'd spurned his offer of marriage before he could even make it, since she'd told him exactly what she thought of it—and of him—and had shoved him out of the door and out of her life.

He hadn't been back.

Was she surprised? Of course not. It was for the best, really, and she knew it.

What surprised her was how much she cared.

She didn't want to care! She didn't want to miss him,

didn't want to remember him sitting on the floor playing with Charlie, didn't want to think about him telling their son a story, didn't want to close her eyes and be plagued by images of him with Charlie in his arms or on his shoulders, the two of them grinning at each other.

She didn't want to remember how proud she'd felt the night he'd got the award for his hospital design, how intently she'd listened when he'd told her about his inspiration for it, how much she heard and understood what he didn't ever say.

She didn't want to think about him—and she couldn't seem to stop.

Now she finished packing her gear bag, slipped on her puffy, bright blue down jacket and headed toward the park.

It was Christmas. A time of hope. A time to put the past behind her and move on. She squared her shoulders, and picked up her bag. Maybe after she'd finished Josie's family's photo shoot, she would go ice skating, meet the man of her dreams, fall in love.

Fairy tales. Would she never learn?

Daisy sighed and headed for Josie's place.

Four generations of the Costello family were ready and waiting. Josie swept Daisy into their Fifth Avenue sixth floor apartment overlooking the park, equal measures eager and apologetic. They were so glad to have her take photos of their family holiday, they were so sorry they were taking her away from her own family today of all days.

"It's all right," Daisy assured them. "I'm glad to do it."

It was every bit the distraction she had hoped. The seven children—cousins who didn't see each other often—along with their parents, grandparents and two great-grandparents, were a noisy energetic mob. And Daisy, intrigued by the possibilities, threw herself into the work.

She did a series of family groups, then gathered them around the table, shot Josie's grandfather slicing the turkey, her grandmother helping the youngest grandson fill his plate.

She caught two cousins playing chess in front of the fire, three little girl cousins playing dress-up with the small trunk of fancy clothes one had got for Christmas.

It was the perfect family Christmas, the kind she'd seen in movies and on TV. The kind she'd always wanted for herself. And especially for Charlie.

She shot their preening and their giggling. She shot four generations of Costello men watching football on television, simultaneously cheering or groaning. She had all the children make a human pyramid that mimicked the Christmas tree.

Then, as soon as she shot that, she said, "Let's go to the park," before things got rowdy, which the human pyramid showed signs of becoming.

The snow was still falling, picture-perfect, when they got to the Bow Bridge. She posed them there and did a couple of formal shots for posterity while passersby, walking off their Christmas dinners, stopped and watched then, smiling, moved on.

Daisy didn't pay them any mind. She glanced their way, then turned back to shoot a series of photos of great-grandpa and grandpa and two little grandsons building a snowman. The girls were making snow angels, their colorful scarves flung out against the snow as they moved their arms and legs. They danced and played and she captured it all—the grace, the laughter—mothers and daughters, grandmothers, great-grandmother and granddaughters. The boys were wrestling in the snow now, pelting each other with snowballs, laughing madly.

Family.

How she envied them their family. She tried to shove the thought away even as it tightened her throat, made her swallow hard. She blinked hard and stopped shooting for a moment, needing to turn away.

Several people who had been watching, smiled at her and scuffed their feet and moved away. She got a grip, started to turn back, then caught a glimpse of someone else out of the corner of her eye.

Her gaze stopped, jerked back, dismissed it. She turned to shoot the snowball-throwing boys again. But her heart was beating faster as she edged around to get a different angle, to look west without turning her head.

He was still there, standing in the shadows beneath the trees.

Lean, tall. Dark wind-blown hair. Wearing jeans and a hunter-green down jacket.

"Lookit me!" one of the Costello boys shouted. He had scrambled up into the crook of a tree and peered down at her.

Daisy turned, focused, shot. Then she swivelled again, taking more shots of the snowball fight, but not even looking at what she was shooting.

She was trying to squint past the camera, to get a better look. He was too far away to be sure. But the last time she'd seen Alex he'd worn a jacket like that.

Surely it wasn't. It couldn't be. It was her stupid fairy-tale-obsessed mind playing tricks on her.

She turned and aimed her shots at the snowman builders now. Grandpa had the littlest boy on his shoulders to loop a scarf around the snowman's neck. Daisy shot it all. That was what she was here for.

When she turned around again, she expected the man to be gone. He was leaning against the tree, hands in his pockets, staring steadily at her.

Daisy raised her camera and pointed it. She zoomed in, and caught her breath.

Slowly Alex nodded at her.

But he didn't move, didn't come closer. Just leaned against the tree, as if he was waiting for a bus or something!

"Are your fingers freezing? Daisy? Daisy?"

She turned, realizing that Josie had been talking to her. "N-no. I'm fine. I— Fine." She glanced back.

He was still there.

"I think we'll call it quits if you've got enough," Josie said. "The little ones and great-grandma are getting cold. I am, too," she admitted, blowing on her hands. "But it's been such fun. Will you come with us? We're going to make cocoa for the kids and hot toddies for the grown-ups."

The panicky desperate part of Daisy wanted to jump at the invitation. Whatever Alex was doing there, he was there on purpose. He had something to say. And Daisy was sure she didn't want to hear it.

But if she didn't hear it now, he'd find another time. And at least she wouldn't have to worry about Charlie overhearing.

"Thanks," she said to Josie. "But I'll just go on home. I loved doing it, though. I'll have the proofs for you by the end of the week."

"Fantastic." Josie gave her a hug. "You were brilliant. And we had a blast. We'll remember it always."

Daisy smiled wanly. She had a feeling she would, too.

With cheery goodbyes and fierce hugs from several small children and a couple of great-grandparents, Daisy began to pack up her gear while the Costellos headed back across the park.

She focused securing the lenses in her camera bag. She didn't look around, ignored the sound of footsteps through the snow. But her heart was going like a jackhammer in her chest. She straightened just as a shadow fell across her.

"Daisy." His voice was soft and gruff, surprisingly hesitant.

Steeling herself, she turned. The sight that met her eyes was a surprise, too. This wasn't the smooth confident man she expected to see. This Alex's jaw was stubbled with at least a day's worth of beard. This Alex's eyes were bloodshot and shadowed. As she stared, his jaw bunched and tightened. He ran the tip of his tongue between his lips, then pressed them together again.

"Alex." She nodded carefully, determinedly giving nothing away, particularly encouragement. The last thing she needed was to fight this battle again.

For a long moment he didn't speak, either, and Daisy wondered if she ought to just step around him, head home. Maybe he'd just been walking in the park, had happened on her by accident. God knew perverse things like that could happen.

"You were right," he said abruptly. "What you said."

Daisy blinked. What she'd said? What had she said? Uncertainly she shook her head.

"That I didn't want to love. That I pushed people away." He answered the question before she even had to ask. He said the words quickly, as if he needed to get past them. Then he said again more slowly, "I didn't want to. Then." Pale green eyes met hers.

Then? Which meant...what? Daisy felt herself tense, but didn't move. She searched his gaze, tried to hear the words he never said.

Then he took a breath and said them. "I loved my brother," he said, the words coming out on a harsh breath. "And I thought I killed him."

"What?" She stared at him, aghast.

He shook his head. "We had a fight...over a car. A toy. I was *eight*," he said harshly. "And I gave him a bloody nose. He bled and bled. They said he had leukemia. I thought..." He shook his head, anguished. "I wasn't even nine," he said. "I didn't know."

"Oh, Alex." She just looked at him. She'd known about his brother. She hadn't known this.

"He said I didn't. But he just kept getting sicker. And...then he died." Now she could hear him dragging the words out. "My parents were shell-shocked. Destroyed. They couldn't help each other. They couldn't even look at me."

"It wasn't your fault!"

"I know that now. But we don't talk much in my family, not about..." He swallowed, then looked past her over her shoulder, staring into the distance, his eyes bright with unshed tears. Whatever he was seeing, Daisy was sure it wasn't in Central Park.

He brought his gaze back to hers, his eyes filled with pain. "When I was ten years old I thought I'd killed my brother and ended our family." His throat worked. "I loved all of them."

And she had told him he didn't love anyone.

"I'm sorry." Her words came out as brokenly as his. She wanted to reach out, to touch his sleeve, to put her arms around him. She had no right. "I'm so sorry."

He nodded almost imperceptibly. He took a breath and then another. "I put it away, shut it out of my mind, didn't deal with it. I never talked to anyone about it—except you. Five years ago."

Her eyes widened. "You never—?"

"No. I shut it all out." There it was, the sharp hard edge. She could hear it. It was the way he always shut people out.

He bent his head. "But I couldn't shut you out." His voice was ragged. A faint smile touched his beautiful mouth.

"You certainly did," Daisy reminded him. She remembered his words all too well.

Alex had the grace to grimace. "I tried," he allowed. "Because you got under my skin. Made me feel things that scared the hell out of me."

"What?" Daisy blinked, confused.

"I was…falling in love with you—even back then, that first night." He pulled a hand out of his pocket and rubbed it against the back of his neck. "I was falling in love with you," he repeated, wonderingly, as if he was amazed he could admit it not only to her but to himself. "And it scared me to death. When you started talking about it like it was a good thing— loving—all I could think was, 'I've got to get out of here. I'll destroy her, too.'" His tone was harsh, anguished. And when she looked close she could see his eyes glistening. He blinked rapidly, then gave a quick shake of his head. "So I did." He swallowed. "Hell of a lot safer that way."

Daisy digested that. Drew in a breath, then another, and cocked her head, then asked him gently, "Was it?"

A corner of his mouth quirked up. "It was until I ran into

you again back in September. Then, short answer—no. You're under my skin. I can't get rid of you. Wherever I go, wherever I am, there you are." He made it sound awful, but Daisy suddenly couldn't stop smiling.

Despairing, Alex shook his head. "I couldn't get you out of my mind, though God knows, I tried. I told myself I needed a woman who didn't make me feel all the things you made me feel. But you must have noticed, I couldn't stay away."

"Every time I thought I'd seen the last of you, you came back," Daisy realized. "It made me nervous."

"Because of Charlie?"

"Partly. But really, I suppose, because I'd…never quite got over you." She didn't want to admit it, but if they were being honest, she owed him that. The heat of his gaze was warming her, making her tingle all the way to her toes. At the same time she was still trying to get a grip on the notion that five years ago he'd been falling in love with her, too.

"I wanted you as soon as I saw you again," he told her.

"On your terms."

"Hell, yes. Safer that way. And Caroline was safe. I never felt for her the tiniest bit of what I feel for you. I never wanted her. Never missed her. I knew I could live without her. I can't live without you."

"Alex." She touched his cheek with her palm and he turned his face to press his lips into it, his kiss making her shiver.

"I couldn't ask her to marry me," he admitted. "I was going to, but I never could."

"You must have realized she needed someone else."

He reached up a hand to press her palm against his cheek. He looked down into her eyes, his full of an emotion she'd never dared hope to see there. "Yeah, maybe that was it." He gave a self-deprecating laugh. "No, damn it. I was still in love with you."

Daisy stared at him in astonishment.

"And then I discovered Charlie."

"And you wanted Charlie."

"Yes. I love Charlie," Alex said with an intensity that made her believe it. "Not just because he reminds me of Vass, though God knows he does. I love him because he's yours. And mine. Because he's bright and inquisitive and fun and just knowing he's alive gives me joy." He shook his head slowly. "And I would give my life for him—and for you. I will go to the ends of the earth for you. I will slay dragons for you. I will get hurt for you. I swear it, Daisy." There was wonder in his voice.

Daisy opened her mouth, then closed it again. She didn't know what to say. Her eyes brimmed. So did her heart. Dear God, she'd loved this man for years, but never more than she loved him now, now that he had discovered the love he was capable of, the love he was willing to dare to share.

He reached out and touched her cheek, stroking away a tear she didn't even know was there. Then he wrapped his arms around her and drew her close, let her feel the pounding of his heart, the warmth of his love, the shelter of his embrace.

She leaned against him, letting herself sink into him, loving his strength, his steadiness. She rested her head in the crook between his shoulder and his chin.

"I would have been here sooner," Alex went on. He spoke softly, his lips against her hair. "But I didn't think you probably wanted to talk to me again after what you said the last time."

Daisy raised her eyes to look up at him, feeling guilty. "I didn't know—"

But Alex shook his head. "No, you were right. It was my problem. You gave me a reason to confront it, to deal with it. And I needed to before I could come back. So I did. I had to go to Paris for work anyway. It was a commitment. I spent ten days there. Then I went to see my parents."

Daisy took a quick look into his eyes.

He bent his head, held her closer. "We've…barely talked in years. It was, I suppose, easier for all of us that way. Not to be reminded."

Daisy slid her arms around his back, holding him close, feeling the tension in him.

He cleared his throat, scuffed his boot in the snow, then pulled back a little so he could look down into her eyes. "They're both in Greece these days. Not together. My mother's divorced a third time. My dad is still buried in his books. But I...talked to both of them. About Vass. About...what happened, about what I thought. They were shocked. They had no idea." His eyes were brimming again. He shook his head. "I'm glad I went. And I...expect I'll see them again." He hesitated. "I told them about you...and Charlie. They'd like to meet you both someday...if you're agreeable."

"Of course," Daisy said faintly, her heart spilling over with love for him, thrilled that he'd taken the step to reconnect with his parents, delighted that they might all now find a beginning to their healing.

Alex pressed a kiss into her hair. "Thank you."

Then he drew back and dug into the pocket of his jacket. "Will you give this to Charlie?" He took out a small silver Matchbox car and handed it to her. "I have real Christmas presents for him, but he's got them already. I left them with Cal."

"Cal?" She stared at him in wonder. "You've never even met Cal."

"I have now. I went to your place from the airport. You weren't there. I didn't know where you were. I thought you might be with him."

"How do you know where he lives?"

"I told you once before—" Alex's mouth quirked "—the internet is a wonderful thing."

Apparently it was. "But I wasn't there."

"No," Alex said. "But he knew where you were."

"And he told you?" That didn't sound like Cal. He was generally very protective.

"After he'd threatened me within an inch of my life. Said I'd be sorry if I hurt you. And I believed him. I liked him.

And…I don't ever want to hurt you, Daze." His voice was rough and warm and intense.

And he wasn't hurting her, he was killing her, Daisy thought desperately. She looked down at the tiny car in her hand. Without having to be told, she knew what it was.

"The car you fought over," she said.

He nodded. "It was Vass's. He gave it to me before…before he died." Alex choked on the words. "I've carried it with me ever since."

"Your hair shirt?" Daisy asked gently.

"I didn't think so then, but yes, it was. I lived with the guilt a long time. I might have lived with it forever—without you."

"Oh, Alex." She nestled close again.

"Charlie should have it. He doesn't need to know its past. Only that it's for him—a gift from the uncle he'll never know. Vass—" Alex swallowed "—would have loved him."

Daisy blinked furiously, her fingers tightening around the tiny car. "Yes." She tucked it into the pocket of her jacket. "Oh, yes."

"I have something for you, too." He fished in his other pocket and pulled out a small box, the sort that jewelry came in. A ring box?

Daisy's heart hammered furiously. More manipulation? Or were they past that?

Alex held it out to her. "This is for you. I saw it at a little shop in Paris and I thought of you. Of us. It's the way I'd like us to be." He looked into her eyes and pressed it into her palm, then closed her fingers over it. Snowflakes dusted his dark lashes, settled on his midnight hair. He smiled gently. "I love you, Daisy. I hope someday you believe it."

Then he drew away from her, turned and set off through the snow.

Numbly, Daisy stared after him. *What?*

He was just going to leave her here? He was going to tell her he loved her, give her his heart, then walk away?

No insistence? No demand? No renewed proposal?

She looked down at the tiny box in her hand, then fumbled to open it. Inside was a silver necklace—real silver, unlike the Porsche—of two interlocking, entwined open hearts.

I thought of you, he'd said. *Of us.*

Two open hearts entwined.

Daisy bit down on her lip. Her fingers trembled. She clutched the box with the necklace in one hand and her camera bag in the other and broke into a run. "Alex! Alex, wait!"

He stopped, turned. Looked at her, half stricken, half hoping. She recognized that look now. She skidded to a halt bare inches in front of him, blinking furiously into the sun, into the dawning hope in those beautiful pale green eyes. "Ask me."

He frowned. "Ask what?"

"You know what!"

He raised a brow. A corner of his mouth quivered, almost smiled.

"Ask," Daisy demanded.

Then he took a breath. "Will you let me love you?" he asked. "Forever?"

"Yes." She threw her arms around him.

"Will you love me?" he asked as she kissed him. His voice was suspiciously hoarse.

"Yes!" She breathed the word against his lips.

"Will you marry me, Daze?" He barely got the words out because now he was kissing her back.

"Yes, Alex. Oh, yes, yes. Yes."

Daisy didn't miss Charlie that night as much as she'd thought she would. She took Alex home and didn't even open the other Christmas present he'd brought her from Paris.

She put on her necklace—or, rather, he put it on for her. Then she took him upstairs to her bedroom. There, slowly, he took off her sweater, her jeans, her shirt, her socks. Then he lowered her to the bed, and, smiling, began to take off everything else she wore.

Everything but the necklace. Daisy wouldn't let him take off that. But the rest—oh, yes. She shivered with pleasure at the way his fingers traced the lines and curves of her body, the way his lips followed and his tongue, as well.

When he unfastened her bra and slipped it off her shoulders, then bent his head to kiss her breasts, she lifted her hands and threaded them in the silky softness of his hair.

Alex kissed his way across her breasts, laved her nipples, made her tremble with longing. Then, smiling at her reaction, he dropped kisses down the line between her breasts, on down to her navel and beyond. And Daisy quivered with need for him.

"Alex!" She squirmed when he peeled her panties down, tossed them aside, then ran his fingers back up her calves, then her thighs, then touched her—there. "Wait. My turn. You're overdressed."

He lifted his head and smiled. "Am I?"

"Oh, yes." And then Daisy set about unwrapping the Christmas present she wanted more than anything—him.

"I love you," she whispered as she tugged his sweater over his head. "I've never forgotten doing this." She tossed his sweater on the bedside chair, then quickly disposed of the buttons of his shirt.

"You're faster at that than I remember." Alex kept his hands at his sides as he watched her, but there was a flame of desire in his eyes.

"Practice," Daisy said, beginning to work on the zip of his jeans.

"Practice?" Alex frowned.

"Charlie couldn't always dress himself."

He grinned, then sucked in a quick breath when she made quick work of the zipper and her fingers found him. He swallowed hard, then shrugged off his jeans and came to her on the bed, settled next to her, stroked his hands over her with an almost hesitant wonder.

And Daisy felt the same. "I love you," she whispered, glorying in being able to say it, to acknowledge it, and to know that he wanted to hear the words.

"I know. But not as much as I love you," he said, a tremor in his voice and another in the hands that stroked her sensitive skin.

"I'll show you," she insisted, and rolled onto her back, drawing him on top of her, wrapping herself around him.

"And I'll show you," Alex countered, teasing, tasting, touching. He was so exquisitely gentle, yet possessively so. His fingers found her, knew her, parted her. And then he slid in. "Daze!" His body tensed, froze. And then—at last—he began to move.

"Alex!" Her nails dug into his buttocks. Her head thrashed on the pillow. Her body tightened around him. He made her shiver, he made her quiver, he made her shatter. And he shattered right along with her, his face contorting, his body going rigid, then collapsing to bury his face against her neck.

She stroked his sweat-slick back, then turned her head and kissed his ear and along the whisker-roughened line of his jaw.

When at last he lifted his head it was to look down into her eyes with wonder. "Why did it take me so long to realize?" he murmured, sounding awestruck.

Daisy shook her head. She didn't need to ask why anymore. She had the answer she needed. "I'm just glad you did."

He rolled onto his back then and pulled her on top so that she rested her head on his chest and felt the gallop of his heart beneath her cheek. Softly, rhythmically, Alex stroked her hair.

Daisy didn't know how long they lay like that. She might have slept a little. She thought he did. But when they roused and began to touch, to love again, he raised his head from the pillow and peered down his nose at her. "Is this the sort of match you try to make?" he asked, giving her his heart with his eyes.

Daisy returned his gift full measure. But then she shook her head no.

"It's better," she told him, rising up to meet his lips, to love him, to share the wonder once more.

* * * * *

MILLS & BOON®

Mills & Boon have been at the heart of romance since 1908... and while the fashions may have changed, one thing remains the same: from pulse-pounding passion to the gentlest caress, we're always known how to bring romance alive.

Now, we're delighted to present you with these irresistible illustrations, inspired by the vintage glamour of our covers. So indulge your wildest dreams and unleash your imagination as we present the most iconic Mills & Boon moments of the last century.

Visit **www.millsandboon.co.uk/ArtofRomance** to order yours!

MILLS & BOON®

Why shop at millsandboon.co.uk?

Each year, thousands of romance readers find their perfect read at millsandboon.co.uk. That's because we're passionate about bringing you the very best romantic fiction. Here are some of the advantages of shopping at www.millsandboon.co.uk:

* **Get new books first**—you'll be able to buy your favourite books one month before they hit the shops

* **Get exclusive discounts**—you'll also be able to buy our specially created monthly collections, with up to 50% off the RRP

* **Find your favourite authors**—latest news, interviews and new releases for all your favourite authors and series on our website, plus ideas for what to try next

* **Join in**—once you've bought your favourite books, don't forget to register with us to rate, review and join in the discussions

Visit **www.millsandboon.co.uk**
for all this and more today!